A quick motion at the edge of her vision was all the warning she had. Then something white flapped across her face and caught heavily in her hair. A feral white face with a nimbus of cobweb hair, milky wings, a long spidery white hand that reached out and pinched her nose—A trill of laughter sounded ahead of her, breathtakingly sweet and cold . . .

Eddi saw bestial figures, hulking-shouldered and heavy-headed. She saw ethereal ones that glimmered like moonlight on wet grass. She saw uncounted pairs of eyes, all watching her with unfriendly curiosity. She cursed the phouka's ointment that enabled her to see them in the dark.

There's no knowing who the enemy is, the phouka had said. She laid her hand in his, and he guided her through the sullen throng.

Ace Books by Emma Bull

WAR FOR THE OAKS
FALCON
BONE DANCE

Ace Books edited by Emma Bull and Will Shetterly

LIAVEK
LIAVEK: THE PLAYERS OF LUCK
LIAVEK: WIZARD'S ROW
LIAVEK: SPELLS OF BINDING
LIAVEK: FESTIVAL WEEK

WAR FOR THE OAKS

EMMA BULL

ACE BOOKS, NEW YORK

This book is an Ace original edition,
and has never been previously published.

WAR FOR THE OAKS

An Ace Book / published by arrangement with
the author and the author's agent, Valerie Smith

PRINTING HISTORY
Ace Edition / July 1987

ISBN: 0-441-87073-2

Ace Books are published by The Berkley Publishing Group,
200 Madison Avenue, New York, NY 10016.
The name "Ace" and the "A" logo
are trademarks belonging to Charter Communications, Inc.

PRINTED IN THE UNITED STATES OF AMERICA

10 9 8 7 6 5 4

Acknowledgments

Thanks are past due to Steven Brust, Nate Bucklin, Kara Dalkey, Pamela Dean, Pat Wrede, Cyn Horton, and Lois Bujold; they always want to know what happens next. Thanks also to Terri, who thought it was a good idea; Curt Quiner and Floyd Henderson, motorcycle gurus; Pamela and Lynda, for the cookies; Val, for comfort and threats; Mike, for the keyboards; and Knut-Koupeé, for all the guitars.

For the singin' and dancin': Boiled in Lead, Summer of Love, Têtes Noires, Curtiss A., Rue Nouveau, Paula Alexander, Prince and the Revolution, First Avenue, Seventh Street Entry, and the Uptown Bar.

But most of all, to Will, for the whole shebang.

This book is for my mother, who knew right away that the Beatles were important, and for my father, who never once complained about the noise.

Table of Contents

Prologue

By day, the Nicollet Mall winds through Minneapolis like a paved canal. People flow between its banks, eddying at the doors of office towers and department stores. The big red-and-white city buses roar at every corner. On the many-globed lampposts, banners advertising a museum exhibit flap in the wind that the tallest buildings snatch out of the sky. The skyway system vaults the Mall with its covered bridges of steel and glass, and they, too, are full of people, color, motion.

But late at night, there's a change in the Nicollet Mall.

The street lamp globes hang like myriad moons, and light glows in the empty bus shelters like nebulae. Down through the silent business district the Mall twists, the silver zipper in a patchwork coat of many dark colors. The sound of traffic from Hennepin Avenue, one block over, might be the grating of the World-Worm's scales over stone.

Near the south end of the Mall, in front of Orchestra Hall, Peavey Plaza beckons: a reflecting pool, and a cascade that descends from towering chrome cylinders to a sunken walk-in maze of stone blocks and pillars for which "fountain" is an inadequate name. In the moonlight, it is black and silver, gray and white, full of an elusive play of shape and contrast.

On that night, there were voices in Peavey Plaza. One was like the susurrus of the fountain itself, sometimes hissing, sometimes with the little-bell sound of a water-drop striking. The other was deep and rough; if the concrete were an animal, it would have this voice.

"Tell me," said the water voice, "what you have found."

The deep voice replied. "There is a woman who will do, I think."

When water hits a hot griddle, it sizzles; the water-voice

sounded like that. "You are our eyes and legs in this, Dog. That should not interfere with your tongue. Tell me!"

A low, growling laugh, then: "She makes music, the kind that moves heart and body. In another time, we would have found her long before, for that alone. We grow fat and slow in this easy life," the rough voice said, as if it meant to say something very different.

The water made a fierce sound, but the rough voice laughed again, and went on. "She is like flowering moss, delicate and fair, but proof against frosts and trampling feet. Her hair is the color of an elm leaf before it falls, her eyes the gray of the storm that brings it down. She does not offend the eye. She seems strong enough, and I think she is clever. Shall I bring her to show to you?"

"Can you?"

"B'lieve I can. But we should rather ask—will she do what she's to do?"

The water-voice's laughter was like sleet on a window. "With all the Court against her if she refuses? Oh, if we fancy her, Dog, she'll do. Pity her if she tries to stand against us."

And the rough voice said quietly, "I shall."

CHAPTER ONE

Another Magic Moment in Showbiz

The University Bar was not, in the grand scheme of the city, close to the university. Nor was its clientel collegiate. They worked the assembly lines and warehouses, and wanted uncomplicated entertainment. The club boasted a jukebox stocked by the rental company and two old arcade games. It was small and smoky and smelled vaguely bad. But InKline Plain, the most misspelled band in Minneapolis, was there, playing the first night of a two-night gig with a sort of weary desperation. The promise of fifty dollars per band member kept them going; it was more than they'd made last week.

Eddi McCandry stared bleakly at the dim little stage with its red-and-black flocked wallpaper. The band's equipment threatened to overflow it. She'd tried to wedge her guitar stand out of the way, but it still seemed likely to leap out and trip someone. She was glad the keyboard player had quit two weeks before—there wasn't room for him.

The first set had been bad enough, playing to a nearly empty club. The next two were worse. Too many country fans with requests for favorites. And of course, Stuart, as bandleader, had accepted them all, played them wretchedly, forgot the words, and made it plain that he didn't care. They were the wrong band for this bar.

"I think," Eddi said, "that this job was a bad idea."

Her companion nodded solemnly. "Every time you've said that this evening, it's sounded smarter." Carla DiAmato was the drummer for InKline Plain. With her shaggy black hair and her eyes made up dark for the stage, she looked exotic as a tiger, wholly out of place in the University Bar.

"It would have been smarter to tell Stuart it was a bad idea," Eddi said. "Ideally, before he booked the job."

3

"You couldn't know."

"I could. I did. Look at this place."

Carla sighed. "I think I'm gonna hear the 'This Band Sucks Dead Rat' speech again."

"Well, it does."

"Through a straw. I know. So why don't you quit?"

Eddi looked at her, then at her glass, then at the ceiling. "Why don't you?"

"It's steady work." Carla was silent for a moment, then added, 'Well, it used to be."

"Tsk. You don't even have my excuse."

"You mean I haven't been sleeping with Stuart?"

"Yeah," Eddi sighed, "like that."

"Sometimes I take my blessings for granted. I'm going to go up and scare the cockroaches out of the bass drum."

"Good luck," said Eddie. "I'll be right behind you."

She almost made it to the stage before Stuart Kline grabbed her arm. His face was flushed, and his brown hair was rumpled, half-flattened. She sighed. "You're drunk, Stu," she said with a gentleness that surprised her.

"Fuck it." Petulance twisted up his male-model features. She should have felt angry, or ashamed. All she felt was a distant wonder: *I used to be in love with him.*

She asked, "You want to do easy stuff this set?"

"I said fuck it, fuck off. I'm okay."

Eddi shrugged. "It's your hanging."

He grabbed her arm again. "Hey, I want you to be nicer to the club managers."

"What?"

"Don't look at me like that. Just flirt. It's good for the band."

She wanted to tweak his nose, see his smile—but that didn't make him smile anymore. "Stuart, you don't get gigs by sending the rhythm guitarist to flirt with the manager. You get 'em by playing good dance music."

"I play good dance music."

"We play anything that's already been played to death. All night, people have been sticking their heads in the front door, listening to half a song, and leaving. You in a betting mood?"

"Why?"

"I bet the nice man at the bar tells us not to come back tomorrow."

"Damn you," he raged suddenly, "is that my fault?"

Eddie blinked.

"You pissed him off, didn't you? Why do you have to be such a bitch?"

For a long moment she thought she might shout back at him. But it was laughter that came racing up her throat. Stuart's look of foolish surprise fed it, doubled it. She planted a smacking kiss on his chin. "Stuart, honey," she grinned, "you gotta grow where you're planted."

She loped over and swung up on stage, took her lipstick-red Rickenbacker from the stand, and flipped the strap over her shoulder. She caught Carla's eye over the tops of the cymbals. "Dale back from break yet?"

Carla shook her head, then inhaled loudly through pursed lips. "Parking lot," she croaked.

"Oh, goody. The whole left side of the stage in an altered state of consciousness. Let's figure out the set list."

"But we've got a set list."

"Let's make a new one. May as well be hanged for Prince as for Pink Floyd."

"But Stuart—"

Eddi grinned. "I want to leave this band in a blaze of glory."

Carla's eyes grew wide. "You're—Jesus. Okay, set list. Can we dump all the Chuck Berry?"

"Yeah. Let's show this dive that we at least flirt with modern music, huh?"

They came up with a list of songs in a few gleeful minutes. Stuart hoisted himself on stage as they finished, eyeing them with sullen suspicion. He slung on his guitar and began to noodle, running through his arsenal of electronic effects—more, Eddi suspected, to prove to the audience that he had them than to make sure they worked.

Dale, the bass player, ambled on stage looking vaguely pleased with himself. Dale was all right in his own disconnected way; but he liked country rock and hated rock 'n' roll, and consoled himself with dope during breaks. Eddi cranked up the bass on her amp and hoped it would make up for whatever he was too stoned to deliver.

Carla was watching her, waiting for the cue to start. Stuart and Dale were ready, if not precisely waiting. "Give us a count," she said to Carla. Stuart glared at her. Carla counted, and they kicked off with a semblance of unity.

They began with a skewed version of Del Shannon's "Runaway.'' It was familiar enough to pull people onto the dance floor, and the band's odd arrangement disguised most of the mistakes. Eddi and Carla did impromptu girl-group vocals. Dale looked confused. Then they dived into the Bangles' ''In a Different Light,'' and Stuart began to sulk. Eddi had anticipated that. The next one was an old Eagles song that gave Stuart a chance to sing and muddle up the lead guitar riffs.

Perhaps the scanty audience felt Eddi's sudden madness; they were in charity with the band for the first time that night. People had finally started to dance. Eddi hoped it wasn't too late to impress the manager, but suspected it was.

Carla set the bass drum and her drum machine to tossing the percussion back and forth. The dancers were staying on the floor, waiting for the beat to fulfill its promise. Eddi murmured the four-count. Dale thumped out a bass line that was only a little too predictable. Stuart shot Eddi an unreadable look and layered on the piercing voice of his Stratocaster. Eddi grabbed her mike and began to sing.

> *You told me I was pretty*
> *I can't believe it's true.*
> *The little dears you left me for*
> *They all look just like you.*
> *Ugly is as ugly does—*
> *Are you telling me what to do?*
>
> *Wear my face*
> *You can have it for a week*
> *Wear my face*
> *Aren't the cheekbones chic?*
> *Wear my face*
> *See how people look at you?*
> *Wear my face*
> *See how much my face can do?*

They were still dancing. The band was together and tight at last, and Eddi felt as if she'd done it all herself in a burst of goddesslike musical electricity.

Then she saw the man standing at the edge of the dance floor. His walnut-stain skin seemed too dark for his features. He wore his hair smoothed back, except for a couple of escaped curls on his forehead. His eyes were large and slanted upward under thick arched brows; his nose was narrow and slightly aquiline. He wore a long dark coat with the collar up, and a gleaming white scarf that reflected the stage lights into his face. When she looked at him, he met her eyes boldly and grinned.

Eddi snagged the microphone, took the one step toward him that she had room for, and sang the last verse at him.

> *I've seen the way you look away*
> *When you think I might see,*
> *You say I scare you silly—*
> *That's reacting sensibly.*
> *Why should people look at you*
> *When they could look at me?*

It was Eddi who had to turn away, and the last chorus was delivered to the dancers. The man had met her look with a silent challenge that made her skin prickle. His sloping eyes had been full of reflected lights in colors that shone nowhere in the room.

She almost missed Carla's neat segue into the next song. She nailed down her first guitar chord barely in time, and caught Stuart's scowl out of the corner of her eye.

Eddi had wanted to close with something rambunctious, something the audience would like yet that would allow Eddi and Carla to respect themselves in the morning. Carla had hit upon Z.Z. Top's "Cheap Sunglasses." Halfway into it, with a shower of sparks and a vile smell, the ancient power amp for the PA dropped dead.

As the microphones failed, Stuart's vocals disappeared tinnily under the sound of guitars and bass and Carla's drums. Stuart, never at his best in the face of adversity, lost his temper. He yanked his guitar strap over his head and let the Strat drop to the stage. The pickups howled painfully through his amp.

Eddi heard Dale's bass stumble through a succession of wrong notes, and fall silent. She supposed he was right; Stuart had made it impossible to end the song gracefully. But for her pride's sake, she played out the measure and added a final flourish. Carla matched her perfectly, and Eddi wanted to kiss her feet for it.

The dancers had deserted the floor, and people were finishing drinks and pulling on jackets. She swept the room a stagey bow. At the corner of her vision, she thought she saw a dark-coated figure move toward the door.

Stuart had turned off his amp and unplugged his axe. His expression was forbidding. Eddi turned away to tend to her own equipment, but not before she saw the club manager striding toward the stage.

"You the bandleader?" she heard him ask Stuart.

"Yeah," said Stuart, "what is it?"

It's our walking papers, Stu, she thought sadly, knowing that he could save the whole gig now, if only he would be pleasant and concilliating. He wouldn't be, of course. The manager would tell Stuart what he should be doing with his band, and Stuart, instead of thanking him for the tip, would recommend he keep his asshole advice to himself.

And Stuart would make Eddi out the villain if he could. Well, she was done with that now. She finished packing her guitar and tracked the power cord on her amplifier back to the outlet.

"You're that sure, huh?" Carla's voice came from over her head.

"You mean, am I packing up everything? Yeah. You want help tearing down?"

Carla looked faded and limp. "You can pack the electronic junk."

Eddi nodded, and started unplugging things from the back of the drum machine. "You done good, kid. Even at the end when it hit the fan."

Carla shook her head and grinned. "Well, you got to go out in a blaze of *something*."

Over at the bar, Stuart and the manager had begun to shout at each other. "I booked a goddamn five-piece!" the manager yelled. "You goddamn well *did* break your contract!"

Carla looked up at Eddi, her eyes wide. "Oh boy—you mean we're not even gonna get *paid*?"

Eddi turned to see how Dale was taking the news. He was nowhere to be seen.

"Carla, you think your wagon will hold your equipment and mine, too?"

Carla smiled. "The Titanic? I won't even have to put the seat down."

They did have to put the seat down, but the drums, drum machine, Eddi's guitar, and her Fender Twin Reverb all fit. They made three trips out the back door with the stuff, and Stuart and the manager showed no sign of noticing them.

As Carla bullied the wagon out of its parking space, Eddi

spotted Dale. He was leaning against the back of his rusted-out Dodge. The lit end of his joint flared under his nose. "Hold it," Eddi said to Carla. She jumped out of the car and ran over to him. "Hey, Dale!"

"Eddi? Hullo. Is Stuart still at it?"

"Still at what?"

Dale shrugged and dragged at the joint. "You know," he croaked, "screwing up." He exhaled and held the J out to her.

Eddi shook her head. "I didn't think you'd noticed—I mean—"

"Been pretty bad the last month. It'd be hard not to." He smiled sadly at the toes of his cowboy boots. "So, you going?"

"Yeah. That is, I'm leaving the band."

"That's what I meant."

"Oh. Well, I wanted to say good-bye. I'll miss you." Which, Eddi realized with a start, was more true than she'd thought.

Dale smiled at his joint. "Maybe I'll quit gigging. Friend of mine has a farm out past Shakopee, says I can stay there. He's got goats, and some beehives—pretty fuckin' weird." He looked at her, and his voice lost some of its dreaminess. "You know, you're really good. I don't much like that stuff, you know, but you're good."

Eddi found she couldn't answer that. She hugged him instead, whispered, "Bye, Dale," and ran back to the car.

Carla turned north on Highway 35. Eddi hung over the back of her seat watching the Minneapolis skyline rise up and unroll behind them. White light banded the top of the IDS building, rebounded off the darkened geometry of a blue glass tower nearby. The clock on the old courthouse added the angular red of its hands. The river glittered like wrinkled black patent leather, and the railroad bridges glowed like something from a movie set.

"I love this view," Eddi sighed. "Even the Metrodome's not bad from here, for a glow-in-the-dark fungus."

"Boy, you *are* feeling sentimental," said Carla.

"Yeah." Eddi turned around to face the windshield. "Carla, am I doing the right thing?"

"You mean dumping Personality Man?"

Eddi looked at her, startled.

"Hey," Carla continued, "no big deduction. You couldn't leave Stu's band and stay friends with Stu—nobody could. So kissing off the band means breaking up with Mr. Potato Head."

Eddi giggled. "It's a really *pretty* potato."

"And solid all the way through. This'll probably wipe the band out, y'know."

"He can replace me," Eddi shrugged.

"Maybe. But you *and* me?"

"You're quitting?"

"I'm not sticking around to watch Stuart piss and moan." Carla's tone was a little too offhand, and Eddi shot her a glance. "Oh, all right," Carla amended. "Stuart would scream about what a bitch and a traitor you are, I'd tell him he was a shit and didn't deserve you, and I'd end up walking out anyway. Why not now?"

Eddi slugged her gently in the shoulder. "Yer a pal."

"Yeah, yeah. So start a band I can drum in."

"You could play for anybody."

"I don't want to play for *anybody*. You do that, you end up working with bums like Stuart."

With a lurch and a rumble of drumheads, they pulled in the driveway of Chester's. Even in the dark, its bits of Tudor architecture were unconvincing. The bar rush that hit every all-night restaurant was in full force; they had to wait for a table. When they got one, they ordered coffee and tea.

"So, are you going to start a band?"

Eddi slumped in her seat. "Oh God, Carla. It's such a crappy way to make a living. You work and work, and you end up playing cover tunes in the Dew Drop Inn where all the guys slow-dance with their hands in their girlfriends' back pockets."

"So you don't do that kind of band."

"What kind do you do?"

Their order arrived, and Carla dunked a tea bag with great concentration. "Originals," she said at last. "Absolutely new, on-the-edge stuff. Very high class. Only play the *good* venues."

Eddi stared at her. "Maybe I should just go over to Control Data and apply for a job as Chairman of the Board."

Carla looked out the window. "Listen. You don't become a bar band and work your way up from there. There *is* no up from there. It's a dead end. All you can become is the world's best bar band."

Eddi sighed. "I don't want a new band. I want to be a normal person."

Carla's dark eyes were very wide. "Oh," she said.

"Hey," Eddi smiled limply, "it's not like you to miss a straight line."

"Too easy," Carla said with a shrug. Then she shook her head and made her black hair fly, and seemed to shake off her sorrow as well. "Give it time. You don't remember how awful it is being normal."

"Not as awful as being in InKline Plain."

"Oh, worse," said Carla solemnly. "They make you sit at a desk all day and eat vending machine donuts, and your butt gets humongous."

"Now that," Eddi said, "is a job I can handle."

"If you work hard, you get promoted to brownies." Carla set her cup down. "Come on, let's roll."

Outside, the wind was blowing. It had none of the rough-sided cold of winter in it; it was damp, with a spoor of wildness that seemed to race through Eddi's blood. It made her want to run, yell, do any foolish thing. . . .

"You okay?" Carla's voice broke into her mood. "If you don't get in the car, I'm gonna leave without you."

Eddi took pleasure in the dash to the car, the way the wind tugged on her hair. "Roll the windows down."

"Are you bats? We'll freeze."

Eddi rolled down her own, but it wasn't enough. As they drove toward the city, the early spring madness drained away. The wagon's rattles and squeaks, its smell of cigarette butts and old vinyl and burnt oil, took its place. By the time they'd reached the edge of downtown, Eddi felt weary in every muscle and bone.

What should she do now? What *could* she do? It sounded fine to tell Carla that she wanted to be normal for once, but Eddi had never been suited to a normal life. Once she had taken a job as a security guard, patrolling an abandoned factory from four until midnight. Each night her imagination had tenanted the shadows with burglars and arsonists. At the end of a week the shadows were full, and she quit. She typed too slowly—did everything with her hands too slowly, in fact, except play the guitar.

As for a normal love affair, it wasn't impossible. She was reasonably intelligent. She was attractive, though not beautiful: blond and gray-eyed with strong features and clear skin; and she was small and slender and knew how to choose her clothes. But she wasn't sure where to find men who weren't—well, musicians.

"Mighty quiet," Carla said, as if she already knew why.

"I'm . . . I guess I'm beginning to realize the consequences of everything."

"Mmm. You going to chicken out?"

"No. But . . . would you call me tomorrow? Around two-ish? I figure I'll call Stu at one and tell him."

"And you'll need someone to tell you you're gonna be okay."

Eddi smiled sheepishly. "You must have done this yourself."

"Everybody has to, at least once. Don't beat yourself over the head for it."

The light was red at Washington and Hennepin, the corner where Carla would begin negotiating the rat's nest of one-way streets that led to Eddi's apartment. "Let me off here," she said suddenly.

"Wha—why?"

"I want to walk. It's a nice night."

Carla was shocked. "It's freezing. And you'll get murdered."

"You've been living around the lakes too long. You think any place with buildings more than three stories high is full of addicts."

"And I'm right. Anyway, what about your axe and stuff?"

It was true; she couldn't haul her guitar and amplifier fourteen blocks. She was settling back in the passenger seat when Carla spoke again.

"I know, I know. 'Carla, would you mind taking them to your place and carrying them all the way up the back stairs, then carrying them back down tomorrow when you come over to keep me from being miserable 'cause I broke up with my boyfriend?' Sure, Ed, what're friends for?"

Eddi giggled. "If you'd quit going to Mass, you'd make a great Jewish mother." She leaned over and hugged her.

"Jeez, will you get out of here? The light's changed twice already!" After Eddi had bounced out and slammed the door, Carla shouted through the half-open window, "I'll call at two!"

"Thank you!" Eddi yelled back, and waved as the station wagon rumbled and clanked away from the curb. The gold-and-gray flank of the library rose before her, and she followed it to the Nicollet Mall.

Whatever had tugged at her in the restaurant parking lot refused to be summoned back now. Eddi shook her head and started down the Mall, and hoped that the effort would blow her melancholy away. The rhythm of her steps reminded her of a dozen different songs at once, and she hummed one softly to herself. It was Kate Bush, she realized, "Cloudbusting," and she sang it as she walked.

Then she saw the figure standing by the bus shelter across the street.

By the shape, it was a man—a man's broad-brimmed hat and long, fitted coat. He didn't move, didn't seem even to turn his head to watch her, but she had a sudden wild understanding of the idea of a bullet with one's name on it. This figure had her name on him.

You must be feeling mighty low, girl, she scolded herself, *if you think that every poor idiot who's missed his bus is lying in wait for you.* Still, the man seemed naggingly *present,* and almost familiar. And three in the morning was an odd hour to wait for a bus in a town where the buses quit running at half-past midnight.

Her pace was steady as she crossed the empty street. Behind her, she heard his steps begin. *It's not fair,* she raged as she sped up. *I don't need this, not tonight.* She thought she heard a low laugh behind her, half the block away. Her stride lost some of its purpose and took on an edge of panic.

South of the power company offices, Eddi turned and headed for Hennepin Avenue. If there were still people on any street in Minneapolis, they would be on Hennepin. A police cruiser might even come by. . . .

The footsteps behind her had stopped. *There, see? Poor bastard was just walking down Nicollet. I'll be fine now—*

A black, waist-high shape slunk out of the alley in front of her. Its bared teeth glittered as it snarled; its eyes glowed red. It was a huge black dog, stalking stiff-legged toward her. Eddi backed up a step. It made a ferocious noise and lunged. She turned and ran in the only direction she could, back toward Nicollet.

She got one of the streetlight posts on the Mall between her and the dog and turned to face it. It wasn't there. Across the street, in the shadow of a doorway, Eddi saw the silhouette of the man in the hat and long coat. He threw back his head, and she heard his laughter. The streetlight fell on his face and throat and she saw the gleam of his white scarf, his dark skin and sloping, shining eyes. It was the man from the dance floor, from the University Bar. She ran.

The footsteps behind her seemed unhurried, yet they never dropped back, no matter how fast she ran. She tried again to turn toward Hennepin. The black dog lunged at her from out of a parking ramp exit, its red eyes blazing.

This is crazy, she thought with the dead calm of fear. *Muggers and mad dogs. I'm stuck in a Vincent Price movie. Where are the zombies?*

She was running down Nicollet again before she realized that it couldn't be the same dog. But it was insane to think that the man could have known she would walk home, impossible to think he had a pack of dogs. Her breath burned in her throat. She had a stitch in her side. Her pace had become a quick stumble.

She'd almost reached the end of the Mall, she realized. Two blocks away were the Holiday Inn and the Hyatt, and she could run into either, into a lobby full of light and bellhops and a desk clerk who'd call the police. She staggered across the street toward Peavey Plaza and Orchestra Hall.

The black dog seemed to form out of the shadows. Perhaps it was only one dog, after all; surely there weren't two dogs like this. It was huge, huge, its head low, its fur bristling gunmetal-dark in the street light. It growled softly, in macabre counterpoint to the waterfall sounds of the Peavey Plaza fountain. Did the damned dog know it stood between her and safety? How had it gotten past her? She moved sideways, through the concrete planters that marked the sidewalk level of Peavey Plaza. The hotels seemed miles away now. She would have to try to lose both dog and man in the complexity of the ornamental pool and fountains below her, and escape out the other side.

The dog lifted its head and howled, and Eddi thought of the dark man and his laugh. She wanted to curse, to throw something, to be home in her bed. She raced down a flight of steps, then another.

The footsteps behind her were sudden, as was the tap on her shoulder. She tried to turn in midstride and her foot didn't land on anything. Just before she plunged backward and head first down the last of the steps, she saw the man behind her, his eyes wide, his hand reaching out.

Then pain took away her fear, and darkness took the pain.

CHAPTER TWO

Who Can It Be Now?

She heard water running, and two voices. Were she to wake, these would be transmuted into ordinariness—the toilet wouldn't shut off, the neighbors were shouting on the other side of her bedroom wall.

"Fool!" raged a wild river of a voice. "Fool, I say!"

"Careful of your little tongue, dear. I've a mind to bite it off." This was a smoky, furry voice, laughing even as it threatened. Eddi heard a clicking, scraping sound, like a dog's toenails. That reminded her of something—what? Dogs, or toenails?

"You may have killed the mortal!"

"You amaze me," the deep voice replied. "Surely one mortal is much like another, to you?"

"Time grows short."

"Ah, of course. Time. Well, if she's harmed, it was by no work of mine." The deep voice added defensively, "And I softened her landing as best I could."

Her head ached, and she felt something cold and hard beneath her cheek—concrete? The conversation she heard was beginning to sound disturbingly sequential, less dreamlike.

"And if her people find her here?"

"Oh, they'll think of us straightway, I'm sure! They'll think she drank too much and fell."

Fell. Eddi remembered falling—and being pursued. Suddenly she was desperate to shed her lethargy, to get up, to at least open her eyes. . . . She opened them, and nothing she saw made sense. A black shape against gray, moving water . . . The deep voice continued.

"But did you see her? She ran like a deer, Glaistig."

"I care nothing for your sport. Fool of a phouka! Are you ass,

15

as well as dog and man? Do the conditions of your task please you so that you wish to linger at it?''

There was a rumbling growl.

"Ah, have I the right of it?" said the water-voice in a fierce purr. "Does it please you to live in mortal filth and stink? To see the mockeries they build of the bones of the earth?" Then, soft and cold as snow, "Would you be some human's little dog?"

The snarl that answered, full of rage, drove out Eddi's lassitude. She lifted her head to look, and could at last make sense of what she saw.

The black dog stood beside and above her. The forepaw beneath her nose seemed as big as her own hand, with glossy black curls of toenails the size of a parrot's beak. Its hackles spiked upward all down its back, and it curled its lips, growling at the fountain.

Eddi turned her throbbing head to look. *Not the fountain.* A woman rose from the water, tall and slender. She seemed to be standing on its surface, to be a coalescence of water into a woman-shaped pillar. Her long gown looked like water, too, spilling over her breasts and straight down in a current of darkness and green-shot light. Where it reached the surface of a pool, it disappeared into it, indistinguishable. Her hair seemed fluid as well, but snowy white, pouring down around her to her feet. Her face and arms were moon white.

Then she turned her gaze to Eddi and smiled, and Eddi remembered how, as a child, she had fallen through weak ice into freezing water.

"Well," breathed the apparition, "it lives."

"Who—what are you?" Eddi croaked. She raised herself onto one arm, and the pain in her head made her squint. "I'm gonna scream for the cops."

The water-woman gave a gurgling laugh, and bowed to her.

Next to Eddi's ear, the deep voice said, "Do it, then." Eddi turned and found the dog watching her, tongue lolling over its wolfish teeth. *The dog . . . talks. Oh, lord.*

"Summon your police," the dog continued, its lips working in horrible parody. "What will you tell them when they come, and find a dog and a pool of water?" It gestured with its muzzle toward the fountain.

As Eddi watched, the woman sank into the water—or became the water, spreading out until only her eyes glinted in the moonlight, then disappeared.

Eddi rose to her knees and started to back away. The dog took her shoulder in its mouth. She felt the long canines through her jacket, and she stopped moving.

" 'A's 'edder," said the dog, and let go. "Bide with us, sweet, until we give you leave to go."

"Why should I, if I can scare you off by calling the police?"

"Ah, but you can't. True, were you to call them, the glaistig" —with a rush of water the woman surfaced and shook her hair out around her—"would become a splash in the fountain, and I, a straying dog. But what of tomorrow night? Would they believe you, these policemen, if you told them you were haunted, and by what, and bid them stay beside you day and night? We will have you in the end; be wise, and let the end be now."

But by the dog's last word, Eddi had lunged for the stairs. Her vision blacked from rising too fast, but she kept on. This time she would outrun the damn dog or let him tear her throat out. Her outstretched hand found the stair rail—

Strong arms closed around her, pinning hers to her sides. She kicked backward, connected with something, and heard a hiss of pain. Hands fastened on her upper arms and spun her around.

It was the man who had chased her down the Mall, the black man in the University Bar. The streetlights slanted across his face, and she could see his teeth clenched, the tumble of hair down his forehead, the shadows that hid his eyes. She didn't have time to wonder where he'd come from before he spoke.

"Idiot child! Do you want me to lose my temper?"

The words were clearer from the human lips and tongue, but the voice was the black dog's. That recognition must have shown in her face; he bared his teeth, and a dog's growl rose from his throat. Eddi swallowed thickly and closed her eyes.

His little laugh startled them back open. "Can it be?" he said with a taunting smile. "You watch the glaistig melt and never turn a hair, yet let me but change from dog to man, and your courage flies away!"

Fury rose up in her, shouldering her fear aside. "Let go of me," she said, her voice flat and icy. She shrugged his hands from her arms.

"Truly, I mean you no harm," he said.

"That must be why you pushed me down the stairs."

"I did *not* push you," he said, irritated. "You fell." He stretched out a hand as if to take hold of her again. She stared at him until his hand fell back to his side. Then she walked across the pavement, back to the pool and the woman made of water.

"What do you want?" Eddi asked the silver-pale figure. Up close, the moonlight face was not so perfectly beautiful; the features were sharp and elongated.

"Your service, until we release you."

"Doing what?"

The water-woman smiled, a sweet, cruel expression, and Eddi saw that she had delicately proportioned fangs. *But vampires don't like water,* she thought with a shiver. "Doing whatever you're told, child of Man. Is that not the nature of servitude?"

"Glaistig!" said the man-who-was-also-a-dog.

"You raise your voice to me," the woman said haughtily, looking past Eddi to where he stood.

"I would raise my leg to you, were you worth the effort. Leave be, Glaistig. Tease her, and she'll learn to bite." He stepped forward to the edge of the pool. He had to look up to meet the woman's eyes—he was not much taller than Eddi, though his ominous presence had made him seem larger. "I say there is no harm in telling her what we require."

"And if she mislikes the sound of it?"

"Why, perhaps she'll spit in your eye, Glaistig, and you can drown her. There's a treat for you, eh?"

"I would as soon not trouble." The water-woman turned an evaluating look on Eddi. Then she inclined her head, an approving gesture, and Eddi felt a rush of pleasure. She was startled by the woman's fluid silver beauty. All the cruelty she thought she'd seen in those features was gone.

"Your pardon," the water-woman said, her voice still cold, but now full of the cadences of old rivers. "We will treat you very well, but you must not plague us with questions. Our concerns are greater than yours, and beyond your ken."

Eddi didn't agree—and yet, what in the water-woman's speech was unreasonable? These were great and noble beings, it was clear, and her business should be to do as they told her.

The woman watched her intently; the dark man, his face blank, looked from Eddi to the water-woman as if waiting. They wanted a response. Eddi could feel a nod pulling her chin down—and at last shook her head, though she didn't know why.

"You are a stupid little beast," the water-woman said pleasantly, with the force of absolute truth, "and will do as you are told."

Is that any way for a great and noble being to talk? Eddi thought. She felt as if she'd been drunk and was now suddenly sober. The woman in the pool was thin and witchy again.

"That's enough," Eddi said, and regarded her two captors warily. "Tell me what all this is about."

They were staring at her. "Well, Dog," the water-woman said at last, though she kept her eyes on Eddi, "you've chosen well and ill in equal measure. She is indeed more than she seems, though by Oak and Ash I cannot say how much. But you saw how she slipped the glamour as if it were a torn net. You'll have no easy task."

The dark man looked up at the water-woman as if he had a great deal to say and resented not being able to say it. Then he turned back to Eddi, and some of the same expression remained. "Eddi McCandry, the Seelie Court goes to war, and needs the presence of mortal blood to bring death to its enemies."

The phrase "mortal blood" sent a shooting cold through her, but she said, "That sounded like gibberish to me."

He hissed something under his breath. "I'll begin again. We are not human."

She couldn't help it—she laughed. They couldn't, of course, *not* be human. Nothing else had that shape. And they couldn't possibly *be* human, because nothing human had more than one shape. The might indeed be werewolves and vampires, but she had no desire to hear them say so. She could see the seams of the world around her begin to ravel and part, and the things waiting outside to pass through the holes were at once terrible and ridiculous. It was like being tickled—an unpleasant feeling that by some perverse reflex brings on laughter. "So what are you?" she gasped.

"We have many names," said the water-woman. "We are the Gray Neighbors, the Good People, the Strangers, the Fair Folk—"

"The *Little* People," drawled the short, dark man.

"Fairies," said Eddi, her laughter strangled. The resulting silence was so complete that she was afraid they'd struck her deaf.

"Had we come to grant a favor, the sound of that name would drive us off," growled the dark man. "Use it again at your peril."

"But that's what you are, isn't it?" Eddi turned to the water-woman. "Isn't it?"

Slowly, the pale head inclined, the attenuated white hands with their long nails rose and turned palm up. Yes.

Fairy tales. That was all she could remember about fairies, and as she tried desperately to recall the ones she'd heard or read, she realized she knew of few with fairies in them. And the two before her were nothing like Rumpelstiltskin or Cinderella's fairy godmother. Elegant Oberon and Titania, silly Puck— Shakespeare was no help, either. These two, with their changing shapes and their offhand cruelties, had their roots in horror movies.

"Are you going to kill me?" Eddi whispered. The mention of mortal blood was taking on more significance.

"Not necessarily," replied the water-woman, as if it were a question of purely intellectual interest. "Let the phouka finish."

"That is what my kind is called," said the dark man. "Phouka. You may call me so; it's name enough. She"—he nodded toward the woman in the pool—"is a glaistig, and so you may call her. For all that she may deny it, she and I have much in common."

Eddi ignored the glaistig's scowl, and said to the phouka, "And you turn into a dog."

"And a man," he grinned. When he was satisfied that he had startled her, he added smugly, "I have been credited with horse and goat as well, but I take no notice of it."

The glaistig shook her hair irritably, and it foamed in the soft light. "So, introductions all around. These amenities will outlast dawn if I leave this to you, Dog."

He snapped at her. The gesture was a grotesque fit for his human jaws.

"We are of the Seelie Court, noblest blood of Faerie," the glaistig continued. "We are the guardians, the rulers"—here the phouka snorted—"and to us are reserved the sacred grounds of hill and spring, the magical herbs and trees."

"But of course," the phouka broke in, "where there are those who think themselves noble folk, there must be some poor sod to play the commoner. . . ."

"Dog—"

"And in our case, we have the Unseelie Court, the most sodden lot you're like to see."

"Am I . . . like to see?" Eddi said weakly.

"Oh, yes. You're certain to, betimes. They've laid claim to territory of ours," he went on, in a voice edged with satire. "We've resolved to water it with their blood."

"That's nice." Eddi felt a queasy forboding. "What do you want me to do? Referee?"

The phouka flung his head back and barked laughter. "Ah, sweetling, you are fresh as the wind, if not as quick. The Unseelie Court are as immortal as we are. We could strike off all their warty heads tonight, and have it all to do again tomorrow. How would you slay an immortal?"

"I wouldn't."

"A sweet sentiment." He smiled fondly at her. "But there is a way. Were *you* upon the battlefield, you would bring to it the taint of mortality. All wounds would be true ones, and some would be fatal."

Eddi said slowly, "You want me to help you kill each other. And all I have to do is stand there."

"For all that it's inelegantly expressed, yes."

"Good. I hope you all die to the last man—or elf."

"Tsk. Oh, did I neglect to say that the Unseelie Court, being less than fond of parting with their loathly lives, will be eager to prove your mortality and rob us of your talismanic presence?"

"Ah," said Eddi. "I suppose I would have figured that out eventually." *So this,* she thought, her stomach clenched with fear, *is how it feels to be drafted.*

The glaistig spoke again. "The phouka has been assigned as your keeper, that we need not hunt you out when you are wanted. He will be at your side always. He serves also as your bodyguard," she continued, before Eddie could protest. "Spies for the Unseelie Court will learn of you soon." She raised her sharp white face to the sky. "Dawn is almost upon us, and I am tired. Begone." And she melted back into the pool with a rush.

Eddi saw that she was right about the dawn; the windows across the street reflected pink-tinged gray. She was aware, suddenly, of the reality of the buildings around her. This was the same Nicollet Mall that had been here yesterday. The difference, the unreality, must lie with her.

But she felt real. She ached from falling down the steps, she was tired, the fingertips of her left hand smarted from playing guitar. . . . *Carla,* she thought. *I could call her right now, and she'd answer the phone and grunt at me, and say, "Are you crazy, girl? It's—'is it six?'—six o'clock in the goddamn morning!" And I'd tell her what just happened, and she'd say—*

"Rowan and Thorn, woman!" came the voice of the phouka from the street above her. "Do come along, or I'll fetch you!"

Climbing the steps felt like mounting a scaffold. When she got to the top, there was no sign of the phouka. Then, three feet away, the black dog rose from behind a planter and turned his red eyes on her.

"Stop that," she said. "Change back."

"Indeed not. I'm to be your bodyguard, am I not? Many's the mortal in this city who'd envy you your fine big guard dog, poppet. See?" And he leaped between her and some imaginary assailant, his head lowered and hackles bristling, stiff-legged, a rumble in his throat that seemed to shake the pavement. "Oh, what a terror I am! But a puppy-gentle with my mistress." He bounded back to her, tail wagging, and licked her hand.

Eddi snatched it away and wiped it on her jacket. "Cut it out, you hear me? Don't touch me again!"

His ears drooped, and he rolled his fearsome eyes upward. "She rejects my doggish loyalty. Ah, my heart, my heart." He turned and began to prance down the Mall ahead of her.

"Where are you going?"

"Why, home with you, my sweet."

"How do you know the way?"

He looked at her over his black-furred shoulder. "Did you think, perhaps, that I wandered into that vile hole last night by chance? You've been my study, Eddi McCandry, for many a day. I know where you live." And he set off once again.

She was furious. What else did these—things—know about her? The color of her rugs? The contents of her refrigerator? That she talked to her reflection in the bathroom mirror?

"What makes you think I'm going home?" Eddi said sweetly.

He looked back and cocked his head. "Aren't you?"

"No. I'm going to the Pound. There's a dangerous dog loose in this neighborhood."

His lip began to curl back from his teeth. "Eddi. . . ."

She didn't think he'd let her get as far as the Pound. But she might manage a phone booth—yes, there was the blue-and-white sign on the corner. *Don't look at the phone. And don't run.* She strode across the street as if she meant to keep walking. At the last moment, she ducked into the booth and slammed the folding door.

She braced her feet against the door and her shoulders on the opposite wall.

"May I lend you a quarter?" said the infuriating voice. The black dog sat beside the booth, ears up, head tilted inquiringly.

Eddi felt foolish, but she didn't take her feet off the door. "This call's free."

"Ah. You don't mind, do you, if I listen? I want to know what you'll think of to tell them."

She let her breath out slowly. "I'm going to call the cops. The squad car will come, and whether you're a dog, a man, or not here at all, I'm going to the station with them. If they won't take me, I'll hit one of them and they'll *have* to take me."

The phouka's look of patient attention only intensified.

"And once I'm there, I can use the same techniques to get them to keep me there. Then if you want me, you can break me out of jail."

Why she hadn't already dialed 911, she didn't know. Perhaps it was the expression on the phouka's face, polite, intelligent, and doggy.

"Very good," he said at last. "And I, for my part, could break one of these glass walls and sever the cable on that telephone before you could say hello." Eddi began a surreptitious move toward the receiver. "But I'd much prefer not to. It would set a bad precedent."

"You mean like chasing me down the Nicollet Mall?" she snapped.

To her surprise, the phouka's ears drooped a little. "If you were to call that ill-considered, self-indulgent idiocy, I would probably allow it to be true."

Eddi would not have chosen any of those words, so she said nothing.

"But let us reason together, sweet. I have *not* tried the walls of your fortress." He indicated the phone booth with his nose. "I have not offered you violence." Eddi snorted, but let it pass. "Will you not deal fairly, and let me bear you company, at least until I *do* transgress?"

"Did it occur to you to try this approach down at the other goddamn end of the Mall?"

He looked offended and embarrassed, and both expressions sat oddly on his dog face. "No," he said irritably.

Eddi decided it would be unwise to laugh. "What if I don't want to deal?"

He stood. "I do not predict the future."

Eddi stared at him. Her shoulders were getting sore, and one of her feet was asleep. She was cold. For all she knew, he never got cold or tired. She would feel like a perfect idiot if she stepped out the door and he strangled her. But just now he didn't have hands. She unfolded the door.

"You gladden a poor dog's heart," he said. He trotted to the curb and looked back; after a moment, she followed him.

The phouka seemed oblivious to the effect a talking dog might produce; he chattered brightly to her all the way to her apartment building on Oak Grove. Fortunately, they passed no one else. She interrupted him only once, to ask, "Why me?"

"Why you, what?"

"Why are you picking on me? Why not grab some drunk off Hennepin Avenue and drop him on your stinking battlefield? They're all mortal, too."

"Lay the blame on good taste. We're a fastidious lot." But a block later, he said, "I can't explain now. Later, when you know our ways, perhaps I can answer you and you'll understand."

She felt strange holding the front door of the building for him. As she stood at the inner door, fishing in her pocket for her keys, he said, "There's a stink on this place."

"Drunks come in here to get warm."

"No, this is a reek of another sort. I smell rules and laws and Thou Shan'ts."

She pushed open the second door. "Mm. That's Roberta, the caretaker."

"Oho—a threat worthy of your guard dog! I shall go for her throat—GRRAAHRRR!" He bolted snarling down the hall and up the stairs, toenails clattering on the wood floors.

"Shut up!" she hissed, and ran after him. She caught up with him on the third floor, outside her apartment door. "God damn you! If she heard that, I am screwed to the wall!"

He cocked his head and looked doggily innocent. "Have I . . . done something?"

"This is a 'no pets' building, you . . ." Something about his voice lit her suspicions. "You knew that, didn't you?"

Eddi wondered if, had he been in human form, he would have pressed a hand to his breast. "You could believe that of me? Oh, I am wounded to the quick!"

She unlocked the door. "Get in there."

He loped into her tiny, blind-alley kitchen, through the living room, into the bedroom. His voice drifted back, hollow from bouncing off the bathroom tiles. "Charming! A bit cramped for two, but I don't regard it in the least! What's for breakfast?"

"Chew off one of your hind legs." She sank down on the

couch and rubbed her temples. Then she heard the sound she dreaded: The clack-clack of a woman's shoes on the stairs.

Eddi opened the door to the firm knock. Roberta stood before her in a robe of salmon velour and white eyelet, and little heeled slippers. "Miss McCandry," she intoned, "I heard a dog."

"You did?" said Eddi stupidly.

"I did. And I heard you, as well."

"You did?"

"Miss McCandry, we do not allow pets here. I wish to inspect your apartment."

"You d—ah, right." But she didn't move.

Roberta frowned. "As stated in the lease, which you signed—"

"I know, I know. Come in."

As if she could smell the trail the phouka had left, Roberta stalked into the kitchen and out, into the living room, where she looked behind all the furniture, and across to the bedroom door. "May I?" she asked as if the answer didn't matter.

With a sigh, Eddi flung open the door.

Roberta gasped in horror, and Eddi followed her transfixed gaze. There on the bed was the phouka. He was lying on his stomach, propped up on his elbows, facing the door. His brown skin was a shocking contrast to the rumpled white sheets, which were drawn across him to barely cover his buttocks. He wore absolutely nothing.

"Good morning," he said with sleepy charm.

Roberta slammed the door.

"Uh, I'm sorry," Eddi began. "He's, uh . . . I mean . . ."

Roberta walked unsteadily to the apartment door, said, "Good day," without turning, and left.

Eddi locked the door behind her and ran to the bedroom. "You get out of my bed and get your clothes on," she hissed through the door.

"Aww . . ."

"I mean it! Right now!"

The door opened, and he stood before her, dressed as he had been on the Mall.

"What are you trying to do?" she wailed. "This is a nice apartment! You think I want Roberta running to the owners with stories about my entertaining strange men?"

"I'm only one strange man."

"God give me strength. I should never have come out of that damn phone booth."

He sighed and said, "I am a phouka, my sweet, and by nature a tricksy wight. I cannot be otherwise."

She scrubbed at her tired eyes. "Oh, hell. Will you get out of there? I want to go to sleep." She squeezed past him and pushed him out into the living room.

"But where will *I* sleep?" he asked plaintively.

Eddi gave him a sweet smile. "Why don't you turn into a dog and curl up on the rug?"

And she slammed the door on him.

CHAPTER THREE

My Boyfriend's Back

Eddi woke up staring at the bedroom ceiling, wondering why she knew that the sky had fallen. Then she heard someone in the living room, and remembered. There was no moment of self-delusion, of believing that it was Stuart who'd come home with her. For one thing, Stuart didn't know how to whistle.

She slid into her robe and opened the door between the bedroom and the bathroom. The other bathroom door, the one that opened onto the living room, was closed. She dashed in and locked it, then locked the one to the bedroom as well. "Of course," she muttered to her reflection in the mirror, "for all I know, he can walk through walls."

Eddi turned on the shower. The rumble of the water covered the clamor that had started in the kitchen, a rattling of dishes and pans and the banging of cupboard doors. She pulled back the shower curtain—and hesitated. All that water reminded her of the Peavey Plaza fountain, and the glaistig with her cold voice and ominous little fangs. What if she could pop up wherever there was water?

It was an uneventful shower. She took the time to dry her hair, and the noise of the blow-dryer shielded her from any sounds from the front of the apartment. It didn't drown out the thunderous knocking on the bathroom door. Eddi jumped.

"Halloo, the pokey hostess! If you want me to eat your share, too, you've only to say so!"

"I'll . . . be right out," Eddi croaked. She made a great business out of putting away the hair dryer before she finally opened the door.

Yes, it was true. There was a dark-skinned man in her kitchen, who wasn't really a man at all, and he was proof that everything she remembered of last night had happened.

This morning he was wearing a bronze-colored jacket, broad-shouldered, that stopped at his waist, and a tight pair of pants to match. Eddi wondered what had happened to the clothes he'd worn the night before. He gave her a huge smile.

"That," said the phouka, in his reverberating low voice, "is a very fetching costume."

It was a secondhand silk kimono from Ragstock, embroidered with green willow leaves on a rust background. She had always thought it rather fetching herself, but she was irritated that *he* thought so. She said, "What're you doing?"

"Making breakfast. A job usually best left to the likes of hobs and brownies, but I fancy I do it well enough."

She peered past him to the stove top. There were what looked like pancakes in her largest frying pan. "What are they?" she asked.

"Flapjacks." He rolled the word off his tongue, clearly pleased with it.

She scowled suspiciously. "Anything in 'em?"

"Why no, they're made of air and dew. Of course there's something in them, or they wouldn't be there." He shot her a disgusted look and flipped pancakes onto one of her plates. It irked her to see him handling her things with such confidence.

The secondhand kitchen table that was her dining room was set neatly for two, with silverware, placemats, and two wine glasses (she only had two) filled with orange juice. It looked cozy and conjugal. Or was she being too sensitive? How was a . . . fairy . . . to know how she would view all this? *Then again, where did he learn to set the table in the first place, from reading Miss Manners?*

There were butter and syrup on the table; she sat down and applied them to her pancakes. The phouka brought his plate out and sat down across from her.

"You're supposed to eat them hot, you know," he said.

Eddi took a bite.

"Well?" he studied her. "How are they?"

She made a noise, grudgingly.

"Now don't say thank you, my flowerlet; we are all made terribly uncomfortable by thanks." He took a bite himself. "Passable, certainly, but not brownie-work. Now with a little forethought and a bowl of milk, a lass like you could have had a stack of brownie cakes thin as leaves and light as air waiting for you when you woke. Sink scrubbed and the floor swept as well, likely. But there, you couldn't know, could you?''

Eddi was doing her best to follow this monologue. She remembered faintly, from her days as a Girl-Scouts sort of Brownie, that the fairy-tale brownie did chores for people. Eddi would have preferred to help fight forest fires. "If you wanted a brownie," she said at last, "why didn't *you* call one?"

He beamed at her. "Bless you, sweet, they won't come for a commoner like me."

She shook her head. "Last night you said you belonged to a Court. . . ."

He sighed and raked his hands through his hair. "You must learn to pay no mind to the glaistig. Or at least, you must learn *when* to pay her any mind. She has delusions of rank, but it's not true. Rowan and Thorn, my dear, she has goat feet!"

Eddi thought about that for a moment. "Goat feet. Is that some kind of fairy insult?"

The phouka blew through his lips like a horse. "You don't know *anything,* do you?"

"No. I know absolutely nothing." She rapped her knuckles on the side of her head. "Solid clear through, see? I don't know how to call brownies, ignore glaistigs, or accept insults from a dog!"

"I am not a—"

"And if you're so disgusted with me, you can damn well leave." She stuffed another bite into her mouth and chewed furiously. Then she remembered that he'd made breakfast. "Thank you," she said sweetly.

He did look uncomfortable. More, he looked angry. He wrapped her wrist with his first finger and thumb, and pulled her arm down to the table with no visible effort.

"There's no profit in trying my patience, Eddi," he said. His voice was soft, but his slanting dark eyes were narrowed.

"If somebody wants to blow me away," she said, trying to keep her voice even and failing, "he has to get you first. I'm sure to die happy."

An expression flicked across his face, and was gone before she could identify it. He released her. She started to say thank you, then remembered and bit it off.

"I . . . forgot myself." The phouka was looking out the window. Eddi doubted, since the view was of the backside of the building across the alley, that he was really looking at anything.

She finished her pancakes in silence, while the phouka continued to stare at nothing and look thoughtful. They *were* very good pancakes, even at room temperature. Would it be safe, Eddi wondered to say so? Wouldn't that be the same as thanking him?

"How long are you . . . staying here?" she asked.

He started a little and blinked at her. "Until you go out," he said, and smiled.

She took a deep breath and tried again. "How long are you going to guard me?"

"For as long as you need it, my primrose, nor shall I count the cost."

"I can stand the dodging around," Eddi muttered. "It's the smug tone of voice that gets me."

"Thank you," he said. But he relented at last. "We fight a war, Eddi, and wars go on for as long as they will. But among the Folk, warfare is something of a recreation, and has as a consequence more rules, more ritual. The campaign will begin on May Eve, and end no later than the eve of All Hallows. If by then neither side has the victory, both will withdraw and lick their wounds until next May Eve. I will be with you until the business is done, win or lose."

"I take it May Eve is the last day of April. All Hallows is . . . Halloween?" Eddi counted, horrified. "That's six months."

The phouka looked uncomfortable. "We, or they, might well prevail before All Hallows."

"Six months?"

He spread his fingers on the tabletop and looked at them. "And the time until May Eve."

"Oh, God."

"It's no trouble, really," he beamed.

Eddi put her hands over her face and moaned.

The phone rang then. Before Eddi could do more than uncover her eyes, the phouka bounded out of his chair and snatched up the receiver.

"Don't!" Eddi cried, too late.

"McCandry residence," he said pleasantly. "May I help you?" By this time Eddi was trying to pull the receiver away from his ear. It didn't budge. "A very good friend of Miss McCandry's," he continued. "Who wants to know? . . . Ah."

"Dammit, give me the phone!" Eddi said through clenched teeth, but the phouka only planted his free hand on her chest and held her at arm's length. Eddi could hear an agitated voice from the earpiece.

"Splendid!" said the phouka brightly. "Eddi has told me about you. We'll be waiting." And he hung up the phone.

"You—you—you *son of a bitch!*"

"Bow-wow," he said, smiling.

"Who was that?"

"Who was what?"

"On the phone!"

"Oh, that. That was your boyfriend."

"That . . . was Stuart?" Her stomach gave a nervous clench.

"B'lieve that's his name. The ornamental fellow with no talent?"

Eddi reviewed the phouka's half of the phone call. "Shit. Oh, boy."

"Come now, sweet. Do you really want to spend your time pandering to that spoiled boy's vanity?" He cleared the table briskly, and called back from the kitchen, "Now, thanks to me, you can dismiss him from your life. Poof. Simplest thing in the world."

Eddi felt rooted to the floor, rage and confusion fighting for control of her. "Simple? What's simple about it? He's going to think I've been sleeping with you!" She'd planned to break off with Stuart, yes, but sadly, quietly, trying not to hurt him. Not like this . . .

The phouka stuck his head around the doorway into the living room, his large tilted-up eyes wide. "Oh, my primrose, are you so innocent? Lads like that can only be replaced. Anything else is too subtle for them. If you told the boy that your love had faded, he'd think you were only being difficult. He won't go away until you show him a rival and tell him he's been supplanted."

"This is none of your business."

He rolled his eyes and disappeared back into her corridor of a kitchen. "I should let you try it your way and prove it to you," he called back. "But it would take too much time. This way he'll be out from underfoot, and you'll be the better for it."

"I hope I get the chance to do *you* a favor some day," Eddi said at last, when she could trust herself to speak without screaming.

"I feel obliged to point out, sweet, that greeting the boy in your dressing gown will not, in this case, improve his temper."

"Get stuffed!" Eddi growled, and stomped back to the bedroom.

Sometimes, she reflected, she dressed for courage, sometimes for success, and sometimes for the consolation of knowing that whatever else went wrong, at least she liked her clothes. This promised to be one of the latter times. She dug through her closet for the long pink pleated skirt she'd found at Tatters. She added her favorite lace blouse and a man's gray suit vest, pink socks and white sneakers. "Better," she said to the mirror over the chest of drawers, and bounced a little to get the feel of the sneakers.

If she could get the damn phouka to go away and let her handle Stuart . . . But perhaps it was true; this was a sharp, short pain, a little misunderstanding to prevent a larger one. Stuart's hurt pride—and there was so much of it to hurt—would drive him away.

She felt the ache in the back of her throat that was the first warning of tears. She wasn't in love with Stuart, not anymore, not really. They'd been together a year, and what was love had turned, unnoticed, into habit. But she could remember being in love with him. They had shared words and phrases that made them laugh because of how or where they'd heard them. He'd sent her dumb cards, for no reason . . . no. Better not to remember. She found herself sitting on the end of the bed, and wasn't sure how long she'd been there. Stuart would arrive soon; she ought to be collecting her wits, not scattering them. And she ought to be doing something about the phouka—

Her door buzzer bleated from the living room, twice, three times. Eddi dashed out of the bedroom and pressed the button that unlocked the front door. The phouka was slouched in her only upholstered chair, looking pained.

"Hideous noise," he said.

"Then why didn't you get it?"

"Get what?"

"The door!"

"Was that what it was?" he said with an air of academic interest. 'I wonder that anyone could welcome company, if it's always announced so."

"It's not welcome this time," Eddi muttered, but the phouka ignored her. His feet were propped on the trunk that served as her coffee table, and he seemed to be engrossed in a copy of *The Face*. He looked entirely at home. Eddi suspected that he was setting a tableau for Stuart's benefit, but there was nothing she could do about it now. She heard Stuart running up the stairs.

She opened the door before he could knock. Stuart was breathing a little hard from the climb, and one lock of brown hair, longer than the rest, had fallen forward over his forehead. He looked pale, his eyes wide and unguarded. Eddi felt the ache again in her throat. *Damn you, Stuart,* she wailed inside, *please be angry.* But it was too late. He would be angry, he would say cruel things, but she would remember his cut-adrift look and be unable to hate him.

"Come in," she said finally, and then, as if that had unstoppered her voice, "I was going to call you, this morning, but you beat me to it. I wanted to—I'd like to talk, Stuart, about . . . the band . . . and . . . oh, shit."

As she ran down, his gaze went past her and hardened. She sighed and turned.

The phouka was unfolding himself gracefully, propping his elbows on the chair back and his chin in his palms. "Stuart Kline, yes?" he said with a drowsy smile. "Please to meet you."

"Get out of here," Stuart said tightly. "This is private."

"On the contrary," said the phouka, "I believe it concerns me . . . intimately."

"Get the fuck out."

"You're being impolite, my little fighting cock. Why should I leave? *You're* the visitor."

Stuart went paler still. "Is that true?" he said to Eddi. "Has he moved in already?"

"No!" Out of the corner of her eye, she saw the phouka cock his head. "Oh hell—yes, but not like that!"

Stuart's jaw went a little crooked, and Eddi knew he was grinding his teeth. "Like what, then?" he said, looking at the phouka.

"I'm not sleeping with him." She had a wild urge to tell him, "He followed me home."

"Well, you'll just have to get your sleep someplace else, won't you? How goddamn stupid do you think I am?" His voice rose in volume and pitch, and he took a step toward her. "What, you want to pass this son-of-a-bitch off as an old friend? Then why the fuck didn't you introduce him last night?"

"Last night?" the phouka's voice broke in, all its laziness gone.

"You shut up!" Stuart screamed at him, and turned on Eddi again. "You think I didn't see him last night at the club? The two of you watching each other?"

"That," said the phouka softly, "is precisely what I'd thought."

"Well, think again. Are you from Jamaica, or what? You talk like a fucking faggot."

"For God's sake, Stuart!" Eddi grabbed at his arm, frightened by the phouka's stiffness, Stuart's overflowing rage.

"What do you say, Eddi?" Stuart asked sweetly, still watching the phouka. "Is he a faggot? Is that why you're not fucking him? I mean, you would otherwise, wouldn't you? As long as he could get it up."

She let go of his arm. "Anything would be better than the way we've been the last few months," she said through clenched teeth.

She watched the swing of Stuart's arm, the fist sweeping toward her face, and thought, *All those fights, and he never hit me*. . . . She was too surprised to feel the blow at first, but it knocked her down. As she fell, she saw the phouka move from his chair to Stuart. Then Stuart was face down on the floor, one arm pinned behind him and the phouka's knee in his back. Stuart's face was white and pinched with pain.

"Don't. Do that. Again." The phouka's voice was soft, but with each word he tugged gently on Stuart's pinned arm. Stuart's breath hissed between his teeth.

"Let him up," Eddi croaked.

The phouka looked at her with another of his unfathomable expressions. He released Stuart and stood.

Stuart rose slowly. He straightened his coat and dragged his fingers through his hair; then he took several shaky steps to the door. He paused in the doorway, as if he would turn and say one last thing. But he raised his head and disappeared down the hallway.

Eddi struggled to her feet and lurched for the door. The phouka moved to follow her.

She turned on him. "You! *Stay!*"

As she ran down the hall, she wondered which of them was more surprised at his obedience.

She caught up with Stuart on the second-floor landing. "Stu, wait!"

He didn't turn. When she came up beside him, she saw the stopping-up of his emotions in his face.

"I'm sorry, Stu. That . . . that wasn't what I wanted."

"You didn't want to break it off?" There was no flicker of hope in his eyes or voice. She winced away from his stillness as she hadn't from his upraised hand.

"I didn't want to do it like that."

He shrugged and looked away. "Too late now."

"Yeah." She exhaled, gulped air. "I . . . the band . . ."

"Yeah, I know. Carla, too, I suppose?"

She was startled, and only nodded.

He rubbed a hand over his face, and Eddi thought some of what he was holding in might escape. But the hand dropped, and his face was closed and hard. "Right. I gotta go."

"Good-bye, Stu."

He shrugged again, and went on down the stairs.

When she got back to her apartment, she found the phouka in the doorway. He opened his mouth.

"I don't want to hear it," she said. She saw his eyes kindle with anger, before he turned sharply away. She stayed leaning against the doorjamb, too weary to move.

"I was going to say, 'I'm sorry,' " the phouka said at last.

Eddi stared at him.

"I hadn't thought he would strike you." Then he gave a bitter little bark of a laugh. "There are many things I hadn't thought he'd do. Earth and sky guard me from the consequences of my error."

Eddi sank down on the couch. She was trembling. The phouka had gone to stand at the window. It seemed a long time before he spoke again.

"I missed what I should have seen, and my only excuse is that he stood in your shadow."

"What?" said Eddi.

The phouka turned, but backlighted as he was, Eddi saw only his silhouette. "When I heard you, I was drawn, forgive the coarse and common simile, like a moth to flame, and when I saw you, you glowed like the moon's own face and blinded me. I should have seen that Stuart, too, had a certain . . . luminosity. But I did not, and that folly may prove costly. For what it's worth, you have my apology."

"I don't understand anything you're saying."

The phouka turned back to the window.

The phone rang then, and Eddi picked it up warily. "Hello?"

"Hullo, kid. It's Carla."

"Carla," Eddi said; then her throat constricted and she couldn't speak.

"Eddi? You okay?"

She took a deep breath. "Carla, can you come over?"

"Shit, yes. I'm at the Seven-Eleven around the corner. Be there in three." And Eddi heard her hang up.

For three minutes there was silence in the apartment. When the door buzzer went off, the phouka stalked over and pressed the button.

It wasn't until Carla appeared in the doorway that Eddi realized she hadn't shut the door after Stuart. Carla stopped and looked from Eddi, still sitting on the couch, to the phouka, who was standing by the bedroom door.

"Well," said Carla. "Hi."

"Come on in," Eddi said.

"I'm already in. You've seen Stuart, I take it."

Eddi nodded.

"I also take it from your semicatatonic state that it was grisly."

Eddi wanted to burst into tears and fling herself upon Carla's bosom. "Yes," she said instead.

"Uh-huh. So. Who's this?" Carla pointed her chin at the phouka. "Friend of yours? Or are things even stranger here than they feel?"

Eddi licked her lips. "You won't like it."

"You're getting a bruise on the side of your face. If he has anything to do with that"—Carla jerked her head toward the phouka—"you damn betcha I won't like it."

"Not exactly. I mean, that wasn't his fault. Carla . . ." There was no way to ease gently into the subject "Carla, he's a phouka."

Carla stared at her, then looked at the phouka. "A—phouka?"

"You know what it is?" Eddi asked.

Carla looked at her dubiously. "The last time I heard that word, Jimmy Stewart was using it to describe a six-foot white rabbit." And she looked back at the phouka.

"Let me tell you what's happened since I left you last night," Eddi said. She saw the phouka scowl and open his mouth to interrupt, but she didn't let him. She told Carla the whole story.

When she'd finished, Carla shook a cigarette out of her pack and lit it. "Dear," she said, frowning, as the smoke rolled out of her mouth, "I love you like my own sister. Which is why I won't hesitate to tell you that I don't believe it."

"How much of it don't you believe?" Eddi asked.

"What do you mean, how much of it? The unbelievable parts. Starting with your gentleman caller here turning into a dog. On the other hand, I doubt that breaking up with Stuart has left you a few stairs short of the landing."

Eddi looked at the phouka. "I don't suppose you'd prove it to her."

He scowled and stepped away from the wall. "It would serve you right if I shook my head sadly and said that you'd been like this since I found you in the street this morning. Watch closely, I won't do it again."

And he changed. Eddi realized as he did it that she'd never seen the process, and she felt suddenly embarrassed, as if she'd asked to watch him undress. The transformation from man to dog wasn't instantaneous, nor was it a slow metamorphosis of man's arm into dog's leg, man's face lengthening into dog's muzzle. There was a sparkling whirl of air around him that seemed to dissolve him, and with it a fleeting fragrance of warm earth and fresh water. The dog-form coalesced, and the confusion of air seemed to be absorbed back into it, until all that stood before them was an enormous black dog.

"There," said the phouka in his furry dog's voice. "Look your fill and be done; I don't feel especially doggish just now and would like to change back."

"Mary Mother of God," Carla said in a flat voice. "Change the hell back. Please."

Eddi, for no reason she could explain, felt comforted by that. "Get used to him. He says he's going to be my shadow until they finish their war."

The phouka returned to human form, and Carla took a long shaky drag on her cigarette.

"Can I talk you out of taking *her?*" Carla said at last to the phouka.

"No." His gaze was fixed on the floor, and his voice was soft.

"If . . . if anything happens, I'll get you. I swear I will."

He met Carla's hard look, and nodded. "All right."

Eddi looked at Carla's profile and saw her filling slowly up with some dangerous resolve. The vision chilled her. She remembered the sight of Stuart in the doorway, his eyes asking for reassurance, and she remembered him leaving, the way he'd straightened his shoulders before he stepped out into the hall.

She had been drafted by the fairies. But wars have a way of coming home, she knew, and not all the shots are fired on the battlefield.

CHAPTER FOUR

I've Just Seen a Face

Eddi took a deep breath and said to the phouka, "I don't suppose you'd go for a walk or something for half an hour."

He stretched in his chair. "No indeed. But it's sweet of you to think of it."

"I want to talk to Carla in private."

The phouka looked elaborately hurt. "Oh, my heart, what can you say to her that you may not say to me?"

"Do you expect to listen in on every conversation I have for the next six months? Because if that's true, you can find yourself another sucker."

He shrugged. "There's the bedroom."

"This is *my* living room. Why don't *you* go sit in the god-damn bedroom?"

The phouka cocked his head. "Are we going to have a fight?"

Carla bounced out of her chair and grabbed Eddi's arm. "Don't beat him up, kid," she said lightly. "It'd probably give him some kind of moral satisfaction.

"And *you*," she added to the phouka, "can quit bugging her. What good does it do you to be such a jerk?"

He shrugged and made a regretful face. "It's the way I'm made, I suppose. For centuries, my kind have delighted in luring travelers off the path and into the marsh for the sheer pleasure of seeing them wet their feet."

"What," said Eddi, spitting out each word, "does that have to do with my living room?"

"Nothing, but it serves to explain why I've done a necessary thing in an unnecessarily annoying fashion."

"Can I have my living room to myself?"

"No," said the phouka.

"Are you going to tell me *why not?*"

He laughed, not at all unpleasantly. "I hadn't intended to, but see how sweetly you beguile me?"

Eddi made a disgusted noise.

"If the two of you sit in the living room and I in the bedroom, my primrose, you might take a notion to try to slip out the door. I wound find you and bring you back, of course, and you would be embarrassed. See the suffering I have spared you?"

"My," said Eddi, "I guess a pair of handcuffs would make me the happiest girl in the world."

"And," said the phouka, "not incidentally, as long as I am between you and the door, I am also between you and anyone who might come in."

"What does that mean?"

"It means, my child, that the Unseelie Court will find out about you. Soon, unless I miss my reckoning. When they do, they will want—how shall I say this?—to do you a mischief. Should they choose a bold attack over a sly one, I would rather be the one to meet them at the door."

"In her own damn apartment?" Carla said, but the phouka paid no attention.

Eddi pushed her hair back with both hands and stared at him. "I'm not safe here."

"Not really."

"Oh." Eddi supposed she ought to be afraid, but in place of fear she found only a simmering anger. *This bastard chases me all over downtown, moves into my apartment, mauls my boyfriend, refuses me my own living room—and tells me he's just protecting me from somebody worse? If these are the good guys, who the hell are the villains?*

She looked down her nose at the phouka and said, "All right, play guard dog if it makes you feel good. I'll go climb out the bedroom window." She turned and started away.

"It's painted shut."

"How do you know?"

"Gracious, pet, I'm a supernatural being."

"You're a shithead," Eddi said sweetly, and led Carla off to the bedroom.

Eddi paced the tiny space at the end of the bed, and Carla drew her feet out of the way in mock alarm.

"Don't worry, I won't tell him how to handle you."

Eddi glanced at her deadpan face. "I don't think I want to know this."

Carla shrugged. "Anytime I want you to do something, I convince you it would be stupid and annoying."

Eddi laughed and sat on the bed beside her. "You *don't* want me to start a band?"

Carla shrugged. "Sometimes I forget."

Eddi pulled a strand of Carla's shiny black hair. "Silly bitch." Then she grew solemn. "Listen, kiddo, you don't want to be in on this—this war, or whatever it is. Really. You're afraid I'll screw up without you. And you're probably right."

"You betcha."

"But whatever else these guys want, they seem to want me in one piece. I'm taken care of." *I hope.* "If you get mixed up in this, I don't know if they'll care so much what happens to you. So why don't you pretend that I've gone to Europe for the summer?"

"What, and not even any postcards?"

"Carla—"

"It's an idea, though," Carla said, rolling backward on the bed. "Why not go to Mexico or something, and give these guys the slip? We'd get the money from someplace."

"Money is not the problem. The problem is getting past the warden out there."

"You mean Rover?"

Eddi fell back on the bed, giggling. "Jesus, Carla, don't call him that to his face!"

"Why not? What can he do to me?"

Eddi had a vivid memory of the speed that had brought Stuart down, and the careless strength that had held him there. "I don't want to know. And neither do you."

"Listen," Carla said firmly, poking the air with her finger for emphasis, "I will buy that he's one bad dude. I will *not* buy that he's invincible."

Eddi sighed. "There's probably something short of a stick of dynamite that'll move him out of that living room. But whatever it is, I don't think either of us have it."

Carla propped herself up on her elbows. "Why are you so sure?"

"Carla, this is a guy who turns into a dog."

"So you might as well give up?"

"You didn't see him last night."

"No, I didn't. All I *have* seen is a guy who turns into a dog, and I'm not even sure about that. I'll bet Steven Spielberg could get the same effect."

Eddi blinked. "In my living room?"

"All right, all right. But that still doesn't make him unbeat-able. And it doesn't prove anything about this fairy war jazz."

"There was the glaistig. Who walked on water, by the way."

"In the dark."

Eddi threw up her hands. "Okay, it's all wires, or mirrors, or hypnotism. But if they're not who they say they are, and they don't want what they say they want, what's going on?"

"What do you mean?"

"Carla, why would anybody go to this much trouble and expense to get me? Either they're who—and what—they say they are, or I'm whacko and imagining the whole thing."

"You could ask me to go back to the damn Seven-Eleven and call the cops for you."

Eddi shook her head. "When the police got here, all they'd find is a chick keeping a dog in a no-pets apartment building. A weird unemployed rock 'n' roller chick."

Carla made a face. "Maybe they'd take him to the Pound?"

"No. I'd just get kicked out of the apartment." She rumpled Carla's hair. "Don't worry, kiddo. We *will* think of something."

"Well, all right. As long as you promise to keep thinking."

"I promise."

"Good. What was Stuart like? Awful?"

Eddi thought of all the things she could say. None were small enough to get past the lump in her throat. She pressed the bruised side of her face lightly. Maybe if she hated Stuart she could wring out of herself all the righteous anger that had to be in her somewhere. "Let's not talk about it now. I think sometime soon I'll have a nice burst of hysterics over Stuart. But not now."

"Do you suppose Bowser would let you go out to eat?"

"God only knows. You're hungry?"

"Yeah, and you cook like a guitar player. I didn't have breakfast. Come to think of it, what did *you* do for breakfast?"

Eddi jerked her thumb at the living room. "He made it."

Carla raised her eyebrows. "He makes breakfast for his hos-tages? And you didn't even have to sleep with him?" Then she frowned. "You didn't have to sleep with him, did you?"

"The subject didn't come up."

"Huh. Well, if it does, and you don't want to . . . just don't be a wimp about it, okay?"

"I am *never* a wimp," Eddi said grandly.

"Hah. C'mon." Carla jumped off the bed and grabbed her hand. "Let's go ask him."

"Ask him what?"

"If he'll let you go eat, you gas-head. Evrything looks better after dinner." She pushed the bedroom door open. "As my grandma used to say, 'You feel better, you eat-a some a dis nice-a lasagne.' "

"Someone is discussing food," said the phouka. He lay crossways on the couch with his head on the trunk-coffee table, his bare feet propped against the wall. His jacket had disappeared; in its place he wore a green tank top that displayed rather a lot of corded brown muscle. He was reading a copy of City Pages, leaving the sections strewn on the floor as he finished them.

"Jeez," said Carla, "I haven't seen that pose since all those cute Fifties illustrations of 'Teenager on the Phone.' "

Eddi stalked over to the couch, grabbed up scattered pages of newsprint, and stuffed them in the trash. "If Roberta saw you getting footprints on the wall, she'd have heart failure."

"That's the harpy downstairs, yes?" He smiled brilliantly. "I think I shall set myself to charming her."

"The hell you will! You stay away from Roberta, do you hear me?"

Carla started to giggle.

"What?" Eddi snapped.

"You look like me yelling at the cat."

And, of course, she did—the phouka still had his head on the trunk, and he was beaming up at her while she stood over him and shook her index finger. She gathered up her dignity and went to sit in one of the straight-backed chairs.

"As I was saying—," Carla began.

"Ah, yes. You were going to talk about lasagne."

"Nope. I want to know if you'll let Eddi out of your sight long enough to go to dinner with me."

"Me? I am grate—"

"No, *not* you. Eddi."

"Ah." He nodded. "It is, however, the same answer. You must think of Eddi and me as if we were new lovers. I shall not be parted from her for more than a moment."

Eddi rolled her eyes.

"Look," said Carla. "I give you my word of honor that I'll bring her back."

His smile became a roaring laugh. "And easy as that, you expect to trick the trickster? No, sweet child, try again!"

Carla glowered at him.

"However," he said at last, "I shall not deprive you of your dinner. We shall *all* go."

"I'd rather starve," said Eddi.

Carla considered for a moment. "Well, I wouldn't. And the thought of eating something out of *your* refrigerator makes me queasy. I say we go for it."

"Carla, are you crazy? We can't take him out in public! God knows what he'd do!" The phouka looked achingly innocent.

"Hmm." Carla frowned and paced to the window and back. "We'll go to the New Riverside Cafe. He can do anything he wants and nobody'll notice."

"Gnnng." Eddi pulled at her hair. "Weird vegetarian eggplant food."

"Maybe they'll make you a nice Wonder Bread and Skippy sandwich," said Carla.

Eddi glared at the phouka. "Why me? What did I do to deserve you?"

The phouka looked, for once, genuinely regretful. "We cannot always choose what life brings us, or how it is brought."

"Platitude."

"There may be truth in platitudes."

"Gnnng."

"Go get a jacket," Carla scolded.

The phouka was smiling a little, and something in that smile, the tilt of his head, offered Eddi a lazy challenge. She narrowed her eyes at him and went to the bedroom.

She put on her big denim jacket and turned the collar up. "Tough girl," she said to her reflection in the bathroom mirror, and tried out a sneer. It made her feel better.

Carla's wagon was parked at the bottom of the hill that was Spruce Place. In the shadow of the apartment buildings that lined the street, the air was chilly. "Don't you need your jacket or something?" Eddi asked the phouka. The skin of his arms and shoulders was smooth as melted chocolate, without a goosepimple in sight.

"What jacket?"

"The one you had on earlier. Aren't you cold?"

He tipped his head back and laughed.

"Excuse me for asking." She wasn't really annoyed—not

until they reached the car. Then she looked up from yanking open the slightly sprung passenger's side door, and found him eyeing the car, his lip curled.

"What's wrong?"

He made a face, as if he'd stepped barefoot on a dead squid.

Eddi leaned back against the car. "If you want to walk, we'll meet you there"—she smiled sweetly—"maybe."

"I . . . will not be comfortable in that."

"Gosh. I should have told Carla to bring the Mercedes."

Carla stuck her head out her door and looked at them over the roof. "Hey, Rover—we'll roll the window down, and you can ride along with your tongue out."

Eddi looked quickly back to the phouka, but he seemed to have missed the "Rover" entirely. He said only, "I would feel much better with the windows open."

It was a cold ride. The phouka sat in the back seat, and though he didn't quite lean out the window, he sat very close to it. Eddi slumped in the passenger seat, her shoulders hunched against the breeze, and whistled all that she could remember of "Won't Get Fooled Again."

Carla took the U of M West Bank exit, and said cheerfully, "Hey, you in the back seat! If you really can do magic, find us a parking space!"

"That is not one of the things I can do."

"Then what good are you?"

The phouka, to Eddi's surprise, made no reply. She turned and looked at him over the seat. He'd leaned his head back and closed his eyes.

"You okay?" she asked.

"Yes." He cut the word off neatly at the end.

"You don't sound like it." *What do I care?* she wondered, surprised.

The seat bumped her under the chin as the car bounced over something. Eddi turned around and found that they were lurching into the gravel lot across from Mixed Blood Theatre. "Remind me," Carla muttered, "to stay off the West Bank on a Saturday night."

"And out of downtown, and Uptown, and off of University Avenue. I always do. You always ignore me."

"Heh." Carla parked the car at the far end of the lot and flung her door open. "Look out for puddles."

Eddi, mindful of her sneakers, did. The phouka was fumbling his hands across the inside of the car door, his face tense.

"What's the matter?" Eddi asked him.

"I'm afraid I don't know how to open this." His black eyes were round, and made his little smile look like a falsehood.

"You could turn into a dog and jump through the window," Eddi suggested. She opened the door for him. "Here," she pointed to the inside handle, "pull this toward you to unlatch it. If that doesn't work, it means you have to pull this up first." She pointed to the knob that worked the lock. "And if that doesn't work, it means that the door's buggered up, and you can yell at Carla." Then he swung his feet out onto the gravel, and she stared. "You're not wearing any shoes!"

He straightened up, and his chest swelled with a long intake of breath. "That's true."

"No shoes, no shirt, no service," Eddi said with relish as Carla appeared at her elbow. The phouka looked baffled. "You can't go into a restaurant in bare feet," she explained.

"Tell you what," Carla said. "You turn into a dog, and we'll tie you up outside while we eat. And we'll bring you a doggy bag."

The phouka turned his gaze on Carla, and even in the light of sunset Eddi could see her pale. "A pity I have to deny you that pleasure. Come along." He strode off across the gravel.

Eddi touched Carla on the shoulder, but Carla's eyes were still on the phouka. She pointed after him. The phouka now wore low black boots.

Carla said, her voice wobbling "He must have got 'em on when we weren't looking."

"Hypnotism," Eddi assured her. "Special effects. Mirrors."

"Right," said Carla—but she stayed wide-eyed.

They caught up with him at the corner. "I have decided to forgive you," he smiled hugely as they came up. "I even waited for you."

"Meaning," said Eddi, "that you couldn't find the place by yourself."

The phouka cocked his head. "You said the New Riverside Cafe. That"—he pointed down the street at a set of dark green awnings"—reads 'New Riverside Cafe.' How could I miss it?"

"You can read, and you can't open a car door?" Eddi said.

He nodded at a piece of construction machinery parked off the road. "You can read. Can you operate that?"

"It's a little more complicated."

"Not to whoever operates it." He smiled. "Come along. After you've eaten, you won't find so much pleasure in posing silly questions."

Eddi had to admit that the Riverside was not as bad as she herself had described it. The most recent renovation had brightened and enlarged the room; it no longer looked like the kind of place where wistful sixties anarchists reminisced about bombing the student union. And tonight's dinner was vegetarian pizza, with, blessedly, not a trace of eggplant.

"I'm buying," Carla said, "so don't starve yourself."

"Does that offer include me?" the phouka asked.

"Do you have any money on you?" said Carla.

"Not a penny."

"How'd you pay the cover charge last night?"

"By magic," he said happily.

Eddi and Carla exchanged looks. "Don't get anything expensive," Carla sighed.

The phouka shook his head. "Ah, gone are the days when your people gave to my people freely and with good heart."

"Yeah, stuff like a nice job picking cotton," Carla muttered. The phouka only laughed his throaty laugh.

They took their loaded trays to a table near the stage. Eddi found herself arranging a band on it.

"Nothing bigger than a five-piece," Carla's voice cut across her thoughts.

Eddi grinned sheepishly. "You read my mind."

"What mind?"

"Bitch. I think you could get six people up there."

"Not with keyboards and a full drum kit."

"Mmm. Anyway, it's not my problem anymore." She tore into her pizza.

"So you say. What are you gonna do if you're not working in a band?"

"I'll find a job, for godsake."

Carla shook her head. "The whole town's on unemployment, and you're gonna find a job."

Eddi looked up from her pizza and found the phouka gazing fixedly at her, as if she were a movie in a foreign language. "Having fun?" she said.

He nodded solemnly.

A slender, brown-haired man came out of the back hallway that led to the alley, clutching a drum case to his chest.

"Isn't that the drummer for Boiled in Lead?" said Carla.

Eddi studied as much of the face as she could see. "I think so."

"So that's who's playing," Carla said. "Windows are gonna rattle tonight."

"Mmm," said Eddi, concentrating on her pizza. It was natural to feel a momentary pang of jealousy. She felt it every time she saw another band play when she couldn't. It was a habit now, and would go away soon. A few months, at most.

"How are you gonna go about it?" Carla asked.

"About what?"

"Finding a job."

"The usual ways."

"Uh-huh. What are you going to tell 'em when they ask about your skills?"

Eddi regarded her bleakly. "I guess I'll have to tell them I can type."

Carla looked sympathetic. "And answer phones, don't forget. You answer a mean phone."

"Want to go apply for food stamps with me?" Then Eddi saw the phouka's smile. "What's your problem?"

"Why, nothing at all. In fact, this sounds amusing, and even educational."

"Not for you, buster," Eddi said, but she felt a cold spot growing in the pit of her stomach.

"No, really. I've never applied for food stamps—or employment, for that matter. Where do we go?" He tipped his head to one side and gave her one of the innocent, clear-eyed looks that she was beginning to dread.

"I can't find a job with you along" she said slowly.

"I promise to be on my very best behavior."

Eddi clasped her hands firmly under the table. "No matter what behavior you're on, you can't go with me. You don't go job hunting on the buddy system."

"Oh." He wasn't disappointed; he was . . . speculating. "Tell me, then—what will you do if someone offers you work?"

Eddi identified the cold spot in her stomach. Her jaw clenched as she stared at him, as he stared back.

"As I said to Carla, you must think of us as new lovers, my primrose. I can hardly be parted from you for minutes.

I'm afraid separation for all the daylight hours is out of the question.''

Eddi felt her anger pushing the tears up behind her eyes, and she shook her head hard and turned away. She would hate to let him see her cry, even from frustration. She rubbed her eyes, and winced when her fingers met the bruise that Stuart's blow had left. *God*, she thought, *I suppose I look like a battered woman.*

Carla was scowling at the tabletop, but the phouka was watching Eddi. "What are you thinking?" he asked suddenly.

"Me? Thinking?" Eddi said.

He reached out and grabbed her wrist lightly. "You. Thinking. I would very much prefer that you not cause me trouble over this. ''

"Let me go. Please." She said it a little louder than necessary, and saw the couple at the next table turn to look. Carla was looking, too, and frowning. *Follow my lead, kid*, Eddi prayed.

"No," said the phouka softly. "I suspect you'll do something foolish if I do.''

Eddi pulled against his grip. "Please, you're hurting me!" He wasn't, but for an instant his fingers loosened. She stepped back, knocking her chair over.

The cafe manager appeared behind the phouka. "Do you need any help?" he asked Eddi, and rested a restraining hand on the phouka's shoulder.

She reached to touch her bruise and hoped it looked like an unconscious gesture. It was easy to draw a shaky breath. "Yes," she said. Then she met the phouka's eyes, and saw them widen. "I won't go back with you," she said loudly, and hoped it would carry. "I won't let you hit me again.''

For an instant the phouka sat wide-eyed. Then he rose out of his chair with a snarl. Carla yelled, "Stop him! He'll kill her!''

As Eddi turned and ran for the door, she saw the manager grab the phouka's arms as a broad-shouldered patron stepped in front of him.

She twisted through the crowd lined up at the serving counter, thinking, *There's a taxi stand across from the Cedar Theatre. Oh, God, let there be a taxi there. . . .* She would go as far as she could afford to, and worry about a destination later.

The sky over Cedar Avenue was indigo, and the night air was a welcome slap against her skin. She sprinted across Riverside Boulevard, dodging traffic. Far down the street she could see the roof light of a taxi. Past the flower stand, past the bank—

From the inset doorway of a shop, a figure stepped into her path. Eddi thought for a fleeting moment that it was a drunk, a panhandler. Then it raised its smiling face—it was short—and she saw the silvery gray skin stretched across the bony features, the snoutlike nose and mouth, the double row of pointed ivory teeth that the curling lips revealed. It had milky-white eyes, like those of blind fish in deep water.

The gray skin-and-bones arms came up. In the filthy, broken-nailed hands was a small double-curve bow of translucent white. The apparition sighted at her down the shaft of an arrow that glittered like glass and running water.

She heard the absurdly familiar snarl behind her, just before the phouka struck her from behind. She tried to get her hands in front of her before she hit the sidewalk, and found a pair of brown arms there before her, cushioning the fall. Running footsteps rattled away down the sidewalk and disappeared.

"Are you hurt?" said the phouka's voice next to her ear. Would he let her lie on the sidewalk and have hysterics? No, he had an arm around her and was hauling her up. "Come, sweetling, we can't stay here. They'll be calling out a flock of redcaps next. And your knights-errant back in the cafe are no doubt picking themselves up and summoning the police."

For a moment she couldn't remember what he was talking about. *Oh. The Riverside.* "Did you hurt them?"

"I tried not. Please don't just hang like a sack, my heart."

Eddi got her feet under her. Then she started to shake. "That thing . . . they're really trying to goddamn *kill* me!" she gasped.

"Shhh, shhh. They failed. You're all right."

She realized suddenly that he had his arm around her. She stepped quickly away.

Carla was standing a few feet behind him, her eyes enormous. "You!" the phouka said to her, as if it was enough insult. "The next time you assist in such a lackwit, ill-considered, dangerous little trick I shall knock you into your next life and regret it later, if then."

"What *was* that?" Carla asked, and her voice broke.

"That, oh my innocents, was the enemy. I'd expected they would find out soon," he murmured, more to himself than to them, "but Oak and Ash, not so soon as this."

"Are they . . . are they all like that?" Eddi asked.

"No." He looked down at her, and his eyes were sad. "The Unseelie Court wear many shapes, and have many powers. Not

so different from the Seelie Court, indeed." Then he seemed to
remember his anger, and took her by the shoulders. "Do you
see, now, that I *must* stay near you? I am all that stands between
you and the likes of that!"

Eddi pulled away from his hands. "Well, goddamn, just how
did I get along without you?" she snapped. Extra adrenaline was
making her whole body throb. "The only reason the 'likes of
that' are after me is because the likes of *you* found me first!"

He looked away. "That, unfortunately, is quite true." He bit
off the end of each word.

"So let me go."

"I'm sorry." He shook his head. "I cannot."

It was her turn to look away. On the sidewalk, she saw a spark
of reflected light. She picked the bright thing up. For long
moments, she couldn't tell what she was holding. It was the
color of mica-flecked stone, but smooth as metal, heavier than it
looked, and burning cold. A little shorter than one of her finger
joints, it was an elongated cone, flattened at the narrow end.
Then she realized what it must be: an arrow point.

"Elf-shot," said the phouka, his voice colorless. "Had it
found its mark, you would have felt a bursting pain in your head,
and never a thing more."

There was a buzzing in her palm. With a single sharp, sweet
note, the little point shattered in her hand, and all three of them
jumped. Nothing was left of it but gray dust.

"Now, sweet," the phouka sighed, "will you come away? Or
will you wait until they send another message of good will, and
see if I can stop that one, too?"

They went back to the car. On the way, the phouka paused
long enough to break a green twig off a locust tree in front of the
oriental grocery. "Not as much as I could wish," Eddi heard
him mutter, "but it will help." He tucked it jauntily over his
ear. "And what," he said to Eddi, "are you staring at?"

"What is that for?"

He looked haughty. "Do you tell me everything?"

She smiled a little and shook her head, and climbed into the
passenger's seat.

As they pulled out onto Cedar, Eddi spotted a police car
cruising slowly toward them. "Get down!" she hissed at the
phouka.

"What?"

Eddi reached back and pushed his head below the level of the windows. The car went past and pulled up in front of the Riverside.

As she turned onto the freeway, Carla pointed out, ''They wouldn't have stopped the car even if they saw him. Domestic violence, y'know.''

''Domestic, hell,'' Eddi sighed, slumping down in the seat. ''For all I know, half the people in the Riverside are prepared to file an assault charge.''

They rode in silence until Carla reached the Hennepin-Lyndale exit. Then the phouka said, ''Do you still want gainful employment?''

''If I don't find some gainful something, I won't be eating in six weeks.''

''Hmm. And if I remain in your company, I will suffer a like fate. Something must be done.'' Eddi could hear the amusement in his voice. ''You have to make money, and I have to stay by your side. Now, how can both imperatives be satisfied?''

''You can rob liquor stores and take me along as a hostage.''

''Interesting. No, I have a better idea.'' He paused. ''Why don't you start a band?''

''Haven't I heard that before?'' Carla said.

''Oh, shit,'' said Eddi.

CHAPTER FIVE

You Can't Always Get What You Want

The boulevard trees moved restlessly overhead, strobing the streetlights across the windshield. The air smelled like ozone. "You want to come up?" Eddi asked Carla as they turned onto Oak Grove.

"That's why I'm looking for a parking space."

"Two of 'em, for the Queen Mary here."

"Hemph," said Carla cheerfully, and swung into the curb near the creamy-gray front of the Loring Park Office Building.

The phouka sprang onto the sidewalk before Carla turned the engine off, and stood brushing imaginary dust off his trousers. "I feel I ought to warn you," he said, "that it's going to rain. You'll have a long, wet walk back to your car if you leave it here."

"Yeah, but the scenery makes it all worthwhile." Across the street, where Carla pointed, the undulating bowl of Loring Park was dotted with the orange globes of its post lamps, faceless jack o'lanterns that gleamed on the sidewalks and reflected in the ruffled pond. From somewhere beyond the footbridge, a dove called nervously and fell silent.

"Yes," the phouka said softly, "I can see that it might." Then, as if to break the mood, he pulled the sprig of locust from the black curls behind his ear and presented it to Eddi with a flourish.

At the door to her apartment, the phouka held out his hand for her keys. Eddi drew back and frowned at him. "Why?" she said.

His smile was brilliant and dangerous. "I want to see if you've had uninvited guests. Don't you think I should, before I let you go in?"

She pictured something gray and toothy in her living room,

waiting. Carla put a hand on Eddi's shoulder and squeezed comfortingly; then she took the keys out of Eddi's hand and gave them to the phouka.

He squatted and studied the lock before he put the key into it and turned it delicately. Then he stood up and rested his head against the door.

Eddi began, "Is there—"

He touched his finger to her lips and shook his head. Then he opened the door and slipped through it.

"D'you get the feeling he's seen too many 'Man from U.N.C.L.E.' reruns?" Carla whispered.

"You're the one who gave him the keys."

Carla shrugged. "Hey, if he wants to sneak around your apartment, it's no skin off our noses." Then she grinned. "Besides, I can empathize. I always wanted to be Emma Peel."

"Emma Peel? In a *station wagon?*"

"You can't fit a whole drum kit in a Lotus Élan."

"Poor thing," Eddi smiled. Then she looked at the closed door and shivered. "What's taking him so long?"

"Maybe he found a cat to chase."

Then the door opened and the phouka was there, bowing low. His jacket had reappeared on him, and he was exquisitely out of place in her shabby apartment. "Enter, my little snowdrop. All is in order."

Everything did seem to be all right. The kitschy lamp by the sofa—the one with the copper quarter horse statuette for a base—was on. By its light Eddi could see the magazines neatly stacked on the trunk, and the sofa cushions smooth. "How about the bedroom?" she asked.

"I checked there, too. You may sleep the sleep of the efficiently protected."

"Yeah," she said, "but did you find anything?"

"If I told you 'yes,' you would be frightened, and if I told you 'no,' you would think you didn't need me. Silence is my wisest course." He finished with one of his taunting grins, but Eddi thought she'd seen some other expression in his eyes for a moment.

Carla had headed for the stereo. Now the opening bass riff of the Untouchables' "Free Yourself" kicked out of the speakers. "Easy for them to say," Eddi muttered.

"You want coffee?" she asked Carla.

The phouka turned to Eddi. "You make *coffee?*" His voice was full of longing. "Oh, I love coffee."

"Oh, God, just what we need." Carla sighed. "A mad dog with coffee nerves."

Eddi ignored that. "Why didn't you say something this morning? We could have had it at breakfast."

He looked embarrassed. "Yes, well, that was my treat, you see. And I don't know how to make coffee."

"You can make pancakes, and not coffee?"

"Pancakes, my inquisitive flower, are a profoundly primitive and practically universal item, in one form or another."

"So's coffee," said Carla.

"Not," the phouka said disdainfully, "where *I* come from."

Eddi looked at the phouka's brown skin and giggled. He raised an eyebrow at her. "I'm gonna go make some now," she said, and headed for the kitchen.

The growl of the grinder blotted out the music for a minute; when she turned it off, Rue Nouveau's "I Was a Witness" was playing. Carla liked it for the artsy drum part. Eddi plugged in the coffeemaker and went back to the living room.

Carla sat hunched forward on the sofa, her index fingers following Rue Nouveau's drummer on the edge of the trunk. The phouka was stretched out on the rug on his stomach. He poked his thumb toward the speakers as the lead vocalist began the second verse. "She's very good."

"That's nice. Why don't you draft *her*, and I'll stay home?"

The phouka shook his head and looked uncomfortable.

Eddi sat down on her heels in front of him. "I've asked this before, and you never answer it. Why me?"

His index finger burrowed a path through the rug, and he seemed to be watching it intently.

"Was there some particular reason? Or did you just stumble on me, and now that you've decided, you can't throw me back?"

He looked up at her through his lashes—ridiculously long, and so thick they rimmed his large almond eyes like eyeliner. "Don't ask me, please," he said, barely loud enough for her to hear over the stereo. "If you ask me again, I shall tell you, and that would be the wrong thing to do."

Eddi heard the appeal in his voice and shrugged angrily. Yet she didn't repeat the question. "Will you ever be able to tell me? I'd feel better knowing I wasn't in danger out of sheer dumb luck."

"After May Eve—after the battle," the phouka replied. "If you still want to know, ask me then."

The coffeemaker gave the death rattle that meant it had done its job. "Better than a timer," Carla murmured.

"I'll get it," the phouka said, and went to the kitchen.

Carla murmured, "Careful." Eddi looked up. "He may be trying to make up for those first impressions," Carla said.

Eddi plowed her fingers through her hair. "I feel like a Russian dissident under house arrest. And no matter how nice a guy the jailer is, it's still a jail."

"Comforting to hear you say so."

Eddi grinned. "What, you thought I was on the rebound from Stuart?"

"Maybe. All I know is, this kid's cuter than Prince, when he wants to be."

"Nobody's cuter than Prince."

The phouka came out of the kitchen with three mugs of coffee. He *could* be a fairly decent—well, human being, for lack of any other description—when it suited him. But he was mercurial, he loved to playact. Were his kindnesses artificial, and all his infuriating ways his true nature?

"So," Carla began, having sent the phouka back to the kitchen for cream and sugar, "what kind of a band is this gonna be?"

Eddi grinned up at her. "It should be a rich and famous band."

Carla nodded. "And?"

"And it should have a recording contract."

"That's part of being rich and famous."

"Oh, come on, Carla. I'm joking, for godsake."

"I'm not. Okay, maybe you can't set out to have a rich and famous band. But I do think you can put a band together that no way in hell can *ever* be rich and famous, no matter how good it is."

"You mean, like InKline Plain?"

Carla wrinkled her nose. "Yeah. So if you say you want to be rich and famous, this automatically means no Top 40 crap, and no country rock bars."

Eddi blinked. "Promise?"

"I get the feeling you're not going to be a lot of help," Carla sighed.

"This is something I have to get used to. By 'no Top 40 crap,' do you mean no Top 40, or no crap off the Top 40?"

"Hmm. I mean, nothing we have to play just because people heard it on their car radios."

The phouka came back with the cream and sugar, shaking his head at Carla. "Criminal," he said solemnly. "Cream is for cats." He sat down next to Eddi on the rug.

"Nah. Cream is for chocolate mousse." Carla doctored her coffee.

"Chocolate mousse?"

Carla nodded. "Yep. Trust me. It's better than sex." To Eddi's surprise, the phouka looked quickly away. "Anyway, quit changing the subject. We're creating a band here."

"Eddi should sing practically everything," the phouka said.

"Who asked you?" grumbled Eddi.

"Of course she should," Carla nodded firmly. "In fact, she should be able to put down her guitar sometimes. This sort of calls for five pieces."

"Composed of what?" asked the phouka.

"Does anyone care what I think?" Eddi said piteously.

The phouka turned an inquiring look her way. "You don't agree?"

"Well . . . yeah—"

"Good," said Carla. "Let's see, someone on sticks—that's me—and a primo bass player. A good, versatile guitar player with plenty of rock 'n' roll savvy. A keyboard player with great hands and electronic imagination. Most, if not all, of these people should be able to do backup vocals. Am I missing anything?"

"Yes," said Eddi. "Everything between your ears."

"Oh, come on. What do you want, a horn section?"

"No, that's a great shopping list. Where are you going to *find* these people?"

Carla looked smug. "Only need two of 'em. I already know the keyboard player."

"Who?"

"Danny Rochelle."

"Jeez almighty," Eddi said. She'd heard Dan Rochelle. "But he's still with Human Rights. Isn't he?"

"Nope. LeeAnn and Whatsisname moved to Louisiana, and Danny's out of a job."

"D'you think he'd go for this?"

Carla looked, if possible, even more smug. "We'll just have to ask him, won't we?"

"So," said the phouka, "that leaves . . . what, a guitarist and a bass player, yes? How does one go about finding them?"

"Ads, word of mouth. Then you audition people."

Eddi sat up straight. "Audition? My God, where? We don't have any practice space!"

Carla shrugged. "Now that you've put your mind to it, you'll think of something."

Rain began to pat against the windows. "Oops. Looks like Rover was right," said Carla. "I'm gonna get wet."

"I'd offer you the couch," Eddi said, "but it's on long-term lease." She scowled at the phouka.

"Nah, I'll run for it." Carla gave her a hug, and turned to point a finger at the phouka. "Watch your step," she said.

The phouka looked busily at both feet.

When she'd gone, Eddi drifted into the kitchen with the cups. She heard the phouka in the doorway behind her.

"She would take care of you, if she could," he said.

"Anything wrong with that?"

"No. But she cannot deal with what the Unseelie Court will send."

Eddi unplugged the coffeemaker and turned to face him. "Why are you saying this?"

"Because I want to make certain you know it." His pose was casual, one shoulder propped against the frame of the doorway. The way he met her eyes was not casual at all.

"So now I know it."

"She'll want to help you get away from us."

Eddi laughed; she couldn't help it. "Good guess."

He closed his eyes and nodded. Then he went into the living room. After a moment, Eddi followed him.

He turned off the lamp, and stood looking out the rain-streaked window. "I wish. . . ." He fell silent, tapping his fingernails on the window glass in irritation, or restlessness, or indecision. At last he said, "I wish she could."

"Could what?"

"Get you away. But the Unseelie Court would be baying at your heels before you could go half far enough."

"Why?" Eddi cried. "Why should they stop me from running away from you? Aren't they better off if I'm gone?"

"Ah, my primrose, you don't know them. They know now that you are our choice." His voice cracked a little on the last word.

"Yeah, it comes back to that. If it weren't for you, I wouldn't be in danger at all."

"I know that!" He whirled and spat his words out through his teeth. "I know it all too well, and it does neither of us any good to repeat it. I have led mankind's nightmares to your door."

"Then leave me alone," Eddi said desperately, "and they'll go away!"

"They will not. Yes, we could declare our minds to be changed, withdraw our protection, and leave you be. And the Dark Court, suspecting us of treachery, or hungry for a grisly joke, would murder you. Now that they see we have found you fair, they would like nothing better than to march into battle against us with your head as a standard." He turned away and began to toy with the cord that worked the blinds.

Eddi sat down in one of the kitchen chairs, and felt her anger and fear plunge to her stomach and coil there.

"But we need you," he said at last, softly. "There is power in a mortal soul that all of Faerie cannot muster, power that comes from mortality itself. We can use that against the Unseelie Court."

"Why should I side with you? Why should I care if you win?"

The phouka raked his fingers through his hair. "You have seen one of them, one of their forms. That is what seeks dominion over every natural thing in this place. We of the Seelie Court are capricious, and not always well-disposed toward humankind. But would you hand this city over to the likes of what you saw tonight? That is the Unseelie Court. If we fall, every park, every boulevard tree, every grassy lawn would be their dwelling place."

Eddi sighed. "It's not just for you, it's for the entire seven-country metro area. Couldn't we just let them have St. Paul?"

The phouka made a disgusted noise.

"All right. What if they did take over? Would we all be eaten in our beds?"

He shook his head. "There are places," he began slowly, "that belong to them. Have you ever passed through some small town, surrounded by fertile country and fed by commerce, that seemed to be rotting away even as you watched? Where the houses and the people were faded, and all the storefronts stood empty?" Eddi remembered a few. "Or a city whose new buildings looked tawdry, whose old ones were ramshackle, where the streets were grimy and the wind was never fresh, where money passed from hand to hand to hand yet benefitted no one?"

His words were quicker now. "This city is alive with the best magic of mortal folk. The very light off the skyscrapers and the lakes vibrates with it. If the Unseelie Court takes up residence here, this will be a place where people fear their neighbors, where life drains the living until art and wit are luxuries, where any pleasant thing must be imported and soon loses its savor." He felt silent, as if embarrassed by his own eloquence.

Eddi rubbed her hands over her face, trying to rub away her confusion, her anger, her fear. Finally she asked the only question she had left. "Can't you get somebody *else?*"

The phouka began to laugh weakly. "Oh, go to bed, Eddi McCandry. You could befuddle a stone. Go to bed, and sleep soundly, and tempt me not into some foolish and fatal flap of the tongue."

She stood up and stalked off to the bedroom, wondering if she'd been insulted. She turned on the light, and looked back over her shoulder.

The phouka smiled crookedly, and winked. "Good night," he said.

But she did not sleep soundly. Half an hour later, she left off peering through the dark at her bedroom ceiling, and read the clock instead. Midnight. *Too much coffee,* she told herself. *Or the thunder.* But it wasn't the thunder she lay awake listening for, or the rush of the rain on her window. She strained to hear any small noises from outside, and wasn't reassured by their absence. She kept imagining faces in the irregular plaster of the walls. All the faces had an uncountable number of teeth.

At last she flung the covers back, pulled on her robe, and opened the bedroom door a crack. The living room was dark. Something moved near the windows, and she felt her muscles lock up with fear.

Then she recognized the motion—the phouka's silhouette, a black shape against the slatted gray square of the window. He was watching the back of the building through the blinds. The bedroom windowsill would be visible from where he stood.

She didn't want to go out and keep him company; he'd only say something annoying. She wanted to go back to bed and try to sleep. Yet she stood peeking through the barely open door like a spy in her own house, fascinated by the sight of him in an unguarded moment. True, she couldn't see much of him; there wasn't enough light coming through the blinds to fill in color or even details. But Eddi suspected that, if he knew he was being watched, he would turn away from even so inadequate an inspection.

His forehead, under the thick spill of curls, was high and straight, his nose unexpectedly long and aquiline. His lips were full, his chin jutted decidedly, and when he turned his head a little those ridiculous eyelashes made a sharp punctuation to the vertical lines of his face. He seemed at once real and unreal, as out of place as a celebrity seen in person. She frowned and thought again longingly of sleep.

Then he raised one slender hand and rubbed his eyes. It was an ordinary gesture. But it was eloquent of weariness and sorrow in a way Eddi had never seen, and she was filled with the shapeless melancholy that music sometimes evoked in her.

He lowered his hand and lifted his chin, and became a sentinel again. Eddi's fingers ached from clutching the doorframe. She pried them loose and went back to bed, and couldn't remember when she fell alseep.

Dan Rochelle was an attenuated black man with an incongruously round face and a grin like a Buddha on speed. His hair was cut in an oversize flattop, and he wore glasses because he needed them. The frames looked like Lalique crystal, clear plastic brushed to a translucent matte finish. When he took them off, his face looked half-built. He liked to wear Hawaiian shirts.

He'd been working in professional bands since he was sixteen, too young to drink in the clubs he played. And he could play the keys. He had a pile of equipment that Eddi only half understood, including three synthesizers, a digital sampler, a sequencer, and a few pieces of equipment that might have been stolen from NASA. Or maybe he'd built them himself, to frighten away guitar players. Under his hands it all came alive with some grand electronic passion. Dan's mild face would be transformed then; he might have been hearing choirs of angels, or the singing of galaxies. Dan was tasteful, tuneful, and wildly imaginative—a better keyboard player than Eddi had ever hoped to work with.

Dan accepted everything with cheerful good will, even the phouka. "You from England?" he asked. "Plenty of brothers over there doing good music. You play?"

"No," the phouka said, with a show of charming regret. "I'm afraid I'm only the roadie." The relish with which he used the word seemed obvious to Eddi, but Dan didn't seem to notice. The phouka put out a hand. "I'm pleased to make your acquaintance."

'Yeah.'' Dan shook the offered hand vigorously. "Uh . . . you got a name?''

The phouka smiled, an expression of unholy satisfaction that Eddi had learned to dread. "Robin Goode,'' he said.

Eddi, waiting for some awful utterance, let out her breath.

Dan had a solution to the problem of practice space: the third floor of a building on the down-at-the-heels manufacturing end of Washington Avenue. Dan's former band had broken up before the rental on the space expired, and Dan had the key.

Eddi and Carla agonized over the ad for the classifieds in the *Reader* and *City Pages*. They settled on:

Lead guitarist and bass player wanted. Strong backing vocals a must. Experienced pros only. New music, many originals. No metal-heads, cowboys, or wimps.

"I don't know,'' said Eddi. "Wimps?''

Carla looked stern. "Well, you *don't* want any wimps, do you?''

Eddi had to admit that was true. Carla delivered the ad to the papers, and for good measure, posted the same information on bulletin boards in places where musicians shopped—vintage clothing boutiques, music stores, and record shops. Then they loaded Carla's drum kit and Eddi's guitar and amp into the station wagon, and went to look at the practice space.

The phouka leaped out of the car when they arrived, and shook himself fiercely. "Oh, there must be a better way to get from place to place than shutting oneself in a metal box.''

"What do you want to do? Fly?'' said Carla. "So buy a motorcycle or something.''

He cocked his head. "An interesting thought.''

Eddi led the way up the iron stairs that climbed the back of the building. Dan had arrived before them, and the door at the top was unlocked.

The first floor was devoted to a foundering drapery manufacture, and the second to its warehouse. In the company's better days, it had probably had a use for the third floor as well, but hard times had turned it into an empty, open space under the rafters big enough to rehearse a dance company. The right- and left-hand walls were studded with windows, some of which weren't stuck closed. On the street side of the room, double metal-clad doors would have led to the second floor, if they hadn't been barred and padlocked. Bedsheets, put up by the last band to soften the room's acoustics, hung from the beams and vent pipes like the ghosts of walls. Industrial carpeting lay loose on a large section of floor; under it were oak planks nearly a foot wide, sturdy enough for a machine shop.

Eddi smiled down at the floor. "Do you get the feeling that nobody downstairs could hear us unless we played *real* loud?"

Dan was moving around in his equipment, turning things on. "The Dead Kennedys could practice up here. It's like havin' the planet to yourself."

Carla rubbed her hands together. "I'm gonna bring up the rest of my stuff."

They didn't have a proper PA, but they ran a couple of microphones through a little mixer of Carla's, and used her drum machine speaker for output. In half an hour, they had a rehearsal setup. Eddi pushed a hand through her bangs and looked at Carla sitting behind her cymbals, checking the reach to all of her drum heads; at Dan, wearing headphones, playing chords and checking heaven knew what; and at the phouka, who sat cross-legged on the floor watching her expectantly.

"Oo-kay," Eddi said, and slung on her guitar.

They started out, a little tentatively, on Prince's "When You Were Mine." Dan unrolled the melody in front of them. Eddi kept the guitar pared down, letting Dan take over most of the effects. She sang the first four lines very simply, almost without style, feeling for the approach that would grow out of this instrumentation, this chemistry of musicians.

The simplicity became a style in itself. The pure notes she sang enhanced the stark, bitter lyrics and made them bite even deeper. After the first chorus she let roughness creep into her voice, to bring in anger and outrage and trust betrayed. They went into the lead break with exhilarating power. Eddi let some fuzz sneak into her guitar mix, and Dan twisted the melody back on itself, adding buzzing overtones to notes that had once been precise and clear.

Coming back into the verse, Eddi opted for another sort of clarity; she sang the last verse and chorus in a ringing clarion voice. Then she handed the melody off to Dan, and they wended their way out of the song with an instrumental recap and a final fade.

"Awright," said Dan.

"Yeah." Eddi nodded. "Not too shabby."

"Well, I want a bass player," Carla sighed. "I could break a leg trying to keep you guys steady all by myself."

"We'll get you a bass player." Eddi turned to the phouka. "Whataya think?"

"Play another one," he said.

Carla got her wish two days later. He called, saying he had seen the notice at Oarfolk and wanted to audition.

"Or at least, I think that's what he said," Eddi told Carla, while they waited for him in the rehearsal space. "He sort of mumbled, and faded off at the ends of sentences."

Carla shook her head. "This doesn't sound promising."

"Maybe not. But I figured it was worth a try. We don't need him to talk on the phone."

There was a very small knock at the door, and the phouka answered it. The kid on the other side was the most unimpressive human being Eddi had ever seen. He was small and narrow-shouldered, olive-skinned, with haphazardly cut brown hair and heavy straight brows. His eyes were brown, too, half sleepy and half sullen. His cheeks had the sort of hollows that have less to do with bone structure than with lack of food. He was carrying an electric guitar case that looked as if it had just come from the store.

Eddi stood up and stuck out her hand. "Hello, I'm Eddi McCandry. Are you . . ." She realized that he hadn't given her a name over the phone.

He mumbled, and Eddi caught the words "audition" and "bass."

"Right." She turned to Carla, who raised one eyebrow. "This is Carla DiAmato, the drummer. That's Dan Rochelle." Dan was playing something through his headphones; he glanced up, looking vague and friendly.

The phouka stepped forward and put out a hand. "Robin Goode," he said, grinning. "A pleasure."

The kid's face opened suddenly into a huge, sweet smile around a set of substantial teeth, and he shook the phouka's hand.

"I've been meaning to ask," Eddi whispered to the phouka as the kid brought in his case. "What is this with the name?"

"Don't you think it's a nice name?"

"Oh, it's a swell name. Where did it *come from?*"

"I confess, I borrowed it. But I can't imagine that its owner would object, under the circumstances."

Eddi rolled her eyes. "Forget it."

"Instantly," he said.

The kid was unpacking a brand new Steinberger bass. Eddi shot a look at Carla, who raised both eyebrows this time. He opened the accessory box in the case and took out a heavy-duty coiled cable, still sealed in its plastic bag. Then he mumbled something and went back out the door.

After a moment of silence, Carla said, "He's going to come back in here with a new Mesa Boogie amp with the warranty tag still tied to the handle. Do I hear any bets?"

Carla was wrong; it was a large Roland amplifier. But it was certainly new. He plugged it in (the shipping kinks were still in the power cord), slung the bass over his shoulder, and plugged in the cable. Had he stolen it all the night before? She was afraid to ask.

She did ask him how long he'd been playing, and who he'd worked with. He mumbled a little.

Eddi reminded herself that this was not the only bass player in Minneapolis. The ads hadn't even appeared yet. "Ahhhh . . . listen," she said at last. "I'm not sure you . . . that this is a good idea."

And he raised his eyes from his bass just enough to look at her. His eyes were more fluent than his mouth; they blazed contempt and hostility, they pleaded for her forbearance, her indulgence.

She winced and picked up her own guitar. "Ever heard Bram Tchaikovsky's version of 'I'm a Believer'?" He shook his head, but continued to watch her, his fingers poised over his strings.

"Start it," he mumbled finally, and Eddi shrugged.

The song did kick off with only guitar. Then Carla dropped in after a few measures with a series of snare drum punches, and Dan's synthesizer yowled across it all.

Then, in precisely the right place, the bass came in. It began as if the Rocky Mountains had begun to walk. It sounded like the voice of the magma under the earth's crust, and it picked up the whole song and rolled it forward like water exploding out of a breaking dam. They were suddenly tight, all four of them, as if they were a single animal and that monster heartbeat was their own. Eddi listened wonderingly as they played the complicated stop beats in the chorus with respectable precision. She was dimly aware that she was playing some of the best guitar of her life.

When they were done, Eddi looked around and saw her own amazement on Carla's and Dan's faces. "Well," she said, and, unable to think of anything to add, said it again.

No one declared the newcomer to be the band's bass player. It would have been beside the point. Eddi only wanted to see if they could make other songs sound like that. She had no idea if he could sing; given his willingness to talk, it seemed unlikely. But for bass like that, she could sacrifice a harmony voice.

When they took a break she asked him, "Um, do you . . . I don't think I ever heard your name."

He looked up—he was about Eddi's height, but he always seemed to be looking at the floor, or his feet, so any time he looked at her, it was up. All she caught of what he said was "hedge."

"Hedge?" she repeated desperately.

He nodded, and his smile seemed cautious, but satisfied.

CHAPTER SIX

It's So Easy to Fall in Love

When the ads they'd composed appeared in the two weekly entertainment papers, the phouka accompanied her downtown every day to check the reply boxes. At last, she'd sorted out three guitarists to audition, and asked them to show up on the third floor at scattered hours on Thursday.

Four o'clock's candidate had superb technique—he was one of the fastest and cleanest lead players Eddi had ever heard. But he didn't seem to listen to the rest of the band, and his lead breaks, though complex and flashy, were too often just a collection of notes in the right key, as if he despised the melody.

The six-thirty guitarist intruded his riffs on other band members' showcase bits, and wanted to do most of the lead vocals. (He told Eddi that club owners in Minneapolis didn't like to hire bands with female lead vocalists. Eddi smiled and told him she didn't think he'd fit in. He left angry.)

Eight-thirty was the best choice, Eddi decided: a woman with cropped red hair and a white Stratocaster whose solemn expression had seemed older than her face. After she'd left, Eddi called a break. Carla ran down to the Qwik-Stop for take-out coffee, Dan settled down to work over the patches on a synthesizer, and Hedge went for a walk. Eddi sat down on the edge of the carpet and resolved to liberate some seating for the place—if they found a guitarist and became a band.

The phouka dropped down with his usual boneless grace beside her. Tonight he had chosen, from whatever mysterious closet he conjured his clothing, a double-breasted shirt of black-shot red, slim black brocade pants, and snakeskin boots. "So the tale is told? These are the three choices?" He'd found a Hershey bar somewhere; he held it out, and she broke off a chunk. She remembered to not say thank you.

"Mmm. Either we go for the third one, or we run the ad for another week," Eddi said.

"What did you think of her, then?"

"She had the chops, and she seemed like a decent human being. A little young, maybe. I'm tempted to go with her just for the sake of having three women in the band."

"But . . . ?"

"I don't know. She had something missing. Maybe a lack of imagination or something." Eddi sighed and fell back onto the rug. "Maybe I'm being too picky," she said to the rafters.

"No. You can afford to wait. Find precisely what you want."

"All of today wasted, then."

"Why do you feel so pressed for time?" he asked. His voice was a little sad, and she looked at him in surprise. "If the band distresses you so, then you need not have one. I only threw in my lot with Carla because you seemed to want work."

Eddi shook her head. "Carla knows me better than I do. I would have gone bats without this. It's the only thing I really know."

"But it seems to swallow you up. You've gone forward like a horse in blinders, seeing only ahead, only the band."

She frowned at him and looked away into the shadowed rafters. She realized with a rush of fear that there might be room there for something to hide—and knew the answer to the phouka's question.

"What is it?" he said.

"What's what?"

"I thought I saw you shiver."

Eddi shook her head. "Oh, hell," she said finally. "Why act brave? If I think about the band all the time, you see, I don't think about. . . ."

The phouka looked stricken. "Ah. About my people's little quarrel, and your part in it. Are you so frightened, then?"

Eddi discovered that ignoring the problem for several days only made her feel worse now. "Oh, for godsake, a bunch of people out of a horror movie want me dead! And I'm not supposed to be scared?"

The phouka took both of her hands in his. His grip was hard, but not painful.

"Eddi," he said, "I will protect you. They will not—they cannot—get past me to strike at you."

She laughed hollowly. "You know, a girl learns to tell when a guy is making her a promise he can't keep."

"Haven't I kept it thus far?"

"I don't know. Have they made any more tries at me?"

He scowled and looked away.

"Have they?"

He nodded, a curt bob of his head.

She drew her hands out of his. "Oh."

"I hadn't meant to tell you. I thought to spare you the worry."

"Wouldn't it be easier," Eddi asked after a moment, "if you didn't have to guard me *and* keep me in the dark about it?"

"Yes," he agreed, but hesitantly.

"Well, then," Eddi said, "let's get all the skeletons out of the closet."

The door to the outside swung slowly open.

The phouka was on his feet blindingly fast, standing between Eddi and the door. She looked past his kneecap and saw a man framed in the doorway, caught in the darkness between the outside and inside lights.

"Excuse me," said the man, "I should have called first. A friend told me you were looking for a guitarist . . . ?"

His voice was the first clear impression Eddi had of him. It was low, resonant, and musical, with what seemed like a pleasant accent, until she realized that it was an *absence* of accent. Then he stepped into the room and the light. Eddi thought for a moment of porcelain, but she had never seen anything made of porcelain that looked delicate and rugged at once.

He was tall and slender and interestingly pale. His face was longish, with high, wide cheekbones and a pointed chin, and his eyes, under black lashes and brows, were a breathtaking green. Shining blue-black hair spilled over his forehead in appealing disarray, and Eddi saw that what she had at first taken for reflected light was a wide white streak in his hair, a little off center. He wore a black leather jacket and tight black jeans. Somehow they seemed to bring color into the room.

"Come in," Eddi thought to say, once she could speak at all.

The man looked at the phouka, who hadn't moved since the door opened, and nodded. Then he turned away to bring in the things he'd left on the landing, and the phouka stirred and flexed his hands. Eddi wished she could see his expression.

The man in black returned with scuffed guitar case, a good-sized amp, an accessory bag, and a smaller case that he carried

under his arm. He set them down and came over to Eddi, who
scrambled to her feet. The phouka stepped to one side.

"My name's Willy Silver," the new arrival said. "I don't
know how my friend got this address but—are you looking for a
lead guitarist? Have I come at a bad time?"

"No! Not at all. You want to audition?" Eddi recognized it as
a silly question, and hurried on. "Go ahead and set up. The
drummer and the bass player should be back any minute." That
reminded her of Dan, and she looked for him in his little fortress
of equipment. He was staring at Willy Silver as if the latter were
a famous sculpture that had just appeared, and Dan hadn't
decided whether to admire it or worry that someone would
accuse him of stealing it.

Carla came rattling up the stairs with four cups of coffee. She
stopped at the sight of Willy Silver unpacking a guitar made of
some dark red wood, and looked as stupefied as Eddi. The
phouka took the tray of cups away from her gently, and Eddi
made the introductions.

By the time Willy was set up and in tune, Hedge was back and
hunched over his bass. He seemed as oblivious to Willy as he
was to everything, and barely nodded when he was introduced.
Eddi found that comforting.

Willy took off his jacket to reveal a high-collared, creamy
white shirt that Eddi suspected was silk. He rolled the sleeves up
to mid-forearm and hung his guitar on again. Then he looked at
Eddi, an open, dazzling gaze from his green eyes. "Where
shall we start?"

Eddi resisted the temptation to tell him, and said, "Do you
know, 'Thrill of the Grill'? Kim Carnes?"

"Well enough."

Eddi left her guitar in the stand and went to the mike. Carla
gave Willy a pair of four-beats, and he led off with a fast
rhythmic fuzzed-out riff. Carla spiked it with her high-hat cymbal on the two and four counts, and it sounded so fine that Eddi
almost forgot to sing. He cut way back during the verse to leave
room for her vocals and Dan's vaguely demented repeating melody between the lines of lyrics. Between them they gave the first
verse a feeling of breath-holding anticipation. Then Carla kicked
in with the drum fill that signaled the chorus, Hedge and his bass
came into the mix, and the waiting was over. Willy's voice
added new weight to Carla's and Dan's harmonies. The bridge,
when they got to it, was nice and tight, and Willy's lead break

was manic, crisp, and tasty. Eddi could feel them all catching fire off each other, responding to each other's experiments. Carla ended the whole thing with a Keith Moon-like percussive frenzy.

"Ah," said Carla, when the last chord had faded. "Better than sex."

Eddi found herself blushing.

"Speak for yourself," Dan said. "But yeah, that was all right."

"All right? Come on, Rochelle, loosen up," Carla sighed. "We were terrific. We charmed the bolts out of the rafters." She turned to Eddi, and pointed at Willy Silver. "Where did you find this guy?"

"Just lucky, I guess." Eddi looked at Willy and looked away, feeling unaccountably shy. "Still interested?"

"Maybe—but you haven't heard it all yet." He opened the smaller case at his feet and lifted out an electrified violin.

There was a question in his face, a challenge. He wasn't asking if she wanted him to play the violin; he was daring her to think of something for him to play it on.

"Oh, let's do some nice cobwebby David Bowie," Eddi said, and picked up her guitar. "Can you play 'Suffragette City' on that?"

A fierce, lopsided grin washed across his face, and he propped the violin under his chin.

It was superb. Willy and Dan worked out the balance between fiddle and synthesizer by what seemed telepathy, and Eddi kept her own guitar playing at something just beyond percussion. They were demented, they were loud, they were ridiculously theatrical. Carla threw her sticks in the air and caught them on the fly. Dan hunched over the keys like Frankenstein over his monster. Hedge wrinkled his nose and showed his teeth occasionally, which for Hedge was the rim of hysteria. Eddi did Joan Jett cheerleader leaps. And Willy . . . he jumped, he swaggered, he danced, he mugged shamelessly. He was beautiful.

When it was over, Eddi flung her head back and laughed for sheer excess adrenaline. Then she saw the phouka.

He was standing very straight against the right-hand wall. His chin was a little tucked, in a way that made him look wary. His black tilted eyes were wide, and they met hers before his gaze slid downward, before he could shutter away his look of dread and longing behind his eyelids.

Her mood faltered as the phouka walked out of sight behind a hanging sheet. Then Dan started up a sustained, electric gospel chord on the synthesizer, and intoned, "Dearly beloved, we are gathered here today to get through this thing called Life. . . ."

Willy laughed, set down the violin and grabbed for his guitar. He shot Eddi a sideways glance and a teasing grin as he slid the strap over his shoulder. Eddi's insides gave a curious, not un- pleasant lurch. Then they both turned to watch Dan ham his way through the introduction to "Let's Go Crazy."

Carla started the drumbeat, and they poised for the leap into the song. Dan got to, "In this life, you're on your own!" and with a pointing finger, handed the lyrics off to Eddi as Willy and Hedge began the slashing low-end rhythms of the guitar intro.

Willy had turned to watch her, playing everything to her. It egged her on. She matched his guitar riffs, then let him split off into a burst of single notes, then matched him again. She began to mimic his movements and he noticed and responded, until they'd established an improvised choreography. Sometimes they were shoulder to shoulder, the necks of their guitars parallel as railroad tracks, and she thought she could hear him breathing. She sang into whichever mike was nearest, and on the choruses they sang into one mike, their faces close to keep within the pickup range. They mugged at each other, baring their teeth like a pair of snarling cats. His green eyes glowed like deep water.

They led the band through the song as if it were a circular staircase they ran up. At its peak Eddi let him go, let him tear into a solo that seemed to rend the air apart. His whole body went into it, arching backward like a parenthesis, and she could see the moment at which he became unconscious to anything but sound. The last chord was both the resolution they had rushed eagerly toward, and the bittersweet end of it.

Carla whistled and cheered, and Danny sprang out of his fortress and ran over to thump her on the back. Hedge looked judicious, and nodded.

Willy wiped tendrils of damp hair off his forehead and licked his lips, catching a bead of sweat that sparkled near the corner of his mouth. Eddi's shirt was sticking to her back.

Willy grinned suddenly at her. "Thank you, ma'am."

"Wanna join a band?" she said.

Willy nodded. "Good idea."

None of them could resist trying a few more. They did the Beatles, "I'm Happy Just to Dance With You" as the Ramones might have covered it. As they came out of it, Willy said, "Oh, hell,'' and cranked up the characteristic lead line for ''Johnny B. Goode.'' When they were done, they did it over as snaky blues. At last Eddi declared them officially off duty, and Carla suggested going out for coffee.

''Not Embers, not Perkins, and Chester's is too far away,'' Eddi said.

''Nope, nope, let's go where everybody goes to gossip about everyone else's band. The Ediner. Calhoun Square.''

''They got room to sit six people?'' Dan asked.

Eddi remembered the phouka, and looked around. He was not in sight. She propped her guitar in its stand and went the way she had seen him go earlier, around the wall of sheets.

He was looking out the grimy windows at the passing lights of traffic on Washington Avenue, one forearm against the glass to pillow his head. He looked up when he heard her, and smiled.

''Sounds wonderful,'' he said.

She licked her lips. ''Are you okay?''

''Always, my primrose. What, have you decided that I'm in need of protecting, too?''

''No, I just . . . I wondered where you'd gone, was all.''

He stepped forward and took both her hands. ''You missed me,'' he said. ''Admit it. Tell me you cannot live without me.'' His lips were twitching.

''You're a jerk,'' she sighed.

''And you love it.''

Willy looked around the sheet. ''Sorry to disturb,'' he said. ''I'll meet you at the restaurant.''

''Right,'' said Eddi, and drew her hands out of the phouka's loosened grip. ''You've got a ride?''

''No problem,'' Willy smiled, and disappeared behind the sheet.

''You want to go for coffee?'' she asked the phouka.

''No, I have to wash my hair. Of course I want to go for coffee, my pet. I never leave your side, after all.'' His lips curved in a taunting smile.

Eddi blinked at him. He never left her side. A new wrinkle to that sprang suddenly to mind. ''Oh,'' she said.

''Oh, what?''

There was no delicate way to address the question. *Why didn't I think of this before? Because I gave Stuart the boot, that's why, so little things like privacy didn't matter. Oh, lord.* ''Nothing,'' Eddi croaked, and hurried back to the band equipment.

"He gave Hedge a ride," Carla told her, not needing to say who "he" was. "And Danny already left." Willy's guitar was in its stand, his amp turned off, his effects rack pushed neatly to one side, and the violin lay ready in its case. He'd left his equipment. It was a sort of silent promise.

"Jeez, you say 'coffee,' to this bunch, and they're gone," Eddi said. "Well, let's go see if the wagon has rusted away yet."

"Hey!" Carla squawked.

The phouka looked thoughtful. "It *is* downhill to the resturant. Isn't it?"

"Oh, God, not you, too. Leave my car alone!"

Eddi and Carla plunged down the stairs giggling, and the phouka followed more slowly. He was quiet in the car while Carla and Eddi talked band. Eddi went from feeling nervous about him to being annoyed. The blasted band had been half his idea, after all; now that it was assembled, did he want to spoil her pleasure in it?

Dan was standing guard over a table for six and a pot of coffee when they arrived. Carla plunked down next to him. Eddi and the phouka squeezed behind the table and onto the banquette.

Willy came down the aisle with Hedge close behind him, and Eddi was suddenly embarrassingly conscious of the empty seat beside her. It didn't seem to embarrass Willy; he slid next to her. The phouka leaned forward and beamed at Willy. Willy only nodded at the phouka and snagged an empty coffee cup.

Eddi turned to the phouka and whispered, "What are you doing?"

"Me? Nothing at all."

"Good. Keep it that way."

He batted his eyelashes at her.

The talk was all business, but with an eager edge—what to name the band, what songs to do and in what way, what connections they could count on for bookings. Particularly what to name the band. They began with jokes like "Free Food" and "Girls in Lingerie 24 Hours" ("Hard on the lingerie," Carla said gravely), moved on to serious ideas, lost control and made more jokes. All the while Eddi stole glances at Willy beside her, seeing the way his green eyes squinted when he laughed, the way he bit a corner of his lower lip when he was thinking, the way his hands moved when he talked. Sometimes she would find him watching her.

Dan stood up at last and said he had to get home. "You're a party pooper, Rochelle," Carla said.

"Ain't my problem you can't have fun without me." He reached for the check, but Carla twitched it away from him. "I love rich girls," he sighed, and sauntered away.

"Tsk." Carla shook her head. "Eddi? Want a ride?"

"We're closer to your place than mine. I figured I'd ride the bus or something."

Eddi could almost see Carla's thoughts. A raise of the eyebrows, a glance toward Willy—then a blink and a glance at the phouka.

"Okay," Carla said. "Last call for the taxi. Hedge?"

Hedge shook his head and mumbled, and wandered off down the aisle and out of the restaurant.

"He's cute," Carla said drily. "He wouldn't be if he didn't play bass like that, but he does. Oh, well. See you tomorrow, kids."

She waved the check, and Willy snagged it from her fingers. He followed her as far as the cash register.

Eddi stood by the phouka for a moment, staring at the floor.

"I'll see you tomorrow morning," the phouka said in a tight voice, and Eddi looked up, startled. His face was expressionless, his eyes a little hooded. "Don't do anything foolish, my primrose."

"But what about—" she began. She summoned up a wobbly smile. "I mean, what kind of a bodyguard are you?"

"You'll be . . . protected," he said softly through his teeth. He ventured a bitter smile at her. "And I may be annoying, but I'm not stupid." Then he brushed past her and down the aisle. She saw Willy turn to look at him when he strode out.

"Anything the matter?" Willy asked when she joined him at the door. She shrugged.

They walked past the darkened stores to the stairs. The phouka was nowhere in sight. *He promised,* she wailed to herself. *He said he'd protect me, he'd watch for them, and he's gone away—* But would he leave her in danger now, after working so hard to keep her safe? She shot a cautious glance at Willy, trying to see him without prejudice. He, at least, must be safe, or the phouka would never have let him near her. Would he?

"How far away do you live?" Willy asked as he held the outer door for her.

"Loring Park. Fifteen blocks or so."

"Hmm." He scanned the clear night sky. "If you were up for it, I'd walk you home."

They wandered down Hennepin, through the Uptown streetlife. They paused to listen to the man playing conga drums on the sidewalk outside the drugstore. They crossed the street to listen to an acoustic punk trio by the library, and even sang along when they covered the Replacements' "Kids Don't Follow." Willy admired a shirt in a store window on the corner of Twenty-eighth Street. Then they caught each other's eye.

"I've got to look," she said.

"You're right," he said.

So they went around the corner to Knut Koupeé to peer through the door at the handmade electric guitars on the wall. "Look at that," Willy said, pointing to a black-and-white checkerboard flying vee. "I won't last the week without it."

"Vulgar," Eddi declared.

"Well, yeah." He grinned sheepishly. "That's why I like it."

She laughed and ran back to Hennepin. He caught up with her just around the corner, and grabbed her hand to slow her down. He didn't let go when they walked on.

At Twenty-sixth Street she stopped. "Hey, how did you get from practice to here? Are you abandoning a car somewhere?"

Willy smiled and shook his head. "Borrowed transportation. I returned it on the way—the owner lives around here."

"Convenient. Oh, lord, are we going to have to get a van? Carla's junkyard dog can't transport the whole band."

"And we need a PA," Willy reminded her.

"Shit. And a PA. Why do you have to be rich to get rich?"

He swung their joined hands. "You watch. We'll make everything work." He smiled down into her face, and she felt butterfly wings in her stomach.

By the time they reached Loring Park, the wind was sneaking through the seams of her denim jacket.

Willy must have seen her shiver. "Cold?"

She shrugged. "It's not far now."

She slid out of his jacket and wrapped it around her shoulders. She could feel the heat of him still inside it, and when she shivered again, it was not from cold. He kept his arm around her shoulders.

Eddi wondered if he could feel her heart beating. She looked at his white shirt front to keep from meeting his eyes, and said, "You'll freeze."

"It's not far now." Her words had changed in Willy's mouth to something tantalizing. His breath stirred her hair.

They stood for a moment looking out over Loring Park. Spring had come to the city like a bomb, and the trees had exploded into leaf in a matter of days. Now the wind made the park rustle, and the branches cast patterns of black lace across the orange globe lamps. Eddi remembered the phouka surveying the same view, his pleasure at it, and felt a sudden unfocused guilt. "Let's go," she said quietly, and they headed up the hill.

They ran up the front steps of the apartment building, and stopped at the door. Eddi fumbled slowly for her keys. "D'you want to come up?" she said, her eyes on the top step.

Willy curved one of his long white hands around her chin and tilted it upward. Even in the dark, his eyes were green. "Do you want me to?"

She stepped away and leaned against the bricks, trying to take deeper breaths. "I don't do this." She shook her head to clear it. "Not like this, so fast. And if we . . . if we don't work out, we might not be able to make music together either, and the band's important to me."

Willy nodded. "There's no way we can know what will happen. Not from here." He raised one hand as if to reach for her, and stopped. "Do you want me to come up?"

The butterflies threatened to shake her until her knees gave way, until the buzzing of their wings made her deaf. She wanted him to touch her face again. "Yes," she whispered.

They went up the stairs with their arms around each other. But they exchanged no kisses until her apartment door closed behind them. There was no comfort in it; when Willy's mouth left hers, she felt as if she were all pulse, and her skin ached to be touched. He took her face in his hands, smoothed the hair away from her temples with his thumbs. She turned her head quickly and kissed his palm. Willy inhaled sharply.

He picked her up in a single swooping motion, and she grabbed his neck in surprise. He crossed the living room and reached for the knob on the right-hand door.

"Huh-uh," she whispered. "That's the bathroom."

Willy eyed the door as if he'd never seen one. "Ah. No. I don't think we want the bathroom." He sounded as breathless as she was. She giggled into his collar.

He opened the bedroom door, and looked down at her. "Second thoughts?"

Her eyes widened. "What would you do if I had them?"

"Set you on your feet, kiss you chastely on the forehead, and leave."

"You could do that?"

Willy's laugh was shaky. "Just barely."

She reached up to trace the edges of his lips with her index finger. "No second thoughts."

"Good," he said hoarsely. "Offer withdrawn." And he carried her into her bedroom.

Willy didn't stay the night. He kissed her lips and her eyelids when he rose, and she heard him dressing in his leather and denim and silk. He whispered, "Tomorrow," in her ear, kissed her again, and was gone.

She fell back asleep. Her dreams were odd, restless ones, from which she woke with a start. It was still dark. She felt a sudden, dreadful conviction that she'd dreamed Willy and his music and his passion. Or worse, he was real, but irretrievably gone. Then she remembered his equipment set up neatly on the third floor, ready for his return. And she had the key to the rehearsal space. It was, she reflected, a very odd pacifier.

She fell asleep again, and didn't dream at all.

CHAPTER SEVEN

Goin' Mobile

Eddi woke slowly, hearing kitcheny sounds from the next room. For a moment she wished that what she heard was Willy in the next room, but she knew it wasn't. It was the phouka. The knowledge brought comfort and annoyance in equal parts. She threw off the covers and went to take her shower.

It was like, and unlike, her first morning with the phouka. She spent a long time in the bathroom, avoiding him. He would make some rude comment about her social life, or her taste in men; or perhaps he'd leer, and be elegantly crude. Or he might be hurt. . . . No, if he turned a wounded face to her, it would be a contrived one, meant to tease. And why the devil did she think he might be hurt?

She took refuge in thoughts of Willy. The memory of him leaning over her, his eyes luminous green in the light of the bedside lamp, made her shiver pleasantly. He had made love with an overwhelming intensity, as if his attention was wholly absorbed in pleasing her and himself. There'd been none of the uncertainty between them that was natural to new lovers.

He'd said he would see her today. What if it was different between them today? Or fine between them everywhere but in the band? *Calm down, girl,* she told herself. *You knew all that last night, and it didn't stop you. It's time to live with the consequences.*

Eddi made rude faces in the bathroom mirror. She towel-dried her hair. She pulled on the corners of her eyes to see how she'd look if she were Chinese. She stared at the contents of her closet. Finally she faced the truth: she couldn't stay in the bedroom all day. It would look cowardly. She put on a pair of dark green leggings and a pale violet shirt that reached halfway to her knees, and went out into the living room.

The phouka was lying on the rug in front of the stereo, wearing her headphones. When he saw her, he lifted them off, and she could hear Curtiss A.'s latest album playing through them.

The phouka contemplated her. He did not seem disposed to be rude, crude, or wounded. That might be good—or it might mean that he was going to be something worse. "Wholly adorable," he said at last. "You look like an iris in bloom."

Yes, definitely something worse. "I think I'll go change."

"What, and break my heart? Not to mention impugning my taste. No, no, you have to eat." He sprang up and led her to the table.

The table distracted her from replying as she ought. There were fresh cantaloupe and strawberries, a wedge of cheddar, milk, and a plate of something covered with a clean dish towel.

"Sit," the phouka ordered, and whisked the towel off the plate.

"They're scones," Eddi said.

"Precisely. *Do* sit down."

She did.

"I confess, I had to seek out expert help for those. Eat one, my primrose, and tell me if it was worth it."

Eddi took one off the plate; it steamed fragrantly when she broke it in half. She took a bite. "My grandmother used to make these," she said absently, and took another bite. "Hey, what do you mean, expert help? I thought you said they wouldn't do anything for you?"

"Who?"

"The . . . brownies," she said, stumbling a little, and scowling at him for making her do it.

The phouka smiled benignly and held up a battered book. "Oh," Eddi said, recognizing her mother's old copy of *The Joy of Cooking*.

"Those the brownies will not help, must learn to help themselves."

"And the fruit?"

"I have it on good authority that anything that can be got at all can be got at Byerly's."

Eddi quailed at the thought of the phouka turned loose in the most lavish supermarket in Minneapolis; then she found herself wishing, rather wistfully, that she'd been there to see it.

"But do eat up," he continued, snagging himself a scone.

"Not only will the cold things get warm and the hot things cold—oh, which reminds me." He bounced out of his chair again and popped into the kitchen. When he came out, it was with two cups of coffee.

"But I thought. . . .," said Eddi.

The phouka looked embarrassed. "I've been watching whenever you brewed a pot."

"Oh," she said. He set the cup down in front of her, and watched her hopefully.

She took a sip, not caring that it was too hot. "It tastes just right," she said, and thought sadly, *He doesn't need me to make coffee anymore,* while he beamed.

"So, as I was saying," the phouka went on, hacking a piece off the cheddar, "you have a busy day ahead of you, and should be well fortified. Breakfast is very important"—he leaned to look out the window at the sky—"even if you eat it at midday."

"What do you mean, busy day?"

"While you wandered the meadows of sleep, my seminocturnal flower, your private secretary has been taking your calls." Eddi coughed, and he ignored her. "Carla will be here in a quarter of an hour to discuss a gig—quaint, that; it used to mean a small carriage—for the band."

"We don't even have a name yet, and already she's found us a job?"

"You'll have to ask her." He looked at the ceiling, as if reading off it. "And Willy Silver telephoned."

Perhaps Eddi only imagined the pause after that, the fragment of silence as loud as a voice. She was certain that it wasn't as long as it seemed to be.

"What'd he say?" she asked.

"He wanted to know, since there's no rehearsal this evening, if you would like to go dancing."

And, of course, she would like to. The phouka was still staring at the ceiling, his expression perfectly neutral.

"Would it be dangerous?" Eddi asked him. She wasn't certain why she did; surely the wisest course was to treat the news casually and change the subject.

He gave her a long, sardonic look. "Dangerous to what?"

"Me."

"Oh, I know that, my sweet, but dangerous to what portion of you? Your physical self? Your sanity? Your immortal soul? Or, perhaps, your heart?"

Eddi couldn't help but flinch a little at that. "Don't be annoying. You know what I mean."

"Yes," he sighed, "I do. But are you certain you don't want the answers to the others as well?"

"No. Not from you, anyway."

"I didn't really think you would. No, my iris, you may go dancing fearlessly and with the utmost lightness of foot. You will be as safe as if you were at home with me."

"How safe is that?" Eddi asked.

The phouka's gaze was measuring. "My, you're full of many-faceted questions this morning."

Something in his expression made Eddi look away. She raised her coffee cup for a long swallow.

"And," the phouka said briskly, meeting her eyes over the rim of the cup, "after Carla's visit, we're going to go out and buy a motorcycle."

Eddi choked on her coffee.

He leaped up and gleefully thumped her on the back. "Just imagine: the wind in our hair, the thrilling sensation of speed and power, the independence of motion it will give us—"

Eddi set down her cup and leaned back in her chair. "I would *love* to have a bike," she said firmly. "But no."

"Nonsense, my sweet! What reason could there be for such self-denial?"

"I can't afford one."

He waved a hand dismissingly. "Can you operate one?"

"That has nothing to do with this."

"Is there anything in mortal law that would prevent you from owning one?"

Eddi wanted to lie to him, but he was being so rational that she hadn't the heart. It would be cheating. "No. I'm licensed."

"Well then—"

"Why don't you get *yourself* a motorcycle, and I can ride on the back?"

He settled his chin on his crossed hands again. "I would, my sweet, if only to save us this brangle. But things that take their power from explosions contained in iron, things operated by an intricacy of mechanical devices—I mislike them, I'm afraid, and I mishandle them more often than not. Some of humankind's creations trouble me not at all. The ones that deal in directing the flow of electricity, for example." He indicated the stereo with a turn of his hand. "But the internal combustion engine . . ."

"But why would it bother you to drive one, and not to ride it?"

"A reasonable question, though I'm not sure it has a reasonable answer. I've—a mental block? A moral objection?—to being in control of such a machine. Being borne along on one I can put up with."

"But cars make you uncomfortable."

He raked his hands through the black curls at his temples and smiled crookedly. "I am a creature of earth and air," he said. "Enclosed in a car, I feel sickened and weak, and as panicky as an animal that chews through its own leg to escape a trap."

Eddi stared at him, surprised. She knew he'd been uncomfortable in the car, but she hadn't dreamed that he'd been as uncomfortable as that.

His gaze dropped to the plate in front of him, and he toyed for a moment with the bread knife. "I hate to raise a question you might prefer unasked . . ."

"Go on."

He looked up at her again. "How did you intend to reach the battlefields?"

It took Eddi a moment to make sense of that. Then time and trouble caught up to her. "I . . . hadn't thought that far," she confessed.

"The first engagement will be several miles to the south and east of here," he continued, "at the place called Minnehaha Falls. I could reach it on foot and still be fresh when I arrived, but I doubt you could do the same." He sounded almost apologetic.

"If they want me there so bad, why don't they arrange transportation?"

"Would you mind if you arrived bruised, wet, muddy, and airsick? The glaistig, for one, would laugh herself ill, but I know you wouldn't care about that." He popped a piece of cheese in his mouth and smiled at her.

"What? I don't—why—"

He chewed and swallowed quickly. "I've told you that I'm a tricksy wight, and I am, my sweet. But there are those in the Seelie Court who would make me seem a very perfect knight. It is these who would come for you, if you were unwilling to come on your own. One trip with them, and you would walk halfway 'round the earth to avoid another."

"And these are the good guys?" Eddi muttered. The phouka

shot her an odd, intense look. "I suppose taking a bus is right out?"

"I would rather have my ears pierced with a railroad spike."

"Gotcha."

After a moment, he said, "You wouldn't, I hope, have begged a ride from Carla?"

"No," Eddie snapped, "I wouldn't have." *Because if I did Carla would know when the battle is, and where. And nothing would keep her from getting mixed up in it.*

"I am comforted," he said, a little sharply. "Your judgment is unimpaired."

"Why should it be anything else?"

The phouka smiled, his head tilted a little to one side, and replied, "Love has a way of turning mortals stupid."

She had to prod herself into being properly annoyed. "What the hell do you know about love?"

He leaned forward. His eyes were dark as water under a moonless sky, dark as a windowless room just after the lights go out. "What," he said softly, "do you know about me?"

The intercom buzzer cut the air to ribbons. The phouka sighed and said toward the door, "You're early."

Eddi jumped up and thumbed the speaker button. "Carla?"

"Is Madame receiving?" said Carla's voice.

"There's a straight line in there somewhere," Eddi said, and pressed the button that unlocked the front door.

"Now, about this motorcycle," the phouka murmured.

"I can't afford one."

He contemplated the ceiling. "That, my flower, is no barrier to your heart's desire."

"What do you mean?" She moved toward him warily.

Carla stuck her head in the door. "You called?"

"He's up to something," Eddi said, pointing at the phouka. The phouka looked innocent.

Carla shrugged. "The Pope's Catholic, they tear up the highways in the summer, and he's up to something. So?"

"It's not as bad as that," the phouka assured her. "Do you know anyone with a motorcycle for sale?"

"A what?" said Carla, entirely off balance.

"A motorcycle. And it should, ideally, be someone you dislike."

Eddi and Carla stared at him.

"Ah, well," he sighed at last, "I suppose I can do it myself.

May I ask of you, then, that you have your tête-à-tête in the bedroom?'' At that, he crossed the living room and opened a window.

Eddi folded her arms. "Why?"

"I'm calling on my sources," the phouka smiled at her. "But they're inclined to be shy. So do me the kindness of shutting yourself in the bedroom, sweet, and biding there until I call. Please?"

Carla looked mutinous, but Eddi grabbed her arm and tugged. Finally Carla snorted and followed her to the bedroom.

Carla bounced angrily on the bed as Eddi closed the door. "Damn it, are you gonna—"

Eddi put a finger to her lips. She'd closed the door firmly and with an audible bump; now she eased it open, agonizingly slow, until she could put an eye to the crack and see the phouka sitting at the table. Carla slid off the bed and scrambled silently over. She sat on the floor and peered through the opening, too.

The phouka took a scone off the plate and cut it in half with the bread knife. Then he held the blade against the middle finger of his right hand and flicked downward. Blood welled bright tulip red against his brown skin. Three drops fell and soaked into the white surface of the bread. He picked up the half-scone and set it on the window sill, then sat back down and watched it, licking his wounded finger absently.

Eddi saw Carla look up toward her. She held up a warning hand, and kept watching.

Something appeared over the offering on the windowsill. At first Eddi thought it was an enormous moth, its wingspan greater than the length of her palm. But the quick-beating wings had none of the powdery whiteness of a moth's. They were full of the suggestion of other colors, with a gelatinlike sheen. Then it landed on the sill, folded its wings, and Eddi could see it clearly.

In rough outline, the tiny thing that stooped over the scone and appeared to sniff at it was human. It might even, at a glance, seem female. But it was a nacreous white all over and fraily built, with a triangular face occupied mostly with shining dark eyes, hair like cobwebs and steam, long spidery hands on which the fingers and thumbs were all the same length, and long feet with toes that gripped like bird's talons. It raised its head and stared at the phouka for a long moment, its mouth a little open. Then it dug its fingers into the scone, tore out the stained parts, and devoured them. Eddi saw the phouka's shoulders drop a little, and realized that it was tension going out of him.

The creature wiped its mouth with the back of one hand, a sharp and sudden gesture. Then it launched itself, landed on the table in front of the phouka, and crouched there. It glared inquiringly up at him.

The phouka's lips moved, though Eddi could hear nothing, not even the occasional sibilance of a whisper. Still, the little creature winced. Or at least, Eddi corrected herself, it looked like a wince. She could no more interpret this thing's expressions than she could those of a bird. The phouka sat perfectly motionless as he spoke to it.

At last the creature curled its lips at him and flung itself into the air and out the window. The phouka blew an audible breath, and his body shuddered back to life.

Eddi closed the door as slowly as she'd opened it.

"Jesus," said Carla, looking at the bedroom door.

"What do you suppose it was?" Eddi wondered.

"Well, it wasn't Tinkerbell, honey. I'm never gonna watch *Peter Pan* again."

"I don't know. It was . . . beautiful, in a creepy sort of way."

"The way it scarfed up that . . . Jesus." Carla twitched her shoulders. "What was going on out there?"

Eddi decided to make that a smaller question than Carla had meant it to be. "It has something to do with motorcycles."

"Motorcycles?" Carla repeated faintly.

"He's decided I should buy one."

"What the hell does *that* have to do with motorcycles?"

"I'm not sure," Eddi replied. "I think he's sent that critter off to find one."

Carla shuddered. "Thank you, but I'll use the want ads."

Eddi patted her hand and grinned. "Maybe we should have told him about 'em." *There,* she thought, *now let's pretend to forget about all that and go on.*

"What about your band business?" Eddi asked finally. The band, at least, was a purely mortal concern, something of Eddi's that her magical allies couldn't control. "The Beast said something about a gig?"

"The b—oh, you mean Rover." Carla grinned. "Right. Wanna play at the reception for the senior show at MCAD?"

"Good grief! How did you do this, with a new band and no demo tape?"

"I called in a favor," Carla said smugly. Eddi raised an eyebrow. "Yes, I did, don't look at me like that. Turned out it wasn't that hard to get, either." Carla leaned forward and poked her finger at Eddi. "Do you have any idea what people think of you?"

"Jeez, I'd rather not know."

"I told the guy who books MCAD events that I had a band he was sure to like. I told him who was in it. And he offered us the gig."

"He recognized Dan's name," Eddi suggested.

"Of course he did, but he's no fool, kid. He wanted to know who was fronting the band—Danny's not that sort of performer, and neither am I. I gave him your name, and he gave us the job."

"Maybe he wants to make a pass at me."

"He's the boyfriend of a guy I took drum lessons from."

"Oh." Eddi found it pleasantly unnerving that someone she didn't know would recognize her name.

"So, do we take the job?"

The Minneapolis College of Art and Design would be a good place to launch the band. Some of the best progressive and art rock bands in town had started at MCAD receptions and openings. It was an informal, low-pressure setting, and the audience would be appreciative and possibly influential. "We'd have to rent a PA," Eddi said finally.

"So we rent a PA. Yes?"

"Yes. In fact, I'm so impressed that I've decided to make you business manager."

"Hell, I knew that. You don't like to do it, and Danny *can't* do it, with his mind off in the Van Allen Belts somewhere. And Hedge and Willy are unknown quantities. That leaves *petite moi*." Carla drew her knees up under her chin and shot Eddi a sideways glance. "Speaking of unknown quantities . . ."

Eddi hadn't actually jumped at the mention of Willy—at least, she thought she hadn't. But she knew that look in Carla's eye. "What about 'em?"

"Did you, ah, get home all right last night?"

"Yeah," Eddi said slowly, and Carla began to fidget so obviously that Eddi laughed and relented. "Willy and I walked back here," she told Carla, "and I invited him up."

"Lawsy me, girl, what done got into you? That's pretty sudden."

"I know." Eddi raised her chin a little. "But I don't regret it. Yet."

"Mmm. Can't imagine why. I mean, he's the best-looking man I've ever *seen,* he plays guitar better than God, and he doesn't act like an asshole. Now, I don't know what he's like when you get him alone . . ."

"I do."

". . . But honey, the boy's clearly too good for you."

Eddi looked at her more closely. "Are you . . . I don't know how to put this. Are you jealous? I mean, did I—"

"Dummy," Carla giggled, and shook her head. "No. He's not my type. It's sort of like seeing a famous painting, and really liking it—but not wanting it in your living room. Too much responsibility or something. I like comfortable men."

"Like who?" Eddi prodded.

"Nobody particular," Carla said, fixing her attention on rolling down the cuffs of her socks. Then she leaned back against Eddi's headboard and grinned. "And anyway, he was paying attention to you from the minute he walked in."

"What? Who?"

Carla sighed. "Willy, dear."

"He was?"

"What were *you* paying attention to?"

"Hah. He knew I was the one he had to impress to get into the band."

"Ladies," said the phouka's voice from the other side of the door, "my business is concluded, if you'd prefer the living room."

"Anything more you want to say in private?" Eddi asked softly.

Carla bit her lip. "Well . . ."

"Out in a minute!" Eddi called to the phouka.

"Now it's *my* turn to worry about how to say this," Carla grumbled. "What . . . what happened to house arrest?"

"What?"

"Him," Carla said, with an impatient nod at the bedroom door. "The Shadow. Where was he last night?"

"I don't know."

"After all that hoopla, he just disappears for the night? They could have killed you!"

Eddi shrugged. "He said it was all right. That I would be protected." *Why am I jumping to defend him?* she thought.

Carla might have heard that thought, to judge from her next words. "He's not as bad as he used to be, is he?"

"The phouka?"

"Yeah. He doesn't throw his weight around as much. He's even—God, dare I say it?—fun sometimes."

"Careful," Eddi said, "don't get carried away."

"Mmm. But are you . . . I mean, okay? Is all this getting to you?"

What could she say? Yes and no? She was used to living alone, and she hadn't been really alone now for weeks. Her life was in danger. And yet . . .

"No, Eddi said. "I'm in good shape. Come on, kid, let's go keep the pooch company."

The phouka was standing in what passed for a casual pose, staring out the living room window. Then he turned, and the look he gave Eddi stopped her at the threshold. It was a delicate curl of a smile and a raised eyebrow. Just the sort of expression he would use if he knew they'd been spying at the door. Eddi shrugged at him.

The phouka favored Carla with his most adorable grin. "Might I ask a favor of you, in the interest of sparing you such favors in future?"

"That sounds mysterious."

"I always am."

"What do you want?"

"A ride, for the two of us," and he gestured at Eddi, "to the north side of Saint Paul." So the creature had found the phouka his motorcycle, in whatever way such things were done. Carla was watching her, waiting for her to second the phouka's request. "Yes," Eddi told her, "Saint Paul it is."

Her reward was the relief in the phouka's face.

It was a black Triumph Bonneville, a street bike of dignified pedigree. Eddi immediately ached to ride it. It was parked next to a metal shed behind a tall, sway-backed house. Eddi looked reluctantly toward the sagging back porch. "D'you suppose we should tell someone we're here?"

The phouka shook his head. "Wait for him to come to us. And when he does, let me speak to him."

To Eddi's amazement, he reached into a pocket and pulled out a pair of blackout sunglasses.

"Why? *I'm* the one who knows—"

"Hey!" said a voice from the alley. A girl of perhaps eight or ten, her features and coloring marking her as Native American, sat on her heels in the brown weeds by the shed. She shook tangled black bangs out of her eyes with a quick motion. "You gonna buy that?"

Eddi found herself searching the girl's face for some sign of elfin blood. She seemed more fairylike than the phouka; she squatted comfortably in the weeds as if she'd materialized there. "Don't know yet," Eddi said at last. "Do you know whose it is?"

The girl made another quick head motion; this one pointed her chin at the house and moved her hair, too. Eddi admired her economy.

"He's a a-hole," the girl said. "You wanna watch it, he mighta ripped off that bike."

Eddi raised her eyebrows at the phouka.

"Do you really think that's likely?" he asked the girl, sounding rather pleased.

She shrugged. "He ripped off some socket wrenches from my ma's boyfriend. He said he didn't have 'em, but he was lyin'. An' he threw a bottle at me once, when I was on my bike."

"Tsk," the phouka murmured. The girl unfolded from the tall grass and went to pace her way around the Triumph, studying it as seriously as any customer.

Then Eddi heard the adult's voice she'd expected earlier, from the direction of the house. It was not the speech she'd thought to hear.

"Get the fuck away from that bike, you hear me?"

The man coming down the walk was large, and probably strong, but no one could suggest he was in good shape. His T shirt strained across his middle, and struggled to meet the tooled belt that held up his jeans.

He was scowling over Eddi's shoulder. She turned to see the girl disappearing behind the garage across the alley. The phouka leaned a proprietary hand on the motorcycle.

"Sorry 'bout that," the man said, and wiped a hand on his T shirt before extending it to Eddi. She shook it limply. "Them Indians steal anything that ain't nailed down."

Eddi tried to imagine a ten-year-old girl making off with several hundred pounds of motorcycle, and failed.

The man looked at the phouka and frowned. The phouka smiled and inclined his head in lordly condescension. His costume contributed to the effect: gold-and-black frock coat, black ruffled shirt, skin-tight black pants and high-heeled boots.

The man didn't offer to shake hands with him. Instead, he returned his attention to Eddi. "So, honey, you lookin' for a bike?"

Before she had a chance to ask him not to call her "honey," the phouka spoke.

"Ms. McCandry would like to test drive your vehicle." He looked to Eddi as if for confirmation. The dark glasses were wonderfully enigmatic. She wanted to laugh at him; she managed to nod instead.

The big man rubbed his nose. "You know how to ride one of these, honey?" His eyes went quickly to the phouka, then back to Eddi. She knew that look; club managers would do it when they wanted to hustle her and were wondering if Stuart would object.

Eddi gave the man a warning stare, and let it stay on him until she was certain he didn't understand it. "I can ride a motorcycle," she said.

"The key," said the phouka, and held out a languid hand.

The man ignored him. Grinning down at Eddi, he said, "Maybe I oughta go with you, to make sure."

The phouka stepped forward. He was shorter than the bike's owner, and possibly a hundred pounds lighter. But he moved the dark glasses down his nose just enough to look over them, and the larger man stopped grinning.

He produced a key on a wire ring. "Take her 'round the block, sugar," he said. "You know how to start one of these?"

Eddi clenched her teeth on the reply that tempted her most. "Can I borrow a helmet?"

"Ain't got one."

That didn't surprise her. She straddled the bike and rocked it off the stand, then went through the start-up checks. With a last glare at the owner, she folded out the kick-start lever, jumped down, jumped again, and the engine fired.

The Triumph ran splendidly. Eddi took a route that included a stretch of highway, and delighted in the lash of the wind against her face. She could hear and feel the steady firing of the engine (what had the phouka said, about explosions contained in iron?), and the clean shifting of the gears.

Then, on a residential street, she braked so suddenly that the back wheel skittered. She stopped at the curb, turning one thought over and over.

She was alone.

She looked around, half expecting to see a dreadful thing or two converging on her. Nothing appeared; the bike's rough purring was the only break in the neighborhood's peace.

I could head for the highway, drive like hell, and be in Wisconsin in an hour, she thought. *Unless the Unseelie Court caught me first.* The phouka would be furious. So, for that matter, would the owner of the bike, who would call the police. *What's the penalty for auto theft? It'd almost be worth it—I'd like to see the Seelie Court break me out of the Ramsey County jail for their damn war.*

The phouka would be in a towering rage if she ran. (Funny— she'd never seen him in a rage, but she was certain he was capable of one.) She wondered if he'd be a little sad, too. She imagined him standing in that square of weedy grass and mud, waiting restlessly, anxiously—and realizing that she wasn't coming back. He would know long before the big coarse man who waited with him. And when the big man threatened to call the cops, the phouka would walk away. . . . No, she would never know what he'd do. She wouldn't be there, after all. . . .

She put the bike in gear and headed for the sagging house.

The phouka was leaning against the shed, the picture of disreputable ease. The black-lensed glasses almost hid his expression. Only a one-sided quirk of his lips hinted at amusement, and relief. The owner of the motorcycle stood several paces away from him, rubbing his palms against his pantlegs. Eddi wondered what the phouka had done to torment him.

"Well?" the phouka said when she switched the engine off.

"It'll do."

The phouka nodded.

"So," said the owner, "c'mon in the house, have a beer, and let's deal."

The phouka seemed to think over a selection of responses. Then he shrugged and said baldly, "We would not be comfortable in your house. We'll conduct our business where we are."

The bike's owner turned white, then red. "You too good to come into my house and drink my beer?"

"I didn't say that."

The big man's eyes narrowed, and his jaw worked around some particularly fine insult. "I don't haveta take shit from no faggot nigger,' he said at last, and smiled.

The phouka fingered the frames of his sunglasses, as if threatening to lower them again. "Ah, but it won't bother you at all to take my money, will it? How much do you want for the motorcycle?"

Eddi watched anger and greed quarrel in the big man's face. "Eleven-fifty," he said smoothly.

The phouka tilted his head and put his hands behind his back. There, where the other man couldn't see, he tapped his thumb against each fingertip, one, two, three. . . . Eddi understood. She reached over as if to examine the bike, and brushed seven of his fingers lightly with her own.

"Now, now," he said. "Seven hundred."

"I ain't gonna bargain with you. I know what this bike is worth." Then the big man showed his teeth. "But I might let you have it for a thou—'cause I like the li'l lady."

The phouka's mouth became a hard line, and one of his hands bunched inside the other. "That's your last offer?" he said with frost in his voice.

"Yeah."

The phouka turned toward the alley. Eddi followed after him, wondering how they were going to get home. Then he turned back.

"Here's *my* last," he said. "Eight hundred." He paused before he added, "Cash," and smiled so fiercely that Eddi expected to scc his dog-fangs.

For a few moments the big man stared at them. Then he shrugged.

The phouka reached into his coat, drew out a slim leather folder, and flicked it open. He licked the tip of a finger delicately and counted out eight hundred-dollar bills. He held them up casually, fanned to display them to best advantage. "Anything else?"

The man scowled, licked his lips, and shook his head.

"Title," said Eddi.

He curled his lip at her. "His money and your bike, huh?" He shook his head and went back to the house to get the title.

The papers were filled out, and the eight bills left the phouka's hand. "Nice doin' business with you," the big man said, crumpling the money in his fist. The weight of his steps as he went back to the house made the mud splatter.

The phouka shivered like a dog shedding water.

"Well!" Eddi sighed. "You said you wanted to find someone despicable to buy a motorcycle from. If I'd known you'd do it so well, I wouldn't have come."

"I'm not certain *I* would have," he replied as he folded up his sunglasses. "Had I been my dog-self, I would have bitten him."

"Let's put some distance between him and us." Eddi kick-started the bike and beckoned to the phouka with a nod of her head. He looked at the half of the seat behind her. "Come on," she said, "or you'll have to run behind the whole way home."

He glanced at her through his eyelashes. "Very well." And he settled in behind her.

"You put your feet on those—and watch the pipes, they get hot. Hang on around my waist until you get used to the acceleration," Eddi told him.

He made a noise, something between a word and a cough. After a moment, he circled her waist carefully with his arms.

She wanted suddenly to turn and look at him; she wanted equally suddenly not to meet his eyes. She put the bike in gear instead.

They didn't talk on the way back; the wind and the engine noise were a good excuse. Eddi did nerve herself to say, when a stop sign gave her the chance, "You let me take it out alone."

She felt the tension in the arms around her waist. "That nice man would have been nervous, surely, if we'd both ridden off," the phouka said lightly. "I was hostage for your good behavior."

Eddi frowned over her shoulder at him and said, "Were you playing with me, ready to reel me back if I tried to run?"

He closed his eyes, and she saw a muscle work in his jaw. "That must be it. I could not have chosen to trust you."

His voice was calm, distant. She did a very sloppy job of accelerating away from the stop sign.

Eddi turned into the alley behind the building and parked the bike near the back door. "Think somebody'll steal it?"

"I believe I can promise you that no one will touch it."

" 'Warning: this bike protected by attack fairies.' All the gay guys in the neighborhood would get a kick out of that."

The phouka frowned at her. "It would be easier for me to arrange if you didn't say that name aloud, in the open air."

She was confused, until she remembered that she wasn't supposed to call them fairies. "Sorry."

"Come along, then," he said shortly. She followed him up the stairs, or rather, followed the sound of his high-heeled boots as he ran on ahead of her.

She washed, put on some makeup, and changed into a white tank top, a short white denim skirt, and a burgundy satin Chinese jacket. Then she spared a few minutes to tidy the bedroom. She didn't think too much about why she did that.

The phouka was in the kitchen washing dishes when she came out. "You don't have to do that," she told him.

He didn't look up from the sink. "I might as well, as long as I'm here." He sounded cheerful.

"Any of that cantaloupe left?"

He nodded toward the refrigerator. "Sliced and waiting."

She took a piece into the living room, where she put Boiled in Lead's "Hotheads" album on the turntable. After a song, she realized she was pacing back and forth between the sofa and the window.

"Impatient?" the phouka said. He was leaning in the kitchen doorway, wiping his hands on a dish towel. He'd taken off his amazing jacket, and the high throat of the black ruffled shirt as unbuttoned to his breastbone. She could see curls of black hair on his chest. She swallowed and looked away. Then he said, "Or nervous, perhaps?" in such a soft voice, that she looked back. He smiled at her.

"I think so. Dumb?"

He shook his head.

"Hey, where *did* that money come from?"

"You don't want to know," he grinned wickedly.

"Why don't I?"

"Oh, very well." He looked pleased with himself. "Sometime after midnight, our lad may want to run his eight hundred dollars through his fingers and gloat. Then he'll open his wallet, and find, not his lovely money, but eight wilted maple leaves. It's the nature of fairy gold."

Eddi stared at him. "We just stole a motorcycle?"

"No, how did we? We've traded something for something, and if the money he took did not remain money, then it's only a judgment on him for his wicked ways."

"But . . . but you knew, when you gave him the money, that

it was an illusion. That makes it no better than counterfeiting. You didn't *really* give him any money. We ripped him off.''

The phouka looked puzzled. "Sweet, he's done as much to others, and would have done to us, if he could.''

Eddi slumped onto the couch and pulled her hair. "Shit. Leave him out of it then. Listen." She leaned forward, trying to ignore his stubborn look. "Maybe he's got a wife, or a girlfriend. Maybe he gave her one of those hundreds for housekeeping money. She thinks maybe now she can get the window fixed in the back door, with what's left over from groceries and bills and stuff.''

The phouka frowned from the kitchen doorway. "Or maybe," she went on, "our guy went to the all-night supermarket, and spent one of those hundreds. The kid at the checkout puts it in the register.

"So what happens at midnight, or the next day? The kid rings out the register and comes up a hundred bucks short, and the manager takes it out of the kid's check. Or the guy's wife looks in *her* wallet and finds a goddamn leaf. How does she tell him that a hundred bucks just went up in smoke? How does she get through the week if she doesn't?''

The phouka seemed wholly absorbed in the kitchen towel he pulled back and forth through his hands.

"Don't you see?" she asked him. "Maybe the guy does deserve to get shafted by somebody. But can you be sure that nobody else is getting screwed along with him?''

She dropped her gaze to the floor between her feet, searching for words eloquent enough to reach him, despairing of finding them. Then the toes of his boots appeared in her field of vision, and he knelt on the rug before her.

"I do see," he said. "I didn't know—ah, sweet, not tears. I never meant to cause you those." He blotted one delicately away with a fingertip.

"It's just frustration," she smiled weakly. "I always cry when I'm frustrated.''

"Oh dear." He shook his head. "I'll surely have to mend my ways now.''

He was holding one of her hands lightly. His other hand maintained its fragile touch on her cheek. His smile was mocking, but as if out of habit, something left over from some other mood.

The door buzzer made them both jump. He tossed the kitchen

towel into the air. "Ash and Thorn, I hate that thing," he muttered, and disappeared into the kitchen again.

"Hello?" she said into the speaker.

"Hullo. Should I have called first?"

A tingle shot along her skin. Even rendered up by the intercom speaker, Willy Silver's voice was rich as chocolate, full of music. "You did, this morning. C'mon up." She unlocked the downstairs door.

There was silence in the kitchen. "Phouka?" she said, and realized from the feel of it on her lips that she'd never called out to him before.

After a moment, he came to the kitchen door. "Mmm?"

They stared at each other. "Nothing," Eddi mumbled.

He grinned ruefully and raked a hand through his hair. "If you're wondering what to do with me, don't fret, my sweet. I'll be discreetly absent when you get home."

"That's . . . I wasn't thinking that."

The knock came at the door, and Eddi opened it.

"Good evening," Willy said, a little shy. The hall lights gleamed in his black hair, fired an uncanny glow in his eyes.

"Come on in," she smiled at him. Willy smiled back. It made her dizzy.

The phouka was still standing in the kitchen door, but Willy seemed to ignore him. For a moment Eddi wondered if he'd made himself invisible.

"Any objection to First Avenue?" Willy asked her.

"Who's playing?"

He shrugged, making it an elegant gesture. "It's danceteria in the main room, but Summer of Love is playing downstairs in the Entry."

"Good choice." Her gaze slid self-consciously to the phouka.

Willy looked at him for the first time. "How's it going?" he said, friendly but distant.

"Fine. Want to do a few dishes?"

"Silly ass," Eddi laughed. Then she noticed Willy's measuring look. "He's a good friend," she told Willy, and wondered why she felt she should tell him anything.

Her words provoked another exchange of looks between Willy and the phouka, none of them decipherable. "I am, in fact, an excellent friend," the phouka said. "And you?"

"Good enough," Willy replied.

Eddi looked nervously from one to the other. "Um . . . we should go."

The phouka held the door for them. "Don't stay out too late, children."

"Right, Pop," said Eddi, and led the way out the door. But once Willy was in the hall, she stuck her head back into the apartment and glared at the phouka. "You'll get yours," she hissed.

The phouka smiled. "I certainly hope so."

Eddi blushed and slammed the door.

CHAPTER EIGHT

Lucky Girl

Eddi breathed the night air, savoring the smell of damp earth and bark, the satiny texture and temperature of the breeze. "Ye gods, are we really going to have spring this year? It's not just a tease?"

Willy laughed, a sound like some well-played wind instrument. "You'd think it never happened."

"You must be new in town," Eddi said.

"Relatively."

"I thought so. If you'd been playing guitar like that around here, surely I would have heard."

Willy made a little dismissing motion with his hands. In anyone else, Eddi would have thought it nervous. "I played a lot back East."

"Where *are* you from?"

"All over."

Eddi raised her eyebrows. "Aren't we all."

He had the grace to look embarrassed. "I'm sorry. It's complex—and little tense, I guess. My family's British, but I was born here."

"In Minnesota?"

He shook his head. "Western Virginia. But I left when I was young and did a lot of traveling." He fell silent for a moment, then added, "I'm the family oddball, you see. Not a black sheep, I haven't done anything dreadful. They just don't know what to do with me, exactly." He shrugged and gave a wistful little grimace. Then he turned his face away, his eyes on the darkening sky over the rooftops.

"I grew up in Winnipeg," Eddi offered in trade. "Moved here with my mother when my parents divorced, went to the U.

of M.— where I met Carla—dropped out at the end of my third year, and been rock 'n' rolling ever since.''

"Your mother still live here?"

Eddi shook her head. "She's out in Washington state, living in a cabin and being a forester." She made a face at Willy. "Why am I telling you all this?"

" 'Cause I like to know,'' he said, and his smile made her skin tickle. "So no other family here? No brothers or sisters?"

"No. My brother stayed with my dad in Canada."

Willy nodded, as if this made some sort of sense independent of the words themselves. Eddi took advantage of his distraction to study him again. He looked elegantly underdressed in black pleated trousers, a black-and-white Art Deco print shirt, and a black chalkstripe vest, which he wore unbuttoned. His black leather jacket hung over one shoulder. His hair was rumpled and slightly damp, as if just washed, and Eddi caught an herbal-soap scent, rosemary and elder-flowers, when he shook his head.

"So," Willy said, "why no spring?"

"What? Oh! We just don't."

"Everybody has spring," he said, like a religious man chiding her for saying there was no God.

"The joke goes that we have two seasons: road repair and snow removal. Or is that snow repair and road removal?" To her surprise, he looked a little shocked. "Well," she amended quickly, "it's not always true. Sometimes they run out of money for snow removal."

They were walking north toward downtown. Willy eyed the featureless backside of the Hyatt-Regency Hotel and said, "That's the kind of thinking that leads to buildings with windows that don't open."

If it did, Eddi decided it must be by a circuitous route. She studied his preoccupied expression. "Is something bothering you?"

A frown flew across his face and was gone; the apologetic grin that followed almost made her forget it. "Not exactly. And nothing to do with you. It's"—his smile took on an ironic cast—"sort of a family problem."

"Does that translate as, 'None of your business?' "

Willy seemed to find this uncommonly funny. "Sort of," he said at last.

Eddi stared at him, wondering what to say. She knew she should be annoyed, and even had a vague notion that she was.

But it seemed—inappropriate? "All right," she sighed. "I won't ask."

He caught her hand. "Didn't mean to hurt your feelings," he said, rueful and coaxing. Light caught in one of his eyes, edging the iris with pale green fire. The laughter melted from his face as he looked at her. The intensity that fascinated her so seemed to shine from him like candlelight through alabaster.

"You're very beautiful," he said softly.

That was confusing; she knew she wasn't. She shook her head.

"You don't believe me? For shame."

As a relief from his eyes, she looked down at the hands that held hers—long and pale, smooth, pleasantly cool, with neatly trimmed nails. Stuart had bitten his fingernails.

He raised her head with a finger under her chin, then put both hands around her waist and drew her close. He kissed her as if intending to burn the caution out of her.

She stepped back after a few moments and laughed shakily. "Do that again and you'll have to carry me downtown. That does funny things to my knees."

He laughed, and tucked her arm into his own.

They crossed over to Hennepin Avenue on Tenth Street. Hennepin was still changing from its daytime clothes to evening ones, from office bustle to party strut. Men and women in suits waited for buses that sucked them in and deposited suburban high school kids, dressed for Friday night, in their places.

Willy stopped in front of the painted scenic windows of the Rhinehaus. "Dinner?"

"This is a little steeper than I had in mind."

"I'm buying tonight, so it's my pick. German food." He held the door for her, and gave a little bow, which made her laugh. It also, annoyingly enough, reminded her of the phouka in one of his courtly moods.

"Something wrong?" Willy asked.

"No, why?"

"You frowned."

Eddi shrugged. "Just thinking about—my friend. Back at my apartment."

"Mmm."

The Rhinehaus was atmospherically gloomy. Hurricane candles quivered in their jars, isolating each heavy pine table in its own pool of uncertain light. The corners of the room disappeared, and the few clearly seen details took on the fascination of *objets d'art*. A painted-glass picture of a stag and hounds seemed to billow like a tapestry; an ornate cuckoo clock seemed as full of fluttering as a pine tree sheltering a flock of sparrows. In the dark air redolent of wine and unfamiliar spices, thought itself was muted and mysterious, and all its sharp edges were planed down.

They ordered things they'd never tried or never heard of, sausages with rich and silly names, hot salad, cold soup, bread as brown as the phouka's skin. They debated the merits of beer and wine with the concentration of executives planning a corporate takeover. They chose mulled wine. The waiter brought it well before the food, and the smell itself seemed to fill Eddi's head with a glimmering haze.

Willy stretched a hand across the table and laid it over Eddi's. She felt a pleasant nervous discomfort. "So," he said softly, as befitted the dark room, "what about your friend?"

She stared at him.

"Back at your apartment," he added helpfully.

"Oh, the—right. What about him?"

"That's what I asked," Willy said, looking patient. "Am I stepping on any toes? Should I expect a nasty scene?"

Eddi wasn't certain, given the phouka, that she could deny the possibility of some kind of scene. But it wouldn't be the sort that Willy meant. For a moment, she wondered if Willy cared whether *she* would be subjected to an ugly quarrel. That, however, was surely splitting hairs. "He's a friend."

"An old one?"

Eddi had a ridiculous itch to tell him the whole thing. She shrugged instead.

"Just wondered. I mean, he does your dishes."

She felt an absurd irritation on the phouka's behalf. "Remember the women's movement? We don't always have to do the dishes nowadays."

That made him laugh. "Okay, I was just making sure. Wouldn't want him to gather his friends and go looking for me."

And his friends would amaze you, Eddie mentally assured him.

They ordered linzer torte and coffee, and Eddi asked, "What *are* we going to name the band?"

Willy winced and pushed both hands through his black hair.

The white streak flashed between his fingers. "Dino Lessons," he said finally, grinning.

"Good God—like dinosaur? Where'd you get that?"

"Something I overheard."

"Well, I don't think so. But it's . . . arresting. How about Love and Rockets?" Eddi asked, thinking of titles in Carla's comic book collection.

Willy shook his head. "Already used."

"Are you serious? Dirty rats. Gargoyles? No, too metal."

"Mmm. So's Wages of Sin. I don't know, I *still* like Free Beer."

"No," Eddi said firmly. "The Sneakers?"

"Too . . ." Willy made a graceful gesture with shoulders and hands. ". . . frivolous."

"Behavior Modification."

"I kinda like that. Long, though."

"Too long." Eddi sighed. "And not quite it. Well, maybe something will come to us when we know what we sound like. Oh, did I tell you? Carla got us a job."

Willy looked impressed. "When?"

"Good grief, I didn't ask her. It's at MCAD, though, for a student show and reception."

"MCAD?"

"College of Art and Design. You'll like it. And better still, they'll like you."

"Well," he grinned, "of course. Artists have taste and refinement."

"And musicians have an ego problem."

"Me?" he grinned, and paid the tab with a couple of crisp bills.

Out on Hennepin, the evening had begun. Cars cruised—little imports, shiny pickup trucks, and big American cars with lots of rear suspension and very little muffler. Dance music beckoned from the open door of Duff's. A boy with an enormous mohawk and a girl in a torn jean jacket and engineer boots were arguing with an earnest young man in front of the Church of Scientology. Three black kids in front of the Skyway Theater had a boom box with something funky overdriving the speakers.

"I love this street," said Eddi.

Willy shot her a quick look. "You mean that?"

"Too grungy for you?"

"Not quite, no. But love?"

Eddi stuffed her hands in her pockets. "At night," she said at last, "this is the heart of Minneapolis. Uptown, where we were last night, is maybe its feet, where it dances. Hennepin Avenue is like an artery between them."

They'd reached the corner of Seventh and Hennepin. Eddi pointed at two high school girls in trendy haircuts and jeweled denim. "When the suburban kids come in for Friday night, or the outstate kids come to the city, Hennepin is where they go. When the college kids want to play pinball, when the guys on the north side want to hang around and check out the women and when the women want to hang around and show off their new clothes, this is it, this is the place to do it." She grinned and pulled her jacket a little closer. "With all those people, all that energy and emotion and—well, *living,* this place ought to have a life of its own by now." She looked at Willy. "Too much armchair mysticism?"

"No," Willy replied. He gave his head a little shake, as if to throw off a mood, and smiled. "Or at least, I don't think so. How much is too much armchair mysticism?"

"Good question. For all I know, it's like chocolate."

"You never have enough chocolate."

"Exactly."

City Center rose up before them, determinedly bland and blank-featured, hiding three floors of shopping mall under its pink ceramiclike hide. Across the street, Shinder's newsstand was a lively, noisy challenge to the impassive mall.

First Avenue and the street that gave it its name were just a block from Shinder's on Seventh Street. Eddi and Willy shuffled in the outer doors at the end of a short line.

"Isn't this pretty quiet?" asked Willy, with a nod at the people ahead of them.

"It's early. I wouldn't want to be showing up at eleven."

Eddi showed her driver's license to the man at the head of the line, and he waved her through. There was something regal, but not haughty, about the gesture, as if it was backed up by an ungrudging *noblesse oblige.*

The building was cinderblock painted high-gloss black in an effort to disguise its bus station origins. The double glass doors that faced the street were cloudy with the dust that even a few hours' traffic produced, and smudged with fingerprints. Inside the doors were more cinderblock and black paint, a middle-aged cash register on the counter of a bare, bleak-lit cashier's stall, and a long black wall studded with photocopied posters advertising next week's bands. A little video monitor hung from the long wall, showing rock videos, special color effects, and scraps of old monster movies without the sound.

"Ahem," said Willy behind her.

"Oh, so they let you in, did they?"

His mouth quirked at the corners. "I'm old enough to drink."

"What about dancing?"

"Too old. I'd better just watch."

Eddi laughed and tucked her arm through his. "Come along, Gramps. Check your coat and we'll test that."

Once around the end of the long wall, First Avenue appeared to have unfolded, or possibly transformed entirely, while the visitor's back was turned. The main room played improbable games with one's eyes; its black walls made the darkened room seem infinitely large. Three projection screens rolled down from the ceiling to curtain the front of the stage with enormous versions of what the monitor by the door had shown. A second-floor balcony wrapped around three sides of the room. The center portion, facing the stage, was fronted with a glass wall that reflected the light from the screens and blended it with the light from the balcony bar. Neon on the invisible walls seemed to float in midair everywhere. Over the dance floor was a tangle of colored lights, neon sculpture that ignited in quick rhythmic bursts, and flash pots like little short-lived stars. The sound system made the whole unmeasurable space quake.

"Are we going to play the main room?" Willy asked next to her ear, and Eddi jumped.

"We . . ."

"The band." The screen light reflected in his eyes, too, a velvety green-black."

"Damn straight," she said, and it sounded like the truth.

They went downstairs to 7th St. Entry. It was smaller, and had less to do with illusion than with function. On the black, un-adorned stage, Summer of Love had finished setting up.

"Want a beer?" Willy asked her.

"You buying?"

"Yeah," he said cautiously.

"A Dos Equis."

He raised his eyebrows. "And if you were buying?"

"Grain Belt."

"You buy the next round, opportunist," he told her, and headed for the bar.

They sat on the gray-carpeted platforms around the dance floor and drank from the bottles. "So," Eddi said. "Do you write music?"

"Not really. At least, not well. I'm good at arranging, but—no, not original things."

Eddi studied his face, looking for the bitterness that she heard in his voice. "It's all right. Not everyone does."

"But you do."

Eddi shrugged. "Carla and I make a decent team at it. And Dan Rochelle does great music, but he never does lyrics. So don't worry about it."

Summer of Love kicked off their first set then, with a heraldic blaze of guitar and keyboards. "Come on," she said, and took his hand.

"Umm?"

"They close the bars at one o'clock in this town, son. We've got a lot of dancing to do."

Willy danced the way he made love, or played the guitar—with his whole attention, and that glorious leashed energy. He had the perfect, unconscious grace of one of his own lead breaks. They danced three songs in succession, and fell laughing into each other's arms when the third ended. Willy pushed a lock of hair out of his eyes. Then he kissed her. The quick brush of their lips jolted her. From Willy's startled face, she guessed it did something like that to him as well.

"Sit this one out?" he said, his voice a little shaky.

Eddi nodded, and they found a spot on one of the carpeted risers. It was harder to to do now; the room was starting to fill up. Eddi sat without speaking, watching the band. She felt a surprising and delectable shyness that tied her tongue and kept her from looking at Willy. The brush of his fingertip along her jawline finally made her turn. He was studying her, his expression thoughtful. After a moment he turned his attention to the stage. Eddi did likewise, and wondered what had gone through his head.

Willy's presence seemed to wrap her in a mist in which every light had sparkling highlights, every sound made music, and music had an effect on all of her senses. In such a haze of wonder, it was hard to discern much detail. They danced, and drank beer, and talked, and all of it was equally absorbing and hard to remember.

At the end of the second set, they went back to the main room, more out of nervous energy than for any change of scene. They stood leaning on the balcony railing, ignoring the current of people that passed behind them. "This always makes me feel as if I'm in a movie," Eddi said, looking down at the spangled darkness of the dancers below, the glittering bottles behind the bar, and the empty VIP seats in the opposite balcony.

"As the star?" Willy smiled.

"Oh, always the star." She felt a moment's foolish melancholy, and voiced it: "We're only cast as extras in real life."

Willy slipped an arm around her waist, and she decided perhaps melancholy had its place. His breath stirred the hair around her ear.

Then Eddi heard a familiar voice behind her.

"That was fast."

She turned to find Stuart Kline at the top of the stairs. He had the rumpled look he got when drunk. His left hand clenched on the balcony railing; his right was in his coat pocket.

"Hello, Stuart," she said. She wasn't sure what tone to use, and ended up using none at all.

"Who's your new friend?" he asked, with a drawing of the lips that ought to have been a smile.

"No one you know."

She felt Willy move out from behind her. "We'll introduce ourselves," Willy said, and there was a warning in his voice. "I'm Willy Silver. And you're . . ."

"Stuart Kline." Again the stretching of the lips. "Are you Eddi's latest screw?"

The phouka would have snarled at that. "You're a slow learner, Stu," Eddi said as softly as she could and still be heard.

His jaw clenched visibly. "So, is he more fun than the swish black guy?"

"Go away, Stuart." She kept her voice low, hoping Stuart would, too. But he was too drunk to care. The sharp edge of his words made heads turn their way.

"How 'bout you?" he said to Willy. "You like dicking an out of work second-rate chick vocalist?"

Willy said, his voice very even, "Actually, I'm the guitar player for her new band."

Stuart turned white and took three steps forward. Willy met him on the last step and blocked Eddi's view. Someone at the front of the crowd shouted and pressed backward. She saw Willy's shoulders twist. Stuart dropped something, and Willy kicked it away before she could tell what it was. People began to scramble out of range. Stuart threw a punch at Willy's jaw; Willy ducked neatly under it and hooked one foot around Stuart's ankle with the same motion. Stuart hit the floor on his back, hard.

Willy returned to her side, and she saw a smile flickering at the corner of his mouth. His face was alive in a way she'd never seen.

"You'd think you were having fun," Eddi said, shaken. She realized suddenly how fast it had all been.

His expression softened only slightly. "I had to do something."

Stuart got slowly to his feet. The look in his eyes could have melted the wall behind her. "You'll be sorry,' he hissed at Eddi. "You'll be goddamn sorry." And he turned and dived through the crowd gathered around them.

"What a sweetheart," Willy said.

Eddi wrapped her hands around the balcony railing, squeezed it until her bones ached and the knot in her windpipe went away. "He used to be," she managed to say at last.

Willy leaned forward and looked at her curiously. "I hope so. Or I'd worry about your taste in men, and that would hit a little close to home."

"Oh, we couldn't have that, could we?"

"Just a joke."

Eddi shook her head. "I guess I don't feel much like joking."

His right arm went around her, hard-muscled and warm. "Want to make an early night of it?"

She leaned against him, suddenly very tired. "Yeah."

"Come on, then." They went downstairs with their arms around each other, though there wasn't really room for it in the crowd, and claimed their jackets.

They walked back on LaSalle, and the street was nearly deserted. The streetlights took the color out of Willy's pale skin and sharpened the contrast between the black and the white in his hair, until the only color about him seemed to be his eyes. The chill glitter she'd seen in them was not entirely gone, and his beautiful face was grim and distracted.

When they reached Eddi's front steps, she realized they hadn't spoken since they'd left First Avenue. Willy put his hands on her shoulders and broke the silence.

"I'd ask if I can come up, but you might say no. And I think I should."

Eddi almost told him no anyway. But she was only vaguely, wearily annoyed at his taking charge. She turned away from him, fumbled for her keys, and unlocked the door. They went upstairs without touching.

She half expected to find the phouka in the apartment, and was surprised to find herself disappointed when she didn't. She sat down on the couch and let Willy close and lock the door behind himself. He slipped his right arm out of his jacket, then, gingerly and with a little indrawn breath, his left.

"What's the matter?" Eddi asked.

"Nothing."

His left shirtsleeve seemed fuller, seemed to flutter a little. She got up and caught his left hand. He tried to pull away; then his hand was still in hers.

There was a long tear, a slash, in the cloth over Willy's forearm. It matched the long wound on the skin beneath, shallow, but swollen and angry red.

"He had a knife?" Eddi said finally, not believing what she saw. Stuart had dropped something, and Willy had kicked it away. But Stuart had never been the sort to carry a weapon. . . .

"I'm sorry," Willy said very softly, and she looked up.

"For what?"

"I wasn't going to tell you. I thought at first he'd missed, you see."

Eddi shook her head. "It ought to be cleaned."

"Mmm." Willy looked around the dim-lit room, then went to the table and picked up the salt shaker. He took it with him into the bedroom, where he took off his vest and shirt. He could have been alone; he showed no constraint at undressing in front of her, in her apartment. Suddenly she remembered the shy clasp of the phouka's arms around her waist, on the motorcycle. It embarrassed her, and she looked down at her feet.

Willy went into the bathroom, and she heard the sink filling up with water. She followed slowly after him, and found him with his forearm half-submerged in the sink bowl. With his other hand he splashed water over the uncovered part of the wound. The salt shaker stood uncapped on the ledge above the sink.

"Do you wear a hair shirt when you're at home?" Eddi asked him.

Willy looked up at her in the mirror, his face blank and cool. "The salt cleans it out." Then he added ruefully, "But it's true, I wouldn't mind using something that stung less. Except you don't have any of them." He shot her one of his brilliant smiles.

The sight of him, bending shirtless over her bathroom sink, made her feel quite fuzzy-headed. She sat on the end of the bed, staring out into the living room. After a minute she heard Willy drain the sink; a little after that she felt him kiss the top of her head.

"He wouldn't have used it on you," he said.

"I didn't think he would use one on *anybody*." She folded her hands, and refolded them. "Is this my fault? Because I left him?"

"I don't know enough about him."

Eddi looked up at him. "He wasn't like this," she whispered. "He was a good person. He just . . . wasn't strong."

He worked his left hand, wincing when his forearm muscles flexed. "I'm a little biased right now."

Eddi nodded.

Willy dropped another kiss on her hair and said, "Get into bed, and I'll sing you to sleep." The words were paired with a little teasing smile, and she had to smile back.

Eddi found she couldn't match his nonchalance in undressing— she did it in the bathroom. When she came out in her kimono he was sitting on the bed wrapped around her acoustic guitar, playing scales with a quick, light touch. She dropped her robe and slid quickly under the covers.

"Nice axe," he said.

"Charlie Hoffman made it." She felt silly, lying naked in bed and talking to Willy about guitars.

But Willy just smiled a little and said, "I know his work."

"Doesn't that bother your arm?" she asked, meaning the guitar playing.

"Only the barre chords."

He startled her when he slipped into a soft-voiced rendition of Joni Mitchell's "A Case of You"; she hadn't been expecting references to love lost from him. Even leashed as it was, his voice was rich and subtle and full of meaning. The guitar notes hung in the dark room like spray from a fountain.

She could feel relaxation filling her up. Willy's voice went on, so softly that he might have been singing only to himself:

> *True Thomas sat on Huntleigh bank*
> *And he beheld a lady gay,*
> *A lady that was brisk and bold*
> *Come riding o'er the ferny brae.*
>
> *True Thomas he pulled off his cap*
> *And bowed him low down to his knee*
> *"All hail, thou mighty Queen of Heaven,*
> *Your like on earth I ne'er did see."*
>
> *"Oh no, oh no, True Thomas," she said,*
> *"That name does not belong to me.*
> *For I am the queen of fair Elfland,*
> *Where you must go along with me."*

Eddi came to the sleepy realization that she did know a few fairy tales after all, in English ballads. Was there one with a phouka in it?

She didn't realize Willy had stopped until she felt his lips brush hers. "Do you know 'Jack O'Rion?' " she asked him.

"Yeah, but I'm not gonna do it," he replied, a quiver of laughter in his voice. "Too close to home. Do you want to go to sleep?"

Eddi opened her eyes and saw him, naked to the waist, perfect, his eyes full of banked fire. She shook her head.

"I'm glad of that," he murmured with self-mockery that she didn't understand. He set the guitar down gently, and just as gently began to kiss his way down her body.

She did not fall asleep after Willy left, though she tried. It was the fault of too much thinking—about Willy, about Stuart, about the phouka and his fairy war. . . .

From the darkened living room, she heard a clink, like glass against glass. She slipped silently out of bed, wrapped her kimono around her, and tiptoed to the open bedroom door.

He had the blinds wide open, and was sitting in one of the kitchen chairs, his feet propped on the windowsill, looking out at the night. She knew him by the silhouette of the loose curls over his forehead, the stubborn chin, the ridiculous froth of lace that spilled over the hand that held one of her wine glasses.

"What, my primrose," he said without turning, "not asleep yet? Or is it awake again?"

"How long have you been here?" She padded into the room and sat in the other chair.

"Long enough. Or perhaps," he said, scowling at the level of liquid in the glass he held, "not long enough, after all. Pity."

Eddi finally noticed the amber color of the stuff in the glass, and smelled the brandy fumes. "That's for medicinal purposes."

"I'm not surprised. I have been consuming it steadily for the last hour, and I can assure you, it was not made for the sake of pleasurable drinking." He spoke more slowly than usual, but just as clearly.

"Then why," Eddi asked carefully, "have you been drinking it?"

"Perhaps because I needed physicking, my heart. Or perhaps not. Tell me, what do you keep it on hand to cure?"

"Head colds."

"Ah, that's the problem, then. I haven't got one."

She sighed. "Who writes your dialogue, Lewis Carroll?"

He frowned over that for a moment, shook his head, and drained the glass.

"Are you trying to get drunk?" she asked him.

"No. I am succeeding, at least in some measure, in getting drunk."

"I didn't know you could."

"Silly child. That's your problem—you know nothing of history. You are"—he thought about it, and let the word roll graciously off his tongue—"ignorant."

He was trying to annoy her. It made her smile. "Does it help?"

"Does what help?"

"Being drunk."

"Not a bit." He poured the glass half-full, sniffed it, made a face, and tossed it off. "I took care of the money."

"What money?"

"Listen to her," he grumbled. "I go to almost endless trouble, endure a not inconsiderable quantity of embarrassment, and all for some obscure moral position, all for her. And she's forgotten it. For your wretched motorcycle, of course."

"Oh!" Eddi leaned forward eagerly. "You mean it won't change back? It'll stay money? Oh, thank you!"

He sank his face into his hand. "I believe I warned you about saying that."

"Shit. I'm sorry. But I . . . that makes me very happy."

He looked up at her, and smiled slowly. "Now *that* I can listen to with no discomfort at all." He held up the brandy bottle. "Would you like some?"

"God, no. I hate the stuff."

"So do I," he said wisely, pouring himself another glass.

Eddi folded her arms on the table and rested her chin on them. "Then why are you *drinking* it?"

The phouka pursed his lips, and studied the streetlights through his brandy. "There is a children's rhyme, I believe, that tells one how many days there are in each month."

She frowned at him.

"Recite it for me, please."

"What?"

"I did say please."

Eddi sighed and began, "Thirty days hath September, April, June—"

"Thirty days hath April," he repeated, letting the words roll slowly out. "If you check the clock and calendar, you'll find, I think, that we are an hour into April's thirtieth and last day. And what does that make this coming night?"

Eddie felt as if, had the fate of the civilized world rested on it, she could not have opened her mouth, or moved, or blinked.

The phouka shook his head sorrowfully and took another swallow of brandy. "You are a slow pupil, dear heart. Well, I'll give you this one, if I must, but only this once. The night to come is May Eve, my primrose. And we shall know the joy of battle." He turned his face away from the window, turned it toward her, and nothing in it matched the lightness of his voice.

After a long time, she cleared her throat and said, "So you're getting drunk."

"Don't be silly. There's no connection at all."

"You said there was."

"I said no such thing. You misunderstood."

Eddi sighed, and stood up. "Well, now I *know* I won't be able to sleep." She started back toward the bedroom.

The discordant chime of breaking glass stopped her. She turned to find the phouka staring down at the glittering fragments of the wine glass between his feet. "I'm sorry," he said, his voice unnaturally casual.

"It's all right," she replied, and continued on to the bedroom.

She didn't think he'd meant her to hear him, when he whispered, "Would that it were."

CHAPTER NINE

Would I Lie to You?

Eddi swung the bike into the parking lot of the building on Washington Avenue. The early afernoon sun warmed her shoulders through her jacket. She wished it would rain; she was in no mood for cheerful weather. The phouka slid off the seat, and frowned when she didn't.

She pulled off her helmet and rested it on the gas tank. "I don't know if I can face practicing right now," she said at last.

"What a pity. Why couldn't you have decided that on the other side of town and spared me a ride on that infernal contraption?"

"The infernal contraption was your idea."

"It's given me a headache," he grumbled.

"Your headache came out of a bottle of Mr. Boston Five-Star. It has nothing to do with motorcycles."

The phouka looked sullen.

Eddi gazed wearily up at the iron stairs to the third floor practice space. She had slept a little, but only enough to make her feel worse. She felt, in fact, as if every cell in her body was poisonous to every other cell. It was no condition to be in for the band's first practice.

And she didn't want to face Carla. Carla might read her expression and remember what day it was. Carla would want to protect her, to become embroiled in the whole bizarre business. Eddi wasn't going to let that happen.

Unless Carla pried it out of her. Which she could do.

"'Of course you want to practice," the phouka said sourly. "This may be your last chance."

Eddi felt her insides scramble. "I thought you said you'd protect me."

"No one," he glowered at her, "is perfect." He pressed his

115

lips together for an instant, then grinned. "Except, of course, myself."

Eddi watched his face as she said, "Then I *will* be safe tonight?"

"Well," he said slowly, "not entirely."

She realized that she should put the kickstand down now, before her strength drained away completely and she let the bike fall on her. Killed? She put the stand down, and sat staring at the bland face of the speedometer.

Tonight? She couldn't quite believe in dying—though if she didn't, why did her arms and legs seem suddenly to be made of gelatin, and her mouth seem full of glue?

The phouka must have seen her distress. "Oak and Ash. Don't mind me, dear heart. It's the hangover speaking."

"But it's true, isn't it?"

He sighed. "We could *all* be killed. That is, unfortunately, one of the points of tonight's exercise. But anyone with designs on your life will be trying to go through me, and that only after going through a host of folk who fight like cornered badgers."

"It sounds like I'm going to be more trouble than I'm worth."

"You, my primrose, are all that raises this beyond the level of an ordinary territorial squabble. You and the sheer scale of the thing, that is."

"There's a difference between a territorial squabble and a war?" Eddi asked, hoping for an intelligible answer.

The phouka rubbed his temples. "A true war is one in which the blood of immortals is shed. Anything less has all the significance of a hard-fought game of football, to the Folk."

"It sounds just like humanity to me," Eddi broke in impatiently. "We'll even bleed for football, sometimes."

"As I have said, no sense of history. There's magic in spilled blood, my child. Your ancestors knew this, and on occasion even put it to the intended use." The phouka was beginning to warm to his lecturing. "And in immortal blood, which is rather more difficult to spill, there is enormous power. In a war of the Folk, the drawing of blood, the taking of lives, forces the participants to abide by the outcome of the fight. Without that, we can fight on for years over the same issue, the same piece of ground—like mortals. But immortal blood tends to stay in immortal veins, and stern measures are needed to have it otherwise."

He talked about spilling blood so calmly, as if it was something that happened elsewhere to others. And maybe it was, for him. He was immortal. There was nothing abstract about the subject for Eddi. She could feel panic bubbling up inside her like yeast.

"And one of the most effective measures," the phouka continued, "is to have a mortal on the battlefield, one with certain qualities, who is bound to the fight."

"Bound?"

The phouka closed his eyes and covered his face with one hand. "May the earth open and swallow me," he muttered. "Immediately."

Eddi stared at him, alarmed. "What aren't you telling me?"

He glared. "As far as I can tell, precious little, whether I will or no!"

"Just what's involved in being 'bound to the fight'?"

"Bread and blood," he snapped, "and much good may the knowledge do you."

Eddi slid off the bike and jammed the key in her pocket. "Well, it *would* do me good. If you'd just tell me what's going on, I might be more cooperative, damn it."

"And you might not. I've told you a great deal more than I should have in the past weeks. I've flown in the face of tradition, inclination, and direct orders. You'll cozen nothing more out of me."

"I'll . . . what?"

"Cozen," the phouka said bitterly. "Trick. Beguile."

"I've never tried to trick you!"

"Hah."

She looked at him through narrowed eyes. "What if I won't go through with it?"

"With what?"

"This . . . binding. If it was no big deal, you'd have told me about it."

The phouka gave an exasperated hiss. "By earth and air, I've tried to keep you in the dark at very step of the way! Why balk at it now?"

She'd never made him so angry—she wouldn't have believed she could. What had happened to the perfect bastard who'd taken control of her life on the Nicollet Mall? That phouka would have laughed at her, ordered her around. He wouldn't have thought it worth the trouble to fight with her.

She said, "If I got on the bike right now, and tried to ride away—would you stop me?"

He seemed angrier still, and about to speak. Then he turned away, looking back toward downtown and, she suspected, not seeing it. A knot of muscle had leaped into sudden relief in his jaw. He lifted one hand to the side of his face, as if to nurse his headache, and Eddi lost sight of his expression.

At last he said fiercely, "No."

A damp breeze, smelling of mud and car exhaust, fluttered his hair and hers. "You'd get in trouble for that, wouldn't you?" Eddi said.

"Trouble." He spat out some crisp word that Eddi didn't catch, and might not have recognized anyway. "Yes, I suppose 'trouble' would cover it, if spread thin." He swept his hair back from his face with both hands, a movement that seemed equivalent to rolling up his sleeves. It made his eyes slant even more than usual.

"Eddi," he said earnestly, "I haven't much taste for begging, and less skill. But I will happily beg you for this, with all the meager talent at my command. I would even *bribe* you, had I anything to offer. Will you please, *please*, go through with the business tonight?"

"You make it sound as if I have a choice."

He closed his eyes, shut out her angry stare. "You do."

Then he'd meant what he'd said; if she left now, he wouldn't stop her. It made her hands shake. She stuffed them in her jacket pockets.

"You told me once that I *couldn't* get away, that the Unseelie Court would come after me."

"And they would. But they may be less vigilant now, thinking that if you meant to flee, you'd have done it weeks ago. You know more of your enemy now as well—though that may be scant help." He paused, and when he spoke again, it might have been to himself. "And there is more of you to reckon with than I suspected then."

Playacting! Eddi thought. *Isn't it?* "What's involved in this binding?"

The phouka sighed. "If I could tell you and not make it sound worse than it is, I would."

Eddi started across the parking lot to the stairs.

"But I can do this much," he said at last, as if the words were dragged up his throat with a string. "I can enable you to see it all truly, so that what you do, you do by your will and not at the prompting of any glamour.''

Eddi looked at him over her shoulder. How well he was coming to know what mattered to her. . . .

''But in return, you must promise to do what is set before you to do—and you must tell no one that I've tampered with the process. Or I will indeed,'' he grinned ruefully, ''be in trouble.''

''Sounds like it amounts to the same thing.''

''Perhaps to you. Not to me.''

''Why, after all this trouble, would you offer to let me go now?'' she blurted out. ''Is this some last disgusting trick?''

The expression that swept the phouka's face was a little frightening, though Eddi couldn't say what it meant. He turned sharply away.

From behind and above them came the sound of a heavy door opening, and they looked up. Carla was standing in the doorway at the top of the iron stairs.

''Come on, guys!'' she yelled. ''You're late!''

The phouka let his breath out audibly. ''Well! Had I a pot of gold to bestow . . . ,'' he said. ''After you, my sweet.''

Eddi shook her head and rattled up the stairs.

Someone had managed to open a couple of the dusty painted-shut window sections in the rehearsal space. The hanging sheets moved in the breeze, and the room smelled of electrical power and spring.

'' 'Bout time,'' Carla said when Eddi came in the door. She nodded toward the middle of the room and added, ''Much longer, and they would have wandered off into the Twilight Zone and never been seen again.''

Dan, Willy, and Hedge were engaged in playing something that might once have been Dire Straits' ''Tunnel of Love.'' It was not loud, but it was . . . well, weird. Dan was adding and subtracting synthesizer voices and dabbing in sampled sounds wherever a blank spot seemed imminent. Hedge was running the bass through a phase shifter. The bone-resonant notes wove in and out, forward and back, like the breathing of a monstrous asthmatic cat. Willy's guitar was so unmodified as to sound naked; it would follow the other two docilely through the chords for a few measures, then, in something like a musical senility, it would wander off into the lead riff for another song entirely. They were all three absorbed in each other, glancing back and forth for cues. Willy's hair had already fallen into his eyes.

Eddi found herself grinning at them in proprietary pride. "So what are you doing standing here?" she said to Carla.

Carla blinked.

"Let's jam, kid."

And for a while, they did. Carla added a bass drum beat to anchor it all, then found a pattern on the toms that interlocked with Hedge's phasing. Eddi played sparse guitar, high and stringy.

A chord progression opened, like a door before her. It led toward a song she and Dan and Carla had worked on a week ago. She leaned on the rhythm, bending it to the shape she wanted. Carla noticed and followed her; Dan picked it up then started his left-hand riff. Hedge and Willy heard the new drive and unity behind the sound, and added themselves to it.

Eddi went to the mike and heard Dan back off his improvising, just a little; Willy came back to the chords and stayed there.

> *Neon on the frontage road*
> *The red light shines on me*
> *I only want you to be happy*
> *I only want me to be free*
>
> *Midnight on the interstate*
> *I'm on the run from you*
> *I've got a dollar says you're lying*
> *I've got a feeling says it's true.*

She gave Willy the nod for a lead break, and he snagged the melody and carried it away, ran with it as if it were a kite in the wind. Then she pointed to Hedge, Willy, and Dan, and drew a finger across her throat. Everything stopped but drums.

> *You look so sweet when you're asleep,*
> *When your mouth is closed;*
> *The angry things all shut inside,*
> *The kind of things you used to hide from me.*
> *And far away from you, I keep*
> *Pictures of you, posed,*
> *All your good side, all well-groomed,*
> *Chronicles of true love doomed*
> *By what I didn't see.*

Synthesizer, guitar, and bass swelled slowly through the second half of the bridge in answer to her prompting. She heard

Carla and Willy add wordless harmonies, too, and that filled her with reckless delight. The last verse was a ragged but enthusiastic climax.

Water on the motorway
The wipers beat like hearts
Why do you love me best whenever
We're a hundred slippery miles apart?

After that, there was the rattle of critical comment that she'd already come to expect. "I think you want bass on that bridge." Carla said.

Dan said, frowning absently, "Can we try that again? I wanna bend that last note out of shape, like a car goin' by—is that too hokey?"

"We'd *better* do it again," Willy laughed. "We don't know how to start it yet."

Hedge puckered up his face, studied his axe for a moment, and played a couple measures that made a very good intro.

By the time Eddi called a rest, they'd improved the chord progressions and added drum punches to the lead break. Dan had put a rush of white noise into the second verse that suggested tires on wet pavement. Willy and Carla were singing the words on the bridge. They sounded remarkably like a band.

Eddi flopped down on the wooden floor. "We need a couch. And a PA. And a *coffeemaker!*"

"I'll go for coffee," Carla offered. "I need cigs anyway."

Eddi snapped upright and levelled an admonishing finger. "You slack off on the smoking, girl. Bad for your voice."

Carla stuck out her tongue and turned to Dan. "Danny? Wanna come with?"

"Yeah, sure." Dan swept a look over his equipment, like a parent wondering if the kids really were safe by themselves. Carla grabbed her jacket, and they trotted out the door.

"She thinks I'm kidding," Eddi said to the ceiling. "Boy, is she gonna be surprised."

It seemed awfully quiet. She didn't want quiet; it was suitable for thinking in, and right now Eddi had no use for thinking. The music had worked like a drug, wiping away her quarrel with the phouka, her fear of what the evening would bring. Now the drug was wearing off. Conversation was not the all-absorbing distraction that music was, but she would settle for it.

She propped herself up on one elbow and looked around for Willy. She found him leaning against the wall at the far end of the room talking to the phouka. *Oh, God,* she thought, *what mischief is that little jerk up to now?* But there was no spark of wickedness about the phouka. He was sitting on the floor with his chin on his knees, looking as close to gloomy as she could imagine him.

Willy, in contrast, seemed to glow. He was discussing something with great seriousness, and he leaned forward as he spoke, punctuating everything he said with crisp motions of his pale hands. He was full of contained energy, and Eddi found herself envying him for it, and disliking the phouka for not reacting to it, and despising herself for both feelings. She dropped back to the floor, tucked her hands under her head, and closed her eyes.

Her unwelcome solitude lasted perhaps a minute. Then she heard someone approach, and opened her eyes.

It was Hedge. He sat down on the floor next to her, crossing his legs as if it required great deliberation, and stared at her solemnly. He seemed to be waiting for her to open the conversation.

"Hello," Eddi said, trying not to sound cautious.

He nodded.

This was encouraging but not inspirational. "I liked what you were doing on the bass," she ventured.

Hedge smiled his sweet smile, the one that turned his usually closed, ferrety face into something that could light a street. He nodded again.

"Is . . . there something you want to talk about?"

His brown eyes widened a little, as if the possibility hadn't occurred to him. *Why does he play bass as if he were nitro-fueled?* Eddi wondered. *He does everything else on three cylinders.*

Hedge looked as if, at worse times in his life, he'd slept in alleys. His brown hair was clean, but not well acquainted with a comb, and might have been cut with a kitchen knife. His thin face had a sallow cast that, with his underfed build, made Eddi wonder if he was recovering from a long illness. He could have been anywhere from fifteen to thirty years old. He wore a plaid flannel shirt so well-washed it was almost white, and blue jeans with holes in the knees.

"No," he mumbled finally, and Eddi realized he was answering her question.

Of course he doesn't want to talk, she grumbled inwardly. *I*

*wonder if the boy says a dozen intelligible words all week.
Maybe he's afraid his tongue will dry up if he opens his mouth.*
"Do you sing?" she asked him.

To her surprise, he gave a half-hearted nod.

"Why don't you ever sing with the band?"

He blinked at her.

"What does that mean?"

Hedge looked down at his tight-clasped hands, and his jaw
worked, as if trying to form words and test them before letting
them past his lips.

"Are you embarrassed about it?" Eddi asked him gently.

Hedge frowned quickly up at her, looked down, then nodded,
a motion so offhand it might have been a shrug.

Eddi studied the mop of messy brown hair that hid his face.
His fingers tugged at each other in his lap. It was an angry,
helpless gesture, from the hands that played bass lines so thick
with emotion they were almost verbal.

She looked across the room and saw Willy and the phouka still
talking softly. "If there was only me to listen," she said to
Hedge, "would you sing?"

Hedge peered out from under his hair and said, as usual,
nothing. But Eddi felt encouraged.

"Yo!" she called to the phouka and Willy. "How would you
guys like to take a walk?"

"No," said the phouka promptly, smiling. "Thank you."

Willy cocked his head at her.

"How would you like to do it anyway?" Eddi said.

The phouka and Willy looked at each other. Then they turned
back to Eddi.

"All right," she sighed, "what would you think of finishing
your conversation at the bottom of the stairs outside?" Surely
that was close enough for the phouka's standards of good
bodyguarding—the windows were the only other way into the
room.

Willy smiled, an enchanting sight. "Okay, we'll be nice guys.
Come on," he said to the phouka. The phouka, after a dubious
glance at Eddi, followed him out the door.

And it was quiet in the practice room again. Hedge had gone
back to looking at the floor, and was now biting at a fingernail.
Eddi almost began to talk, to put him at ease. Then she remembered that words made Hedge nervous.

"I'm going to rest until Carla and Dan come back," she said

at last. "You don't have to do anything you don't want." She lay down on the floor again, laced her fingers under her head, and closed her eyes.

From the open windows she could hear cars going by on Washington Avenue, and the occasional muted rumble of a bus. Two sparrows started a quarrel under the eaves, finished it, and flew away. A breeze whispered through the pages of the notebook Dan had left open on his amp. All of these only thickened the stillness.

Hedge broke it; he laid his voice on it like a leaf on an unruffled pool, and the song spread on the air in widening circles. His voice was soft and tuneful; he began as if he was telling a story or a piece of history.

> *In Newry town I was bred and born,*
> *In Steven's Green now I die in scorn.*
> *I served my time to the saddling trade.*
> *But I turned out to be*
> *I turned out to be a roving blade.*

The song hung in the air like a gift tentatively offered. But listening was a gift as well, and Eddi gave it. In the exchange, as often happens, both gifts increased in value. Fear and anger were gathered up in each single note, carried in ever-widening circles away from the heart of the room, and evaporated. It was not a lasting peace, but its effects lingered well beyond the end of the song.

"Hark, the evening has begun," said the phouka's voice in her ear, "the nighthawk's on the wing. The enchanted princess wakes."

"Uh," Eddi said, and lifted her head from the pillow. "Wha?" Practice had gone on until five. Then they'd ridden home, where the phouka had made her a sandwich, ordered her to take a long, hot bath, and given her a cup of—oh.

"What," she gritted, and noticed even as she spoke that the cobwebs were clearing from her thoughts with supernatural speed, "did you put in the cocoa?"

His smile was uncommonly white in the dimness of the bedroom. "Didn't you need more sleep?"

"Mmm."

"And would you, under normal circumstances, have been able to get any?"

She frowned at him.

"Well, then!" the phouka said. "Mind, I wouldn't recommend the technique for everyday, but you're none the worse for it now, are you?"

Eddi was, in fact, far from worse. She felt strong, fresh, and clear-headed. Whatever the phouka had used, it wasn't the average sleeping pill.

"Get dressed, now," he told her. "I let you sleep perhaps little longer than I should have, so don't dawdle. Oh, and wear shoes you can climb in, just in case."

She squinted at him. "Just in case of what?"

"Why, just in case you need to climb in them, sweet." He'd shut the bedroom door behind him before she could respond.

The clock radio showed nine p.m.. She turned it on loud and went to the closet. Blue jeans, black high-top sneakers, her denim jacket, and an old turtleneck sweater—she had no idea what she was supposed to wear, but she was grumpy enough to feel that the Seelie Court was not worth dressing up for.

Certainly the phouka's sleeping potion hadn't improved her mood. She was becoming steadily more anxious, in a way that years of stage fright had not prepared her for. She knew how to bring stage fright under control: imagine the worst that could happen, and its consequences. The terror was always out of proportion to anything she could expect. She had no idea what she could expect of a fairy war. Once again, she cursed the phouka comprehensively. He had told her just enough to make her afraid.

The phouka rose from the couch when she came into the living room, as if in salute. He was costumed for the occasion. His heavy, high-necked sweater was olive drab, and had suede gun patches on the shoulders. His pants were olive, too, and tucked into high brown boots. Over his shoulder hung a nicely aged brown leather jacket. He looked like a guerrilla outfitted by Ralph Lauren.

"Never dress better than your date," Eddi grumbled at him, which made him laugh.

"Here," he said. He held out something black.

It was a wool beret with a thin leather sweatband. Fastened to the wool was a pin, a five-petaled, rather Oriental-looking gold flower inside a silver square. She looked suspiciously at the phouka. "Is this part of the uniform?" she asked.

"No, worse than that," he said. "It's a gift."

"From you?"

He looked carefully over both shoulders. "I don't see anyone else."

She looked at the beret again, ran the sweatband back and forth through her fingers. Then she took it into the bathroom. She put it on in front of the bathroom mirror, adjusting the angle carefully. The black wool was severe and elegant against her pale hair.

When she came back to the living room, the phouka nodded. "I have exquisite taste."

"It looks good," Eddi said finally, remembering not to thank him. "I like it."

The phouka made a vague, dismissing gesture, as if it didn't matter to him whether she liked it. True or not, for once, the gesture was more endearing than annoying. *Maybe everything looks better when your life's in danger,* she thought, *even dumb phoukas.*

"You'll have to hang on to it while I'm wearing my helmet."

"I think I might manage that."

"Well," she said, "let's do it."

The phouka nodded, opened the hall door, and dropped her one of his graceful, foolish bows, his face grave. "Forth to honor and glory."

"Get stuffed," she said crisply, and she walked out the door.

CHAPTER TEN

Spellbound

The Triumph shone like new in the alley lights, all black satin and silver. It fired on the second kick. So much for that excuse. The phouka slid on behind her and said, "Do you know the way to the Falls?"

"I know where they are, more or less."

Something in his moment of silence made her look over her shoulder at him.

"You've never been to Minnehaha Falls?" the phouka asked, clearly startled.

"No."

"How long have you lived here?"

With an effort, she kept her voice cheerful. "Not long enough, I guess."

He must have heard the effort, because he sighed impatiently and said, "You're not of a certainty going to your execution, you know."

"Hush," she said, and let out the clutch.

It would have been maudlin to choose a route that passed some of her favorite places. So she was practical and drove straight down LaSalle onto Blaisdell, only to find that everything suddenly seemed precious. The red stone castle at Groveland and the brooding brick church at Twenty-sixth Street became architectural marvels. Even the stucco duplexes, common as field mice, looked gracious and welcoming with their living room windows aglow. By the light of the street lamps she could see gardens planted under apartment house windows, and swollen flower buds on the lilac bushes. She wished furiously that it were November.

She signaled to turn at Twenty-eighth Street, and the phouka called, "Go straight."

"Can't you get there this way?"

"Yes, but you can get there my way, too."

She twisted out more gas, and they sailed through the intersection. "I bet mine's faster," Eddi shouted after a moment.

"Quite possibly. But mine is more scenic."

"I don't want scenic. I want to get there and get it over with."

The phouka's arms stiffened around her waist. "Objection noted," he said haughtily, "but would you mind very much indulging *me?*"

Eddi stopped at the red light on Lake Street and looked back at him.

He regarded her steadily, and without any particular expression. "I would like to see a lovely thing or two," he said, "on the chance that I won't see many more."

Of course. Though she might be in little danger tonight, he would be in the thick of it; he would be protecting her. There was no one at all to protect him. "Oh," she said in a small voice.

South of Forty-eighth Street, Eddi realized they were in a portion of town she'd never seen. The phouka directed her through a tangle of streets that ran in every direction except north-south and east-west. Street lights and yard lamps showed her large, gracious houses with well-kept lawns. Old elms flung an arched roof over every street.

"What about the help you said you'd give me?" she asked, breaking a long silence between them.

"Help?"

"You said you'd do something to keep me from . . . well, being bedazzled by bullshit."

"Ah, yes. Protection from glamour. That should wait, I think, until we've arrived. The effects might interfere with your driving."

"Sounds like drugs," she grumbled.

"It is not." His voice was suddenly stern and cold. "It is magic. You should get used to the idea—immediately, if possible. Faerie cannot be explained away with talk of inebriation, pre-Christian religions, or cave men. Magic is the nature, the tool, and the weapon of the Folk, and nothing makes you so vulnerable to them as refusing to believe in it. Magic will be thick on the ground tonight, and if you are busy trying to explain it away, it will have you by the throat in an instant."

"Sorry."

"Left here," said the phouka.

She knew where she was, finally. They'd turned onto the boulevard that ran along Minnehaha Creek, through a ribbon of parkland, to the Falls. This, she realized, was the true beginning of the phouka's scenic route. She drove a little slower; the Triumph's growl became a mutter.

After a moment, the phouka began to speak dreamily next to her ear. "All things that live are drawn to water, and arrange their lives around it. Humankind is no different. There is water at the heart of every human community—as much as the sea, or as little as a spring. This is the water at the heart of this city."

Eddi had never seen this mood on him, or heard such a voice from his lips. It was resonant but contained, and the words came in the measured cadences of poetry or song. He was talking about Minnehaha Creek. If he'd asked her to pick the most important body of water in Minneapolis, she might have said the Mississippi. Or Lake Calhoun, the largest of the city's lakes. . . .

"Not the largest body of water, or the most useful," the phouka said, still in that brimming voice, but with humor bubbling in it. "I said the city's heart."

"Follow the creek back to its source, and you'll find that it binds together all of what people call Minneapolis. It starts in Grays Bay in Lake Minnetonka and ends in the Mississippi—if anything can be said to *end* in the Mississippi. In between, it runs through woodlands, through unreclaimed marsh, wild in culverts and well-behaved beside suburban backyards. It is not a conduit for commerce; it is the pure spirit of running water, small, but deep and full of secrets."

Deep it certainly was. As the bike idled at an intersection, Eddi could hear the rush of the water, high with spring, against the bridge pilings. And secrets? She supposed that the conflict they drove toward would become one of them. She hoped her body wouldn't end up as another.

Wind rattled the leaves above them, and the phouka's words seemed to weave in and out of that and the sound of the creek. "One might say that, less than a mile from the Mississippi, the creek reaches a precipice and plunges over it—but that would be shading the truth. The creek has made that precipice, shouldering back against the limestone and wearing it away. The Falls move up the creekbed like a child walking backward against the sun to admire his shadow.

"Once the Falls were called holy. Now its priests are the

Army Corps of Engineers and the Minneapolis Park Board, but it is still a shrine, a place of power. It is the city's birthplace and its soul.

"That," said the phouka, in a voice so much more natural that it made Eddi jump, "is why it's the site of the first battle. Control of the Falls brings with it a great deal of magical leverage."

Eddi stopped the bike in the middle of the parkway and turned to look at him. "Leverage? All that loving description, all that—*feeling*—and you sum it up by saying it's got strategic importance?"

"Drive," was all he said.

They passed Lake Nokomis, shining silver-gray in the intermittent moonlight, its beaches like brushed aluminum. Just past Hiawatha, the phouka directed her down a drive and into what a sign declared was Minnehaha Park. She pulled up next to the park administration building and pried off her helmet. "Won't they notice anything tonight?" Eddi asked, poking a thumb toward the door bearing the legend, "Park Police."

The phouka raised an eyebrow at her. "No. They will not." He handed her the black beret.

The sound of running water was a low-pitched thunder; it came to her more through her bones and the soles of her feet than through her ears. The Falls, she supposed, and wondered where they were.

The phouka frowned at the sky. "Rowan and Thorn! Come on," he said sharply, and grabbed her hand. His fingers were cold. He loped her along to a stone wall that bordered the parking lot, and for a moment she wondered if he would go over the top of it. Then he saw a gap, and the top of a heavy iron handrail. They plunged down an old stone stairway, the steps slippery with last fall's leaves. The parking lot lights did nothing for the darkness on the stairs. The air was full of moisture.

They reached a landing, and the phouka grabbed her around the waist and swept her down onto the first step of the next flight of stairs. As he set her on her feet, she saw a line of green light streak along the edge of the landing behind them, climb the stone wall, and course off through the wooded land beyond. A moment later, a low curtain of trembling emerald fire rose from the stripe of green, writhing and flickering like the northern lights in miniature.

"The circle is closed," the phouka whispered. In a steadier voice he added, "A near thing, my primrose. A moment later and we would have been on the wrong side of that. And I would rather hear an Oakman curse than listen to what the Court would have to say then.''

"Can't be late to my own funeral," Eddi said, meaning it to sound casual. But she couldn't draw her gaze away from the cool green sheet-lightning of the barrier on the stairs. All of the phouka's power, even his transformations, seemed sleight-of-hand beside it. Bright as it was, it should have tinted everything around it green; but deep darkness still gathered in the lee of the wall, and the woods beyond remained full of impenetrable night. "What is it?" Eddi asked finally.

"I could tell you what it's called, but I suspect that's not what you want to know. It forms a ragged circle around the valley in which the creek runs, from just beyond the top of the Falls down to the Mississippi. It will contain any forces generated here tonight, and keep even the sound of battle within its bounds. The barrier is invisible to passers-by, but they feel a profound disinclination to cross it. And if a park policeman stood on the stairs above at this moment, he would see not so much as a hair of me.''

"Would he see me?"

"Yes, but in a very short time, that will be tended to. Air and Darkness, I nearly forgot! Here, face me and close your eyes.''

"What? Why?"

"Your ward against glamour, my heart, as I promised you.''

She did as he asked. "To begin with a broken promise," she heard him mutter, as if to himself, "that would have been a fine start to the evening's festivities." A fresh, sharp smell filled the night around her, reminding her alternately of sage and thyme and menthol. His light touch on her eyelids made her start, and left behind a trace of something that made the skin feel cool. His finger brushed her nose, then her lips, and each earlobe in turn. He took her hands, turned them palms up, and touched them, and left the tingling feeling there, too.

"A few seconds for that to take effect," he said. "That should do it. Open your eyes, my primrose." She did.

She nearly fell, out of sheer surprise. She saw color and detail around her, where before there had been darkness. But the colors were not the ones the sun brought out; these were dusky, rich, like the shadows in dark-toned velvets. The details were strange, as well. Eddi felt as if she could see the tree trunks from all sides at once. Elements she'd never noticed in her surroundings had become the definitive ones, and the elements she'd thought most important had receded into near obscurity.

"I see why you didn't want me to drive with this," Eddi gasped at last. It was difficult to finish the sentence when she heard her own voice. It sounded more like it did on tape. . . .

"This is—this is really my voice, isn't it?" she said.

"If you mean, are you hearing it as it sounds outside your head, yes. You'll become accustomed to the effects in a few minutes."

The phouka looked like himself, only more so—that was the only way she could describe it. "*You* don't sound any different."

His smile was slow and sardonic. "That, my heart, is because I have never wanted you to think me anything but what I am."

"No, you never have, have you?" She shook her head. "What is it you've done to me, anyway?"

"Do you think you can walk and listen at once?" he sighed.

"I'm not sure," Eddi said. But she found that, strange as her new perceptions were, they never led her astray. If anything, the stairs seemed less treacherous.

"What you're seeing—and hearing, and all the rest of it—is, simply put, the truth," the phouka lectured over his shoulder. "Your senses are now resistant to illusion, preconception, and willful ignorance."

"How does that account for my being able to see in the dark?"

He sighed again, loudly enough that she knew he'd meant her to hear it. "Do you want me to explain it with physics—lumens, refraction, and the components of your eye? I shall not. It is magic. For the purpose at hand, night-blindness is a preconception. Will you settle for that?"

"Yes, boss,' she said patiently.

"Good. Because there's a great deal I have to tell you, and no time at all in which to do so."

He stopped on the next landing, turned to her, and took firm hold of her shoulders. She couldn't see very far past the surrounding trees, but something about the slope of the iand suggested that they might be near the foot of the hillside.

"Look at me," the phouka said, giving her a little shake, "and pay the closest attention, my sweet. You are about to submit yourself to a ritual of great wonder and not a little terror. You will be asked to do and say many strange things. Balk at none of them." His gaze wandered from hers, and stopped at her shoulder. He seemed to become aware for the first time that his hand was there. A little too quickly, he let go and tucked his hands in his jacket pockets.

"And try, if you can," he continued sternly, "to seem a woman under a glamour. There's no hope that such a masquerade can go undetected for long, but . . ."

"But?"

The phouka shrugged. "I have done the unthinkable in giving the ointment to you. Whether it is unpardonable as well will depend on how well you carry your part of the ceremony tonight. So please, my sweet, even if you can't pretend dazzlement, go through with it all no matter what it may be."

Eddi heard the edge of desperation in his voice, at odds with his casual posture. "I said I would, didn't I? If I wasn't going to, dummy, I wouldn't be here." Her words didn't sound as light as she'd meant them to be—or perhaps it was only the effect of the phouka's ointment on her hearing.

"Well," he said softly, "that brings me promptly to my last three bits of counsel. Tell no lies tonight, to anyone; do not give your word lightly; and do not break it. Lies and broken oaths are weapons in the hands of your enemies. And in the dance we dance tonight, there's no knowing who the enemy is."

Then he turned from her and strode off down the stairs. She settled the black beret on her head, straightened her own back, and followed him.

When she got below the trees, she saw them. They milled restlessly in the steep-sided bowl of land before her, and at first she perceived them only as the many-celled organism of an army. Then faces and bodies separated themselves from the mass.

There was a shrunken, brown figure, too lean and wrinkled to identify as male or female, who wore nothing but a knee-length tunic of rough leather. It carried a wooden cudgel as long as it was, and possibly twice as heavy, and watched her with bright, black, hostile eyes.

Eddi couldn't tell the sex of the next creature, either, any more than she could tell at a glance the sex of a cat. It had short fur the color of toffee and a long-nosed, chinless face. It was squatting on its haunches on a fallen tree, cleaning the curving edge of something that looked like a wooden sickle. When Eddie met its eyes (large, without whites, and bright blue), it ran a long pink tongue over its lips.

A quick motion at the edge of her vision was all the warning she had. Then something white the size of her hand flapped across her face and caught heavily in her hair. She stumbled backward and nearly tripped over the last step. Her hair swung in front of her eyes, and with it a feral white face with a nimbus of cobweb hair, milky wings, a long spidery white hand that reached out and pinched her nose—It launched itself into the air with a fierce kick to her chin, and she recognized it as a creature like the one the phouka had summoned to her windowsill.

A trill of laughter sounded ahead of her, breathtakingly sweet and cold. It was laughter at her expense, from a slender, pale young man whose brown hair was tucked behind his pointed ears. Then he turned his head a little, and Eddi decided she'd been wrong; it was a young woman. With a last taunting gesture, the young woman looked like a man again, and Eddi was relieved when he/she turned his/her back and wandered into the crowd.

There *was* a crowd. They gathered at the foot of the hill, some perching on the few picnic tables that dotted the grass. Eddi saw bestial figures, hulking-shouldered and heavy-headed. She saw ethereal ones that glimmered like moonlight on wet grass. She saw uncounted pairs of eyes, all watching her with unfriendly curiosity, with cold fascination. She cursed the phouka's ointment that enabled her to see them all in the dark.

Even as she thought of him, the phouka was at her side. His face was immobile with the effort of keeping his thoughts off it. But his body betrayed him; there was eloquence in the way he held out his hand to her, not as a command but as a courtesy offered to an honored guest.

There's no knowing who the enemy is, the phouka had said. Now he stood among her supposed allies, his own kind, as defiant as a prisoner of war. To the rest of the Seelie Court, she was the next best thing to the angel of death; she understood their chilly looks. She wished she could make as much sense out of the phouka. She laid her hand in his as regally as she could manage, and he guided her through the sullen throng.

As the crowd thinned, Eddi could see what the phouka was leading her toward, and the sight made her steps falter.

There were fifteen or twenty of them between the two elms that grew on the grassy mound. All of them were human-shaped and human-featured, but she would never have mistaken them for ordinary men and women. They were tall, slender, and preternaturally graceful; they radiated beauty like a blinding light that seared the eyes and scattered the wits. Their attire was splendid and fanciful. On their clothing and hands, gold and silver flashed, and the many lucent colors of faceted jewels.

A terrible longing swelled in Eddi as she watched them, like a balloon being inflated painfully in her chest. Her vision distorted with tears, and she blinked them quickly away. She had no idea what she longed *for*; but she felt as if the memory of that glittering assembly would remain with her forever, and the rest of the world would look dim and blurred beside it.

At the foot of the mound, the phouka dropped to one knee and drew her down next to him. She vaguely noticed that she'd knelt on a stone. The phouka squeezed her hand, and she turned to find him, head bowed, watching her out of the corner of his eye. Then a clear, low voice sounded above them, speaking a language Eddi didn't know, and she looked up.

Perhaps she was under a glamour after all. Nobody could be as beautiful as this. Wide-set, sloping eyes of peridot-green, dark red hair that spilled over one shoulder in a thick waist-length plait, a white inverted triangle of a face with none of the ruddiness that should have accompanied that hair . . . Eddi remembered words that Willy had sung the night before.

> True Thomas he pulled off his cap
> And bowed him low down to his knee
> "All hail, thou mighty Queen of Heaven,
> Your like on earth I ne'er did see."

For a giddy moment, Eddi wanted to ask this woman if she was the one in the song. But the answer might be yes, and she didn't want to know it.

The red-haired woman wore a fitted jacket of velvet and satin, in a green so pale it was almost white. It was embroidered all over with silver and pearls, and her close-fitting white pants were trimmed with silver down the seams. The silhouette was popular with avant-garde French designers. The effect was that of a padded doublet and hose. A short black velvet cape hung like a partial eclipse from one shoulder, fastened with silver and emeralds.

She lifted her exquisite chin and smiled a little at the phouka. He rose, and Eddi scrambled up after him. The woman spoke again, a lovely and confusing convocation of rounded vowels and rolling consonants.

The phouka drew a long breath. "Might we speak English, Lady?" he said slowly. "My companion does not understand our language, and it would be discourteous to use it before her."

Shocked murmuring rose from the group on the mound. The red-haired woman stared down at the phouka. No frown creased her white brow or marred the perfect shape of her lips, but her green eyes were hard and cold as glass. The phouka went a little pale, but did not drop his gaze.

At last she laughed, a sound like wind chimes or breaking glass. "It shall be as you wish. We would not have it said that we lack courtesy."

But the phouka did not relax.

The peridot eyes were on Eddi now, and she felt small and grubby under their piercing regard. "We are pleased to have you attend us, Eddi McCandry," the red-haired woman smiled. "We have heard naught but good of you."

It was hard to look into that glorious face and not trust its every expression. Compliments from those lips, in that lovely voice, were always true, surely? But Eddi watched the phouka's fingers clench, and said only, "I'm grateful for that."

That seemed to amuse her. "Ah, no, the burden of gratitude is all ours." Which seemed an odd way to put it. "But tell us," she went on gently, "have you come tonight of your own will, or are you constrained to do so?"

The phouka had warned her not to lie. Here was a direct question—and she wasn't sure what the truth was. The phouka had assured her that, if she tried to escape him, she would fall into the hands of one Court or another eventually. He had moved in with her, ordered her around, threatened her.

He had also guarded her with relentless vigilance, saved her life, and cossetted her like a fond uncle. Eddi thought of him, in the throes of a vulnerable drunk, at her kitchen table. She remembered their quarrel in the parking lot before practice—and he'd said then that he wouldn't stop her, if she chose to make a run for it. He had, in the end, begged her to do what he had once been prepared to force from her.

Slowly, she said, "If the obligations of friendship are constraints, then I'm constrained to be here."

The phouka shot her a startled, sideways glance.

"Indeed," said the red-haired woman, and frowned at the phouka. He held his hands out to either side, palms up.

"Come , then," the woman snapped, and turned on her heel. "We'll waste no more time on pleasantries."

Pleasantries, right, thought Eddi. She asked the phouka in a whisper, "What was all that?"

"A test, of sorts," he replied. His eyes followed the red-haired woman as she stalked up the hill. "I think you did very well."

"*She* doesn't."

"Oh, she may come to agree with me yet."

"Hmm. Who is she? She makes me feel like . . . like . . . something disgusting."

"Welcome, then, to a very exclusive club. She is a queen, my primrose."

Eddi tried not to be impressed, and failed.

"She and her kin have been Mab, Titania, Gloriana—and all of those are only shadows of what she is. She is a ruler of the oldest kingdom on earth, and has been so for longer than the span of a mortal empire and all its emperors." A grin flashed on his handsome dark face. "So forgive her, sweet, if she seems a little set in her ways."

"Do you always try to annoy her like that?"

His gaze turned to the sky above the mound, and the full moon that rode the running river of clouds. "No," he said, "I didn't always." Then the stillness was back on his face. "Go up," he told her. "They're waiting."

On the mound, the company had formed into two rows, and the aisle they made led to the two trees at the summit. The redhaired queen stood between them. Light outlined the trees, traced the bark, then leaped across to her like electrical current.

Eddi stepped forward, and stepped again. Leaving the phouka was like jumping out of a plane—he was solid and in his own way comprehensible, and he was the only certain ally she had. All the rest of this was air and danger. But she kept walking.

She was only a few feet from the summit before the queen nodded, and raised both arms. The light from the trees arced out and coursed over her. She felt a snowy chill, heard a single ringing note, breathed in a fleeting scent of some spicy, potent flower. Then the light broke in two, and lay on the grass and in the air above them in a quivering lattice.

"By the Holy Trees," the queen said, and her voice was lovely and terrible, "be these, our words and ways, all sacred here."

The gathered beings rumbled in agreement.

"Join we together in this?" the queen asked.

Silence stretched for an eternal moment, and even Eddi could feel the tension that sprang up. She realized suddenly that it was not only tension. Something swirled unevenly around her, something that stung her skin like a slap wherever it eddied.

"Aye," the assembly murmured at last, and the many pitches and timbres of their voices became, in an uncanny unison, one voice. The something that hovered in the air swept past and gathered itself with an arctic snap—in the queen's person? It was not a wind, though she felt as if her hair ought to be blown back from her face with the force of it.

The lattice of light blazed up, and cast a frosty illumination on the queen's triumphant face. "We ask with one voice, then. Bind over mortal flesh to the service of spirit; bind the magics of the spirit under the yoke of mortal doom."

"We all so ask," said the company.

The queen swept them with a pale green stare. "What is dearly wanted must be dearly bought.

"Name the fee."

The queen's eyes fixed on Eddi, the fierce, challenging look of birds of prey. "I speak aloud, that none should say he did not know the cost, that all shall know the size of our need by the price we pay." Eddi thought she could feel the crowd stir nervously. "Mortal flesh and mortal doom be one, and mortal will may rule them. Spirit shall reside in flesh, doom reside in spirit, and all shall bow before will."

Great. What does it mean? She knew it was important—she read it in the queen's face, the watchers' unrest. Was she meant to understand it? She thought not. She committed a shorthand version of the queen's last sentence to memory, as she did when learning song lyrics, but she hadn't time to do more.

"We will pay the price," the eerie voice-of-many-voices rose up around her.

One of the ladies of the court approached the queen. Her sea-green calf-length skirt whispered sweetly of silk when she knelt. Her honey-colored hair was cut very short, except for a layer at the top which fell to her shoulders on all sides like a translucent veil. She held a white dish so thin that light came through it, with a little round cake on it the color of old piano keys.

The scent of that cake reached Eddi, and all her senses were subordinated to her sense of smell. Perhaps it was something she'd eaten as a child, and loved, and forgotten. No, surely she'd never smelled that before, as surely as she knew she had. Its fragrance was warm, spicy, cool, and mild, and she knew it would be creamy on the tongue and crisp between the teeth. It was difficult to concentrate on anything else.

Then Eddi realized that the cake lay in the queen's palm, white on white. The court lady had rejoined the watchers. An unfamiliar collection of sound dragged Eddi's attention aside: a rhythmic jingling and a soft clatter. They came from the tall figure that stepped up to the queen and bent the knee. The sound of armor.

It was not the metal plate of Hollywood knights; this was both simpler in its lines and more complex in its construction. It was an impossibly harmonious collection of Japanese samurai garb, biker's leathers, and costuming for a science fiction movie. There was golden metal mesh so fine it might have been cloth; shining quilted leather, dyed dark green; and solid plates over the shoulders, torso, and lower legs that looked and sounded like brilliantly lacquered wood. The head was covered by a lacquered helmet that suggested what might have been an animal's face. She couldn't be sure; it was not an animal she'd ever seen. Eddi saw no sign of wear on the armor.

From the figure's gauntleted hand the queen took a knife. It looked like silver, with a short, thin blade. She held it point down over the little cake in her palm. An instant before the motion, Eddi saw what it would be from the tightness in the queen's face. Then the queen plunged the knife into the cake and her own hand, and Eddi was too shocked to cry out.

Blood welled up and stained the white morsel. *Bread and blood, and much good may the knowledge do you.* The queen watched without expression, but her gaze never left her hand, as if she found her own blood fascinating.

The scent of the cake changed. It ceased to be like food at all, or like anything Eddi knew, but it was exquisite and to her horror, she longed for it. This, she knew suddenly, was the part of the ceremony most changed by the phouka's ointment. Without it, she would have wanted the bloodstained cake and felt no horror at all, like some undiscriminating animal.

The queen took up the dreadful morsel and held it out. Eddi remembered another part of the phouka's words that afternoon: she would do what she did here of her own free will, but she would have to do it just the same. And there was that fragrant, gruesome cake. . . .

"Open your mouth," the queen said, as if to a recalcitrant child. She was frowning.

Eddi had promised the phouka that she would go through with this. And he had warned her about the dangers of broken promises. No, she couldn't do it. To hell with the consequences. But the phouka had said that the consequences would fall to him. What would they do to him? And she *had* promised, after all.

She opened her mouth. *Let me not gag,* she prayed.

The cake evaporated like smoke on her tongue and left behind the flavor of burnt toast. *All that agony and it doesn't even taste good,* Eddi thought vaguely, then had no time for thought or nausea. Pain swatted her to her knees, a blazing hurt all over her. It was the force she had felt stinging in the air only minutes before, but magnified.

It's magic. The magic of all these people, inside me, doing whatever it is they want done.

How do I know that?

CHAPTER ELEVEN

Helter Skelter

There was cold grass under her, and someone was supporting her head. She opened her eyes (though she couldn't remember closing them), and found the phouka looking down at her. It was one of his knees she felt under her head.

"Hullo?" she said faintly.

He looked relieved. "Sorry. Had I known that would be the result . . ."

"Finish your speech, do," said the queen of Faerie politely.

Faerie? Eddi wondered. *Now where did that come from?* She turned her head a little and saw the pale queen, whiter still with fury, her eyes so cold they burned. The full strength of her rage was directed at the phouka.

"What would you have done, manikin, knowing the results of your actions?" the queen continued, her voice still tea-table calm. "Left well enough alone? Give us leave to doubt it. Perhaps you would have compounded your error instead, and told your little mortal all you knew. Perhaps you would have given her a stronger medicine than simple truth."

The phouka closed his eyes, as if in pain, and Eddi saw his teeth clench. "Lady, in spite of me she has done all we would ask of her. We are none the worse for it."

"Is that now yours to decide, manikin?"

He bit his lip. "No, Lady."

From somewhere on the hillside above them came a piercing call. It laid silence over the crowd, and yanked the queen's gaze away.

"Saved," whispered the phouka. "Up, my primrose, and dust yourself off." He helped Eddi to her feet. Her legs felt a little too flexible, and her thoughts seemed inclined to chase each other through her head, but the pain was gone.

141

The armored figure who had given the queen her knife stepped forward. "Sentry, Lady," he said. "They come."

Eddi saw a subtle transformation in the queen—she became, through some inexplicable change in posture or expression, a martial figure. "Aye, they would have scented this. Commanders, order your troops as we have instructed. Oberycum, see to our cavalry, and be our marshal, that we may know when all are in place."

The armored man bowed, and joined the scattering men and women of the court. Eddi saw many of them dressing in light armor, and some buckling on scabbarded swords.

The queen's attention had returned to the phouka. "Go," she said coldly. "You have done a merry bit of work this night. Should it go awry, I shall see that you eat first of whatever fruit it bears."

The phouka bowed, and the queen whirled away and strode down the hill.

"Swords," Eddi muttered. "These people have swords. What am I doing here?"

"For the moment, nothing more demanding than staying alive," the phouka replied. "And to that end, I suggest we remove from this indefensible bit of grass and find a rock to hide under."

"Does that mean I don't have to be right in the middle of everything?"

"By 'everything,' I assume you mean the fighting? Then no. You only need to be on the field, and we fulfilled that requirement as we came down the stairs."

Eddi followed the phouka toward the side of the bowl. Around them the creatures of the Seelie Court bustled, arming themselves, hurrying to their positions. None of them had the leisure to pay attention to Eddi.

"Oop," the phouka said. "Move quickly."

She heard them even as she dashed the last few steps to the bottom of the slope—the sound of many horses' hooves.

They poured like white-crested water from behind the mound, as if they'd come out of the hill itself. After a moment Eddi realized that there were only twenty or so of them, that their constant motion, their size, and their glowing whiteness multiplied them. But she could not dispel that first impression, that this was a host that might ride out against any army, and barely notice as it fell beneath those shining hooves.

The horses were the color of heavy cream, and big as the

Belgians that shook the state fair horse barns with their tread. Their manes were long, and their tails would have dragged the ground like brides' trains if they hadn't carried them so high. Their saddlecloths were banners of satin, richly colored and trimmed, and their tack was of gold and silver and bright-dyed leather.

Their riders were armored in the broad-shouldered, vaguely Oriental style that Oberycum wore—and in fact, he rode at the head of the cavalry. Eddi recognized his green-and-gold, and the symbol inlaid in his breastpiece, a disk of some golden metal with three green disks inside it, like a three-petalled flower.

Each rider wore his own color: scarlet, deep blue, gray-blue, wine, poppy-orange, violet, butter yellow, and every shade of green. There was even a rider in black, made bright with liberal dashes of white and the three interlaced silver crescent moons on the breastplate. They wore scabbarded swords and carried long white lances that gleamed in the moonlight like a forest of sapling birches.

They passed with a din of hoofbeats and jingling harness, with a smell of clean horse and oiled weapons. "Good God," said Eddi, watching after them.

"Appropriate enough. They were called gods, once."

"What are they called now?"

"Why, what they've always been. They are the Daoine Sidhe—or a sampling of them, anyway—the high lords of Faerie. You see them in their working clothes tonight, my heart. The sight of them on holiday, with bells and whistles in their horses' manes, jewels on their harness, and all their fine clothes on, would quite strike you blind."

"Are you jealous of them?" Eddi asked, surprised.

"Wouldn't you be? Come along, I don't want the slope at our backs."

Eddie hurried after him, and nearly bumped into a little brown woman with nothing on. "Och, mind how ye go," scolded the apparition, squinting up the length of her enormous nose. Her accent reminded Eddi of her grandmother's. "Bloody grrreat oaf," she muttered as she stalked off, boney elbows jutting, drooping breasts swinging furiously.

Eddi caught up with the phouka and grabbed his jacket. "Yo—what about her?"

The phouka looked where Eddie pointed, at the little woman disappearing into the crowd. "What about her?"

"Nobody expects her to fight, do they?"

The phouka grinned. "Silly girl. Believe me, you'd rather face the cavalry. That's Hairy Meg. She can reap a field in the space between midnight and a summer dawn, carry home a lost cow over her shoulders, and chop the winter's wood before a strong man can split the evening's kindling. There aren't many like her here—brownies prefer to choose a household or a territory and not stir from it, not even on the orders of the Sidhe."

"Why is she different?"

The phouka nodded at a low stone wall, part of the bottom section of a stairway. "There," he said. "In the angle of the wall and that fallen tree. We'll be unobtrusive, but we'll be able to move as well, if we need to."

They settled in behind a mat of brush. Before them the army of the Seelie Court spread out across the grass, perhaps two hundred of them, arrayed for an attack from the far slope. They moved restlessly, like grain in the wind, but except for a horse's nervous whinny and the occasional clatter of weapons, they were quiet. While Eddi picked a burr out of her sock, the phouka said, "Meg had a farm in Strathclyde that she watched over—"

"In Scotland?"

"To the best of my knowledge, though I suppose they might have moved it." It was half-hearted sarcasm; the phouka's attention was on the distant hillside. "Unfortunately, there is very little for a brownie to tend on a stretch of motorway, which is what the farm is now."

"Oh dear. But how did she get to America?"

"There are ways. Head *down,* sweet!"

Then the drums began. Eddi couldn't see the drummers, couldn't even tell if they were in the hollow or on the hillside. The rhythm was a wild, rolling march, quick as a racing heartbeat. Like the best dance music, it sent a thrill through her like an electric current, made her restless to move. A shrill battle-yell went up from somewhere in the front of the army, and suddenly the air was full of howls and shrieks and bellows from those ill-assorted throats. With a wail that transformed itself into music, the army surged forward up the slope.

"Bagpipes?" Eddi whispered in the phouka's ear. He nodded.

The far slope was wooded, and the trees kept Eddi from getting any clear view of the front ranks. But there was a terrible din suddenly, of shouting and shrieking, of sounds less human but with the same meaning. Horses neighed like furious trumpets, and metal rang against metal. She saw flashes of light through the branches, and knew that some of those were moonlight on swords and lances. But there were lights too bright for that, and Eddi wondered what other weapons were being wielded on that slope.

The phouka's hand came down hard over hers. "Shit," he said precisely and with uncanny calm. She looked and saw what he had seen.

Past the mound with its twin trees, deep in the upper end of the bowl, a column of dark figures slipped through the trees toward the army's flank. They were too far away to show much detail, but there was no doubting their intention.

The Seelie Court had no rear guard; all that wild army's attention and effort was bent on the slope before them. The phouka's gaze swiveled desperately between the two forces. Then with a strangled cry he was on his feet. He threw something, a stone perhaps, at the rearmost soldier in the swarm of the Seelie Court. It was too far, no one could throw so far—but she remembered the strength in the phouka's arms. The missile struck the soldier lightly between the shoulder blades, and he turned. Eddi could see his expression, the change from anger to shock as he saw the advancing enemy troop. He shouted. Others turned, and a drum changed beat, and another.

Then the phouka staggered and dropped to his knees next to her. He half fell against her shoulder, a hand pressed to his left temple.

"What is it? Are you—"

"Sorry," he gasped. "I'm afraid I've given away our position."

"*Sorry*? My God. Are you all right?"

He gave his head a dismissing little shake. "We have to move, quickly—"

It was too late. Above the trunk of the fallen tree rose a grinning yellow-gray face, its eyes crazy-wide, every dirty tooth in its manic grin pointed as a shark's. There was a jaunty red cap atop it, like a gruesome joke. The thing gave a rasping shriek, jumped onto the trunk and launched itself and its enormous knife at Eddi.

The phouka flung himself between them. The knife flashed somewhere above his upraised left arm. Eddi grabbed a rock, dashed under the phouka's other arm, and brought it down as hard as she could on that red cap. The creature sat down hard, fell backward, and lay still. Eddi started at the rock in her hands.

"Good God," she said weakly.

"Don't stand there!" the phouka roared. "Get behind me!"

Two more red-hatted horrors leaped up from behind the tree. The phouka snatched one of them up by the neck, and Eddi heard an awful crack. It dropped limp from the phouka's grip, mad eye staring and blind. The last redcap received the first's knife in his belly, and with a look of mild surprise, he fell backward and out of sight.

The phouka whirled, grabbed Eddi around the waist, and half carried her down the slope. Several things whistled through the air close to them.

"Can you swim?" the phouka shouted over the racket of battle. He dodged as one of the white horses flew wildly out of the struggling mass of creatures to their left. It ran unevenly, trailing its reins. There was blood streaked on its shoulder that did not seem to come from any wound.

"Yes—"

"Good."

Then Eddi caught sight of the shining stain on the left side of his face. "You *are* hurt!"

"Take a deep breath and keep your mouth shut," the phouka advised, and threw her into the creek.

The water that closed over her head was fast and barely above freezing. She tried to go limp and float, but her lungs were empty and her heart seemed stilled with cold. She thrashed and prayed for the feel of night air on her face.

Her jacket pulled up around her neck with a yank, and a moment later her prayer was answered. Breathing made her sane again. Then she realized that more than the current was pulling her downstream.

"Phouka?" she gasped, and got a mouthful of water.

" 'iet. And don't t'rash avout." It was the phouka's voice, very close to her ear—and furry. She felt the shape of him against her shoulder, his dog-shape. Of course—he had the collar of her jacket in his teeth. She concentrated on keeping her nose above water.

The sound of fighting was loud and horrible. There were none of the bloodless screams of Hollywood warfare; each cry from the bank, however inhuman the throat that made it, seemed to describe to Eddi a wound or a killing stroke. There was a stink of burning in the air that she couldn't account for.

A face rose suddenly next to hers, and she choked on creek water. Sharp, witchy white features and wet white hair that spilled down behind . . . The creature opened its mouth to speak, and Eddi saw the delicate little fangs. The glaistig.

"Well, Dog," said the glaistig in a voice like water boiling, "are you reduced to carrying the Court's baggage?" She laughed, turning her ice-colored face up to the moonlight.

The phouka's growl shook Eddi's collar.

Something like an animated tree limb, twisted and vivid green as moss, lashed out of the water, and the glaistig's face filled with dismay and rage. She arced up like a leaping fish, like a waterspout, and fell upon it. They disappeared beneath the surface. Eddi saw the turbulence subside as the current and the phouka surged on.

Something blocked her view of the sky, and they stopped moving. She put out her hands, found slippery stone under them, and hung on.

"Bridge," the phouka said softly. "We may rest here, though not for long—they, too, have taken to the water, it seems. Would you mind holding on to me for a moment? I swim fairly well in this shape, but I tread water badly, and if I stop paddling long enough to change, the current will have me halfway to the river."

Eddi put an arm around his neck and back. "Shut up and change."

She found herself holding on to something not quite solid, that prickled even through her jacket and sweater like a series of small static shocks. Then the phouka's human head was in the crook of her arm, his thick black curls sleek with water.

She hadn't realized, when he'd been in dog form, that she'd end up hugging his human shape against her, or that his face would be so close to hers. Moonlight reflected off the water and into his eyes, and they seemed deeper than the creek. Eddi knew she should let go of him, maybe say something. But the moment when she could have done that went past. He opened his mouth to speak, shut it again, and shivered under her arm. "Ah, well," he whispered, with a little catch in his voice.

Then he pulled away and ducked under the water. His head broke the surface again and he shook the water out of his hair with a snap. "I'm a fool," he said calmly. "Come along, my nemesis. If we stay here, we'll freeze to death. Or perhaps worse." He let the current pull him away from the bridge piling, and Eddi, after a moment, did the same.

The creek diverged suddenly, and they held to the right-hand fork, where a gravel bank promised shallows and safe footing. The phouka scrambled to shore and stood still for a moment, listening to the sounds of fighting on the far bank. He shook his head as Eddi came out of the water.

"I wish I knew who was getting the worst of it," he said. "If they've taken the bridges and are on this side, then the issue is as good as decided. We could go home and lick our wounds." He pushed the wet hair out of his eyes and winced when his fingers hit the gash on his temple. His hand came away with a little blood on it, and he stared at it for a second. "The wages of folly," he said.

"What do you mean?"

He shrugged. "I showed myself to the enemy, and the enemy showed their appreciation. There's folly, surely."

"Oh, of course. A smart guy would have sat quiet and watched the other side sneak up and slaughter his buddies."

"I had no right to endanger you."

Eddi snorted. "The only stupidity I've seen out of you tonight has been right here on this bank. Come on, let's find out where we are." And she stalked off up the path.

She was annoyed beyond all logic, and she was grateful for it. It kept her from puzzling over the phouka's behavior, and it enabled her to ignore the cold. Her hands were stiff with it, her feet felt like blocks of wood, and her wet clothes were like an ice pack around her. She stamped down the trail to bring the feeling back into her toes.

Suddenly she stopped. The phouka bumped into her. "What is it?" he said softly.

"I don't . . . know." Nothing moved ahead of them except the trailing fronds of the willow on the creek bank. The wind made a weary soughing through its new leaves. But there wasn't that much wind.

The phouka grabbed her arm and pulled her off the path behind a rocky outcropping, away from the creek. "There's an answer to my question," he hissed. "They may not have crossed the water, but their magic has."

"The wind?"

"That wasn't wind. The willows are walking."

Eddi heard a shrill squeaking at the creek's edge. The phouka moved to stop her, but she peered over the top of the boulder in time to see one of the willow tendrils swing up from the bank, coiled around what might have been a muskrat. It struggled and squealed, and another drooping branch rose and twined around its neck. Muskrat fur bulged on either side of the coils. After a moment, the animal stopped moving.

The phouka tapped her shoulder and pointed up the steep incline away from the path. They scrabbled up the rocks slippery with limestone mud, trying for silence. *Just like nightmares,* Eddi thought. *There's something behind you, but you can't move fast enough, and you're afraid to look back.* She kept listening for the sound of wind in leaves.

About twenty feet up from the path, they turned parallel to it, making their way back toward the Falls. In places, harder rock jutted out through the limestone in a smooth outcrop, forcing them over or under it. At last they reached a stretch of nearly vertical slope, where the footing was crumbling and treacherous.

"The path again, then," the phouka whispered.

Eddi started down the hill crab-fashion, half-sitting, using her hands to hold herself back. Her feet still skidded from each outcropping, and she was glad when a deadfall braced against two living trees stopped her slide. She paused for breath and to nurse her scraped palms. Then she heard a volley of curses below her. She ducked under the dead trunk and found a clear view of the path below.

There were three figures, one backed to the edge of the retaining wall where the creek churned by. The two with their backs to Eddi were gray-skinned, their form a distorted parody of humanity. It was a familiar distortion, she realized—and knew from where, when one of them turned its head a little. The elongated jaw, the many sharp, discolored teeth, the milky eyes like cataracts—these were creatures like the one that had tried to kill her outside the New Riverside Cafe.

Her mouth was dry. She recognized their intended victim, too. It was the brownie, Hairy Meg, who was backed against the lip of the wall. She was spitting inventive epithets at them in her broad Scots accent, and shaking an outsized brown fist whenever they came close. But the two gray creatures had long knives.

Then a dripping green-gray hand shot out from beyond the retaining wall and grabbed the brownie's ankle. Meg gave a despairing wail and bent to claw at it, while her other two attackers closed in.

Eddi grabbed the trunk of the dead sapling and yanked, and the rotted wood broke loose from between the two bracing trees. She pinned it under her arm like a battering ram and leaped down the hill much too fast.

This, too, was like a dream: flying over treacherous ground and by some miracle not falling; those gray faces turning, one at a time, to fix their clouded eyes on her and raise their long knives. Everything seemed to be moving so slowly. Surely her target would step aside, and she would fall into the creek, into the green arms of whatever was in the water.

With a shock that wrenched her arms and buffeted her ribs, the end of the tree trunk slammed into a gray belly. The thing went backward over the wall. The green hand freed Meg's ankle and whipped snakelike out of sight. Water frothed on the surface of the creek.

Eddi swung her tree trunk at the second gray demon, and it stumbled backward into the phouka's grip. The phouka flung that one, too, over the retaining wall.

For a moment, no one moved or spoke. Then the phouka sat down hard in the middle of the path and sank his face into both hands.

"That," he said at last, "was what is called an unnecessary risk. If you continue like this I shall be the first immortal to die of heart failure."

Eddi, who was nursing a hand full of splinters and a pair of quaking legs, did not dignify that with an answer.

Hairy Meg's black eyes darted between the phouka and Eddi. She snuffled rudely at last and wiped her enormous nose with a knobby brown knuckle. "Tha's no so ill done," she said grudgingly to Eddi. Then she cackled and loped off down the path.

The phouka unfolded and tried to brush some of the mud off himself. "You could have waited for me before you made your charge, you know."

Eddi meant to shrug, but shivered instead. "I guess I knew how she felt."

The phouka nodded. Then he lifted his head sharply. "A curse on this!" he spat after a moment. "Come, my sweet, this is the last leg, and I'm afraid we must run it all. Can you do it?"

She felt tired enough to lie down and die without help from any outside agency. "No. But I will."

If the previous scenes had been from nightmares, then what followed was hell itself. Eddi pretended that her aching legs belonged to someone else; it was the only way she could keep running. After a moment, she, too, heard pounding feet and shouting and the clash of fighting behind them. After a few moments more, all she could hear was her own heart. Trees and path and night sky seemed to fly by on all sides, regardless of up or down.

The path twisted, and before them was a scene lit red with flames: a gently bow-backed stone bridge across the creek bristled with the enemy's advance. At the end of the bridge, where the path widened, a ragged rear guard of the Seelie Court fought to hold them back. Patches of grass and clumps of dead brush on both banks were blazing, and something draped over the near side of the bridge was also burning brightly. It looked as if it had once been alive. Behind it all was the wild white curtain of Minnehaha Falls, slamming down the cliffside with a sound like angry thunder.

The phouka paused a moment, and Eddi saw the dismay on his face. Then he shook his head sharply. "Make haste, then, love," he said. "We must get to the other side of that, and our only hope is speed."

He grabbed her hand and plunged forward. On the bridge, an unholy chorus of voices howled. At the head of that dreadful host was a huge figure, possibly eight feet tall, with girth and shoulders disproportionately large even for that. His hair hung tangled to below his waist. He carried a club in one hand and a spear in the other, and from his belt dangled a collection of old severed limbs. He let out a bellow that shook stones from the cliff, and led the attackers in a charge.

The Seelie Court's forces met the shock of that charge and held, but barely. Eddi saw one of the Sidhe cavalry at the fore, the one in black and white armor. The white shaft of his lance was dark with blood, and the white leather over his ribs was slashed open down one side. He spurred his horse forward and couched his lance for a thrust at the monstrous enemy captain. But something darted beneath his horse's belly. The animal reared, and the point of a spear thrust up and took it behind one foreleg. With a near-human scream, the horse crashed sideways.

Beside her, the phouka made a strangled noise and faltered. A redcap leaped off the bridge and onto the fallen horse. Eddi couldn't see the rider, but the redcap surely could, was surely preparing his knife for the rider's throat. Then the bloody-shafted lance thrust upward, into the redcap's lower jaw. The redcap rolled backward into the creek.

The rider pulled himself from under his dead horse. He had lost his helmet. His black hair was in disarray, but the moonlight and firelight picked out the lock of white that streaked it. There was a smear of mud across the bridge of his perfect nose and down his beautifully sculpted cheek. His teeth were bared in a fierce fighting grin, and his eyes flashed like emeralds. With flawless grace he sprang onto the wall of the bridge and slashed his lance across the enemy captain's belly, and the creature fell like a shattered tree.

". . . Willy?" Eddi heard, in her own voice.

Perhaps it was coincidence; perhaps some trick of battlefield acoustics carried her voice. But he turned and met her shocked stare. His pale face grew paler still, his green-fire eyes widened. For a moment longer he stood, while his expression darkened. Then he turned and drew his sword, and plunged back into the fight.

The phouka pulled her away. Behind them on the path were more of the Unseelie Court, and they could not afford to slow down. Stone stairs twisted up the hill in front of her, apparently forever. Each landing offered a scenic view of the Falls, and a carrion bird's view of the fighting at the bridge. The Seelie Court was retreating up the stairs. In the commotion, there was no determining who was alive or dead.

"Wake up," said the phouka, and he shook her. "Once you leave the circle, the battle is over, the killing is done for tonight. That's all the help you can give him now."

The fog cleared a little from her vision and mind, and she stumbled up the stairs. A last turning, and she saw the flickering green barrier that edged the landing above. It grew, and grew, and suddenly disappeared, and her shoulder struck something hard and cold.

"That's my lass," said the phouka's voice, weak and ragged. "Come on, on your feet one last time. I'm afraid I haven't the strength to carry you the rest of the way."

She sat up and found the green light dying into the stones at her feet. The quiet around them was frightening—it felt like being deaf, after the sounds of battle. Then Eddie realized that she could still hear the roar of the Falls. Far away, across a broad field of trees, a car went by on Hiawatha Avenue. She pulled herself upright.

After what seemed a long time and several stops to rest, Eddi and the phouka reached the park building. The Triumph sat where they'd left it, untouched, unchanged, her helmet hanging from a handlebar. That seemed so absurd to Eddi that she began to giggle. Then she found that she couldn't stop.

The phouka cradled her face roughly in both hands and shook her a little, and the giggles subsided long enough that she could breathe. Then she began to cry. "Don't do that," he whispered, and began to cry himself. They held each other, leaning into the embrace, and it was as much to keep from falling as for comfort.

CHAPTER TWELVE

Makes No Sense at All

Eddi drove home slowly. She was tired, and inclined to doubt both her perceptions and her reactions to them. Briefly she wondered what time it was; the plunge into the creek must have stopped her watch. The streets were nearly empty. The phouka rode with his arms around her waist and his head on her shoulder, and she suspected that for much of the ride he was half-asleep.

They reached the apartment building and made their way wearily up the back stairs. The phouka went in the apartment first, as usual, and Eddi propped herself up against the hallway wall to wait for him.

Then she realized that the door hadn't closed completely behind him, and that she didn't hear him moving around the apartment. She stepped out from the wall, feeling like an actor in a particularly silly spy movie, and pushed the door open slowly. The phouka stood with his back to her, just inside—he was watching something in the dim-lit room. She moved to see past him.

Willy Silver sat in one of the kitchen chairs facing the door, the picture of simulated ease. He wore a black suit and a white T shirt, and his long legs were crossed and stretched out in front of him, his hands deep in the pockets of his trousers. He shifted his gaze lazily from the phouka to Eddi. She could read nothing in his face, or rather the half of it that she could see well in the lamplight.

"You're out of uniform," Eddi said as she shut the door behind her.

"It's awfully conspicuous," Willy replied.

And so, of course, was he, even without his black-and-white armor. How had she missed the otherworldliness of him? No one had eyes like that, or that pale, clear skin like porcelain; no human moved with that extraordinary grace.

But the phouka had given her truth, touched it to her eyes. However she had missed the marks of Faerie before, she couldn't do it now. "What do you want?" she said finally.

Willy dropped his head back and laughed. It was not the bright music he made when he was amused. "I don't know, actually," he said softly to the ceiling. His voice was calm and frightening. "I know I have something to discuss with our little friend here"—and he fixed that burning green look on the phouka, who lifted his chin—"but I suppose that could have waited. No, I think I came as a favor to you," he said to Eddi.

"To me?"

"Mm-hm. So you could say all those things you're dying to say to me."

Eddi let the silence hang between them until it broke of its own weight. "You could have saved yourself a trip."

Willy raised his eyebrows.

"I don't want to say anything at all to you. Not tonight, anyway. I'm tired. I want to take a shower and go to bed."

Willy closed his eyes. "Maybe I should take up my quarrel with the phouka, then."

"No," Eddi said. Willy's eyes flew open. "He needs a shower and a night's sleep worse than I do."

"And if you will both pardon me, I think I'll start with the shower," said the phouka. He headed for the bathroom door, and Eddi wondered how much effort he was expending on holding his head up like that. Willy looked as if he would have liked to call him back, but Eddi stepped between them on the pretext of claiming a chair.

She stripped off her soggy denim jacket. It had taken more damage than creek water and mud; it was torn in several places, and one armhole seam had ripped. Her jeans were in similar shape. One knee was torn, and the skin beneath was scraped raw. *When did all this happen?* Eddi wondered. *You'd think I'd remember the knee, at least.*

Willy was silent. Eddi looked to see why, and found him with his chin on his chest and his eyes closed.

"You, too, huh?" she said.

Willy didn't move. "I'm all right."

There was a bruise darkening along his jaw and a scrape across the bridge of his nose. Something at the corners of his mouth and eyes suggested weariness and pain, though Eddi couldn't have said what. His jacket hung open, and where his T shirt should have lain smooth over his ribs, there were the ridges of a bandage.

"We could audition for the Spirit of '76," she said. Willy ignored her.

She was in the kitchen measuring water for coffee when Willy came and leaned in the doorway. "Do you have any idea what he's done?" he said in a low voice.

"The phouka? Some." She poured water into the coffeemaker and got the beans out of the freezer. " 'Unthinkable,' is how he put it."

"Oh, not unthinkable. It's even happened before, that the ointment of sight has been used on a mortal. But he could be banished from Faerie for it."

"I don't know how stiff a punishment that is." She turned on the grinder.

Willy chose not to try to talk over the noise. "Stiff," he said when it stopped. "But that's not all he's done." He shook his head—Eddi couldn't tell whether that was outrage or admiration. "Apple and Oak, forcing the Lady to speak English . . ."

Eddi frowned at him. "He didn't force her." The idea that the phouka could force the queen of Faerie, that icy splendid being, to do anything—he'd only asked, as a kindness to Eddi. Hadn't he?

Willy pursed his lips, as if he might smile otherwise. "Do you know anything about the ancient laws of courtesy to a guest?"

"Not unless they're in Miss Manners." Eddi sighed, and scrubbed at her face with both hands. "You aren't changing the subject, are you? The phouka brings up courtesy in front of witnesses, and she *has* to do the right thing?"

"Very good," he said with a mocking grin. Then he shrugged. "Anyway, how he did it doesn't matter. You entered into the ceremony tonight with . . . with your eyes open, as it were. You understood what was said, you saw everything as it was. That's never happened before. Any number of unpleasant things are . . ." He thought for a moment, and whatever was in his head seemed to afford him some bitter amusement. ". . . possible, as a result."

Eddi tapped the ground coffee into the filter. "Why are you telling me this?"

"Because either you or he will have to answer for any foul-

ups. If you can convince me that none of this was your
idea . . .''

She set the filter basket in place and plugged in the coffeemaker.
The apartment lights dimmed. She wiped her hands on the dish
towel and turned to Willy finally. ''I don't have to answer to
you. For anything.''

Willy's eyes narrowed.

''Okay,'' Eddi said. ''I should be patient. But all three of us
have just spent the last—however long it was—with people
trying to kill us. It frays your temper. So if you want to discuss
the night's events, do it. But if you'd rather play B-movie
gestapo officer, you can play somewhere else.'' She'd meant to
stay calm, but tension and exhaustion and delayed fear drove her
voice up until she was spitting words at that impassive pale face.

There was burning in his eyes. *Eyes don't really do that*, she
told herself. But these were living jewels out of Faerie, and God
alone knew what they could do. Belatedly she remembered what
he was: a warrior of the Sidhe, a lord of the Seelie Court. It
would be easy to be afraid of him.

So she met his eyes, and by some inexplicable magic it was
Willy who looked away. Eddi pushed past him into the living
room and sat down. She could hear the shower running.

Willy came to join her at the table. He limped a little when he
walked, and there was something stiff about his carriage. He
must have noticed her scrutiny. ''Takes a little of the spring out
of your step, when a horse falls on you,'' he said. He closed his
eyes tightly. ''Air and Darkness, I can't believe I lost a horse.
Those horses are worth more to the Court than I am.''

''You're exaggerating. Aren't you?''

His smile was sad. ''I wish.''

Eddi picked up the salt shaker from the middle of the table and
studied it blindly. ''Well. Who won?''

''At the Falls?'' Willy made a noise too weak to be a snort. ''I
suppose, strictly speaking, they did.''

''Strictly. What do you mean?''

''They did what they meant to do. They pushed us over the
creek. When you left the field and everyone stopped dying, we
were backed into the cliffs and making last stands at all the
bridges. If it had gone on . . .'' Willy shrugged stiffly.

''So they won,'' Eddi said, feeling something heavy inside her.

''Mmm. But from what I saw of the casualties, it was a
Pyrrhic victory.''

Then Eddi realized what made his movements stiff. "Why are you keeping your hands in your pockets?"

He looked surprised. "I don't know. Maybe because they hurt." He drew his hands out of his trouser pockets at last and leaned his forearms on the table. Both his hands were neatly bandaged; only his fingertips showed. Willy stared at them as if they belonged to someone else.

"Good God. What . . . what happened?"

"They're burned," he said with great detachment.

Eddi remembered the smoldering remains she'd seen on the bridge, and decided that she didn't want to know. "Will you still be able to play?"

As soon as the words left her mouth, she felt like an idiot. This was not her lead guitarist sitting across the table. He had been an illusion. This was a prince of Faerie, and someone else entirely. Someone who might not care about music at all.

But he answered as her guitarist. "We heal fast. I'll be a little stiff, but I can play tomorrow."

"You're still in the band, then?"

"That's up to you, isn't it?"

"Is it?"

He raised one eyebrow. Eddi studied his face and wondered if he was laughing at her. No, whatever that expression meant, it wasn't that.

"If none of this had happened, would I still be in the band?" he asked.

"Of course."

"Well?"

"But the whistle's been blown. The jig is up. Is there any reason for you to be hanging around playing rock 'n' roll?" That was dangerously close to asking why he'd played his damn charade in the first place. So she did. "Were you just keeping an eye on me, or what?"

Willy asked a question with his eyebrows.

"When you walked in and auditioned—" Eddi swallowed the words "under false pretenses," "—why did you do it?"

"To play guitar," Willy said with a little edge to his voice. "I do, you know."

"That wasn't all glamour then?"

"Not a bit."

"But still . . . why didn't you just have the phouka bring you in? Why pretend to be human, to . . ." She stopped then, because she wanted to accuse, to scream about lying, about playing her for a fool—in short, all the things that he'd expected when she came in the door. She hated the thought of fulfilling his expectations.

"First," he said coldly, "I don't ask a phouka to make my introductions."

"Beneath your dignity?" she snapped.

"Yes." He waited, but Eddi refused to rise to the bait. "Second, would you have let me into the band if you knew what I was?"

She wanted to think that, once she'd heard him play, she would have accepted him if he'd had three eyes and duck feet. But she'd fought so hard against the phouka's encroachment on her life. She'd been pleased that the band was under her control and out of Faerie hands. That memory brought a bitter taste to her mouth.

"And third," he said, just when she'd thought the discussion was over, "I wanted to meet you." The light slid across his face from the side and ignited emerald green crescent moons in his eyes. They were beautiful, powerful—but they were just eyes. If he had meant to weave illusions around her, Eddi couldn't tell it; her own eyes still wore the phouka's ointment.

"What do you mean?" she said wearily.

"When he found you," Willy tipped his head toward the bathroom door, "he reported to the Court. He told us what you looked like, how you sang. . . ." He shrugged. "I decided to see for myself."

"And?" Eddi said, almost against her will. She didn't really want to hear his opinion. She wanted some clue to her value for the Seelie Court—she wanted an answer to her longest-running question: Why her? But she didn't know how to ask that, not of this cold-voiced stranger.

"And I found out he was right."

"About what?"

Willy looked at the floor and seemed to be weighing answers. When he met her eyes again, his face was full of mockery, and she didn't know why.

"He said that you weren't pretty, but that you attracted attention anyway. And that you weren't the best musician he'd ever heard, not in a technical sense. But with half a chance, you were able to grab and hold an audience."

A cloud of steam and the phouka came out the bathroom door.

He was wearing an extraordinary robe, a Victorian men's dressing gown in brown-on-brown silk brocade that reached the floor.

"Believe me, my sweet, Willy's just given you the greatly expurgated version." The phouka smiled placidly at her and stalked across the room to the kitchen, following the smell of coffee.

"I don't suppose you'd let me borrow your robe someday," Eddi called after him.

"Yours is quite nice enough, greedy girl." He came back in with two cups of coffee, set one on the table in front of her, and took the other with him to the couch. Willy narrowed his eyes at the phouka's back, but didn't speak.

The phouka dropped onto the couch, leaned against the cushions, and sighed.

"How do you feel?" Eddi asked.

"Infinitely weary, sweet, but it's true that a quantity of hot water poured over the head is a sovereign remedy for most ills." He rubbed the space between his eyebrows and smiled at her.

Eddi stood up. At the table, Willy stirred restlessly, and she took pleasure in ignoring him. "Let me look at your head," she said to the phouka.

"It's right here," he replied, pointing. "Look all you like."

"Don't be stupid. Never mind, I suppose that's too much to ask." She lifted his wet hair carefully off his forehead. At her touch, the phouka closed his eyes and drew a long, irregular breath. The gash on his temple still seeped blood. "What did they hit you with, anyway?"

"A big rock," he enunciated carefully. "Nothing but the most sophisticated weaponry can prevail against me."

"I'll put something on it," Eddi said, and started for the bathroom.

Willy said crisply, "We might all be better off if he bled to death."

"I'm afraid I can't oblige you this time," the phouka murmured.

"Too bad," Willy replied.

"What did he do that's so goddamned awful?" Eddi had not, she decided afterward, so much lost her temper as set it aside. "As far as I can tell, he did exactly what he was supposed to do—namely, keep me alive. So excuse me if I'm a little unsympathetic."

The phouka smiled. "Go take your shower, my primrose."

Eddi studied first the phouka, then Willy, then the phouka.

"No," she said finally, and sat down in the armchair. "You only want me out of the way."

"And do the wishes of a wounded man not count with you at all?" the phouka said plaintively, but he followed that with a warning look.

Eddi ignored it. "Nope."

"Well, it was worth the attempt."

Willy rose from his chair with a snap and strode to the window, stood there with his back to them. The phouka sipped coffee and pretended to be at ease.

"I want to know," Willy said, slow and soft, and he raised one bandaged hand to the blinds, remembered and jammed it back in his pocket, "I want to know why you did it. Why you gave her the ointment."

"I made him do it," Eddi said. "More or less." Willy fixed her with a baleful stare, and it made her falter for a moment.

"Interesting. How did you manage that?"

Eddi swallowed. "I was about to back out at the last minute. He had to offer it to keep me in the game." She looked hard at Willy and added, "I guess he's figured out that I hate to be lied to."

Willy almost smiled. "No, no. One argument at a time." He turned to the phouka. "Is that how it was?"

"More or less, yes."

"I'll ignore how many things you could have resorted to before you got to that one. But I wonder: Did you think of the ointment of sight in the pressure of the moment? Or did you have it in mind all along?"

Eddi was about to answer that. Then she stopped. How devious was the phouka? Could he have maneuvered her into it, let her think she'd forced him to give her something he'd meant to give her all along?

When the phouka hesitated, then cast a sideways glance at her, she felt a little sick. But he said, "No. I'd intended . . . something else. No."

Willy stood in the middle of the room, tight as a string about to break. "What is worth that?" he asked, and the fury in his voice was matched with something that, in someone not so proud, Eddi might have called pleading. "You've put the keys in her hands, and taken them out of ours. You may have started a wedge into us that the Dark Court will use to split us like kindling. What can you *possibly* get that's worth that?"

The phouka looked down at his hands; then he raised them, palms up, empty. "Nothing," he said sadly, "that you'd want."

Willy looked puzzled; then his face hardened. "There's a traitor in the Court," he said. The words were placed delicately like knives.

The phouka laughed bitterly. "Did you just learn that? I would be surprised if there were less than a score of them." Then he turned a sharp look on Willy. "Oh, did you mean for me to take that personally?"

"The thought had occurred to me."

"Then you're an idiot," said the phouka. "Meaning no disrespect, of course."

Willy took a step toward the couch, and another. "If I had reason to believe you were a traitor," he said, horribly gentle, "I could pass sentence on you and carry it out, and no one would think I'd done anything but right."

I would! Eddi wanted to shout, but what was being acted out before her held her frozen in the chair.

The phouka rose from the sofa, his teeth bared. Willy raised one bandaged hand; but the phouka caught his wrist and snarled, "Oh, aye, you'd get nothing but praise for it! And your traitor would sing loudest of all. Have you listened to anything in the last fortnight? No sooner had I found her"—he stabbed a finger at Eddi—"than she became a target for every evil thing in Faerie. Your traitor kept the Unseelie Court informed of her every movement, until I have been driven half-mad just keeping her alive!"

Eddi felt queasy. *How many attempts?* she thought. *And how many came close?*

The phouka flung Willy's hand away, and spat, "So put me to death, Lord, as you see fit. But you'd best find her another guard dog, and quickly, if you do."

Willy smiled thinly. "The only time you use my title, you're being rude. How *have* you lived so long?"

The phouka blew through his lips and dropped back onto the couch. "It's my diet."

The phone rang.

Phones ringing at unreasonable hours were always alarming, but given the context, Eddi found this one positively terrifying. When it rang the second time, Willy and the phouka looked at her.

"Well, why don't *you* answer it?" Eddi snapped at the phouka. The phone rang again.

"It's almost certainly not for me."

Fourth ring. "That never stopped you before," Eddi said, and picked up the receiver. "Yeah?" she said cautiously.

"Are you all right?" Carla's voice. She sounded cautious, too.

"What? Yes. I mean—"

"I lost you," Carla said accusingly.

"What?"

"I lost you. Somewhere below Forty-second Street. What happened?"

Eddi finally understood. "You *followed* me?"

"No, I tried to follow you. Dammit, girl, if you don't tell me what happened and whether you're all right, I'm gonna come over there and see for myself."

"Ah . . . I don't think you should come over just now." The phouka was watching her, his head cocked. Willy was pacing the living room, or rather limping it. Eddi put her hand over the mouthpiece and hissed at him, "Sit down, for godsake! If you stayed off it, it wouldn't hurt!"

"What?" said Carla ominously.

"Listen, I'm fine. I'm just really beat. And I'd tell you the rest of it, but I can't just now. I'll call you tomorrow, okay?"

"Eddi! No, it is not okay. I was going crazy all afternoon, trying to figure out what to do. And I knew there wasn't any point in asking you about it, because you wouldn't tell me—"

"I wondered why you didn't mention it."

"Anyway, I decided I'd follow you. You couldn't do anything about it if I just showed up. So we sat in the car and waited 'til you left—"

"Wait a minute. What do you mean, 'we'?"

There was a long silence on the other end. "I brought Danny."

"You brought Danny. How much does Danny know?"

Carla made an impatient noise. "What could I do? Tell him, 'Hey, you wanna stake out Eddi's place? Just for fun?' I had to tell him what I was doing."

Eddi sighed. "I suppose he thinks I'm out of my mind."

"No, he thinks I am."

"He's right."

Willy had begun a low-voiced conversation with the phouka, full of half-audible distracting phrases. "Listen, kiddo," she said at last to Carla. "Willy and the phouka are both here, and I have to keep them from eating each other. I *will* call you back tomorrow, I promise.''

''Willy?'' Carla said.

''Oh, hell. Tomorrow, okay?''

''Sheesh.'' Carla hung up.

''. . . it's not as if it was easy under normal circumstances,'' Willy was saying fiercely as Eddi replaced the receiver.

The phouka looked smug. ''You were warned. The glaistig learned that first night that she was . . . less than susceptible.''

''You'll forgive me,'' Willy said, his voice brimming with sarcasm, ''if I point out that I'm rather better than a *glaistig*.''

Eddi could see the phouka mastering his anger. ''Humility does come to you slowly, doesn't it?'' he said at last, deceptively mild.

''What are you talking about?'' Eddi asked.

Willy turned away. ''Nothing you should know.''

''Oh, yeah? That usually means exactly the opposite.'' She switched her glare to the phouka.

''It's not mine to tell, sweet. But I don't think you should stop asking.'' And he grinned fiendishly at Willy.

''Well?'' she said, when Willy glowered at her.

''We were talking about your resistance to glamour.''

She stared at him. ''You've tried it on me?''

''Yes.''

''And failed?''

''Not entirely.''

Of course not. She'd thought him human, hadn't she? But she had a dreadful, growing suspicion that he'd done more than disguise his appearance. ''What did you do?'' she asked, barely above a whisper.

He wore the haughty little smile that she was quickly coming to associate with the Sidhe. ''I made you a little easier to deal with.''

''I told you once tonight, say what you mean.''

''When you objected to something I did or said, I blunted that objection. When you might have thought I was behaving strangely, I clouded your mind, and you accepted whatever I was doing.''

She felt grimy, and she didn't think a shower would take care of it. ''You made me fall in love with you.''

''I did not.''

''The hell you didn't! You pretended to be a different kind of person entirely, and you forced me to believe it. The man I thought I was with when I was with you doesn't exist! What do you think falling in love is?"

"What does that have to do with it?" Willy frowned.

He honestly didn't know. Sadness took a little of the edge off her anger. "So," she said heavily, "what was the problem? Everything you did seems to have worked."

Willy ignored her distress—or perhaps he didn't notice it. "It was damn difficult to keep it up. You didn't stay pacified, and after a while I realized that though I could make the glamour work on you, it never worked as thoroughly as it should." He looked thoughtful. "I'd love to know why."

Eddi shook her head. He'd toyed with reality, bent her perceptions, and showed not the least guilt at the admission. She felt a lingering desire to punch his exquisite nose.

The phouka laughed softly, and Eddi and Willy both looked at him. "A lad so widely traveled as yourself, and you don't know the answer to that?"

Willy's expression was eloquent, even for Willy.

"A great pity," said the phouka. "You'd do well to read Yeats. But I suppose you haven't time, just now."

"Are you going to say anything useful, or are you going to pat yourself on the back?" Willy snapped.

"Both. She has her own glamour, Willy lad. All poets do, all the bards and artists, all the musicians who truly take the music into their hearts. They all straddle the border of Faerie, and they see into both worlds. Not dependably into either, perhaps, but that uncertainty keeps them honest and at a distance."

Eddi found all this uncomfortable to hear. It wasn't that she was being described in the third person; more that someone else was being described, and called by her name.

"Does this sound familiar yet?" the phouka asked Willy, in his sweetest voice.

"Oh, I'd stop you if it did," Willy muttered. "Trust me."

"I am surrounded by people with no appreciation for history. Ah, well. In a time when we were stronger and more numerous, we sought out mortal men and women with that dual vision, kept company with them, and sometimes carried them away with us."

"I know *that*," Willy said.

"We usually did badly by them, in the end." The phouka glanced at Eddi then, and she saw regret or sorrow in his face. "But we cannot resist the lure of that mortal brilliance. It is its own kind of glamour, that dazzles the senses. And once we have found it, we cannot turn away.''

It was explanation and apology at once, and Eddi realized that it was meant mostly for her. She wanted to tell the phouka that it was all right, but Willy was there, and she couldn't do it in front of him.

''So I can't work magic on her because she already has magic of her own?'' Willy was asking the phouka.

''For the sake of brevity, more or less.''

Willy squinted as if with a headache. ''Oak and Ash. And you've . . . what she heard tonight . . . Oak and Ash.''

The phouka leaned back, cradling his coffee cup and smiling.

Willy looked up at him sharply. ''Did you plan all this from the beginning?''

The phouka's smile turned bitter. ''All the parts of it that you're asking about, yes.''

For a long moment, Willy gnawed his lower lip and glared. ''And it's all gone just the way you wanted, hasn't it?''

The phouka's only answer was a crack of harsh laughter.

''I could gag you,'' Willy said.

''You wouldn't . . . ah, yes, I suppose you would dare. Who would teach her, then?''

''No one,'' Willy replied, soft-voiced and precise.

''All my work for naught?''

''If I knew what you were working *toward,* you might get a little sympathy out of me!''

''I work toward a victory for the Seelie Court.''

''Why do I think that's only half an answer? Never mind. I'm too tired to go around in circles with you now.''

''Pity.'' The phouka sighed. ''I was just about to offer you first watch.''

Willy shrugged. ''I can handle it.''

''Good. I very much doubt I could. Wake me at sunrise.'' And he set his coffee cup on the trunk, stretched out on the couch with his back to the room, and appeared to fall instantly asleep.

''Lucky bastard,'' Willy muttered.

Eddi got up from her chair. ''Very interesting,'' she said. ''Teach me what?''

''I'd forgotten you were there,'' Willy said.

''I thought you had. Answer the question.''

"Teach you—oh." He laughed weakly. "No. If I answer you, you'll have had your first lesson, and I won't be responsible for that. But ask him when he wakes up. I've left him free to tell you. Try not to make me regret that, all right?"

Eddi unfolded the afghan from the back of the armchair and threw it over the phouka. He didn't stir. "No promises," she said. "If you want promises, I have to know what the hell you're talking about. And you don't want that, do you?" She headed for the bathroom door. "Practice tomorrow at 4:30. See you there."

"Eddi." His voice stopped her on the threshhold. "About the band . . ."

"Yeah?" She held her breath.

The silence went on for long enough that she turned to look at him.

"Hedge," he said, "is one of us."

Us. It took an instant for her to understand. Then she stepped into the bathroom and closed the door behind her. What, after all, could she say to that?

CHAPTER THIRTEEN

Do You Believe in Magic?

Her denim jacket was mended and clean. Eddi stood in the living room with the thing hanging from her fingers, and squinted at the phouka through a deluge of noon sun.

"It wasn't me," he told her.

"Well, it sure wasn't *me*."

The phouka leaned in the kitchen doorway. He was wearing navy chalk-stripe pleated trousers with cuffs, a pink band-collared shirt with the sleeves rolled up, and suspenders embroidered with—were they? Yes, they were. Palm trees.

"The Godfather meets Miami Vice," Eddi muttered. "How's your head?"

"Perfect, of course," he said. He swept his hair back from his forehead to show her a short, pink scar.

She felt comforted. "It's more than you deserve. Well, if neither of us did this"—she flourished her mended jacket—"who did? Willy?"

The phouka made a dismissing gesture with his coffee cup. "Once you're fully awake, I trust you'll recognize the folly inherent in that suggestion."

"I wasn't serious."

"I also trust you'll observe that it's not just your jacket."

Eddi looked around. The sun streamed uncommonly bright through the blinds. That held her attention for a moment. "The windows are clean," she said at last, wondering.

"Very good. Don't stop there, sweet."

In fact, everything was clean. And the apartment smelled of fresh bread, which, she realized belatedly, was what had awakened her in the first place. "You made bread?"

"No."

"Then what do I smell?"

"Bread."

She pushed past him to look in the kitchen. There were two round brown loaves cooling on the counter. There was a pot of coffee made, as well. She drew back and looked him in the eye. "And you didn't do any of this."

"None, I'm ashamed to say."

"So?"

He sucked in his cheeks and looked thoughtful. "If I were required to be forthright, which, thank earth and air, is rarely necessary, I would have to say that you've acquired a brownie."

Eddi stared at him. "That's silly," she said after a bit.

"Possibly. But just in case, don't offer up any thanks for all this. I don't really enjoy washing dishes."

Eddi paced the apartment, touching things. Perhaps she'd had so many intrusions into her life lately that she'd gone beyond resenting any more. Or perhaps the nature of this intrusion was different—its character was so clearly a smoothing of the waters of daily routine. Whoever had come and gone had left nothing in the way, nothing that wasn't useful, nothing that Eddi had to rearrange her life around. The message of the clean apartment, the bread, the mended jacket, was, "The irritants are gone, the mundane details are taken care of. The important matters are left to you."

She couldn't say thank you. But she remembered how pleased the phouka had been at praise. "This is great," she said softly. "The place never looked so good."

Eddi stood at the window, not really seeing the rooftops and the waving trees of Loring Park. It was more than just clean windows and mending. She felt as if her future was back in her hands. She was not just baggage for the Seelie Court, an amulet that brought death but had no life of its own. She had allies, however uncertain. And she had knowledge, and would get more.

So she had her own glamour, did she? And Willy had found that alarming. He'd made a great fuss, also, over her un-bedazzled state during the binding ceremony, and over the Queen of Faerie speaking English. . . . All pieces of the same puzzle. The clearest part of it was that she shouldn't have understood the ceremony. The bread-and-blood of it tended to overshadow the words—what were they?

Mortal flesh, and doom, and something else, there were three things mortal. Spirit in flesh, spirit in doom—no, that was

wrong, the other way around. And all of them under . . . will?
Yes, that was the third mortal thing. It sounded like heavy metal
lyrics, or imitation Aleister Crowley. Flesh, the body. Will, the
mind. Doom? Mortality, fear of death? That made sense. It was,
after all, what the Seelie Court wanted her for: to bring death to
the battlefield.

Why had the Seelie Court supplied the mortal? Did the Unseelie
Court not want their enemies dead? Or was it just the good guys'
turn to bring the party supplies? But that was a digression; one
thing at a time.

Spirit—the soul? But then the whole thing became metaphysi-
cal, and hardly dangerous for her to know. Spirit, spirit . . .

"Magic," the phouka said behind her, and she realized she'd
spoken her last throught out loud.

"Spirit is magic?"

"Or more exactly, the power of Faerie. If, as I think you are,
you're quoting the Lady."

Then Eddi remembered the context of the quote, and another
puzzle piece came to her hand. This was the price of Eddi's
services as Angel of Death, this was the risk worth taking.

"Damn," she said. "What were her exact words?"

The phouka watched her as he spoke, something eager in his
expression. " 'Mortal flesh and mortal doom be one, and mortal
will may rule them. Spirit shall reside in flesh, doom reside in
spirit, and all shall bow before will.' "

"Impressive. Do you have the whole ceremony memorized?"

"No, my sweet. Just that crucial bit." He was biting back a
grin.

"I bet you could tell me what it means, too."

"But it's much more fun to watch you do it."

"You jerk. Okay. Mortal flesh and doom are one—humans
die, it's part of the business of being human. What was the next
bit?"

" '. . . And mortal will may rule them.' "

"Hmm. Mind over muscle, sure—but is that saying we control our own deaths?"

"Have you never heard of those who seem to lose their will to
live?"

Eddi considered this. "I suppose. Now, spirit resides—"

"*Shall* reside."

"Picky, picky."

The phouka shook his head. "This, remember, was her warning to the assembled Court: Spirit *shall* reside in flesh, as a result of what we would do here.''

Eddi could feel her scalp begin to tingle. "Repeat the whole last half, that begins with 'Spirit shall reside in flesh.' ''

'' 'Spirit shall reside in flesh, doom reside in spirit, and all shall bow before will.' '' The phouka looked at her expectantly.

"My God," she whispered. "She wasn't lying—?''

"In the midst of a piece of ceremonial magic? No, my primrose. She was not lying.''

Eddi raked her hair off her forehead. "Then . . . I've got the power of Faerie, Faerie's got my mortality, and if I want, I can control both of those?''

"Close," the phouka said. "Faerie still has its power, and you are still mortal. But you have become, conditionally, part of Faerie, as symbolized by your acceptance of food from the Lady's hand. Our power is thus yours by right, as it would not be had we taken you captive. You are not a captive—your answer to the Lady last night made that clear. Your answer also showed that you had not come as a willing sacrifice. You were there as an ally of Faerie, assuming the bonds as a formality.''

"Wait, wait, wait—which answer was this?''

'' 'If the obligations of friendship are constraints, then I'm constrained to be here.' ''

Good God—he memorized that? "But I didn't mean friendship with Faerie. I meant . . .''

He gave her that grin, and that wicked look through his eyelashes. "You're a poet, my sweet," he said. "Surely you know that sometimes your words have more meaning to others than they do to you. And as for your ability to control what goes on . . . well. You have exactly as much control over magic as you do over your body, or your fate.''

"I haven't had much control of that lately.''

"If you believe that, it's true, and you have no magic," the phouka said harshly. "And I have been as much a fool as Willy Silver claims I have.''

"Is that my fault? What do you think I—''

His voice overpowered hers. "But I don't think you truly believe it. If you did, you would not have fought back when the redcaps threatened to overwhelm us. You would have curled up and let death ride over us all. I chose you in part because you were strong. I believed you would fight for your own life, if for nothing else. Now I believe you would fight for a great deal more.''

"If you think that not dying is just a matter of not wanting to," Eddi sighed, "then boy, have you got a surprise coming."

He wouldn't smile. "Do you understand me, my heart? I offered you the key to magic, and you responded with denial. I cannot let that pass, even once. You must believe that what I have made possible, *is* possible, or we have already failed."

Eddi paced the living room rug. That she was a part of Faerie now—it was surprisingly easy to buy. She remembered the searing feeling of the Seelie Court's power passing into her through every pore, and the scraps of knowledge that had come with it.

But the phouka was offering her magic, power of her own. Not possible, surely not. Yet why would he want her to believe in the impossible? Was this a trick? Would he make a fool of her? No. He was entirely capable of making a fool of her, but not like this.

"Why me?" she said softly. He looked startled. "You told me I'd get all my questions answered on May first. And that's always been Question Number One."

"You heard what I told Willy. . . ."

"About musicians and glamour? Do you want me to believe that in a town full of musicians, I'm the only one who meets the specs?"

He shook his head.

"Was I the first one you found?"

"No. Do you know how many brilliant musicians are stupid, or crude, or determinedly ignorant, or in some way wholly despicable?"

"Sometimes I feel as if I've met every one of them," Eddi replied. "But the Seelie Court doesn't need someone lovable for this job. They don't even really need an artistic type, do they?"

"No, though the chances are very good that we would have chosen one, simply because we like them. My primrose, before we go on, do you suppose I could at least have more coffee?" He held up his cup and looked pitiful.

"Pour me one, too." He disappeared into the kitchen. She called after him, "And cut a couple of pieces of bread, for godsake!"

Eddi plunked down on the couch and tucked her feet under her. So many things to deal with. Explain all this to Carla, figure out what to do about Dan (what the devil had moved Carla to tell him?). Then there was Willy, and . . . Hedge? That Hedge was another denizen of Faerie made a certain cockeyed sense. It explained his determined air of the outsider, and all that new equipment. What local music store had found a little surprise in the cash register that time? Living with the hosts of Faerie, it appeared, was like running a home for incorrigible children.

The phouka balanced two cups of coffee and two pieces of bread-and-butter into the living room. He seated himself cross-legged on the floor, handed her her coffee, and looked expectantly up.

"Don't give me that cocker-spaniel routine," she scolded. "I want some answers, son."

"Oh, but you have to ask me the questions first, love. It's not in my nature to smooth the way for you."

"I have one pending."

"Bother. I was hoping you'd forgotten." He refolded his legs. "Why you. A short question with a long answer. You met, as I've said, the few requirements of the Court. The rest were mine."

"I kind of figured that out. You have an axe to grind in all this, don't you?"

"Yes." Then he closed his lips firmly and looked stubborn.

"Phouka." She leaned forward and pinned him with her eyes. "You've run a lot of risks, and gone to a lot of work, and all to turn me into a bullet for your gun. But I'm a bullet that thinks for itself, and I want to know why I'm being shot at." He winced. "Are you a traitor?" she asked gently.

"No! At least, I devoutly *hope* I'm not." He massaged the bridge of his nose. "Ah, Eddi, Eddi. If I fail, I will become a major figure in the history of the Seelie Court. Reviled for centuries, I imagine."

"And if you don't fail?"

"Well, that's the cream of the jest. If I succeed, I will be barely noticed."

"What is it you want to do?"

He rubbed his hands along his trousered thighs, as if his palms itched, or were damp. "You may have seen, my primrose, that the Fey Folk are the merest bit class-conscious. We would, by our nature, make very bad anarchists. We do make excellent monarchists, however, under ordinary circumstances." He cut the air with one hand in a frustrated gesture. "There are no mortal structures to which I can compare this. None have lasted so long. A very bad analogy—Do you remember bad King John and the Magna Carta?"

"A little."

"John was not bad, precisely. But he'd a tendency to do as he pleased without regard to the lesser lords whose men-at-arms kept him in power. The situation became untidy for a while, until those lesser lords forced John to be a little more thoughtful."

"And you want a Faerie Magna Carta?"

The phouka shook his head. "As I said, there is no proper human analog. The Sidhe have a habit of rule cultivated over more than two thousand years. What mortal government has lasted so long? And the rest of Faerie has a habit of obedience of corresponding length. Even the most solitary of the Folk will not run directly counter to the will of the Sidhe, though they may, when convenient, fail to hear the expression of that will."

"Like the brownies?"

"And the oakmen, and others. But none of the Seelie Court would rise up, as King John's lordings did, and bring the Sidhe to book."

"Do they need it?" Eddi asked, thinking of Willy, and not knowing what to think.

The phouka drew his knees up and rested his chin on them. "They have ruled for so long, my sweet. They are an unbroken dynasty, and while there have been faction fights and quarrels, there has never been a voice raised to say that perhaps the Sidhe have led us long enough. A thousand years and more of consent. After so long, who can blame them for forgetting the obligations of monarchy, and ruling only for themselves? Who can blame them for thinking that those who never speak are voiceless?"

"Have they . . . done something awful?"

"In time, I think they would. They have forgotten the Folk they govern, and how to feel for them. And so the Folk slip away from them, looking increasingly toward the only other part of Faerie with a tradition of rule." He let out a long breath. "There are high lords of the Unseelie Court as well, you see."

Eddi did see. "This really is a civil war, then."

The phouka looked away to a distant, invisible point. "When I explained why the Seelie Court *must* win—"

"I remember." Visions of bitter, frightened people in gray cities . . .

"But they cannot win if the Unseelie Court lures its warriors to the opposing side, and if the Sidhe help them on their way. The Lady and her kin will see it at last, but by that time the damage will be done, the Court splintered.'' He pressed a hand over his eyes.

"Where do I come in?" Eddi asked, after a respectful pause.

"We need a third element, a possible rallying point for both the Sidhe and the lesser ranks.''

"If this were American politics, I'd tell you that splitting the vote is a lousy idea.''

The phouka shrugged. "Perhaps it is. But what can I do? The Sidhe will not be led by one of their subjects. Nor will their subjects break tradition and lead themselves. But I thought . . . if I found a mortal, unhindered by ancient habits, bringing with him no ancient associations . . . And I needed someone who might command the respect and admiration of both the high and low ranks. When I found you, I knew you could do all that, if only I could arrange for you to have the chance. So I informed the Court that I had found their mortal.''

"Dear me,'' Eddi murmured. "And Dad always said I'd never get anywhere playing rock 'n' roll.''

He choked on his coffee. "Eddi McCandry, you are infinitely more than I deserve. Do you forgive me for not telling you all of this immediately?''

Eddi shrugged. "Much as I hate to give you the credit, I wouldn't have understood a third of that before last night. No, scratch that. I would have understood it all and *still* spit in your eye.''

"But not anymore?'' He cocked his head at her.

Eddi took a bite of bread while she thought about that. "I like these people,'' she said finally. "I like Hairy Meg. Even though I hate his guts, I like Willy. And I like you.'' The phouka looked at his feet. "I haven't seen any lovable qualities in the opposition yet.'' There was another reason, too, though she didn't quite understand it herself, not well enough to explain to someone else, anyway. But she'd been in danger and fought back, fought with the Seelie Court against their enemy. It was hard to be indifferent to them after that.

Then she remembered— "Omigod. And Hedge. Willy wasn't just saying that to drive me crazy, was he?''

The phouka looked shamefaced. "No, he wasn't. I am profoundly sorry, my primrose. I should have told you, I know. But so much was different then, and when it changed, it changed so quickly.''

"Quit apologizing and tell me now. I suppose you thought you needed help keeping an eye on me?"

"Well . . ." The phouka looked at the ceiling. "Yes."

"So you brought a ringer into the auditions, knowing that he was too good a bass player for me to turn down. Did you know about Willy, too, before he showed up?"

The phouka's smile faded. "When he came in the door that evening—I didn't know what to do. I knew who he was, of course. But what he intended . . . No, I didn't know." He looked away, and hugged his knees as if to keep from doing something else. "And when I did know, I wanted to tell you, and I couldn't. There are habits of obedience in me as well, it seems. He is my liege lord, Eddi, and I *couldn't,* though I knew you would hate the deception and perhaps the deceiver as well."

Eddi sat with her chin in her hand, watching him. "I don't blame you," she said. "I don't blame anybody. I'd blame Willy, but . . ." She shrugged.

"But he still doesn't know what he did wrong?"

"Exactly."

"We are an inconstant lot, my sweet," the phouka said. He spoke as if amused, but his face was harsh. "We take love lightly, and we're hard on those who love us. Willy has no model for his behavior but that of Faerie. By that model, he has done nothing amiss."

"You sound proud of it."

"Well, I'm not," he snapped, "and you know it perfectly well." He stood up abruptly and took his coffee cup to the kitchen.

"Do I?" Eddi murmured to the air. Twisty, untrustworthy, mercurial phouka. Oh, but surely some of these emotional U-turns must be genuine, if only in part? If he wanted privacy, she ought to stay out of the kitchen. But he might want her to come jolly him out of the sulks. . . .

She dialed Carla's number and got her answering machine. *Silly broad. I told her I'd call and explain today. Where would she be?* A possibility occurred to her; but she decided against calling Dan's.

"Hi, party girl," she told the recording, "practice and fairy tales at 4:30 today, the old same place." She itched to add, "Did you have fun?" but resisted. "Good luck," also came to mind, but she didn't say that, either. The end-of-message beep sounded, and she shrugged and hung up.

Then she called toward the kitchen, "I'm going to get dressed and drive down for a little solo practice." No reply, except the rattle of dishes, and the thump of the refrigerator door. "You want to come with, or do you want to delegate it to Willy or somebody?"

That got him to poke his head out the door. He asked, sour-voiced, "Would you prefer Willy?"

"No, you little twink," she replied gently.

"Oh." His head disappeared into the kitchen again. After a moment, he said, "Then I suppose I'd best go with you."

Eddi rolled her eyes and went to get dressed.

They rode the Triumph through a balmy afternoon wind, dodging downtown traffic. Eddi swung off Washington Avenue, parked the bike next to the iron stairs, and would have gone up them. But the phouka caught her arm.

"Chivalry, my primrose, must give place to safety. I go first." He trotted up the stairs, and Eddi followed him.

A strand of green vine with starry purple flowers was twined in the door handle. The phouka snorted and pulled it free.

"What is it?"

"A little May Day hate-mail. Pay it no mind." He tossed the vine over the railing.

"Did I tell you you could read my mail? What did it mean?"

"It's nightshade. It would do you no damage; it's purely a message of ill will. and it could be"—he grinned with a great emphasis on teeth—"from anyone." He held out his hand for the keys, and she gave them to him.

She dreaded the opening of the door for a moment, but the room was untouched. She turned on her amp, to let it warm.

"Can they get in here when we're gone?" she asked the phouka.

"Curiously enough, this place is safer with us out of it than in it. It is not a dwelling, you see, and different magical customs apply."

"I'll have to trust you on that," Eddi said. She plugged in the Rickenbacker and began to tune it.

She'd brought a sheaf of song lyrics with her. For the next hour and a half, she made up guitar riffs and fit them together into the melodies in her head, wrapped the melodies around the words. The phouka lay on his stomach on the floor. Just when she would decide he'd fallen asleep, he'd say, "I like that," or "More distortion."

At last she let a long minor chord die away. When the phouka looked up at its last trembling edge, she said, "So how do I do magic?"

He rolled onto his back. "Deceptions, illusions, and tricks of the light, my child," he told the ceiling beams. "That's what you've got from Faerie. A few things more as well, but they come and go. The power to cloud men's minds is always to hand."

"Could I make you believe something that wasn't true?"

He studied her through his eyelashes. "You could make me believe anything at all."

"I believe I'll just play my guitar," Eddi sighed.

Hedge was the first to arrive for practice. He seemed surprised to see Eddi and the phouka.

"Afternoon," Eddi said. "How are you?"

Hedge shrugged and mumbled.

"Take any direct hits last night?"

Hedge peered at her, narrow-eyed, then turned to the phouka.

"Willy told her," said the phouka. When Hedge scowled at him, he added, "Don't blame me, old hedgehog. I was asleep when he did it."

"Didn' think y' were 'lowed to sleep," Hedge said darkly. Other than his singing, it was the clearest utterance Eddi had ever heard from him.

"Lighten up, troops," she ordered. "There's no harm done." She turned to Hedge. "I don't know how long you promised to play in a rock 'n' roll band and keep an eye on the mortal chick. But as of right now, that contract is void. Fizzled. Poof."

Hedge's eyes got round for just a second. Then they squinted again, and his face was sullen and shuttered.

"I want you in my band," she said to him. Hedge blinked, and all his shutters seemed to come a little unhinged. "But it's *my* band, and you don't have to play in it because he says so"—Eddi pointed to the phouka—"or because the Sidhe say so. You stay if you want to. If you don't want to, you're free to walk."

Hedge looked sideways at her. "Wha' 'bout Willy?"

"As soon as he shows up, he gets the same choice. That's no concern of yours. In the band, you answer to me."

Hedge shot a glance at the phouka.

"You'll get no help from me," the phouka said. "Except that she can't get rid of me, I am her slave in all things."

The decision hung in the air for a moment. Then Hedge startled Eddi with a growling chuckle. With no more comment than that, he picked up the black Steinberger bass, plugged it in, and turned on his amp. He started up a fast pattern in the key of G, and Eddi shook her head wonderingly and followed him into it.

Carla came in a few minutes after that, and Dan behind her. They were carrying a snakepit's worth of cables and patch cords, and a wedge-shaped, suitcase-sized box with a handle. . . .

"A mixing board?" Eddi squeaked.

Carla and Dan looked equally pleased. Dan said, "Dude in South St. Paul had a backup board. He needed some studio work. So we did a little trade."

"What about speakers?"

"You can help carry 'em up," Carla said, wrinkling her nose. "They're heavy as boxcars, but the cones are JBLs."

"I'm impressed. Come on, gents." Eddi nodded at the phouka and Hedge. "Let's make like roadies."

When they came out, Willy was leaning on the railing at the bottom of the stairs. At first glance, he looked insufferably proud. Then she saw his face, and how much his expression resembled the closed and guarded one that Hedge often wore.

With an effort, she grinned at him as she sailed past. "Oh, good. You're just in time to carry some nice heavy speakers." Out of the corner of her eye she saw the surprise wash his features, and she wondered what he'd been expecting.

Carla opened the wagon's rear gate. The speakers were home-made and odd-looking, but not excessively large. "Don't let 'em fool you," Dan warned, rubbing his arms.

Hedge slid one onto the tailgate. He nodded shortly; then he looked at Eddi and raised one heavy eyebrow. "Go for it," she told him.

He swung the thing easily to his shoulder, and held it there with one arm while he crossed the parking lot to the stairs.

Dan stared after him, and whistled finally. "But he's a *little* sucker . . ."

"We're all just full of surprises," Willy replied. He slid the other speaker out of the wagon and followed Hedge.

By some unspoken armistice, they devoted themselves to setting up the PA, and ignored all the questions and mysteries. Eddi saw them working together, not quite a team yet, but no longer

quite an unrelated group, either. It hurt her and warmed her at
once. So much unresolved, so much danger.

"All right," she said, when all the mikes worked and the
monitor speakers had stopped feeding back. They all turned to
her. Carla's thin, mobile face and big dark eyes; Dan, wired and
vague at once, peering earnestly through his square-framed glasses;
Hedge, taciturn to the point of sullen, all street-kid looks and
supernatural origins; Willy Silver, whose splendid face didn't
hide his feelings as well as he thought it did. Eddi realized, faced
with them all, that this was the closest she would ever come to
her dream band.

And the phouka, of course, sitting cross-legged on the floor
looking wild and fey and foolish. He turned his eyes up to hers
just then and grinned. She gathered up her courage and began.

"We're not all of us what we seem," she said. The phouka
snorted. "Carla, how much did you tell Dan last night?"

Carla shrugged. "That you were mixed up in a battle that was
being fought by elves. You can probably guess what he said."

Eddi turned to Dan. "Did she convince you?"

He shook his head. "I figure *she's* convinced. Somethin'
funny's going on, but I'm not buying little elves, girl."

"I resent these comments about my height," the phouka said.
Dan looked narrowly at him. "It's quite true, you know—all
except the 'little.' "

"He's one of them," Eddi said apologetically. "He's a phouka.
That much Carla knew. What she didn't know"—and here she
directed the apology at Carla—"is that Willy and Hedge aren't
human, either."

From Carla she got a round-eyed stare. Willy looked uncomfortable. Hedge seemed to be getting a certain wry enjoyment
out of the whole tableau. Dan said nothing, but frowned narrowly at Eddi. She decided she preferred his vague look.

"No kidding?" Carla said weakly.

"I just found out last night."

"We've been had."

"Fast-forward this shit," Dan said suddenly, not loud but
harsher than Eddi had ever heard him. "You all in on this?"

Eddi blinked at him.

"Yeah, I get kinda zoned out sometimes," Dan continued,
when he got no answer. "But I'm not brain-damaged. So if you
think you can play games with the dumb nigger, you can find

another set of keys." And he began to turn off power to his equipment, snap, snap, snap.

"Dan!" Eddi said, and he stopped. *Follow it up, girl, or you lose him.* She was no good with clever arguments—but she was very good with the truth. "This band means too much to me to mess with. I'm not lying, and I'm not playing jokes. If anybody here is being tricked, it's me. But I don't think I am. These people"—she made reference, with a sweep of her hand, to Willy, Hedge, and the phouka—"really *aren't* human."

Eddi nodded toward the phouka. "You're the obvious proof," she said reluctantly.

"Certainly," said the phouka at once.

Willy made a sharp noise through his teeth. "Why go to the trouble? He can believe it or not. We don't have to jump through hoops for him." Then he stalked away across the room.

"Do it," Eddi told the phouka.

There was a dark sparkle all around him, the preface to his change, and Eddi wished she could stay and watch. No, she had to leave the phouka with the job of convincing Dan. Her problem was Willy.

She caught up with him at the other end of the cavernous room and grabbed his arm. She would have liked to take him by the shoulder and spin him to face her, like something from a Clint Eastwood movie. But the effect was the same. He rounded on her under his own power, teeth bared. He was suddenly the person who, the night before, had pulled himself out from under that horse, blood fresh on his lance.

Eddi poked him hard in the breastbone, before he could speak. If she let him speak, she would never get him under control again. . . .

"Don't you dare," she said, low-voiced. Any louder, after all, and her voice would shake. "Don't you ever fucking *dare* show that kind of contempt for anybody in this band. Do you play guitar better than Dan plays keyboards?"

After a moment, he shook his head angrily.

"Do you play better than Carla plays drums, or Hedge plays bass? No, I didn't think so. Then you better not care if they're fey, human, or little box turtles. They're your equals here, and you'll treat them that way."

"And what about you?" he said at last, through clenched teeth.

Now there was a question, indeed. "I'm the one who had to

tell you this. I'm the boss. I keep the whole thing together. And don't you forget it."

He breathed like a man in a fight—which, she supposed, he was. And so many things to fight against, no matter which way he turned: Eddi, the Sidhe, the music in his hands that demanded an outlet. In an instant, he'd choose sides. She had to make him choose the right one.

So she stepped back. "I'm sorry. I'm assuming things. There's no reason for you to put up with this."

He looked startled. Good.

"Nobody can force you to be in this band," Eddi told him gently. "I won't. Your queen can't, because if your only reason for being here is her orders, I won't take you." When he looked dubious, she added, "I *won't.* She doesn't rule here. This is *my* band. She can get down on her lily-white knees and beg me to take you, and I won't do it. But if you want to play rock 'n' roll with these guys, and you'll take directions from me and leave the Seelie Court out of it—" Eddi shrugged. "Up to you."

Willy inhaled, let it out. "What about us?" he said, and his voice had something in it that made the meaning clear.

Eddi bit her lip. "You knew the first night that whatever happened between us had nothing to do with the band. That's something else you have to accept, if you stay."

Willy dislodged himself from the wall where she'd pinned him, and paced the length of the room. His head was down, and Eddi couldn't see his face.

At the opposite wall he turned, as if at bay, and said, "All right. It's a deal."

Eddi let out her breath at last. As close as she would ever come to her dream band . . .

The rest of the dream band watched them fixedly and in silence. The phouka, in his black-dog-from-hell form, sat in the middle of them like a statue of Anubis from an Egyptian tomb. He cocked an ear at her.

"Convinced?" Eddi asked Dan.

Dan looked thoughtful. "Hell of a piece of evidence," he said, pointing a thumb at the phouka.

"Am I not?" the phouka said, sounding pleased and furry.

Eddi frowned him into silence. "So you believe me?"

"Guess I gotta. But jeezus, girl . . . !"

Carla giggled. "Yeah, that's how I felt."

"Do you mind it all?" Eddi asked, since someone had to.

He looked down at one of his synthesizers, ran a finger across its display. "We're a good band," he said finally.

That, it seemed, was all that needed to be said. Eddi flexed her fingers, startled by the feeling of power in them, the current of elation that made her light-headed. She picked up her guitar. "Let's make some noise, then," she said softly. The microphone filled the room with her voice.

CHAPTER FOURTEEN

Shall We Dance?

After three weeks of practice, they were better than any band Eddi had ever worked with. She suspected, half-elated and half-afraid, that by the end of the summer they might be better than any band she'd ever heard. If they all lived that long.

She stood in front of the bathroom mirror, putting on eyeliner. Her hands were inclined to shake. She wore skinny white jeans and a vintage beaded sweater with padded shoulders. "Jesus," she muttered at her reflection. "I look too pale. I look dead. Oh, godohgodoh—"

"That's enough," the phouka's voice came from the living room. "You'll be fine. You will, in fact, be exquisite, since I have never seen you otherwise."

Eddi felt as if she had a flock of sparrows loose in her ribcage. "Did we pack the guitar tuner?" she called.

"It's in the case with Willy's effects switches. Which is in the back of Carla's rolling horror of an automobile. Now that's something worth worrying about," he said, sounding thoughtful. "If Carla's horror chooses tonight to *stop* rolling, you'll be reduced to whistling through the set list."

She wailed, flung herself out of the bathroom, and threw a bar of soap at the phouka. He dodged it placidly. "Does that mean you can't whistle?" he inquired.

"You're an idiot." Then she saw him properly. "A good-looking idiot, though."

And he was. He wore a black suit with very narrow pants and a waist-length double-breasted jacket. His white high-collared shirt was open at the throat. He'd finished it off with black high-heeled boots and a white silk opera scarf. His black hair shone in short curls around his face, and hung to his collar in back. What might have been a ruby winked in one ear, a tiny point of scarlet fire.

He shrugged off her praise, but couldn't keep from blushing.

"You need a red carnation," Eddi told him. "You could get some cute art student to paint one on your lapel. MCAD girls have a secret fetish about men in suits, you know."

"Where is that bar of soap?" the phouka frowned.

"Gonna throw it at me?"

"Or wash out your mouth. I hadn't decided."

"It'd ruin my makeup." She took a deep breath. "Time to go?"

"I'd say so."

She put on her denim jacket and tucked her helmet under her arm. Door keys, wallet, a cache of extra guitar picks . . . She went out the door as if stepping into the deep end of a pool.

The Triumph growled them through the twilight. The air was crisp and cool as clean bedsheets, and Eddi took long breaths of it. Would the evenings be like this, if the Unseelie Court ruled in Minneapolis? Would the wind feel as good, smell so much like a promise of summer?

She circled the clustered facilities of the College of Art and Design and the Institute of Arts. At last she found a spot to park the bike, a little further from the campus than she would have liked.

"Is the protection of Faerie in effect here?" Eddi asked the phouka.

"Such as it is, my sweet. Why?"

"Because if the bike gets stolen, I want to know who to blame."

"For shame," the phouka replied. "I shall remember, in the future, that stage fright makes you testy."

"Get stuffed."

"You see?"

They would be playing in the new building, in the midst of a showing of students' paintings. Eddi wasn't sure if the band was intended as dancing or background music, but she'd decided that they would play what they liked, regardless, and play softer if they had to.

The stage was a platform set up at the end of the gallery, with double doors, now open, behind it. To Eddi's relief, Carla and Dan were already there, and the wagon was backed up to the doors. Carla was setting up her drum kit. Dan's keyboards,

stand, and miscellaneous intriguing junk were in a daunting heap
just off the platform.

"What'll I carry?" Eddi asked.

"Nothing," the phouka said, before Dan could answer. "I
take my duties as roadie very seriously, my heart. I will bring
you your axe, and you may tune it."

Carla stared after him as he went out the double doors. Then
she sighed, tossed a drumstick in the air, and caught it. "Why
can't *I* find one like that?"

Eddi wrinkled her nose. "Act your age, DiAmato, not your
stick size."

"Besides, they wouldn't take you," Dan told Carla. "The
Pook says they only dig cute girls."

"You wanna walk home, Northside?"

"Who you callin' Northside, Northside?"

Eddi smiled indulgently upon them, and wondered how the
hell Dan and the phouka had come to discuss any such thing.

The phouka came back with a load of equipment and Willy,
who was likewise burdened. They both looked serious and a
little preoccupied. Eddi relieved the phouka of her amp.

"Who died?" she asked them.

"What?" said Willy, startled.

"Something's up, yes?"

The phouka nodded. "I'll let Willy tell you, my primrose. My
strong back is needed elsewhere."

"All our strong backs are needed. Tell me while we set up."

Willy shrugged, and trailed after them.

It was the dinner hour, and the gallery was sparsely populated.
Eddi located the nearest electrical outlets and began to run
extension cords. Willy followed in her wake, plugging in equipment. As he worked, he talked. Carla, Eddi noticed, was listening with a frown, Dan with a wondering look.

"Council of War last night," Willy said. "The whole bloody
fight will last well into fall, if last night's discussion is typical."

"Why's that?"

"Everyone's stalling," Willy said. "After the bloodbath at
the Falls, nobody's willing to set the next battle until one Court
or the other thinks it has an advantage."

"Wonderful. But what advantage are they waiting for?"

Willy sat back on his heels and regarded her skeptically.

"Oh, come on," Eddi sighed. "I'm pretty quick for a human,
all right?"

"True enough," Willy said with a rueful quirk of an eyebrow.
"All right. There are certain days associated with magic. Halloween, May Eve, the solstices and equinoxes, a few others. Some are more favorable to one Court than the other. The next big event is Midsummer's Eve, which is a good one for the Seelie Court. The Eve itself is a truce period. But the Sidhe would like to hold off and fight soon after that, when we're still strong."

"But you said that *both* sides are stalling?"

"The Dark Court is pressing for a battle on June first—hoping that our weakness will be worse than theirs, I suppose. If they don't get that, they'll delay as long as they can. And I doubt they'll get June first."

Eddi stared at him. "They *negotiate* times and places for these things? How do they get anything done? How did they agree on Minnehaha Falls?"

"If it's something both sides want, they manage. And both sides want this war, and the spoils from it. One Court will accept a less favorable time in exchange for a site that offers them some advantage. It's not very different from rival mortal nations."

Eddi sighed. "I guess I'm used to self-propelled wars. This all sounds too reasonable to be believed."

Willy smiled crookedly. "Oh, yes. All very gentlemanly and fair. With assassinations and guerrilla tactics between times."

"I thought you were one of the guys who made the rules," Eddi said, very soft.

That brought his black eyebrows down, made his hands stop. Then he tossed her the power cord for her amp, and she plugged it in.

"I don't like it," he said finally. "I've never seen anything like what happened on May Eve. I don't look forward to seeing it again, and sitting around waiting for it doesn't make it any better." He rose suddenly and walked away, went to the edge of the stage to unpack his guitar.

The phouka watched him go, looking thoughtful. Hedge had arrived sometime in all that, and was watching as well, slouched and silent. His chin was tucked—a protective pose—and his eyes followed everything from behind the veil of his ragged brown hair. There was hurt in the lines of his body, and fear. Eddi wondered what the battle at the Falls had been like for him. But before she could go to him and draw him aside, he shuffled away to set up his bass.

They did Rue Nouveau's "I'm Not Done Yet" for a sound check; the phouka alternately adjusted the mixing board and paced the room to check the results. The first chord startled the few bystanders in the room. But none of them left, and by the end of the song all of them were tapping feet or swaying in place. Willy plugged in his fiddle, and they did some blues improv in A. People began to accumulate in the room, multiplying from nowhere in the fashion of crowds-to-be.

At last the phouka gave Eddi a thumbs-up, and she called a halt. "Showtime in five, troops," she told the band.

Eddi stepped off the stage and turned to study it, ticking things off mental checklists.

"You're fretting," said the phouka over her shoulder.

"Was that supposed to be a pun?"

He smiled. "I refuse to say. But I'll repair the damage: You're worrying."

"Of course I am. It's my job. Keeps everyone else from having to do it."

"I'd spare you it, if I could."

Something in his words, so lightly spoken, sounded like more than merely band matters. "When I'm so good at it?" she said with a little laugh.

He let the subject turn, and Eddi told herself she wasn't sorry. "As long as your heart's set on worrying, then, tell me how you think it will go tonight."

"I think . . . good. We'll be a little raggedy in places, but not much. And we'll be a little cautious, maybe, but not as much as some bands that have been together for two-three times as long as we have."

He looked pleased with his thoughts. "Tell me—does the reaction of the audience affect your performance?"

"Hugely. Why?"

"Curiosity, sweet. What sort of effect does it have?"

Eddi frowned. "Well, about what you'd expect. You feel better in front of a crowd that's enjoying what you do. You work harder. Playing for an audience that hates you is like wading through swamp water up to your chin."

The phouka made an appreciative face.

"And sometimes," she continued, "on a good night, there's a . . . I can't explain it properly. Something that happens between the performer and the audience at the best times. Both sides get a little wired." She flourished her hands. "I really *can't* explain it very well. But you can feel it when you get it, and it makes you crazy.''

He watched her intently through all this, a little smile at the edges of his mouth. "May you get it often," he said at last, and touched a forefinger delicately to her chin. "Now, go call your band—I believe it's time.''

The band came on without fanfare or theater. Eddi slid the Rick over her shoulder and wiped her hands surreptitiously on her jeans. Carla snapped out four counts of rim shots on the snare, then four more seasoned with the sharp *tsk* of her high-hat cymbal. Eddi and Hedge began to pound their low strings, and Dan swelled the synthesizer up under them in a growl almost too low to hear. Dead stop, then Carla swatted her big drums. Willy flung out a trail of high guitar notes like stars—not cold points of light in the dark, but suns, the burning and beginning of everything.

They sailed into Richard Thompson's ''Valerie'' and Eddi could almost see the sound of it, a broad arc of light that unrolled over the crowd, wound around and under them. . . .

It was a good opening song. Eddi would tell herself that when the night was over, and she could look back and be rational. But now the music had her, and the playing of it. She traded wild low notes and vampy looks with Hedge until he, by God, *laughed*. She posed and danced with Willy like his short blond shadow. They all leaned into their microphones at once, and Eddi heard in their voices the same open-throated power that she felt in her own. As they split into harmonies, she climbed for the top one, until she was an octave above Willy's tenor, out on the edge of her own range.

People in the crowd were starting to dance, more of them as she watched. That, too, was an observation she would examine only later. There was no time now for anything but the music. That was a train that wouldn't wait for her. Doors open, closed, gone—no. The music wouldn't wait, because she didn't want it to. She was herself the power to the wheels.

They spun another song from the threads of the last, one Eddi had written. The dancers would quit, of course—it took more dedication than most people had to dance to a song they'd never heard. But she couldn't stop now, even for them.

> *Drinking coffee,*
> *Have to stay awake and think of you.*
> *Aching awfully,*
> *Knowing my perceptions aren't true.*

If you were what I've made you
Not as your acts betrayed you
How could I keep away?
But things still lead me on,
A word, and then it's gone.
What lives here, and what's stray?
Tell me, please, what's signal and what's noise?

A brown-haired girl near the front of the stage spun like a ballerina; Eddi saw delight in her open mouth and closed eyes. Her partner, a blond boy in a painted T shirt, grinned and bit his lip, dancing with narrow-eyed concentration.

She spotted the phouka near the mixing board, the glow from its meters adding underlight to his dark face. He watched the crowd, and his eyes moved in quick, restless patterns. She knew what he was doing. *Give it up, phouka. Nobody can touch me now. Not now.* His gaze, in its travels, met hers, and he smiled as if her thoughts had reached him.

Dan played crackles and pops with one keyboard, a string quartet from space with another. Then he grabbed a fistful of brass, and Willy made his axe chatter and whine. Eddi went back to the mike with lyrics swelling in her throat.

Her lyrics. They weren't just sounds to be made; they were a sliver of experience, with photographs in her memory for illustrations. If she wanted, she could summon back every emotion. But it was her audience she wanted to give them to, once she'd called them out.

Interference
Or is that the broadcast that I've got?
Your appearance
Renders me incapable of thought.

Here's your voice on the phone,
Your sweet and sullen tone,
What am I to believe?
Did you blow me a kiss
Or was that just tape hiss?
When I hang up, will you grieve?
Have pity, now, what's signal and what's noise?

Here's your photo,
I found it cleaning out my bottom drawer.
When you wrote, oh,
I couldn't keep from wondering what for.

Through the gray, through the grain,
A picture taken in the rain,
That doesn't show your face.
Connected dots don't make a line,
You confuse me every time,
Confusion has its place,
But just this once, what's signal and what's noise?

Yeah, like that. She let the band pause for breath between songs, but not much more. Then they swept on, like heroes in search of glory and plunder, and those who watched and danced followed after.

It was the end of the first set before Eddi discovered how her band worked.

The revelation came with their cover of a Nate Bucklin song, "She's Getting Desperate." It opened with Hedge's galloping, grumbling bass notes and Willy's lead vocal. Eddi stepped back and let them take the spotlight. She turned to Carla and Dan, to gather them up with her eyes and launch them into the second verse. Carla was half dancing on her drummer's throne, sticks poised, barely contained. Dan's dark fingers hovered twitchy over the keys. They were ready.

Eddi leaned into the harmony vocals on the last two lines of the verse, and gathered Hedge and Willy as she had the other two. Hedge rocked contemplatively over his axe, unruffled but not unmoved by the rhythm. Willy sang strong and crisp and clean, biting off each word. His left hand curled over the chord on the neck of his guitar, and his right hung above the strings, prepared to strike. His hair had fallen over one eye; the other eye blazed.

They'd practiced the transition from first verse to second until it was flawless, until she woke up two days in a row with it running like a loop through her head. Last word of the verse, and three beats. Then the rest of the band would come in like the end of the world, just when the audience thought it was safe.

That was exactly what happened. Not with the offhand perfection of a long-rehearsed band; it sounded like the hot improvi-

sation of a solo artist. One with ten hands. Eddi knew, with a
rush of warm and cold, that she was responsible. Four people
watched her for cues, relied on her to keep them together,
counted on her to let them run amok when it was right and leash
them when it wasn't. Four artistic, anarchic personalities had
placed themselves under her rule.

She nearly forgot her harmony part.

If they hadn't scheduled a break after that, they would have
had to take one anyway. They'd worked themselves up to an
emotional peak that was hard to abandon, and they needed night
air to cool the sweat off their faces and blow the crazies away.

So it was out the doors behind the stage once again. Carla
plucked a cigarette and lit it with a trembling match. "Holy
shit," she said on a mouthful of smoke. "That was kinda fun."

Dan laughed. "Yeah." He said it again, softer, and tapped a
beat against his thighs. Willy leaned against the white stone
wall, hands in his pockets, head back, eyes closed. He was
smiling.

Hedge was the last one off the stage, the last out the door by a
long minute. When he came into the night, it was with his head
down, and no attention paid to any of them. He sat down on a lip
of stone, a little removed from the group.

Eddi felt her elation weighted down with something in the
region of her stomach. She debated the issue for a moment, then
she went to sit next to Hedge. She tried not to look too purpose-
ful about it.

For a little while they sat in silence, and Eddi watched his
knuckly hands massage each other. Then she asked, "You okay?"
Not profound, but to the point.

His smile was not the one that sometimes lit his face; this one
looked hard to do, and fragile.

"Can I help?" She knew better, at least, than to ask if he
wanted to talk about it.

Hedge shook his head and made knots with his fingers again.
" 'S too good," he muttered after a moment. "Nothin' so good
lasts."

"Oh, come on," Eddi grinned at his bent head. "That's not
true. Why shouldn't it last?"

Hedge looked up again, and this time he made no pretense of
smiling. " 'Cause it won't. Nothin' so good c'n last."

There was something almost oracular in the intensity of his
voice. His eyebrows pulled together, as if some idea or lack of

one frustrated him. Eddi understood suddenly what prompted grownups to promise impossible things to children.

"I'm going to try to make it last," she said. "I know what the odds are, and I know what I'm up against, and I'm still going to try."

He gave her an impenetrable look from the covert of his hair.

"But it would help . . . well, if you believed in me. Hokey as it sounds."

He blinked, looked down again, and after an oppressive bit of time, nodded once.

"Good enough," Eddi said. She wondered if she should pat his shoulder or hug him or *something*. But she didn't feel quite comfortable about it. Instead they sat for a minute or two in what became a companionable silence.

Eddi broke it at last with, "Have I told you lately that you play *great* bass?"

This time his smile was brilliant and genuine.

"Five minutes, ladies and gentlebeings," said the phouka, poking his head out the door. Then he grinned. "And the dancers need every second of it, poor things."

Willy's eyes grew round. "Hazel and Thorn. I forgot."

"Forgot what?" Eddi demanded, alarmed by his tone.

It was the phouka who replied. "Have I told you about the Faerie rings? No? Well, now is certainly the time. We are fond of music and dancing, as you know."

He smiled benignly, and Eddi fastened on a warning glare.

"On occasion, mortals have, knowingly or inadvertently, crashed the party. They quickly discover one of the most notable characteristics of Faerie music: it makes one dance."

"So?" Eddi said.

"You don't understand," Willy interjected. "It *makes* you dance."

Carla frowned and raised a finger as if to question that. Then she stopped, her mouth open and eyes wide. Dan got it at about the same time. "Shit. I mean . . . you mean . . ." He stared at Willy and the phouka. "Shit."

It made a certain appalling sense. The crowd had danced to the first song, they'd danced to the originals—in short, they'd shown a remarkable willingness to dance, even under the worst conditions. But . . .

"What makes this Faerie music?" Eddi asked.

The phouka cocked his head. "Two of you are fey. One of

you is closely tied to the Folk. The other two''—and he grinned at Carla and Dan—''have picked up an uncanny lick or two out of sheer proximity. Oh, the effect isn't perfect yet. It's possible to resist the urge to dance, and possible to stop when one is wholly exhausted. But try to have a little mercy on the poor things in the second set, won't you?''

Dan stared at the phouka, then turned his now-what-do-I-do expression on Eddi. Carla looked at her hands and started to giggle. Then she began to laugh. She staggered over to the wall and slid down it until she was sitting in the grass, still laughing.

"Carla?" Eddi said. "Carla, calm down. Are you hysterical, or what?"

"No, no, it's—oh, God, you'll kill me. I can't tell you." And she burst into another fit of giggles.

"Carla . . ."

"Eddi and the Fey!" Carla squeaked, and had another attack.

"What?" said Eddi.

Willy rubbed his chin. "Not bad."

"Quite good, actually," the phouka seconded.

Dan began to grin. "Sure doesn't make us sound like something we're not."

Hedge seemed to be trying not to smile.

Eddi looked around at all of them, wondering if they had gone mad simultaneously. "What? You mean—good grief, as a *band name?* You're all crackers."

"Nah," Dan said. "It'll be great."

"Eddi and the Fey," Willy said, wrapping his splendid voice around it and making it resonate.

"Hell, I'm smart," Carla sighed happily.

"I suppose form demands that it be put to a vote," said the phouka. "All in favor?"

Three fey hands and two mortal ones went up, as Eddi flapped hers helplessly. "Who said this was a democracy?" she wailed, and no one paid the least attention. It wouldn't help a bit, she reflected, to rule that the roadie couldn't vote. Besides, it was growing on her. Eddi and the Fey. It embarrassed her, putting her own name in the band's. But it was her band. . . .

They'd fallen silent, and watched her eagerly. "Nobody'll know what it means," Eddi warned.

"Jefferson Airplane," Carla intoned. "X. The Psychedelic Furs. At least this one you can look up in a dictionary."

"Well . . ."

"And it's a lot better than InKline Plain."

"Okay," Eddi said. "But if anybody laughs, I'm gonna tell who made it up."

"You're late," said the phouka, and they scrambled for the door.

Eddi used the new name to introduce the band. No one laughed; they applauded and yelled.

She led off alone on the intro to "When You Were Mine," her guitar thin and high and lonely. Then the rest of the band swelled up under that, with Willy on his electric demon fiddle. Carla and Dan had come up with a bizarre percussive patch for one of the synthesizers, and hung it on the end of the fiddle's phrases. The effect was that of a succession of violins being bitten neatly in half.

Eddi found that the single-minded frenzy of the first set had passed. She still had the crackling energy, but she had a clear head to use it with as well. She tried to make every note glow; she felt the rest of the band respond to that and stretch like a racehorse seeking that one winning length. And they listened to each other. A sudden musical discovery by any one of them would be picked up immediately by the others, so quickly it must have looked rehearsed.

The party was supposed to end at 11:30, but with the encore they ran late. "An encore," Carla grinned. "These people must all run marathons in their spare time. Jesus Christ." But they played it, wringing wet and panting, and if the crowd was reduced by weariness to a sort of vigorous swaying-in-place, nobody seemed to mind.

Afterward, people came up to the stage and told them they were a wonderful band. Eddi had forgotten that things like that happened. It was all she could do to say, "Thank you," instead of, "My God, aren't we?" Was Hedge right? Was all this too good to last? *Let him be wrong, let him be wrong,* Eddi prayed.

They tore down their equipment; then Eddi went to the ladies' room and washed the sweat off her face. She studied her badly lit reflection in the mirror and grinned. No, she looked exactly as she had when she left her apartment that evening. Well, exhausted. But she still felt as if the night's work should have changed her. "Great band," she told the mirror, and went back to the gallery.

Something was wrong. The phouka stood at the lip of the stage, one of Willy's cables half-coiled between his hands. Willy was on his feet, too. The double doors were still open, but the station wagon was gone—no sign of Carla or Dan. Hedge stood in the doorway, and if Eddi were to believe his face, someone had glued his feet to the sill and he wasn't happy about it.

Their attention was fixed on a woman who stood on the dance floor, looking up at them. Her back was to the gallery door, and all Eddi could see of her was the smooth, shining coil of her black hair, her gray trench coat cut long and full, sheer black stockings, and black lizard pumps. She carried a wide-brimmed black hat in one hand.

From behind, she was elegant but nothing more. The phouka, however, was in front of the woman, and his expression . . .

He was afraid. It was difficult to tell at first; but he looked past the woman in the trench coat and saw Eddi, and she was sure. The phouka was afraid, and for her.

Willy's chin was up in that haughty way of his. Something about that seemed odd, but Eddi hadn't time to think about it. She stepped warily toward the stage.

She could have sworn that the woman had seen the phouka's look, and knew Eddi was behind her. But she didn't turn. She was speaking in a low, pleasantly hoarse voice, and as Eddi drew near she heard her say to the phouka, "Well, my compliments. I couldn't have done better myself."

The phouka bit his lip for an instant, then lapsed again into stillness.

"This is no business of yours," Willy said, but not with any great certainty.

"Isn't it? Perhaps you don't think so." Eddi heard laughter in the woman's voice as she turned a thin hand toward the phouka. "But I'd bet he wouldn't agree."

Eddi took a deep breath. "May I help you?" she said crisply. "I'm the bandleader."

The phouka closed his eyes.

The trench-coated woman inclined her head, as if thinking about Eddi's offer; then, in no discernible hurry, she turned around.

Not beautiful—she was too feline for anyone to comfortably call her beautiful. Her gleaming black hair was scraped severely back from her face, which made her gray almond eyes look as huge as a cat's. Her eyebrows were thick and black, and their high arch gave her a look of perpetual gentle surprise. She had a small, narrow nose, dwarfed by the rest of her face, and a wide, well-shaped mouth painted the color of cyclamen petals. Her cheekbones were pronounced, and her chin was pointed. She was tall, wide-shouldered, and narrow-hipped, and looked very good in the cream-colored suit under the trench coat.

She tipped her head and smiled. "You must be Eddi, then—oh, unless it's one of *those* band names."

"No. No, it's . . . I'm Eddi." In the fourth grade she'd had a teacher like this, gracious of manner, elegant of person even on a teacher's wages. Eddi had adored her.

"So pleased to meet you. Your band is fabulous." The woman extended one of her thin hands to Eddi.

Of course, the teacher's wages had, as it turned out, been supplemented. . . ."Thank you. But I think you'd better get to the point." Eddi put her hands in her pockets.

Those black arched eyebrows climbed a little more. "I beg your pardon?" Her voice remained pleasant, and for a dreadful moment Eddi doubted.

But she pressed on anyway. "They'll tell me all about you as soon as you leave," Eddi said, pointing at the phouka and Willy. Hedge, she saw, now stood openmouthed behind the stage. "I know all the things I'm not supposed to know. So there's no point in pretending."

The woman looked at Willy and the phouka, neither surprised nor displeased. Then her attention returned to Eddi. "How did you guess I wasn't just another audience member? For the sake of my curiosity, you understand."

"The way Willy acted. One of his redeeming social graces is that he almost never subjects mortal strangers to that nose-in-the-air routine. I saw him do it to you when I came in, and it bothered me, until I realized that either you weren't a stranger, or you weren't mortal."

She laughed. "Or both. But why did you assume I wasn't one of your allies, and decline to shake my hand?"

"The way the phouka behaved," Eddi said.

The woman turned another look, longer this time, on the stage. "Ah, of course, your watchdog. Don't trust too much to one guardian—he's not incorruptible, my dear."

"Who is?"

The woman's throaty laugh was quite genuine. "Exactly! I've built a very old reputation on that principle."

Hedge took a step forward, his hands curled into fists and

raised. Eddi and the dark woman turned almost in unison, each equally wary, it seemed, of breaking eye contact.

The dark woman stared at Hedge, then smiled one of her quiet smiles. He glowered and turned his face away.

"Leave him alone," Eddi said quietly. "We're not on the battlefield now."

"No, we aren't—quite." The woman returned her attention to Eddi. "And there are better targets."

She set her black hat on her head at a striking angle, casting a diagonal of shadow across her features. "Again," she said to Eddi, "a marvelous band, and I was delighted to meet you. I'm sure we'll see one another soon." And she left the gallery, her heels making small, sharp noises with the measured cadence of her stride.

"Front door's locked," Eddi said thoughtfully.

"Oh," Willy replied, "she'll get out."

The phouka sank down on the edge of the stage and buried his face in his hands. Eddi hurried to him, alarmed.

"Phouka . . .?"

"Heart failure," he murmured through his fingers. "I warned you, my primrose, that I would be like to die of it, should you go on as you have."

She made a disgusted noise and pulled his hair. He lowered his hands and grinned wickedly up at her.

"Creep," she said. "All right, guys, who was that?"

Hedge looked at his feet. The phouka drew breath to answer, but it was Willy who spoke first. "The Queen of Air and Darkness," he said. His voice was soft and pitched low, but every surface in the room seemed to catch his words and whisper them back.

Willy was standing at the back of the stage, his eyes fixed on the empty oblong of the gallery door. He rubbed his hands absently over his upper arms, as if he suffered from cold and knew there was no relief for it.

"She scares you," Eddi said.

"She scares anyone with any sense," Willy replied sharply. He stepped off the back of the stage and went outside through the double doors. After a moment and a long inscrutable look at Eddi, Hedge went, too.

"Where are Carla and Dan?" Eddi asked the phouka after a respectful silence.

"On their way home."

"No mass outing for coffee?"

"They didn't seem in need of it," the phouka said.

Eddi raised her eyebrows. "Which didn't they need, the caffeine or the camaraderie?"

"They seemed quite happy, and almost incapable of beginning a sentence, let alone finishing one."

"You're right. They need to sleep. Well, then tell me who the Queen of Air and Darkness is."

"You don't—? Ah, of course. Never mind. She rules the Unseelie Court."

Eddi took a deep breath; it wobbled when she let it out. "Oh." Then she added, "I guess I understand why you might feel heart failure coming on."

"I should not have said that," he said seriously. "You managed that confrontation very well indeed, my sweet. I suppose I spoke out of a spasm of guilt—here was the villain of the piece, and I had done nothing to prepare you for her."

"Is she really the villain?" Eddi sat down on the stage next to him. "I kind of liked her."

With a rueful snort, he replied, "It would hardly be to her advantage, my primrose, to be repulsive."

"Why did she tell me you could be corrupted?"

"Oak and Ash," the phouka muttered, "do you remember everything that's said to you? She was sowing at random, hoping that a seed of doubt would find fertile ground in you."

"Well, it didn't," Eddi said crisply.

The phouka turned and studied her face. She resisted the sudden shyness that urged her to look away. "Thank you," he murmured.

"Any time," she said lightly, but she thought, *If I'm not supposed to thank him, what the hell does it mean if he thanks me?*

"If you're interested," Willy's voice came from behind them, "there wasn't any fertile ground here, either."

"What?" The phouka looked confused; then his frown disappeared and he turned to Willy, who stood in the door. "Ah, that's right—she aimed a bolt or two at you, didn't she?"

Willy strolled in and sat next to Eddi. He was trying to seem at ease, his equilibrium recovered. It was very different from the real thing. "I don't think she seriously intended them to work," Willy said. "She was shooting in the dark, probably, just to see if anything would break."

"So you no longer think I might be her agent?"

"She wouldn't have made the crack about not doing better herself if you were."

"I shouldn't point out, I suppose, that she might have done it to lay your suspicions."

Willy looked disgusted. "Don't be a pain in the ass."

"I thought I was being a devil's advocate." The phouka looked brightly at Eddi. "Are they synonymous?"

"Don't be a pain in the ass." Eddi smiled and shook her head at him. Then she turned to Willy. "Where's Hedge?"

"He's gone home."

It occurred to her that she didn't know where or what Hedge considered home. "We should follow his lead. It's been a long night, kids."

"Now there's a suggestion with merit." The phouka bounced to his feet and held out a hand to Eddi. When she took it and stood up, he executed one of his casual bows. She copied it back at him. It made him smile.

"Eddi?" Willy said behind her. The phouka looked over her shoulder, raised an eyebrow, and shrugged.

"I'll be outside, my primrose," he said, and went out the door without another word.

She rounded on Willy. "Did you send him away?"

"No. Or at least . . . I looked as if I *hoped* he'd leave, and he did. You tell me."

"Given your rank, doesn't your wish become his command?"

Willy snorted. "For the phouka? You've seen him in action. No, I think he decided to do me a favor."

"So are you grateful?"

"Yes, yes, I'm grateful. Eddi—" He rubbed the space between his eyebrows. "Air and . . . I don't suppose we could start the last minute and a half over again?"

"Not really." But she felt sorry for him, and sat down again. "What is it, Willy?"

He sat for a moment, watching his right thumb stroke the edge of his left. "I . . . It's been a long while. . . ." He pulled his hands apart suddenly, and they made a pair of half-finished, frustrated arcs. "I've run out of charming euphemisms. Eddi . . . I don't want to sleep alone tonight."

He met her eyes (oh, those speaking green gemstones of his), then looked away into the darkened room.

She waited for her emotions to stop flailing, until she knew it was hopeless to wait. Then she said, "No." That was too bald. "I'm sorry. But no." Was that worse? Probably. There was almost certainly no good thing to be said, after all.

He gave her one of his fiery, intense looks, and this time she had to turn away. "Is it still because of the glamour? Because I hid what I am?"

"No. And the problem wasn't that you hid what you are, damn it. It was that you became someone else, and *made* me like him."

"But still, that's not the problem?"

"Oh, hell." One voice inside her said, *I don't need this now.* The other said, *I will not cry, I* will *not cry.* "You don't love me. And I don't want to sleep with you."

Anger crossed his face in a series of tensions and tics, crossed and was gone. "So, you've never slept with someone when you didn't want to?"

She almost told him no, she hadn't. "All right. Yes, of course I have. I'm only human"—he smiled coldly, and she wanted to hit him—"and sometimes you don't realize until afterward that you didn't want to. But why the hell should you want me to repeat past mistakes for you?"

"You're sure they were mistakes?"

"Of course I'm sure! Sex without love is like a goddamn business transaction. And sometimes both parties feel as if they got a good deal, but that doesn't make it any less so. If I go to bed with you as a favor, because you need it—son, I might as well charge you for it, because there are places where they do."

He must have battled his pride, to be able to ask her for this. His terrible lordly pride. Perhaps she should have granted his wish. But combining sex and self-sacrifice—it was obscene, like mixing sex and cruelty. And surely Willy had seen enough people set aside their needs and desires for his? She wished she could be sure.

She stood, before she lost the courage of her convictions. "I'm going home," she said.

He looked up, one eyebrow raised. When he spoke his voice was full of mockery, and Eddi couldn't tell if it was at her expense or his. "No sad speeches about hoping we can still be friends—I'm grateful for that, anyway."

"You've seen too many movies."

"I suppose I have. I didn't get that from personal experience, you know." Bitterness slipped from his voice, replaced with—

surprise? Curiosity? Now that Eddi thought about it, she realized Willy's experience with rejection was not likely to be extensive.

He shrugged. "Safe trip home."

"Aren't you leaving?"

"Soon."

Eddi looked back when she reached the double doors. Willy was still sitting on the stage, staring out into the dark room.

The phouka was a shadow in the shadow of a tree. He detached himself from it and ambled toward her when she came out.

"No, my sweet," he said cheerfully, "don't mind me for an instant. I live to wait for you, outside in the cold and damp." His face, in the streetlight, was at odds with his voice; he looked sad and sympathetic.

"Did you overhear any of that?"

"No, I try not to eavesdrop unless it's likely to profit me. Ought I to have?"

"No, you ought not, and don't you *dare* ask me about it."

The phouka sighed hugely. "And now I haven't even the excuse of stage fright to offer you. Come along, my obstreperous primrose. Everything will be improved by a night's sleep and a day's reflection."

He might have been right, but Eddi couldn't swear to it. She spent much of the night awake, between sheets that seemed unusually harsh and cold.

CHAPTER FIFTEEN

In a Different Light

They were playing the Uptown Bar, one of Eddi's favorite venues. At least, it began with the Uptown Bar, and with the memory of a good first set. Then piece by piece the surroundings turned inside out, until the stage was on the roof of the building, and Eddi and the Fey were gathered around it. Eddi couldn't find her guitar. It was probably still inside, downstairs. Carla called to her from the stage, warned her that it was time to begin. But it would only take a minute to get the guitar. . . .

She stared down the stairs and discovered that the building had grown several floors. On every stair landing there was a party, elegant people of the sort she'd never seen at the Uptown Bar—and of course, it wasn't the Uptown. It was the Guthrie Theatre, with the lobbies and wide iron-railed staircases thronged with concertgoers. A tall, black-haired woman in a cream-colored dress stepped out in front of her. "Great show, Eddi," the woman said. "I didn't think you'd live this long."

"Neither did I," Eddi heard herself saying. "But I have to find my guitar."

Her axe was backstage, of course. But where was backstage? The band would be waiting. If she asked an usher, she'd have to prove she was with the band. No one would believe her.

Eddi pushed her way despairingly through the crowd. Suddenly she saw Stuart Kline, halfway up the next set of stairs. He looked the way he had when she first met him, young and clear-eyed and clever. He wore formal dress, white tie and tails. She waved furiously, and he saw her and smiled, and beckoned. Eddi fought her way to the foot of the stairs and saw him disappearing around a corner at the top.

There was no one on this flight of stairs; Eddi ran up unhindered. At the top of the next flight was a gray metal fire door, swinging closed. Eddi caught it before it latched and pushed it open. Before her was the roof of the Walker Art Center, the Guthrie's sister building. A Calder mobile creaked gently in the wind, its black silhouette like locust leaves against the night sky. So many stars—more than the city lights ever allowed for.

Stuart sat on the low wall around the roof. He had her guitar, the red Rickenbacker, propped on his thigh, and she heard the melody of Peter Gabriel's "Here Comes the Flood." The Rick resonated like an acoustic. Stuart looked up at her and struck discord. He smiled.

"What are you doing with my axe?" Eddi said.

"You were looking for it, weren't you?" He hopped up on the wall, and the wind tugged at his brown hair and the tails of his jacket. He held her guitar by the neck in a gray-gloved hand, out over the street below.

"Why are you wearing gloves?" Eddi asked him.

He looked at his free hand. "They're burned," he said calmly. He shook the glove off, and the wind took it. His hand was charred black. As she watched, the black began to flake away, swirling off bit by bit after the glove, until it revealed the hand beneath, pink and new and much smaller than the old one. Then Stuart turned and walked off the wall.

He didn't fall. He stood in midair like something from a cartoon, smiling and waving her guitar. "Come get it!"

She stood beside the wall, unable to move. Stuart did a little dance step on nothing. "Well, come on. What, didn't your new friends teach you this?" Then his face changed, still Stuart, but cruel and angry. "Oh, that's right. They don't want you to know shit. Your taste in friends sucks, Eddi."

"It's getting better. I used to hang out with you."

"Come on." Stuart waved her guitar. "Before I drop it."

Eddi climbed up on the wall, which was tall and narrow now. The wind caught her under the arms, a warm wind full of the smell of lilacs, and she stepped out.

Stuart was gone, the roof and the street and the traffic, all gone, and she hung above the trees of Loring Park like a kite. She saw the orange globes of the park lights, and the dark glitter of the lake, patterned over with the fluttering brocade of the tree branches.

The phouka lay on the lakeshore. He was asleep, lying on his side with his knees drawn up a little and his head on his arms. His dark skin seemed almost luminous under the moon and lamplight. He looked young and fragile, not at all like the wretched nuisance he was when awake. She felt a deep pain somewhere under her breastbone at the sight of him.

Then she looked down and saw the gray shaft quivering in her chest, the blood welling dark and staining the cloth around it. The archer stepped out of the shadow of the park building, his skin the gray of his arrow, his staring eyes milky white, a grin baring his many sharp teeth. The phouka was not asleep. He was dead, and so was she.

. . . Which brought her wide-eyed awake with her heart banging against her ribs. She rolled over and looked at the clock. Nine A.M. Too early to get up, especially when she could remember most of the hours of the night. But her thoughts rattled like a teletype and wouldn't let her sleep. She flung the covers back finally and grabbed her robe. She would go out to the kitchen, get something to drink. Then she would be able to sleep. And if the phouka asked her what she was doing up so early, well, she'd tell him to drop—she'd tell him to shut up.

The light slanted strangely through the living room windows. It was strange to her, anyway; she was so rarely up when the sun was still low. She didn't see the phouka at first. Then she found him, in dog-shape, asleep in front of the door to the hall. His pointed black ears flicked forward, as if acknowledging her presence, but his eyes stayed closed. *At least somebody gets to sleep in this morning,* she thought. For a moment she watched his sides rise and fall with his breathing. Then she turned back toward the kitchen.

She heard a creak, as if from a cupboard door, and a soft, rhythmic thumping. Eddi crossed the room softly, and inched forward until she could peer around the kitchen door.

Above the sink, a dish towel writhed across the surface of a plate. The plate then skimmed toward the open cupboard like a frisbee, and Eddi clenched her teeth. It slowed and settled on the stack with a faint click. By that time, the towel was at work on a glass.

Her largest bowl wobbled on the counter, rocked by the fury of the spoon flailing the batter inside. The carafe from the coffee maker skidded across the countertop and ducked under a stream of cold water from the kitchen tap. The sponge mop drag-raced down the floor. The curtains shook themselves vigorously, and the resulting dust gathered itself up and puffed out through the kitchen window.

In the midst of it all was Hairy Meg. She was naked, bandy-legged, profoundly ugly, and full of a deep and obvious content-ment. Her pose was martial: arms crossed over her breasts, long chin thrust out, long knobby nose pointing like a finger wherever she turned her head.

Mickey Mouse in Fantasia, *with all those brooms,* Eddi thought. She watched in awe, forgetting that she was in hiding. When she remembered, she wasn't sure what to do next. She could clear her throat . . . no. That seemed like a good way to get the coffee carafe broken. Perhaps it would be better just to sneak back to the bedroom. She leaned slowly back, away from the kitchen door. . . .

And bumped into something hard and soft at once, and warm. Surprise pushed the air out of her lungs and made a squeak of it, the tiniest little sound. In the kitchen, there was sudden, earsplit-ting silence.

"Shhh!" said the phouka, next to her ear. That, too, was probably audible in the kitchen. He was in human form again, blue-jeaned and bare-chested, his hands clasped behind him and a grin on his handsome dark face.

"You could have tapped me on the shoulder or something."

"You would have jumped and squeaked," he said smugly. "Just as you did, in fact."

"You—you little—"

The phouka looked over her shoulder. Warily, she looked behind her.

Hairy Meg stood in the kitchen door, her martial look fixed on Eddi and the phouka.

"Lover's quarrel," the phouka told her.

"I will *not* hit you," Eddi muttered, glaring at him. "It is beneath my dignity."

Meg looked unimpressed. "I'll no' be spied at. Come in, or be about tha business." Then she turned and stomped back into the kitchen.

The noises began again. Eddi shrugged and went to stick her head in the doorway. She hesitated to do more than that. She watched a box of currants hurl itself like a suicide from a cupboard shelf, stop with a lurch above the mixing bowl, and dump its contents into the dough.

"May I ask you a question?" Eddi said, with caution.

Hairy Meg made a horrible face, but said nothing. Eddi decided at last that this was not meant to be discouraging.

"I won't, if it would offend you, or if it's bad manners," Eddi added. "The only things I know about . . . your people are from the phouka. And I don't think he's a good example." She stole a look back over her shoulder, but didn't see him.

Meg snorted. "Proper amaudhan, that 'n'." Eddi, having no notion what that was, did not reply. "Tha'll get nobbut nonsense out o' him, for all he means nae ill."

Eddi watched the mixing bowl tip over on a floured countertop. The dough wriggled and stretched out a little; then it folded over onto itself and stretched again, and folded, on and on.

Would she truly get nothing but nonsense out of the phouka? She couldn't be sure, but she didn't think his explanation of matters in the Seelie Court was nonsense. On other subjects, perhaps—but he was so changeable, how could she tell? He showed her a multitude of faces. Were any of them true?

"Nay, never mind, lass," said Hairy Meg gruffly. "Th' had summat to ask, then."

Eddi looked quickly into that wrinkled brown face. Meg was scowling at the counter, where the dough was dividing itself into eight neat ovals. "It's not really important, I guess. But . . ."

Meg tapped her foot.

"I don't . . . I don't knock things off the counter anymore. Carla came over to dinner last week, and I drained the pasta without spilling it all down the sink. She tried the sauce and asked if I'd sent out for it. I used to burn myself in this kitchen maybe twice a week, and it hasn't happened for the longest time." Eddi took a deep breath. "Is that on account of you?"

By the end of that speech, Meg was staring at her, and the lumps of dough sat still. "A' course it's ta my account, ye great ninny," Meg said at last. "I'm a *brownie*."

"That's . . . what brownies do?"

"Nay, lass, we hang arse-up in gorse bushes, whistlin' pop'lar songs. Whisht, now, take tha speiring tae yon silly phouka, he's a fancy for it. I've work tae do."

"Yes, ma'am," Eddi said meekly, and backed out of the kitchen. As she did, the little mounds of currant-studded dough rolled onto a baking sheet, like children rolling down a hill.

The phouka was sitting on the couch, slid low down with his feet on the trunk. He smiled at Eddi and patted the cushion beside him. It seemed like an intimate gesture, to sit next to him. She sat on the couch and tried to pretend that she hadn't thought about it first.

"Did you know it was Meg?" she asked him.

"Your brownie?"

Eddi shrugged off a little irritation. "She's not mine."

"And why not?"

"Because she doesn't belong to me, for heaven's sake!"

"Oh, but she does, in the sense that she would use the word. Or perhaps 'belong with' would express it better." The phouka smiled, as if at a thought that pleased him. "It's the custom of brownies, in the common way of things, to attach themselves to a household or a person. Of course, your situation cannot be called quite in the common way. But the effect remains the same."

Eddi frowned at the floor. "Do you mean she thinks she owes me this? I saved her life, maybe, but I didn't buy her."

He didn't answer, and she looked up at him. He was wearing another of his inscrutable faces. "All of this is more amusing than you can know, sweet," he said at last. "No, you've not bought her, though the Folk understand fair exchange, and we've an obsession with paying our debts to the penny, meeting the obligations of favors and barter. What we're bad at is gratitude. It is a cultural phenomenon of many parts, some of them contradictory. In a world where each word is powerful, still the words 'thank you' are not thought sufficient to cancel a debt. We have no concept of giving without thought or need of return."

The phouka fell silent. He seemed absorbed, as if his explanation continued in his head and he was listening to it.

"What does this have to do with Meg?" Eddi asked him, but gently.

"Ah. We've lived close to humankind for long and long. Things of which we cannot conceive sometimes become part of us anyway. Sometimes we find ourselves with an obligation that has no clear value, with a dreadful itchy feeling of indebtedness that cannot be bartered away. We feel *grateful*. And having no reliance on those two precious human words, we each deal with that feeling in whatever way suits best." He smiled then. "I believe Meg is dealing with hers."

She found herself looking into his black eyes, unnervingly close. A stillness fell over her, and over him as well, it seemed; the smile slid from his lips, and she saw the quick motion of his chest as he drew a breath.

Eddi remembered another such moment, under a bridge at Minnehaha Falls. She found herself wanting to ask, *And how do you deal with your gratitude?* The answer that occurred to her was good and logical, at least by the crackbrained logic the phouka swore by. Why should such a clever insight be so depressing?

She stood up abruptly, and was careful not to look at the phouka as she did it. "I have to call Carla," she said. It was too early in the day to call her, but she didn't think the phouka knew it.

So she told Carla's answering machine that Carla should call her back. Then she hung up the phone, and stood for a moment with her hand on the receiver. The mood in the room had changed. *I ought to say something. We should iron it out now.* She went to the bedroom to get dressed instead.

She put on jeans and a sweatshirt, and brushed her hair. Her face looked pale and unfinished in the bathroom mirror. "Tough," she told it. "Nobody you have to impress."

She sat on the bed and stared out the window. Then she took the Hoffman from its stand and cradled it in her lap, put it in tune, and played a few careful, random chords. *So these are the hands that make people dance. Hah.* An arpeggio spilled from her fingers, as if of its own volition. She followed the notes around for a while, until she realized that she was staying in a minor key.

Why should it bother you if he's playing at being in love? God knows he does it better than Willy did. Hell, he does a better job than Stuart, and for a while at least, Stuart really was in love. She chopped out a flurry of barre chords down the neck. *Is it that you wish he weren't playing?*

She put the guitar down and left the bedroom.

The phouka was leaning by the window. Something in his pose said that it was only a rest from pacing.

All that was left of Meg were the currant buns in the kitchen wrapped for warmth in a cotton towel; a pot of coffee; and a drainer full of clean dishes. Or at least, that was all of Meg that Eddi could see. Did she leave the apartment? If so, she didn't seem to do it by the front door.

Eddi gathered up plates, the buns, and the butter dish, and took them out to the table. The phouka stayed at the window. After another trip to the kitchen for the coffee, she sat down and began to butter a bun. "Breakfast," she said.

He sat down across from her, but ignored the food. Instead he studied the ceiling, both hands braced lightly against the table edge. "It may be," he said, "that you *should* have a new guard dog."

Eddi found herself staring at the butter knife in her hand. She set it down on the edge of her plate; it made a little ringing sound on the china. "Why?" she said.

"I've done what I meant to do," he replied, quite calm. "I've brought you as far as this, and given you all the advantages I can. Perhaps it's time you had a more . . . comfortable bodyguard."

"Comfortable. You have someone in mind?"

He looked at her warily, possibly warned by her tone. "Nooo. But there are denizens of Faerie who are less provoking than I am, if only a little."

They stared at each other across the table. "I suppose, if there's someplace you'd rather be . . . ," Eddi said carefully.

"One place is much like another," he said, but she saw him bite his lip before he spoke.

After a long, uncomfortable moment, Eddi asked him, "Do you *want* to leave?"

He closed his eyes. "No."

A little knot of tension untied itself in her shoulders. "Then shut up and eat," she said, and handed him a currant bun.

He took it from her as if it was part of some private, solemn joke.

Eddi turned off Twenty-fifth onto Garfield and pulled up to the curb.

"Pleasant," the phouka said, looking around at the boulevard trees, the bits of lawn, and the shabby-genteel old houses. "More so, I regret to say, than your neighborhood." He must have noticed the set of her lips, because he added quickly, "But I'm very fond of your neighborhood, certainly."

"Well, good, because I can't afford this one."

The phouka smoothed back his wind-tossed hair with both hands. "Does Carla have more money than you do?"

"She drives cabs part-time."

The phouka frowned and cocked his head. "Cabs?"

"Cabs are . . . cars you pay somebody else to drive you around in."

"Oh. When I think of cabs, I think of horse-drawn conveyances for hire."

"You do?" Eddi said.

"I do."

"How old *are* you?"

The question startled him. "Earth and Air. There are times when you are no more comfortable a companion than I am. The answer to that serves no conceivable purpose, and I refuse to give it to you."

"When I was a kid, I read *Black Beauty*. There were horse-drawn cabs in that. Are you that old?"

He sighed deeply. "Older."

"How much older?"

"Older, older, older. I shall *not* tell you, so you may as well leave off, my primrose."

She snorted. "I think that means I should give up. You've started sweet-talking."

"I am torn," the phouka said, grinning, "between responding, 'Oh, absolutely,' and 'What do you mean, *started?*'" He grabbed her hand, dropped a kiss on the knuckles, and loped across the street. Eddi felt the touch of his mouth on her hand for an inexplicably long time.

Carla lived in what had probably been intended as a duplex. But in South Minneapolis, attics frequently became studio apartments. Carla's had a big arched window at the front of the house, dormers along one side, and a back door to the outside stairway. In summer, she had to open all of them, and was fond of explaining that it turned the place from a conventional oven to a convection one.

Eddi followed the phouka up the front stairway, which was carpeted in faded red and had a comfortably dusty, Victorian smell. On Carla's door, at the top of the stairs, was a door knocker in the shape of a lacquered wooden face with a sappy expression. When the cord that dangled out of its grin was pulled, it opened its mouth and stuck out its tongue with a loud clack. The phouka found this delightful. Eddi had to whack his hand to keep him from pulling the cord several more times.

"Come in!" Carla yelled.

It was a pleasant apartment, all Carla's jokes aside. It was shaped by the angles of the eaves and the stubby fingers of the dormers. The walls were white, the floor a checkerboard of black and white linoleum tiles interrupted by the big rag rug in the front half of the room.

On one wall hung a papier-mâché mask of a unicorn's head with mane, forelock and chin whiskers of curly white hair, and a gilded horn tied with multicolored ribbon; another wall sported an old hooked rug depicting a moose, a lake, and what were either pine trees or pointy green mountains. A collection of little cast-metal toy cars competed for space with books, magazines, and comic books.

Carla greeted them with, "I've got money for last night, and two more gigs, also on account of last night."

"I feel like I'm living in a movie musical," Eddi said. "Is this what I've been paying my dues for?"

"Don't jinx us, girl, we're not famous yet. Anyway, have a seat. Coffee?"

They nodded in unison.

Eddi watched Carla take a couple of running steps and slide sock-footed across the kitchen linoleum. "Ah . . . is it just band business that's made you giddy?"

"Me? I'm not giddy."

"Uh-huh," Eddi said. *Yes, you are. Dan must be a nice guy. If he's not, I'll kick him down the stairs.*

The door knocker clacked, and Dan's voice called out from the other side. "Yo! It's me!" Carla opened it to reveal Dan in the hall, a grocery bag in each arm and his glasses sliding down his nose. Carla pushed the glasses back up and took one of the bags.

"I couldn't find the weird noodles," he told her. Then he saw Eddi and the phouka, and grinned. "Oh, hiya."

Eddi watched them empty the bags on the counter. They seemed at once comfortable and shy with each other—though perhaps the shyness was only because she was there to watch them. Eddi hadn't realized how intimate the business of putting away the groceries could be.

Dan got a beer from the refrigerator and dropped down in a canvas chair across from Eddi. "So, any idea when the other guys're gonna get here?"

Eddi shrugged and looked at the phouka. "You're the one who delivered the message. How *did* you deliver the message, anyway?"

"Paper airplane," the phouka replied.

Then they heard a quick, light tread on the stairs, and knuckles on the door panel. "Bingo," Carla muttered, and called out, "Come in!"

And Willy stood in the doorway, tall, slender, the perfect Romantic hero. He wore a white shirt with the sleeves rolled up and the neck open, a skinny black tie knotted loose, tight black denims, and black high-top sneakers. His hair was in his eyes again, black and white like the rest of him. His gaze fell on Eddi first, though she was hardly in the spot most visible from the door. It was a grave look, but there was no accusation in it, no anger. Eddi felt the phouka's stillness next to her. She smiled at Willy. She couldn't remember ever having to judge a smile so carefully as that one. After a moment, Willy answered with one of his own. Eddi heard the phouka exhale.

"Hullo, all," Willy said. He sat down on a bench under the front windows. The light behind him made it hard to see his face; it lit the streak of white in his hair and made the shoulders of his white shirt glow. "Before we get to business," Willy said, his voice oddly constrained, "I've been directed to invite you all to a party."

They stared.

"A month from last night, exactly, in Tower Hill Park. Fun starts at full dark. And there'll be music; I suggest you bring things to make it with."

"A month from—," Carla began, but the phouka interrupted.

"Midsummer's Eve," he said softly. "It's decided, isn't it?"

Willy nodded. "Three days after Midsummer's Day."

"Where?" the phouka demanded.

"Como Park."

Eddi was watching the phouka's face, looking for clues, wanting to know what was good news and what was bad. This was the date and place of the next battle. But she didn't understand the puzzlement on the phouka's face.

"Como Park is under our dominion," the phouka said at last.

Willy raised an eyebrow and nodded.

"And only three days after Midsummer—Oak and Ash, why has she given us every advantage?"

"What're you talking about?" Dan said.

The phouka explained quickly. "But *why?*" he asked Willy once again. "If the Dark Lady wanted to cede this battle to us, there are easier ways. What does she want?"

Willy shrugged, but his voice was at odds with the gesture. "To throw us off our stride, maybe. To make us nervous. I don't know."

Eddi stood up, paced across the room to a dormer window and back. "What I want to know," she said at last "is who came up with the party invitation?"

Willy raised his head. "Beg your pardon?"

"Who is it who wants the noncombatants involved?" Eddi gestured at Dan and Carla. "Was this the Wicked Witch's idea?"

"Midsummer's Eve is one of the truces," Willy said, but not as if he thought it answered her.

"Big damn deal. Whether there's shooting going on or not, there's no reason for them to have anything to do with Faerie."

"Already do," someone said hoarsely behind her. She turned to find Hedge in the door, glowering at her through his hair. He used his chin to point at Carla and Dan.

"The kid's right," Carla said. "Look at us. Here's bloody Tam Lin on my left"—she nodded toward Willy—"and the Kennel Club's answer to Mr. Ed in front of me. I dunno what Hedge does, but I'm sure it's something good. And they're all drinking coffee and chatting it up in my living room." Carla came out from behind Dan's chair, walked over, took hold of Eddi's shoulders, and gave her a little shake. "And then there's my best friend. Friendship comes from shared experience, right? So what am I supposed to say when my mother wants to know why I don't hang around with you anymore? 'Oh, you know. She got a little fey, and we just drifted apart.' "

Eddi shook her head. "I don't want to have to say that I got a little fey, and you got a little dead."

Carla looked down, and shrugged. "Well, neither do I. But this is a party. If there's a truce on, it's safer than a lot of parties I've been to."

"I can't stop you, can I?"

"No."

"You're a jerk," Eddi said gently. "Watch your step, then. These people are weird."

"I know that. I work with three of 'em." But Carla nodded once, unsmiling, and Eddi felt better.

CHAPTER SIXTEEN

Party Up

It was the reviews that startled her. The quality of Eddi and the Fey was easy to get used to. The almost telepathic musical unity that enabled them to pick up an idea and run with it, their growing sense of showmanship, the development of a group style and a characteristic sound—Eddi felt comfortable with those. It was the reviews that were strange.

They were good reviews; they came as close to gushing as reviewers ever did. What bothered Eddi was the praise for things that weren't there. The additional voices that the reviewer thought were from the digital sampler. The electric fiddle part on a song that didn't have one. The lighting effects.

"What lighting effects?" Eddi wailed from the depths of the couch in the practice space. "I can understand the rest of it—Dan does enough neat stuff with the keyboards that you could mistake it for almost anything. Especially if you were busy dancing, which God knows they all were." She propped herself up on one elbow and lectured Dan, Carla, Willy, and the phouka. "You notice that not one reviewer has admitted to spending the whole night dancing."

"Whatsisname came close, in *City Pages*," Dan said generously.

"Hah. They're all afraid it'll ruin their reputation for critical reserve. But where did they get the lighting effects?"

Carla was tuning her drumheads. "Maybe," (thump) "whoever was running," (thump) "sound was playing," (thump, thump) "with the lights, too."

"The Uptown's got a fixed light setup—once you focus 'em, they're either on or off. They could have done more than that at the benefit, but nobody did."

Willy, who was sitting on his amp, looked at the phouka. The phouka looked at the floor.

215

"Uh-huh," Eddi said, glaring at them both. "Enough with the conspiracy of silence. What have you been doing?"

The phouka smiled up at her, a glowing look that nearly robbed her of breath. But it was Willy who answered her.

"We haven't done a thing. You have."

Eddi stared at him.

"Yes, you have. They're your images. Or in some cases, sounds. When you're wrapped up in making music, there's more of you in it than you think." Willy stretched his long legs out before him and leaned back. "You're casting illusions."

She looked at Carla. Eddi could no longer scoff at the possibility of magic—she'd promised the phouka she wouldn't. But Carla was free to doubt assertions like Willy's.

Carla only said, "She is?"

"Mmm. Just be glad she started with illusions. If her subconscious was dabbling in the elements, she could have set the Uptown on fire."

"Rubbish," the phouka said cheerfully. "With all due respect, of course. You know perfectly well that manipulating the elements is conjuring of a high intellectual order. It does *not* happen by accident." Eddi suspected that the last sentence was for her benefit. She was grateful; it was nice to know that she wouldn't burn down her apartment building in her sleep.

"So, how did I know how to do this?" Eddi asked, more or less of the phouka. "Have you been whispering in my ear?"

He shook his head irritably. "Were you taught to pull yourself upright, or to crawl?"

"It's not the same. Those are normal developments."

The phouka raised one eyebrow.

"This isn't normal," Eddi snapped.

Willy rose from his amp, a quick, impatient movement. "Does it matter? You've got power, you've started to use it. Learn to control it, before somebody does it for you." He ducked under the strap of his guitar and began to play scales.

"How likely is that?" Eddi said.

Willy's hands stopped, and he looked up. His face was suddenly made younger with doubt and concern. "I'm not sure. But I know it can be done. And if I know, then it's certain *she* does."

Eddi didn't have to ask who "she" was. "Then I suppose I'd better start practicing."

There was a rattle of feet coming fast up the iron stairs

outside. Eddi stopped halfway from the couch to her guitar; Willy and the phouka were suddenly still as well. When the door opened, it was only Hedge, and Eddi could see the tension go out of her bodyguards.

"Hello," Eddi said, "you're late."

Hedge ducked his head and looked embarrassed. He was even messier than usual, his brown hair every which way, his gray sleeveless sweatshirt dark with sweat down the middle, grass stains on his jeans. "Sorry," he mumbled, and shot her a look full of appeal.

"It's okay. We haven't started yet, anyway. What kept you?"

He turned his amp on and picked up the Steinberger. "Midsummer's Eve," he muttered, as if that explained everything.

Dan grinned. "Been rollin' beer kegs, huh?"

Hedge turned one of his smiles on, and when he spoke, he was as close to laughing as Eddi had ever heard him. "Beer, whoo! Gonna be s'prised. One big blowout t'night!"

"Uh-oh." Carla shook her head at Dan. "I don't know if I should let you go, Party Boy."

"Gonna have to carry you home—you better let me go."

Eddi turned to quiet them down and start practice. She paused when she saw Willy. He was watching Dan and Carla with an odd, stricken look, a mingling of recognition and regret. Then he dropped his gaze, squatted beside his amplifier, and toyed with the midrange control.

"You guys want to warm up with something," Eddi said gruffly, "or work on the new one?"

"New one!" Dan said promptly. "Let's do some motorcycle music."

They knew the tune and the words; now it was time for the real work, the business of making the song sound like Eddi and the Fey. Eddi gave them her rough outline for the arrangement; they worked the parts over, and put it all together.

Dan played a keyboard line like a question that demanded an answer, and Willy punctuated it with a harsh chord. After two of those, Carla joined Willy with a distant growl of thunder on one of her toms. Hedge's bass began to throb with the hungry rhythm of tuned engines and tires on pavement seams. There was the digitally sampled crash of a cymbal that went on and on, glass breaking in slow motion—and the band welled up behind it like water, into the first verse.

Fantasies of violence,
Breaking bottles on the wall,
Hungry for the motion, for the action,
For it all.

Road noise on the night street,
See the taillights through the blinds,
Out there where your dreams slide
Toward the night side,
For it all.

Eddi launched into the chorus looking for the effects of her magic. She saw, heard, felt nothing. A quick glance at the phouka, where he sat on the dilapidated couch, gave her no clues.

For it all, for it all,
What you're aching for,
Where the magic's real and you're like a fire in the sky,
when the deal calls for a sacrifice
And you know you cannot die.
For the edge the best ones live on,
For it all.

You want to be a hero
With the axe about to fall,
You'd buy it for the love and for the glory,
For it all.

You want to dress in black
And lose your heart beyond recall,
Hunt a dream through rain and thunder,
On your honor
For it all.

Would she feel it? Would there be a tingle, or the stinging feeling she'd had when the Seelie Court's power swirled around her? Another chorus, and the bridge:

In your head, no car is fast enough,
In your heart, no love is true.
Will it ruin all your solitary fancies
If I tell you that it isn't only you?

Keep your ankle off the tailpipe,
Keep your bootheels off the street;
We'll hit the throttle, hit the redline,
We'll find the edge,
We'll make it sweet,
We'll go for it all.

Properly, the song would fade out, with Hedge's bass the last thing to go, roaring off into distance. They simulated it with instruments dropping out one by one, Hedge leaning on his volume pedal, then backing off slowly. Carla added a tattoo on the bell of one cymbal, very soft, at the end.

"Good," Eddi told her. "Keep that. Willy, not so much early Pete Townshend on the lead break."

"Aww."

"Next pass we add harmonies." Eddi looked around her microphone at the phouka. "Well?" she asked him.

He said, "Lovely."

"I didn't mean the song. Did I do anything weird?"

"No," he replied, grinning.

They did the song twice more, taking it apart and putting it back together. After each one, Eddi stole a look at the phouka, who shook his head. "Break," she declared at last, in disgust, and went to sit next to him.

"What am I doing wrong?"

"Nothing, my primrose. It's an excellent song, and it's taking shape wonderfully."

Eddi stared at him sternly until he began to laugh.

"Oh, my heart, my heart. You want magic to dance at the end of a stick for your pleasure. Tell me, are you performing? Are you gathering up the music and flinging it out to your audience, as if it were a truth you wanted them to believe?"

She was furious with him for laughing, and refused at first to follow his logic. But he grabbed her wrists when she moved to stand up, and shook them gently.

"Willy's words to the contrary, matters are not at so desperate a pass. Pay no attention to making magic, Eddi. Make music, and let the magic come when it will."

"What if it never comes?"

The phouka looked down at her hands, released his grip, and glanced quickly up again. "Then perhaps you'll never need it."

Whether or not she would ever do magic, she did none that

afternoon. Once, during the last verse of the new song, she felt the narrowing of her concentration that she often felt onstage—as if the song, and the space in which it echoed, and the duration of it, were the whole world. But when she noticed, wondering *Is this it?*, it was gone.

It was a long, hard practice, and the breeze through all the windows that would open was warm. When she called a halt at seven, Eddi felt like a damp bathroom rug. "Go home, guys," she said. "We've got a party to go to tonight."

"Tower Hill Park at dusk?" Carla asked.

Willy shook his head. "Not dusk. Wait until full dark." His smile had little amusement in it. "The truce begins at sunset. Don't risk getting there too early—you might tempt fate."

Dan stole a glance at Carla. "Oh my. What'll we do to pass the time?"

"Let's go home and soak your head," Carla said, blushing. "We're gone, guys."

Eddi heard them giggling as they went down the stairs, heard their voices, though what they said didn't reach her. Hedge put his equipment away and nodded to Eddi. "See ya," he said, almost clearly, and went down the stairs.

She moved around the room, unplugging the coffee pot, closing windows. Willy, to her surprise, made no move to leave; he sat on his amp, angled over his guitar, playing softly. She recognized the melody after a moment, though she couldn't name it. A folk song, about a woman who swore she'd never marry because her lover was drowned at sea. . . . "Quitting time," she told him gently.

He smiled, but didn't look up. "I'll lock it. You go on home."

Eddi studied him a moment, then looked over his head at the phouka. She nodded toward the door. He frowned. But he went out, and she heard his boots banging on the metal stairs.

"Something wrong?" she asked Willy.

He stopped playing for a moment. "No, not really," he murmured. He began to play again, and she found she knew that song, too.

"There was a battle in the north," she sang softly, and he joined her for the rest of the verse:

And nobles there were many.
And they have killed Sir Johnny Hay
And laid the blame on Geordie.

He shook his head. "Do your people ever write songs about anything besides love and death?" A thread of impatience ran through his voice, side by side with something else.

"Now and then."

"Couldn't prove it by me." His hands were still again, and he looked away, out the window. "And sometimes it seems as if I know them all. Funny, no?"

Eddi studied his profile, sharp as a paper cutout against the lengthening shadows. An earring swung from his left ear—Eddi recognized it as the device on his armor, the three interlaced crescent moons. The silver gleamed like liquid against the dark side of his face.

His shoulders moved with a shrug, or a sigh. Then he turned back to her. "They're in love, aren't they?"

It took her a minute to figure that out. "Carla and Dan?"

He nodded, intent on her answer.

"It looks like it, anyway."

His mouth got tight, and he frowned. "Isn't that enough?"

Eddi began to see what the conversation was about. "It's not that easy, Willy. Only they know if they're in love—and I'll bet that neither of them knows for sure yet if the other is."

Willy stared at her. Then he laughed, as if it was forced out of him. "Oh, Oak and Ash." He looked away again, this time toward the muddle of the band's equipment. "They make each other happy," he said at last.

"It's not that easy, either. They make each other angry and sad, too. If they don't, then it doesn't go as deep as love."

After a long and thoughtful pause, he said, "Were you in love with me?"

"Not . . . really," she said finally, and knew it was true.

"Well, that's something solid to go on, at least." He laughed again, with barely a lungful of air. "After all those damn songs, I thought I ought to understand either love or death. And I'd rather study love."

Eddi wanted to say something comforting, but the conversation made her nervous. She found herself waiting for Willy to suggest they try again, to ask if she couldn't forgive his mistakes and fall into his arms once more. She was completely unprepared for what he actually said.

It was, "And the phouka?"

Eddi stared. "What?"

"Do you love him?"

Her legs had turned either to stone or to Jell-O; the effect was the same. She wanted to stand up and couldn't. And whatever had done it to her legs had affected her mouth as well.

"You tell me that I can't judge by appearances. But if I had to gamble, I'd bet that the phouka is in love with you. And you were very different with me than you are with him." Willy spoke with the intensity so characteristic of him, and his green eyes searched hers as if hunting through them for the truth. "Tell me what all that means."

Her legs did work, after all; she got up and paced to the windows and back. "If you were just a goddamn guitarist, I'd tell you to mind your own business."

Willy shrugged. "Maybe you ought to, anyway."

"Well, as long as you're feeling insightful, what should I do about him?" She heard the edge in her voice and regretted it.

"I think . . . what you did about me."

"Namely?"

His face looked young, innocent, and not at all human. "What you think is right."

The low sun cast hot bars of butter-colored light through the windows. Dust swung slowly through each beam.

"I'll try," Eddi said. She walked across the room to the door, making the dust motes leap and churn. "Don't forget to lock up."

As she stepped out on the stairs, she heard his guitar begin again on "Geordie."

The phouka stood at the bottom of the stairs, his face turned up to her. His brown skin glowed copper in the late sun, and his eyes were round and dark and enormous. The look in them made her chest ache.

"Nothing amiss?" he said when she was close enough, and he could speak softly.

"I don't know. I don't think so." Which was the truth, after all. She hoped.

It wasn't easy to ride a motorcycle in a great deal of skirt. Eddi had tucked most of it under her knees or sat on it. But the two top layers slipped free, and the night wind caught them, until she and the phouka seemed to be riding in a levitating mist of sheer midnight blue, enhanced by the silver crescent moon and embroidered stars that spangled the chiffon.

"Where did you find this enchanting whimsy?" the phouka

said at a stoplight, staring bemused at a drift of skirt across his knee.

"D'you like it?"

"Very much."

"You could try it on."

"Pestilent flower," he smiled.

"I found it at a vintage clothing store. I think it must have come from a dance company or something." She was pleased that he liked it, and embarrassed that she was pleased. "You said I should wear something I can dance in."

"Not precisely. I said you should wear something you *like* to dance in. I think highly of this velvet thing you're wearing on top, too." At that point the light changed, and it wasn't until the next stop sign that he could add, "But the low back—unfair of you, my primrose, decidedly. And me with one arm around your waist, and the other around your guitar."

She let the clutch out a little too fast, and the bike leaped away from the stop sign. "I beg your pardon, I do." He laughed next to her ear. "You needn't toss me into the street. I shall behave."

"Hah!" Eddi replied, but she wasn't sure he heard.

They were past the university campus, very close to Tower Hill Park. Something like stage fright scrabbled across Eddi's stomach. She had shared a battlefield with the creatures of Faerie, but nothing else. She was the Angel of Death. What possible place could she have in their celebrating?

Tower Hill rose up from the middle of the park like a gem from its setting. Green-fire lace edged the sidewalk and the curbing. Inside that barrier Eddi could see lights in subtle hues, and mist like colored veiling lit from within. Each tree was outlined in luminous gold; each leaf was a pale green lamp. At the summit the witch-hat tower that gave the park its name rose against the night-blue sky, and each of the arched, glassless windows around the top gleamed with faint silver.

"Good . . . God," Eddi gasped. She found she'd pulled over and stopped the bike, which was probably wise. "What the hell do the neighbors think?"

The phouka laughed. "Silly primrose. The hill is dark and quiet tonight—not even lovers abroad. And if any should venture by, the place will have no appeal for them."

"And I can see it all." She turned suddenly to the phouka. "Or is all of that illusion?"

"No. It's quite real. Tonight, the dark is illusion." His voice was charged with something she couldn't identify. She revved the bike and swung out from the curb, toward the glittering hill.

Eddi pulled in to the curb on Malcolm Avenue between the park and an old school. "Can we cross that?" she asked, nodding at the green border.

"Come and see," the phouka replied. She followed him across the sidewalk.

Now that she was closer, Eddi saw that the barrier of light was not the same as the one that had circled Minnehaha Falls. That one had been a curtain of deep emerald. These were dancing flames of delicate golden green, with faint lavender showing at the edges. The phouka set down her guitar case and dropped to one knee before the barrier. With a murmured word, he touched a stone that lay just outside the line. The blaze sank and drew back, like courtiers bowing and withdrawing before a king. They stood at the foot of a path that climbed the hill in front of them.

"O most admir'd of mortals," the phouka said, grinning up at her. "If it please you?"

"Silly nit," she said. She took his hand and pulled him to his feet, and inside the barrier of light. It leaped up again behind him.

He looked shy suddenly, which made her feel, unaccountably, the same. His hand was warm in hers, the skin very smooth. She let go of it. "So," she said quickly, "you said you'd change when we got here."

"What would you like me to become?" he said, blandly innocent.

"Hah hah. Dressed up."

"Ah. Turn your back then, my sweet."

After a moment, she did. The taffeta layer of her skirt whispered coolly against her calves in the night breeze, and strands of her hair patted her face. Moonlight lit the slope before her, and street lights, and a certain lambency of the grass blades themselves. She felt weightless.

"Very well," the phouka said carefully, and she turned around.

He stood across the path from her, his chin up, his hands playing unconsciously with a blade of grass. He was transformed. No, he was still himself. But to say only that he'd changed his clothes—it wouldn't explain his air of elegance, or his sudden reserve.

His coat was of dark green brocade, embroidered with flowers and strange creatures in dim, subtle colors. It looked like a garden seen at night. The sleeves had deep turned-back cuffs of black, ornamented with silver buttons. He wore it open, over a black waistcoat and tiers of heavy white lace at his throat. More lace spilled out from under the cuffs and frothed over his fingers, where the silver of rings glittered. His pants were black satin, close-fitting and embroidered with silver down one outside seam.

He moved his head abruptly, and light flashed off silver in one earlobe. For a moment he seemed some haughty stranger. Then she recognized the nervousness in him, and he was once again her phouka.

"Gorgeous," she said softly, as if he were an animal she didn't want to startle. "If you'd worn that on the way over, we'd have a trail of broken hearts behind us."

He laughed, and ducked his head. "Is that a very long way of saying I'm conspicuous? That's why I waited, you know."

"Since when have you cared about being conspicuous?"

"Well, I don't, then. I'd rather be gorgeous." He offered her his arm. They went up the hill together, through groves of young trees with leaves that rang like windchimes.

The path divided, and they took the lower, right-hand one that circled the hill. Eddi heard voices, laughter, music from around the grassy shoulder, and all her earlier doubts and suspicions returned. She stopped beside a retaining wall of railroad ties. "Phouka."

She wasn't sure what he'd heard in her voice, but he turned to her immediately and lifted an eyebrow.

"What am I going to find when I get around that corner?"

"There are no nasty surprises lying in wait for you, sweet. We are under a truce."

"I don't mean *those* kind of surprises. Why should I be invited to this party? How are they"—she nodded up the hill—"going to treat me?"

The phouka sat on the retaining wall. "Are you afraid of them?" he asked her, not as if he believed it.

"No. But if I were one of the Seelie Court, I'd spit in my face. Come on, Phouka," Eddi said, when he continued puzzled, "I'm the girl who makes it possible for them all to die in battle."

"Yes, you are. We sought you out and made you part of Faerie that you might do so." He ran a hand through his hair and smiled at her. "You've set me a devilish task, my primrose. We are never easily explained. We do not live in the past, yet we can hold a grudge for an unimaginably long time. We despise mortals, and we revere them. Is it enough for you, if I tell you that it is no more than your right to be here, that no one will think it odd, that you will have a very good time, and that those around you will do likewise?''

She studied his face. He was happy, she decided, happiness unalloyed with worry or mischief or bitterness. Given the circumstances, she hadn't seen that mood on him lately. "Will you?"

He blinked. "Will I what?"

"Have a good time, dummy. Are you here as a bodyguard, or a guest?"

"Oh, a guest, certainly," he grinned. Then he looked quickly down. "Of course, if you would prefer that I remain near you, I would not object—merely as a courtesy, you understand."

She watched as he nudged a pebble with the toe of one glossy black boot. "Good idea," she said finally. "I don't know a lot of people here."

He raised his head and gave her a brilliant look, and Eddi decided that neither one of them was fooling the other.

They rounded the shoulder of the hill. The sloping land before them was full of color and soft lights. Eddi saw pinpoints of brightness like candles in the branches of shrubs and trees. There were the tinted mists she'd seen from the street, too; they were spangled as if with fireflies, and drifted lazily between the tree trunks or tangled in the leaves. The trees themselves shone faintly. There was a bonfire laid and ready to light in the middle of the open area. Around it, and under the trees, the revellers had gathered.

Eddi had forgotten the wild variety of the hosts of Faerie. She saw a tall, spindly figure that might have been a close relative of birch trees; its swallowtail coat was too short for it, and its broad-brimmed hat too large. There was a little creature dressed in a musk ox pelt, or perhaps its own hair. There was a slender naked woman with blue-black skin and white hair to her shoulders, shining whiteless eyes, and long ears like a fox.

"Someday," Eddi murmured, "you should meet *my* family."

At the corner of her vision she saw a familiar silver-gray, and turned quickly to look. One of the long-snouted, many-toothed creatures, a gray-skinned Unseelie fey of the sort she most feared, stalked through the throng. No one challenged it; no one spoke to it at all. It continued on toward the other side of the park.

"They're here, too?" Eddi found enough voice to say.

"It is a truce, my primrose. And they are as much of Faerie as I am." But Eddi thought it made him nervous, too.

Then Carla loped toward them out of the crowd, with Dan following behind. " 'Bout time!" Carla crowed and hugged her. "You look swell!"

"So do you," Eddi said. Carla wore a red strapless dress that looked splendid with her dark hair and eyes. Dan had found a black tuxedo somewhere, and a formal white bow tie. He wore them with a Hawaiian shirt. "Funky," Eddi assured him.

"Not as funky as Rover here," Carla said, eyeing the phouka's lace with a little grin.

"Well, I like it," Eddi told her.

"Thank you," the phouka said gravely.

"Hedge is here," Carla said. "And my God, so is everything else." She turned to Eddi. "Some of these people are . . . oh, never mind. I guess you already know. But my God, Eddi—!"

Dan gave Carla's shoulders a squeeze. "She means this is some great shit. Weird, though. It's like there's something in the air—like you could get bombed just from breathing."

He was right, Eddi realized. It was as if the altitude had changed, as if the air were thinner, purer, intoxicating.

"Have you been here long?" the phouka asked Dan.

"Nah. Long enough to dump the equipment." He pointed at a heap of things under a bush—a remarkably small heap, for Dan. "It won't get ripped off, will it?"

The phouka glanced at Eddi, an almost penitent look. "No. Whatever our temptations, we don't steal from our guests. We also do not steal from each other, so if no one objects, I'll leave the guitar there as well. Then I'll present you to the Lady."

The Queen of Faerie. Eddi remembered her, in all her icy rage, at Minnehaha Falls. The memory sent her hurrying after the phouka. "Do you have to?" she said, softly enough that Carla and Dan wouldn't hear her.

The phouka said gently, "She won't eat you, dear one, truly."

"Says you. The last time I saw her, she was thinking seriously about it."

"Oh, then." He waved the suggestion away. "I've told you, we've no taste for living in the past."

"And you hold a grudge forever."

"Havers, as Meg would say. What if she is still nursing a sense of ill-usage? She'll not do anything about it tonight, sweet.

Besides—'' He set her guitar case down, turned to her, and put a fingertip under her chin. ''You may attack Royalty, or deny its will, but you must never, never ignore it.''

''Makes her mad, huh?''

The phouka laughed. ''On that heartening note . . .'' He turned to Carla and Dan. ''We got to meet the Queen of Faerie. Be polite, circumspect, and above all, follow my lead.''

Carla and Dan raised their eyebrows at each other. ''Lead on, boss,'' Carla said at last.

They threaded their way through the revellers and around the bottom of the hill. They emerged on the side of the park that faced University Avenue. Here the land was flat and open, the grass still lush even after weeks of summer heat. There was a game of something in progress; two teams of the Folk were engaged in what seemed a cross between horseshoes and field hockey, played with enormous stones. Yelling was apparently part of the game.

Before them, a crabapple tree stood in a smokelike, fragrant cloud of blossom. A bank of spirea bloomed ghostly white beyond it. ''Wait a minute,'' Carla muttered, ''those quit flowering a month ago.''

''Sshhh,'' Eddi warned. The Lady stood beneath the crabapple, flanked by her glittering court. They were watching the game. After one particularly long throw, the queen smiled and made some comment. Clear, breaking-crystal laughter rang out from the group around her. She wore a close-fitting, one-shouldered satin gown, barely tinted the color of new willow leaves. Her blood-red hair was loose, and it fell to her knees. Against that backdrop her shoulders and bare arms were white as new-cut marble. And her face, so inhumanly beautiful in all its curves and angles . . . Willy's was a copy of it, but a copy several generations removed. A little humanity had slipped into his face, if only in his expressions.

They were perhaps ten feet from the gathered court when the phouka dropped to one knee and bowed his head. Eddi followed him, her dark skirts spreading out around her like water. Carla and Dan, after a moment's surprise, also knelt. Eddi heard the hiss of moving satin. The hem of the queen's gown and the tips of her embroidered shoes appeared at the top of Eddi's vision, but she waited for the lovely, cold voice before she raised her head.

''Eddi McCandry. You are welcome among us.''

You couldn't tell it from listening to you, Eddi thought wryly, but only said, "That pleases me, Lady."

Did that white face thaw a bit? "Introduce your companions to us."

Eddi was sure she knew their names already. "Carla DiAmato, Lady, an old friend and my favorite drummer. And Dan Rochelle, keyboard player for Eddi and the Fey."

The queen's lips thinned a little at that. "Presumptuous, certainly, to name yourselves so."

"We didn't intend any disrespect, Lady," Eddi said. In the face of the queen's opposition, she was suddenly delighted with the band's name. "And even Willy didn't seem to think there was anything wrong with it."

"Willy Silver," the queen said gently, looking down her perfect nose, "has not always conducted himself as we would like."

The phouka moved a little at Eddi's side; she couldn't tell if it was impatience or nerves. "Lady," Eddi began, "if you mean losing the horse, he—"

"This is too solemn a topic for a festive night. We shall have dancing soon—may we ask that you and your friends lead off the music, Eddi McCandry?"

"We'd be pleased to," Eddi said, since there was no real reason to refuse.

"Very well." The queen turned one white hand up, managing to indicate the entire park with the gesture. "Partake freely of all that pleases you here, and let your friends do likewise."

Eddi swallowed a "thank you," and said simply, "We will."

The phouka rose, and offered a hand to help her up. "Back up three paces and bow," he whispered in her ear. She shot a quick warning look at Dan and Carla, and stepped backward. It might not have mattered; the queen had turned away. But her attendants still watched, if surreptitiously.

Whatever they did, it must have been good enough. After the three paces, they might not have existed, for all the attention the queen's court paid them. They headed back the way they came.

"Holy shit," Carla whispered. "That really was the Queen of Faerie. Wasn't it?"

The phouka shushed her. His face was full of wicked delight.

"What are you so pleased about?" Eddi grumbled under her breath.

"Later, my sweet. No, don't look daggers at me, I promise to tell you, but later. For now, I'd like a bit of refreshment. Courtliness is dry work."

In a grove of honeysuckle they found the beer, dark and creamy-headed as stout, in a tapped wooden keg. There was red wine, too, with a sharp, smoky fragrance; mead the color of amber; and other things that Eddi resolved to ask the phouka about later. He produced four silver cups from, apparently, nowhere, and Eddi filled hers with the beer.

"Common folk's refreshment," he teased her.

"Well, when all's said and done I'm pretty common."

"You don't look it. And I didn't mean to raise your hackles. I don't, in fact, mean to raise them at all tonight, though I may have set myself a hopeless task."

She swallowed some beer. It was bittersweet, rich enough to make a meal of, and dark in the bottom of the silver cup. Dark as the phouka's eyes. The notion startled her and she looked up, to find those eyes on her.

"Mortals were warned against this, once upon a time," he said softly. "Take no food or drink from Faerie hands. If you do, no other food will please you, and you will pine away for it and perish."

"Is it true?"

"You trust me for the truth, don't you?" He wore a curious twist of a smile. "Strange. And not entirely pleasant. To answer your question then, no, not literally, but there may be some poetic truth in it. What will you do, assuming you live through all of this, when our war is done and we withdraw from your life?"

Eddi took a deep breath and couldn't, for a moment, let it out. "I . . . hadn't thought about it."

"How odd. When first you made my acquaintance, you could think of nothing else."

He turned his cup in both hands, but didn't seem to be looking at it. The eldritch light of magic and the moon polished his hair and face, and brought the garden in his brocade coat to life.

"That was a while ago," Eddi said, feeling strangled.

He raised his eyes, and the mischief was back in them. "Time flies when you're having fun."

"Jerk." She swallowed some beer, and it helped break up the last of the lump in her throat. "Now what were you so pleased about, earlier?"

"After your audience with the Lady?"

Eddi nodded.

"Well, my sweet. Remember what passed, and tell me whom she chose to talk to." He let her think that over for a moment before he said, "Once she would have spoken almost solely to me. Low though my rank may be, I'm at least fey. Tonight she spoke to you, as she might to the emissary of another ruler, and I do not think she knew it herself. But those around her marked it, you may be sure."

Eddi frowned at him. "Which means what?"

"That the Queen of Faerie recognizes you as a power, and has spoken to you with respect. Others will follow her lead."

"Huh. That and a quarter will buy me a gumball." But she was impressed. She turned to look for Carla and Dan, and didn't find them.

"They've gone, I think, to unpack instruments," he said in response to her look. "There's a dancing mood growing on us all, and they may have felt it."

"And do you feel like dancing, too?"

"Oh," he said, raising an eyebrow, "I might."

The phouka offered her his arm, and they headed down the slope toward the unlit bonfire.

Dan had brought a Casio CZ series portable and an amp to play it through. Carla had a kobassa. "It's the only hand percussion in the house," she said ruefully. She gave it a quick slap-and-slide, rattle-and-hiss, across her hand. "I could have brought the snare, I guess, but that just makes me wish for the whole kit."

Eddi shook her head. "Violent Femmes used to use a washtub."

"I don't have a washtub. Maybe I'll beat on your head, instead."

"It's a thought. I'm not using it for anything."

Carla looked curious, but Eddi turned quickly to unpack her guitar. Dan gave her an *E* to tune to. *Now why did I say that?* she wondered. *I didn't mean it. Did I?* She remembered suddenly, unbidden, the phouka saying that love made mortals stupid. *Damn phouka.*

She looked up to find Hedge standing beside her. He wore a black T shirt and clean black jeans—dressed up, for him. At his side was a big-bellied acoustic bass guitar. The finish was dark with age, the fretboard worn, and she knew that this was the instrument that had taught him to draw such fearsome music out of the Steinberger. She smiled at him. He seemed surprised by that; cautiously, he smiled back.

"Only one short, then," Eddi said. "Where's Willy?"

Carla shrugged. "I haven't seen him, but that doesn't mean he's not here."

Eddi looked at the phouka, but he, too, shrugged. "Well, never mind. If he's here, he'll show up when the music starts."

As they moved closer to the bonfire, Eddi muttered to the phouka, "Any idea what might be keeping him?"

The phouka's expression was indecipherable. "None."

"If he's still sulking in the rehearsal space . . ."

"Is that what he was doing this afternoon? No, never mind. That's no business of mine." His brows drew down for a moment, then his face was impassive again.

"He wasn't sulking. That wasn't fair of me. He's pretty confused right now, and he's not used to it, that's all."

The phouka walked with his hands in his pockets, unnecessarily interested in the turf. "I know you haven't . . . been keeping company with him. Not since May Day."

She wanted to laugh, though she wasn't amused; she wanted to snap at him, though she wasn't angry. Balanced between extremes, her voice ended up with nothing much in it. "That's over. We're both content to leave it that way."

Beyond a quick, sharp look, he made no reply. But she found she felt better for having said it out loud.

Then she realized she was at one end of a roughly sketched semicircle of the Folk, with the wood for the bonfire at its center. As she watched, a man and woman of the Sidhe approached the piled branches. The woman was one of the queen's attendants, the one with the white-blond veil of hair. The two caught each other's hands across the unlit wood, right hand to right, left to left, and drew them close together in an interlaced knot of flesh and bone. Then, slowly, they lowered their joined hands. Magic gathered in them—Eddi could feel it, could hear the throbbing silence of it.

They touched the wood. Blue-white fire ran the length of each branch and leaped up. Cheering split the silence, from every fey throat in the circle.

Across the fire the Queen of Faerie turned toward her. In the light of the flames, her face looked warmer, softer, more beautiful still. The Lady nodded, and Eddi knew they were requested to play.

With her eyes, she gathered Hedge and Dan and Carla. She set nervous fingers to the neck of her guitar, and launched them all into a song.

She played the wailing, sliding opening notes of Dire Straits' "Solid Rock," and Carla smacked the kobassa against her hand in half-time. Then Dan pounded piano out of the Casio, Carla put the rhythm into high gear, and Hedge walked a bass line with gorgeous style. The circle became ragged almost immediately with the motion of the dance.

As the lyrics rolled off her lips, Eddi almost laughed aloud. They were about living for things that were solid and true. Around her, fantasies and illusions circled and stamped and spun, in glimpses of flying hair around uncanny faces, extravagant motion of inhuman arms and legs. She threw words at them as if daring them to ignore her.

Dan bounded out of the last chord into the opening riff of Men Without Hats' "The Safety Dance." A figure broke free of the dancers, a thin, foxy, red-haired boy. He pushed a large flat drum and a two-headed stick into Carla's hands, and disappeared into the mob again. "A bodhran!" Carla squeaked, and took up the beat happily, weaving the low thrumming voice of the drum into Hedge's bass.

It was the thin, intoxicating air; it was the moonlight, or the strong beer. Whatever it was, Eddi stood in the heart of the music and the night, and she knew it. She clapped out the beat, and watched her dancers pick it up. Hers. She pushed the guitar behind her and began to work them. She brought power up from her lungs, her diaphragm, put it in her voice, and sent that into every vibrating thing in the park.

"And we can act like we come from out of this world / Leave the real one far behind." She formed her lips and tongue and teeth around the words, made them mercilessly clear and full of meaning. "We can dance if we want to / We've got all your life and mine." Her mortal life and, now, theirs. There were worse things to do with a life than dance it away. She felt feverish, her head light and her skin prickly.

This audience, these fey dancers—they were the other half of the song, as if it were a question and they the answer she'd waited for. They lived for the music for as long as it lasted, and were ruled by it. They danced with wild grace, with all their attention on her. *Fairy food*, she realized. *Once you've tasted it, nothing else will do. Will I waste away for want of this?*

They held still in the opening of Peter Gabriel's "And Through the Wire," and the notes fell on them like a shower of rain. Her voice tore across them like lightning. "And through the wire I touch the power—" Every bolt of lightning has thunder in pursuit. She felt hers up through her feet, against her ears, on the palms of her hands. She heard it in the full-throated singing of Dan and Carla and Hedge.

She didn't understand what she felt. She only knew she had to express it, pass it on. "Overloaded with everything we said / Be careful where you tread—" There was a flash when she almost knew—"Watch the wire!"—but the knowledge dispersed into the song and was gone.

When it was finished she was hot with fever, cold with drying sweat, trembling with weariness. The voice of a wooden whistle rose out of the chasm of silence. Then drums, and shouting fiddles and bagpipes. Her hosts had taken up the music.

Someone took her hands and drew her out of the circle. It was the phouka. His eyes were bright, his lips parted, his whole face molded by some outside force that was only now leaving him. Calmly, she recognized that force: it was in her, too. It had come from her. It was magic.

They went up the slope without speaking, until they reached the honeysuckle grove and the kegs of wine and beer. The phouka poured something into two cups and handed one to her. It looked colorless; if it had any tint, it might be green, but she couldn't tell in the fitful light. Streams of bubbles rose from the bottom of the cup, like champagne. The fragrance was like walking through a field on a hot day, the smell that rose from the crushed grasses underfoot. There was the fiery scent of alcohol, too.

Eddi looked over the cup at the phouka. He was so serious she had to smile. "Is this part of the initiation, or strictly for members only?"

His lips twitched. "Perhaps a little of both. No, don't drink yet, my sweet. You must wish, in silence, something concerning valor or love. Then you must drain the cup, quickly and to the last drop."

"Why valor or love?"

"Because those are the special province of Midsummer."

"What are you going to wish for?" she asked.

"I shan't tell you," he said, smiling, and his cup chimed against hers.

What was it Willy had said? She should do what was right. She wondered which that had more to do with, valor or love. She swallowed the contents of the cup.

It froze the back of her throat and half her chest on the way down. She hadn't expected it to be burning cold. For an instant all her senses were taken up in it, like a burst of brilliant light. Then her vision returned, and the feeling in her hands and feet and tongue.

"Earth and Air," the phouka said, his voice shaky. "There's a cruel pleasure." His eyes were closed, and his face had nothing in it to match his light words.

She felt . . . new, just-made. She felt as if everything she had ever done out of weakness or fear had been undone, and all of her past washed clean. Her future lay before her like the sticks of an opened fan. *Like branching paths in the woods,* she realized. *That's Faerie for you. You wish for an answer, and get fifty to choose from.*

She stepped forward and touched the cascade of lace over the phouka's chest. He took a deep, quick breath, and his eyes opened, wide and startled.

"Come dance with me," she said. She took his hand and led him toward the bonfire light.

CHAPTER SEVENTEEN

I Burn for You

The instruments were bagpipes and whistles, guitars, drums, cymbals and bells, mandolins, fiddles, and something that sounded like a button accordion. The music was anything the night called for. There were jigs and reels—she might have guessed that. But there was hot city blues, too, rock, jazz, funk, and bluegrass full of mountains and whiskey. It should have sounded silly, and didn't. The fusion reminded Eddi of zydeco: wildly disparate musical styles played on inappropriate instruments, all to scorching good effect.

Some of the dances had steps and patterns, and the phouka led her through them. Some of them were as seemingly formless as slam dancing. But mostly, it was just dancing.

Just dancing. For the first time, she heard the power of Faerie music, felt what her own audiences felt. The difference was that she never seemed to get tired. She was full of rhythm and obedient to it. She couldn't put a foot wrong.

And the phouka was always with her. Eddi had the odd notion that they were two complementary forms in space, like the halves of the yin-yang symbol, like the light and dark faces of the moon. That in itself was distracting. Sometimes the movements of the dance would put her hand in his, or his arm around her waist. She wanted then to stop in mid-step, to have time to wonder at the warm, smooth skin of his hands, the cool brocade of his coat sleeve. She knew the shape and size of him, knew always just how far away he was, as if some mental radar bounced her thoughts off him and described him. Yet she was constantly surprised when she looked and found him there.

He was a flashy dancer—but then, so was everyone around her, tonight. Eddi danced *at* him, egging him on as she might have with her singing from on stage. He knew what she was doing, of course. *Did he always know?* she asked, somewhere in the corner of her thoughts. *Was he always quick to know what I wanted, what I meant, what I was trying for?* It seemed like it. He grinned at her and shook a stray black curl off his forehead.

Dan's synthesizer splashed melody against a background of bagpipe drone. It was Dan playing it; Eddi could hear his touch, his voicing and embellishing of chords. Dancing was suddenly not enough for her.

"Can anybody jam at this party?" she asked the phouka.

"No. But invited guests most certainly can."

"Hair-splitter," she said, shaking her head, and whirled her way through the dancers back to her guitar.

Dan had the Casio on a strap around his neck, and boogied in place as he played. The bagpiper stood beside him: a tall, twiggy old woman with a comic Cyrano nose and a head of hair like a disturbed porcupine. She wore a man's frock coat, bottle green and frayed at the too-short sleeves, and a long full skirt of shifting pastels. She exuded a scent of apple blossoms.

Eddi watched Dan's hands for long enough to pick up the key. Then she started playing rhythm, a country-swing flat picking lick. She thought the piper smiled at her—though how she could and continue to blow like a bellows, Eddi didn't know. They played something jiggish. Then, inspired perhaps by Eddi's flat picking, Dan fingered a verse of Hank Williams' "C'est La Vie." He raised his eyebrows at her, and she took up the words.

When the lead break came around, a fiddler took it up. He reminded her of Willy; he was one of the Sidhe, and played with a similar demonic intensity, but a little short of Willy's imagination or irreverence. His hair was white-blond. He seemed older than Willy, though the Sidhe were ageless and uniformly young, to look at them.

They were having too much fun to stop, so they did "Jambalaya" and "Hey, Good Lookin'," too. When they were done, Eddi turned to the fiddler as she would have to any mortal session player. She stopped before her hand was actually extended. Then she decided to offer it, anyway. He shook it. His manner was regally friendly.

"Nice job," Eddi said.

"And to yourself, as well." His voice was deep and clear, an actor's voice. "In another time, we might have met together only for this"—he indicated the revelry with a nod—"and not for the making of war."

Eddi studied him. "It takes two to fight a battle."

"Indeed." His eyes were hooded and cool. "Did we not oppose our enemies, then surely there would be no war. Only slaughter, and darkness."

"Is that it? Two options, either make war, or lie down and be walked on?"

His pale skin flushed—with anger, Eddi suspected. But his tone was perfectly polite. "Ah, have I been too long away from the Half-World? Have mortal men found the remedy for war at last? Tell it me, quickly, that I may never again suffer the sight of a comrade dead in battle."

Eddi winced. "I'm sorry. I . . . I think I spoke as I did . . . because I don't want them to die, either."

"These are not your people. What care you if they die, or how?"

"Some of them are my friends," she said. Then she had to fall silent. The thought of the phouka, dead on a battlefield, thoroughly stopped her voice.

It was his turn to study Eddi. "You are known to me, of course," he said at last, distantly. "I think I am not known to you. I am Oberycum, Consort to the Lady."

Eddi realized now that she had seen him among the courtiers earlier, under the flowering tree. She had seen him, too, at the Falls, in full armor. The pleated silk of his shirt was patterned with his device, the three-disks-in-a-disk, in gold on green. She sank quickly to one knee, wondering if it was the right thing to do.

"You need not," she heard him say, though he sounded faintly pleased. "We set formality aside, once the dance has begun."

She rose, and he nodded to her. "I hope we may play together again, you and I," he said, tucking his fiddle under his arm.

"So do I."

He gave her a shallow bow, turned, and disappeared into the crowd.

"Well!" the phouka said over her shoulder a moment later, and she jumped.

"How long have you been here?"

"Long enough to witness your new conquest, sweet."

"Conquest!"

He grinned at her. "Now where's the pleasure in baiting you, if you rise to the first cast? You do it on purpose, I think, to spoil my fun."

"I would have if I'd thought of it."

"Blast." The phouka shook his head. "I wonder—is it drink that makes me indiscreet?"

"Wish I had that excuse," Eddi sighed. "That little chat with Oberycum wasn't a landmark in diplomacy."

"You think you did so badly, then?" His look was full of contained smugness. "I'd say otherwise, myself."

"Yeah? Were you here when I came damn close to calling him a warmonger?"

The phouka tried not to smile. "You came nowhere near it. Surely a warmonger is one who sells war, as a fishmonger sells fish?"

"Get stuffed. You know what I mean. You heard that, then? And you still don't think he's pissed?"

The phouka nodded.

"Then either I'm luckier than I deserve, or you're dumber than you look."

He was delighted with that. "You're good for my self-esteem."

"The way aspirin's good for a headache?" Eddi said, and realized he was making her smile.

"Precisely. Do you want to dance, make music, or sample a new amusement?"

She could tell from his tone what he hoped. "What new amusement?"

"Oh, there's a competition just begun, 'round the other side of the hill, that you might enjoy watching."

"I love it when you use that full-of-yourself voice. Lead on, son."

Eddi expected to follow the route they'd taken to their audience with the Lady, around the base of the hill near the park's edge. Instead the phouka led her halfway up the slope. To do so, he took her hand and held it—lightly, as if he was afraid she'd object. She cast around for something casual to say. Nothing presented itself. She curled her fingers around his, and used what little attention she had left to keep her feet from tripping over each other.

They crossed the flank of the hill on a narrow gravel path. Young trees and brush were thick on both sides, and the night wind stage-whispered in their leaves. Eddi knew they were in the middle of the city, in the middle of the hosts of Faerie. But the music and voices were faint behind them; the trees shut out all sights but fragments of the dark sky.

"Careful here," the phouka said softly, and squeezed her hand. Ahead of him there was a bit of path washed out, part of a gulley that ran off into the brush on both sides. The phouka stepped over it. Then he turned, clasped her waist with both hands, and lifted her across.

His movement, her instant off the ground, had been quick. It took her a moment to notice that her feet were on the gravel again, that his hands were still on her waist, that hers had fastened on his upper arms and hadn't let go. She could feel his palms and fingers outlined in a pleasant dry heat through the cloth of her blouse. Did her hands feel the same to him? Larger than they really were, their touch important out of all proportion?

Shifting moonlight drew contour lines on his face. She could see the fine texture of the skin around his eyes and over his cheekbones. One black curl shone like a metal shaving on his forehead. His eyes were wide and dark, full of amazement and something like alarm.

She slid her hands up and over his shoulders, the brocade of his coat silky-rough against her palms. When she got to his collar, she tucked her fingers like combs into the hair behind his ears, set her thumbs against the clean angle of his jaw. The sensation in her hands was so strong it was almost painful, as if she'd taken some drug that accentuated touch. She drew his face slowly toward hers. He closed his eyes, in submission or trust, in an excess of pleasure or fear, she didn't know. But she kissed him, a light and lingering contact.

She pulled her head back a little and looked at him. His eyes opened, his chest rose and fell once, quickly, and he whispered, "You needn't stop, you know."

Every motion she made was slow, as if she'd never before put her arms around a man, and didn't know for certain where everything fit. When at last they were pressed close, she didn't think she'd know how to let go when the time came. They summarized the course of passion with kisses: a chaste, half-frightened brush of the lips metamorphosed into something fierce and fast-burning, which in its turn became a more patient, more intimate touch, full of inquiry and shared pleasure.

He held her against him and hid his face in her hair. She heard him whisper something that might have been her name, and she stroked his back. He was trembling a little—with nerves, she knew. She was doing it, too.

"We could have done this long ago," she said at last, her voice wobbling.

He shook his head and murmured, "Not like this, I think."

"No, you're right. Not like this. For a cute guy, you're pretty smart."

He laughed breathlessly and backed off a bit to look at her, smoothed the hair off her forehead with one hand. "All I know of love, I've learned from you, Eddi McCandry. And you've been at pains to teach me since first I saw you."

"I have? Hm. Didn't know that."

"Well, to be honest, neither did I, at the outset." She felt his chest move with silent laughter. "Proof of my ignorance on the subject, surely."

Reluctantly, she remembered her suspicion, that he was playing at being in love. She didn't believe it anymore, not really. But she heard herself asking the hateful question anyway. "How do you know it's love? Maybe you haven't learned anything after all."

She expected a joke, an impassioned protest, an airy denial. Instead he looked gravely into her face and replied, "I've no surety that it is. I know only the parts of what I feel; I may be misnaming the whole. You dwell in my mind like a household spirit. All that I think is followed with, 'I shall tell that thought to Eddi.' Whatever I see or hear is colored by what I imagine you will say of it. What is amusing is twice so, if you have laughed at it. There is a way you have of turning your head, quickly and with a little tilt, that seems more wonderful to me than the practiced movements of dancers. All this, taken together, I've come to think of as love, but it may not be.

"It is not a comfortable feeling. But I find that, even so, I would wish the same feeling on you. The possibility that I suffer it alone—that frightens me more than all the host of the Unseelie Court."

She was shaken by his eloquence, and humbled. Whatever she'd expected of the phouka, it wasn't this faithful, fearless cataloging of his emotions. Though, now that she thought of it, it was just like him. Serious and literal-minded when it seemed least likely, when it proved most appropriate. It was like him, too, to love her and admit to it before he knew if she loved him. Maybe only mortals expected to barter their hearts.

Her silence must have been longer than she thought; the phouka touched a finger lightly to her cheek and looked uncertain. "But it's true that I have faced the Dark Court and lived. I suppose I could survive this peril as well, if need be."

"What? Oh—no. I mean . . ." Eddi faltered and shook her head. "I'm not good at saying this kind of thing. I always sound stupid or too casual or . . ."

"My poet, betrayed by words?" He smiled crookedly.

"I never said I was a poet. Besides, it's not the same thing. This is public speaking." She smiled weakly and looked at his ruffles. He set his hands on her shoulders, but they were motionless and weightless.

"You've kept me alive for the last three months," Eddi began, groping furiously for the words. "You've made me coffee. You've carried my amplifier." A nervous chuckle escaped her. "And you've been good company. Even when you were being a jerk, you were pretty good company, now that I look back on it."

"But," he said, without inflection.

Eddi looked up at him, alarmed. "But? Oh, hell, I told you I was bad at this! No, no buts. You're a wonderful person. Even if you are a supernatural being. Damn it, Phouka, how am I going to tell my mother that I'm in love with a guy who turns into a dog?" She blushed; she could feel it.

A silence of unreasonable proportions followed; the phouka's only response was a quick spasm of his fingers on her shoulders. "Are you in love with him, then?"

"I said so, didn't I?"

"Not quite." There was a smile twitching in the corner of his mouth.

"All right, all right." Eddi took a long breath. "I love you."

"There. Now why should that be so hard to say?"

"Because it sounds like something out of a soap opera," Eddi grumbled.

"Does it? Not to me. The best line from a favorite song, perhaps." His smile softened his whole face in a way she hadn't seen before.

"That's because you're a damned romantic."

He reached up and tucked her hair behind her ear on one side. "Then you're a doubly damned romantic, my heart, since you won't even admit it. But perhaps with my excellent example before you . . ."

Eddi caught at his disconcerting fingers, which were now tracing the edge of her ear, and kissed his knuckles. "You're a jerk,'' she said fondly. ''Where were we going, when we got distracted?''

''Earth and Air, I'd forgotten! It's your fault, you know. The color of your hair in the moonlight, the curve of your waist, the—''

''You're going to forget again.''

''You're quite right. But I'll try not to do so for at least a few minutes. You *will* enjoy this, I think.'' He flashed her a grin and folded his fingers around hers. ''Come along, then.''

When the path widened and the trees thinned into open lawn, he put his arm around her shoulders. In his heeled boots, he was a little taller than she was, and she fit neatly against him when she put her arm around his waist.

They joined a semicircle of perhaps two dozen fey folk seated on the grass. She felt the phouka beside her like a source of heat, the rise and fall of his ribcage against her arm as he breathed.

A slight, pale-haired man stood before the gathered audience, facing outward toward University Avenue. He wore a baggy leather jacket dyed and painted with many colors, and tight white pants. His ears were not the large, foxy ones Eddi had seen on some creatures of Faerie, but they came to a pronounced point.

The watchers were quiet, and the pale-haired man stood, silent and still, as if he were alone. Then he flung his head back and slowly lifted his hands.

University Avenue disappeared. It wasn't covered up; it was gone, like a chalk drawing washed away. What was left was a featureless gray fuzz that seemed to billow a little at the edges.

The grayness began to glitter, and light and dark formed slowly in it. Color appeared, the suggestion of pink and yellow and green. Then Eddi saw the outline, and realized what was quickly taking shape before her.

It was a castle. Not the utilitarian fortresses of the mortal past, not the marzipan-and-plaster illusions of Disneyland; this was a towered, turretted marvel, graceful with flying buttresses, real and rich and impossible. It leaped and twisted into the sky perhaps thirty stories, all of them polished golden stone. Banners hung from its balconies. Clouds snagged on its spires and broke away in tatters into the night sky. A shadowed garden of topiary surrounded its base and marched down to join the edge of the park.

The gathered watchers made noise at last—they applauded the pale man's efforts in whatever ways best suited their forms. He

turned and bowed low, and his creation dissipated in a cloud of
sparkling light, like fireworks burning out.

'Good God!'' Eddi said in the phouka's ear. "That was all
illusion? Of course it was. But there was . . . so *much* of it!''

"Mmm.'' The phouka raised his eyebrows as another figure
separated from the crowd. "Ah hah. I thought so. See what you
think of this, my sweet.''

A woman stood before the semicircle of audience, much
closer than the pale man had. She was tall and thin and steely-
looking, with a hollow-cheeked, pleasant face. Her brown hair
fell loose to her waist, and she wore what looked like mechanic's
coveralls with the sleeves cut out. She did nothing to awe the
watchers; she had no haughty manners, no artistic airs. No
showmanship at all, Eddi thought at first—then recognized the
consummate showmanship in that.

The woman gazed vaguely off into the middle distances, not
so much entranced as absent-minded. Then she smiled slowly, as
if at some happy memory. She turned her right hand palm
upward and studied it.

There was an apple there, suddenly. It was a neighbor's-apple-
tree sort of fruit, small and rosy-red with a little reverse blush of
green on one side, its surface misted over with the unpolished
bloom that never survived the trip to the supermarket.

With a nod, the woman tossed the apple into the air. Eddi
watched it spin through its arc, heard the thunk when it landed in
the woman's hand again. Then she bit into it. The sound carried
faintly to Eddi, the snap of teeth through the skin, the crunch of
the crisp flesh tearing away. It made her hungry. Juice sparkled
on the woman's lips, and a drop ran down the skin of the apple
and fell on the front of her coverall, leaving a little dark spot.
Slowly, with something like regret, the woman held the apple at
arm's length. The white flesh shone wetly in the moon and
lamplight. She blew on the apple as if blowing out a candle, and
it puffed from her hand onto the night wind in a plume of
red-and-white dust.

Eddi knew the stunned silence that sometimes preceded ap-
plause, that was a greater accolade than all the noise a crowd
could make. That was what she heard, what she contributed
to.

''I saw the damn thing appear in her hand,'' she said
wonderingly, ''and I still forgot it wasn't a real apple.''

The phouka nodded. ''It put that poor boy's castle to shame.''

She thought for a moment. "The apple was harder to pull off, wasn't it?" she asked the phouka.

The phouka leaned back on his elbows. "Your imagination filled in the blanks in the castle. The apple was all observation, uncolored by the wishes of the heart."

Eddi grinned down at him. "That's bad art, you know. Copying reality without interpreting it."

"Mmm. But illlusion is not art. It can be a tool for art, but there is nothing of genuine creation in it." He looked distant suddenly, and a little sad. "You'll find precious little creation among us, dear one. For the most part, we are only excellent copyists."

"Why? Is there some reason why you *can't* be creative?"

"Habits of thought. Tradition like a weight upon the chest." He tipped his head back and stared at the sky.

Eddi touched a finger to his lips and saw them soften into a smile. "Don't be bitter," she said.

"No. Not tonight. Tell me then, sweet, if you made an illusion, here and now, what would it be?"

Around them, the knot of audience was unravelling, drifting away across the grass and up the hill. Eddi leaned on one elbow, so that she was stretched out on her side next to him. He began to stroke a finger lightly through her hair, as if it demanded all his concentration.

"Something musical," Eddi said finally. "All those sounds in my head, that the instruments I know of can't make. You'd be surprised at how clearly you can hear something in your head and not be able to reproduce it."

His fingers were motionless in her hair, and he looked into her eyes without smiling. There was meaning in the look, and the need to be understood. "You have already played a piece of the music inside you. You did it tonight."

Eddi remembered playing for the circle of the dance, remembered the feel of it, the power and confidence and exhaustion. "What did I do?"

"The very fire danced in rhythm," the phouka said softly. "There were instruments and voices where there were none to play or sing. But more, the music seemed to fly straight from your heart and mind into all those who heard it, and they understood it without words or images."

"You're sure that wasn't just you?"

He laughed, embarrassed. "I think not, but it's true that I may have felt the effects more than some. You go directly to my head, sweetling, just like your dreadful brandy.''

Eddi laughed, too, and leaned over him to kiss him. The feel of him along the length of her body was like fire running up the bark of a tree, and the kiss became rather more than she'd intended. His arms went round her. Her hands, without any effort from her, found their way inside his coat, where they felt his back muscles through his vest and shirt.

She had hardly any warning at all—only the phouka going tense under her. Then he was off the grass and in a fighting crouch near her head, and she had only the most muddled notion of how he got there.

Past him, she saw the cause of his quick movement. It bared its long, discolored teeth at him, studied them both with its pearly dead-fish eyes. Then it laughed; Eddi had heard Carla make a sound like that by running a drumstick down a ridged, hollow wooden block.

"So charming," it said thickly, as if its tongue and teeth were ill-made for speech. The voice itself was hoarse and dry, and sounded like old bones and dead wood. "Young things rutting on the grass."

"Drop dead," Eddi said, rising slowly and with great care.

It laughed again. "Truce, little things." It was, in fact, shorter than Eddi, but she knew the adjective had nothing to do with size. It spread its long gray hands in a parody of benevolence. "No hostility here, yet you are without a kind word. Is it not truce?"

"It is," said the phouka, his voice perfectly neutral. "Which is why all that stealth makes me so suspicious."

"Stealth? Is it wicked to be quiet by nature? No matter." It turned to Eddi and sketched a bow. She realized that all its movements looked like parodies of human ones, as if it were a computer simulation or a very good marionette. "The Lady sends her invitation to you, to speak with her if you would."

Eddi frowned and looked to the phouka.

He said, his eyes still on the gray messenger, "Meaning, the *other* Lady."

The messenger laughed.

She was here? Yes, of course she would be. Sitting in the midst of it all, unwelcome but impossible to exclude. Would that please her? Hurt her? Make her angry? Eddi knew so little of her. "What," Eddi said finally, "does the Queen of Air and Darkness want with me?"

"Speech," said the gray thing. "It is truce. You will not be harmed," it rattled off quickly, like an arresting officer reciting her rights. "You will not be held against your will. You will not be gone for more than half of an hour."

Eddi looked again at the phouka. "What do you think?"

He shrugged. "I'd not venture it—though those are the reassurances I'd demand. We've nothing to gain from it."

The gray thing curled its lip. "Not so. The Lady has a thing she knows, that you want to know also. A very important thing, and urgent."

The phouka sighed. "It lacked only that, I suppose."

"How do we know it's telling the truth?" Eddi asked.

"We don't lie," the phouka said, sounding disgusted, but not at her. "We'll shade the truth until you'd think that green was red, but we don't lie. And particularly not to each other."

"Well, it's a chance to get to know the enemy," Eddi said with a shrug. She eyed the messenger. "Where is she?"

It smiled, and with an almost graceful gesture pointed up the hill to the tower.

"Now why am I not surprised?" Eddi grumbled, and took a few steps toward the slope. The phouka started to follow—and the gray thing stepped in front of him, grinning. Eddi turned, and they were all still for a remarkably long moment.

"She will *not* go alone," the phouka said, his voice low and ominous.

"Then she remains ignorant," the messenger said. "Her loss."

"What difference can it make that I am with her? As long as you observe the truce, I shall as well. If you intend no harm, you needn't fear my presence."

"Assuredly. But you are still not invited."

The phouka's fingers curled and stiffened at his sides, and his shoulders rose with a long, slow breath. "Why not?" he said through his teeth.

"Because the Lady has no need to speak to you."

The phouka, from his face, might have been considering breaking the truce. Eddi stepped around the gray thing—with room to spare—and touched his arm. "It's your call," she said. "You know more than I do how much they can be trusted, and how much weight to put on this piece of information. I'll go alone, if you tell me I should."

He closed his eyes and turned his face away, but she only moved around to where she could see him again.

"That makes it worse, you know," he said bitterly. "If something happens to you the fault will be mine, for sending you into their hands."

"I know. But one of us has to decide, and I can't."

Without looking away from her face, the phouka addressed the gray messenger. "Will you take me in her place?"

"No," it said.

The phouka winced, then stepped forward and took Eddi in his arms. She wrapped hers around his waist, under his coat. "Be wary," he whispered. "I shall give them their half an hour, and then to the bowels of the earth with the blasted truce. But be wary still, love."

"I will." She kissed his cheek and let him go. "Lead the goddamn way," she said to the gray thing.

It did not go straight up the hill; it followed a level track through the front of the park, until it came to a little-used thread of trail that disappeared among the young trees growing thick on the slope. Then it stepped off the path and stopped.

"Aren't you going to lead me there?" she asked.

It showed its dreadful teeth again. "Only one tower," it said hollowly. "Only one door."

So why go to the trouble of leading me this far? she thought sourly. *Maybe it's seen too many horror movies.* She scowled at it and started up the path, though it made her back prickle to have that thing behind her. When it prickled more than she could bear, she looked over her shoulder. There was nothing behind her but empty trail.

Once between the trees, the track turned steep, and was cut down its length with a washout gully. Gravel rolled under her feet. A wind had sprung up, one left over from October. It sank its cold teeth in her until her ears and bare arms ached with it. Other than the daunting hiss of it in the trees, and her own crunching footsteps, she could hear nothing. On this path, there was no moon in the sky, no streetlight, no eldritch glow from any living thing.

Barely visible from where she stood, at the end of a corridor of darkness, she saw the bottom of the trail. The phouka stood there. His very silhouette spoke of stubborn devotion, and Eddi felt suddenly as if she were on a lifeline. When the time came, when there was need, he would reel her back to him.

In a few more steps, the trees were bare, and she was surrounded by the last bleak breath of autumn. It was an illusion.

She fought against it, but it was too strongly made, or she had waited too long. The only break in its surface was a nighthawk that burst out of the trees, its white wing patches shining in the darkness. She welcomed the start it gave her; it was a summer bird.

She scrambled out of the trees at last onto the pavement that surrounded the tower. The base of it, high as anyone could reach, was covered with graffiti. Previous scrawls and slogans had been covered up with a broad band of white paint, but that had only served as a canvas for the current array. There was a cluster of spray-painted dope leaves, and LED ZEPPELIN, and THE MISFITS over a skull and crossbones. There was a stencilled drawing of two figures, one holding a gun to the other's head and blowing out its brains, with the caption YOU'RE IT! There was the usual collection of initials and names of high school teams, and a few pentagrams and six-sixty-sixes that probably had more to do with heavy metal bands than Satanists.

And there was the door.

It was unguarded, unattended—in fact, there was no one on the hilltop at all, that Eddi could see. She should have been able to see the lights of the city on her right, over the treetops. She saw only darkness there.

It was made of iron, strapped and barred and painted rusty red. It was set in a concrete arch at the top of a short flight of steps. A chain hung through the bars—probably the one that, on other nights, fastened the door closed. Tonight it hung loose. The door stood open by a hand's breadth.

Phouka, she thought, as if it were a prayer or a curse. She walked up the stairs and pushed through the door.

She felt her way for three paces, sliding her foot along the stone with each step and stretching her hands out before her. Then light bloomed along the walls.

They were not wall sconces. They were white living hands holding torches, and they swung to follow her progress. Sometimes the white fingers shifted a little, seeking a better grip, perhaps, and the torchlight wavered unpleasantly. "Beauty and the Beast," Eddi snapped, her voice over-loud against the hard walls. "You ripped this off from Cocteau."

She looked behind her and saw that the door was shut, almost lost in the gloom. With a shrug and a shudder, she went down the hall, and the torches sprang to life ahead of her.

The hall was three times as long as the diameter of the tower,

and perfectly straight. Just when Eddi grew irritated with that, it
ended at the base of a flight of spiral stairs. With darkness above
and below her, isolated in a puddle of torchlight, she couldn't
tell how far up they went, or if they followed the right size
curve. When she arrived at a set of double doors, intricately
carved and curiously hard to see, her legs ached. She saw no
door handles and no knocker; she pushed them open.

The room was round and enormous. It had no walls—only the
pillars of the unglazed arches that were its windows, and the
stone railings, hip-high, in each arch. The circle of arches was
uninterrupted, and Eddi wondered what had happened to the
double doors she'd passed through. From the curve of the ceiling, Eddi guessed it was the tower's witch-hat roof.

An immense red-patterned rug, perhaps twenty feet by thirty,
lay like an island on the stone floor. At the far end of it were a
pair of lamps in the form of great brass bowls on tripod stands.
They might have been burning scented oil or incense; the air was
full of a spicy-flower smell, like peonies. Between the lamps
stood a lacquered black table and a high-backed black wicker
chair, and in the chair sat the Queen of Air and Darkness.

She stood up and inclined her head graciously. Eddi began the
long walk down the rug.

"I'm pleased that you've come," said the dark queen, her
throaty voice rustling in the high ceiling like a disturbance in a
flock of nesting birds. "Though of course, we both benefit from
your presence here. Can I offer you tea?"

"No, thank you." Eddi reached the table at last, wishing
she'd been offered a chair instead. "I think we should do our
business and I should leave."

The queen smiled. She was even more elegant than when Eddi
had first seen her. She wore a dress of silvery twill-weave silk
with a wrap top and a broad sash, like an obi, at the waist. The
sleeves were kimono-like, too, and lined with scarlet. The skirt
was narrow and stopped at the knees. She wore high heeled red
satin pumps. Her black hair was pulled back from her face again,
wound into a complicated knot at the back of her head, and held
in place by two long silver sticks ornamented with what might
have been rubies. On the table before her was a silver-and-glass
dish that held a half-smoked black Sobranie cigarette.

"What do you have to tell me?" Eddi asked, feeling small
and grubby.

The queen picked up her cigarette and glided away to one of

the arches. "Actually, the news is not just for you," she said, letting out a mouthful of smoke. "You, I believe, are the person most intimately concerned with it. I thought it would be wise to tell you first, and in private. But if you will pass it on to my opposite number in the Seelie Court, you would save me a great deal of trouble."

"I can't until you tell it to me," Eddi said, but without much force. She was under no illusions about the woman before her—this was the enemy. But the tower room was full of an emotionless peace, removed from the violence of hate or love, or the need for quick decisions. She didn't feel in any hurry to leave it.

She moved around the table to one of the railings and looked out at the night. A breeze, neither cool nor warm, lifted the hair off her forehead. The sky was a perfect black, ornamented with the white disk of a full moon and clouds of stars like spilled sugar. The treetops below were green-black, billowing like yards of satin until they reached a field of tall grass. It was quiet and relaxing, if a little lonely.

Lonely. The whole city of Minneapolis should have been visible from where she stood, a fierce constellation of lighted windows, streetlights, traffic. It should have paled the sky with its brilliance, excited her just with the sight of it.

"The view up here could put you to sleep," Eddi said, louder, quicker, sharper than necessary. "Don't you ever want something a little more exciting?"

The queen turned a measuring look on her. "I don't come here for excitement." The cool regard of those great, sloping eyes, the gentle satire of the arched brows, made Eddi wish she'd kept her mouth shut. She struggled against that wish.

"I bet you'd be happy if it really looked like this. The whole city gone, poof. What do you have against mortals? You look like us, you dress like us—why is that?" She was flinging words, any words, against the quiescence that threatened her. She scraped her fingernails on the stone railing just to feel the nasty sensation. If she could have smashed the peace of that room with the sound of an overdriven amp, she would have done it gladly. She pulled away from the railing with a jerk, stamped her feet to disturb the unnatural calm of the room.

The Dark Queen was laughing. "How should I dress, Eddi McCandry? Would you prefer this?" She glimmered all over, and was suddenly the wicked queen from Snow White, in a long black gown with trailing sleeves and a tight, helmetlike black hood. "Or this?" Black cocktail dress, bulky white fur, her hair half-black and half-white, cigarette holder between her fingers—Eddi recognized Cruella DeVille. "Or would you prefer the devil you know?" Severe chin-length hair, tortoiseshell glasses, a slate-colored jacket and skirt and a white blouse—she was the epitome of everything corporate and conservative. Then she was in gray and scarlet again, laughing, her head thrown back.

"Is there anything you do that you didn't steal from a movie?" Eddi said softly.

That stopped the laughter. The queen's head came down so quickly that her hair should have come loose, and there was close-held fury in her face. She turned away, back toward the night sky, and pulled at her cigarette. The silence went on for a long time.

Then the queen said, "I hold Willy Silver captive."

She said it as if it were the answer to a math problem—precisely and without emotion.

Eddi considered several responses. "Prove it," she said finally, but her voice was not strong.

"Why should I? Go look for him, and see if you can prove me a liar." The queen shook her head, and smiled. "Oh, why not—I fancy a dramatic gesture now and again." She reached into one of her sleeves and flipped whatever she'd taken from it across the table. It landed glittering on the carpet at Eddi's feet. She picked it up.

It swung from her fingers, catching the light from the lamps. The three interlaced crescent moons, in silver, dangling from a silver ear wire.

Eddi felt vaguely sick. "What do you want?"

"I want the victory at Como Park. A bloodless one."

"I . . . I can't do anything about that."

"No. But you can deliver my ransom terms to the Seelie queen. And you have such a stake, haven't you, in seeing that she accepts them?" Then she smiled, and what Eddi saw in her face made her more horrible than her gray long-toothed servants.

Cold blankness lapped at Eddi's thoughts. "Throw a whole battle to save one person—she won't do it. It would be stupid."

"Really? To save a young lord of the Sidhe? One of the White Lady's own kin? Even in mortal history, a hundred common lives is a fair ransom for a prince. And the Sidhe are so few. . . ."

"What about the truce?" Eddi said, grasping at straws.

"It did not begin until sundown," the queen replied pleasantly.

But she'd seen Willy at sundown—no, she hadn't. When she'd left him in the rehearsal room, sundown had been an hour away. "What happens if they won't ransom him?"

"Then he is of no use to me," said the Dark Queen. For a moment, Eddi misunderstood that, but only for a moment. "You see, I've nothing to lose. If she will cede me the park, I'll return her kinsman gladly. If she will not, I'll kill him, and I will take the park from her by force of arms. Tell her she may have until an hour before the battle to contemplate the wisdom of buying him back. At that time I will meet her messenger in the Conservatory in Como Park, and we will make the exchange. But remind her of this: while she deliberates, he is in the loving care of my most trusted people. I'm sure she'll do the right thing. Aren't you?"

Eddi thought of the gray things; the redcaps; and the green, groping hand that had risen from the waters of Minnehaha Creek. She swallowed the bile in her throat and said, "I'll tell her."

"Go, then," said the Queen of Air and Darkness. And all the light went out.

CHAPTER EIGHTEEN

Red Rain

Eddi's growing rage sustained her as she felt her way through the dark. She slipped and fell down four steps, and kept herself moving with the thought that the Dark Lady would laugh to see her. If she kept on, she would get out, she knew. After all, wasn't that what the bitch wanted, for her to get out and deliver her message?

Still, when she saw the vertical line of light that marked the edge of the door, she nearly cried. She pulled it open and stumbled through moonlight that seemed blinding by contrast, down the short flight of steps and into the phouka's arms.

He swept her away from the door, around the flank of the tower, and onto a park bench. Eddi looked up, out over the rooftops and the summer-clad trees to the blazing skyline of Minneapolis. It seemed the most valuable thing she'd ever seen.

She took a deep breath and got her voice back. "They've got Willy," she said, and the phouka's arms tightened convulsively around her. "I could *kill* her, goddammit!"

"Not easily," the phouka muttered. "What does she want?"

"Como Park," said Eddi, spitting the words.

He stared, transfixed. "Earth and Air. That's why she made no complaint over the date and place of the next battle."

"She's had this planned since then? Jesus Christ, I *will* kill her!"

"No, you won't. You'll come and tell the Lady."

And she did. Surrounded by the bizarre countenances of the Folk of the Seelie Court, in the quivering light of the bonfire, she faced their pale queen. She recited the terms like a sentry reporting during battle, terse and clear; then waited for the martial response.

The Lady did not move, or speak, or even blink. She only

stared, not quite at Eddi. The fire crackled. Finally her lips parted. "We . . . will consider the matter," she whispered.

Eddi frowned. This was not what she'd expected. "She said Willy was a relative of yours."

"He is our cousin."

"Then don't you—"

"It is a great matter, Eddi McCandry—one of which you know nothing. Our response to this piece of treachery is not to be lightly decided."

That, at least, was anger. Eddi was heartened by it. "But in the meantime, he's in *her* hands."

The Lady turned her willow-green eyes on Eddi, as if seeing her for the first time. Then she looked at the assembled Court. "Enough. The revels are ended. Begone." She turned and walked away, and her courtiers followed.

Eddi felt a hand on her shoulder. She turned to find Carla at her side, Dan just behind her. "What do you want us to do?" Carla said.

Eddi scrubbed her hands over her face, trying to think. "Go home. Together. Don't go anywhere alone. I don't expect her to move on anybody else, but God knows we didn't expect this, did we?"

Carla shook her head and looked miserable. "No. Christ, Eddi, we can't just sit and wait for Her Majesty to figure out what the hell she wants to do!"

"Go home and stay by the phone. I'll take the phouka and see what we can find up at the practice space."

"We'll take your axe in the car," Dan said, his voice tight.

"Good. Thanks." Eddi wanted very much to cry. "You guys . . . you're worth any six of these characters," she said, jerking her head at the dispersing fey folk.

"Except for a few of 'em," Carla replied. Just as Eddi realized who she meant, she added, looking over Eddi's shoulder, "Don't let her do anything dumb, okay?"

"I'll try," the phouka said.

They half ran down the path to the motorcycle. As they reached it, Eddi heard thunder. The sky was clouding over. "Melodrama," she muttered, and kicked the bike alive.

It was not far to the building on Washington Avenue; the way Eddi drove then, it was closer still. When they arrived, the phouka grabbed her shoulders to keep her from flinging herself up the iron stairs.

"She would think it a splendid joke," he said, his voice tight, "to leave a surprise for anyone who came to search." He went up the stairs slowly, examining them as he went. Just short of the second landing, he crouched over one of the treads. Eddi heard his breath hiss out. He held out his hands and muttered something. There was a blue-white flash, and he grabbed for the railing.

"Phouka!"

"It's all right."

"To hell with *it,* what about you?"

He smiled down at her. "Fine. Come up behind me, but slowly."

"What would that have done?" she asked as she climbed.

"I'm not precisely sure. The tread might have been slippery. It might even have broken entirely, and whoever was on it would have fallen. It's a piece of idle malice, something like the reverse of Hairy Meg's work." He continued to examine the stairs as they climbed, but found nothing more. Eddi unlocked the door at the top, and turned on the practice room lights.

There was so little out of place. Willy's russet-colored guitar lay face down on the floor. His amp was still on, and buzzed with the contact of the strings against the rug. A microphone stand was tipped over. One of the sheets that had hung from the overhead beams lay on the floor like a cast off shroud. A faint scorched smell clung to the air.

"Oh, God." For a moment she was stuck in place, looking at the guitar. Then she walked over and turned off the amp, and the silence became brutal. She picked up Willy's axe. It was undamaged, though the high E string was broken. She put it in its stand.

"They surprised him," the phouka said, in that contained voice. Eddi looked up and found him still standing against the closed door. "Not as thoroughly as they wanted to, I think, but if he'd had much warning, this place would be a shambles. Given the opportunity, he can be profoundly dangerous." He moved further into the room. "I think . . . yes, here." Eddi came numbly to look where he pointed.

On the brick wall, about a yard up from the floor, was a sooty black spot as big across as her palm. The scorched smell was much stronger. "He'd time for only one blast, and it missed," said the phouka.

"Willy did this?" Eddi stared, puzzled, at the black mark.

The phouka wore one of his unreadable expressions. "Yes." He crossed the room and stood for a moment over the sheet, then knelt beside the fallen mike stand. His hand went out for it, then pulled back.

"This—," he began, stopped, and closed his eyes. Eddi saw his jaw working. With a sudden, strangled noise, he slammed his fist against the floor.

She went to him and touched his hair. "What?"

His voice was controlled again when he said, "More than likely, they hit him with this."

The weighted iron base of the mike stand would have been an effective bludgeon.

"And he pulled the sheet down with him when he fell," the phouka added.

The base of the mike stand might even have broken the skin, to let out the smear of blood in one of the sheet's white folds. The phouka curled forward over his knees as if around a pain. He made no sound.

Eddi stared at the rust-colored mark for a long time. "I thought you said it was hard to draw immortal blood."

The phouka raised his head swiftly. "Eddi—"

"It requires the presence of a mortal bound to the cause, you said. Am I wrong?"

He looked at her with mingled dread and fascination. "I said once that you were a quick study."

"What happened here?"

He looked down at the sheet, and looked away. "There are . . . two mortals bound. One on each side. Ideally, they stand in . . . some relationship to each other. Kin, friends, lovers. If they are estranged, severed one from the other, that is best of all."

Eddi sat down on the floor and stared at him.

"I'm sorry. I'd hoped—" He passed a hand over his eyes. "I'd hoped there would be no need to tell you. And when I knew I should have told you, I feared to do it. I knew I'd made the Unseelie Court's choice inevitable. But I couldn't tell you. It was the one last thing I hadn't the courage to tell you."

"Stuart," Eddi said.

"He must have been present. But I doubt he struck a blow; he is as valuable to them as you to us. They would not have risked him against Willy."

She looked around the room without seeing it. What she saw instead was the balcony in First Avenue, and Stuart lunging at

Willy, the flash of a knife as it fell from his hand and clattered across the floor. "From the first," she said, and her voice seemed to come from someone else, "I wanted to keep everyone else out of this. To keep anyone from being dragged in after me." She laughed weakly. "And from the first, it was a lost cause. Isn't that funny? I think it's funny."

The phouka stood up stiffly. His face was bleak. "I'm sorry. If it's any consolation . . . no, of course it's not. But I would do anything now to undo what I've done to you."

His words were a distraction, and she shook her head to clear them away. "Was he recruited the way I was?"

"Essentially. The binding itself was not the same."

"And did he try to get away from them?"

The phouka looked confused. "I don't know."

"I bet he didn't." She shook her head again. "I bet he thought it was a great way to get back at me. It was a lost cause before you even showed up, and I never knew it."

He knelt again before her. "What are you saying?"

"I'm saying I never knew, all the time I was with him, what a mess he must really be. Poor screwed-up Stuart."

The phouka looked genuinely rattled. "He may not be doing his part whole-heartedly. You weren't, at first."

"Do you think I'd stand by, even *stand by,* and watch you ambush an unarmed man?" Eddi snapped.

Round-eyed, he shook his head.

"Have they hypnotized Stuart? Turned him into a zombie? No? Then don't offfer any goddamn excuses for him." And she turned her face away.

"We cannot know what they've done to him."

"I know. I hope to God there *are* excuses for him. But Stuart has always wanted to be bigger than he is. If somebody offered him what you offered me . . ." Her throat felt hard and hot, and she had to stop talking.

"Do you forgive me?" the phouka asked after a moment, with caution.

"Nothing to forgive."

He sighed, closed his eyes, and let his head fall back. She took his face in her hands and pulled it down again, and his eyes flew open when she shook him a little. "But in the future, would you please, please, *please* tell me these things?"

"Yes. I shall."

"Is there anything else I should know?"

The phouka shook his head.

Eddi stood up and looked around the room. There was nothing more to see, no new clues. She wasn't sure what more she wanted—a map to the bad guys' hideout, maybe. "We have to do something," Eddi said, hearing echoes of Carla's words in her own.

The phouka set his hands on her shoulders. "We can do nothing more now. Wait until tomorrow. The Lady will choose her course then, and it may affect ours. And if she chooses to give up the park, then we need do nothing at all."

"Is she likely to do that?"

After a pause, he replied, "I cannot say."

"But she will do *something?*" Eddi turned under his hands. She needed to see his face, even though she knew he wouldn't lie.

"She will. All of the Dark Lady's arguments are sound. Willy is the queen's kin, and it must prey upon her, to think of him in the hands of her enemy."

Rain spattered on the windows; Eddi went to the nearest and looked out. The street was already shining wet. "What will they do to him?" she asked.

"I don't know."

She leaned her head against the glass, and the coolness of it was a comfort.

"Do you find you still care for him?" the phouka said softly from across the room.

She turned around to look at the band's equipment, at Willy's guitar with its string hanging broken. "He's my lead guitarist," she said finally, with a flimsy smile. "And given a little time, he might be my friend. I don't think he understands friendship yet, but he's making progress. Yeah, I care for him." Then she shifted her gaze to the phouka's wary face, and her voice hardened. "If she'd kidnapped Carla, I'd have dangled her out one of her goddamn windows until she gave her back."

"I see. What would you have done, had it been me?"

"Same thing. Only I'd have held her by one ankle."

His lips twitched. "I'm impressed by the strength of your regard."

"Oh, Phouka," she said, not quite steadily. She met him in the middle of the floor and put her arms around him, pressed her face into his ruffles.

"If you get tearstains on my shirt, my valet will never forgive you." He held her tightly against him.

"Fire the bastard," she said, and sniffed. "Let's go home."

They stopped by a phone booth on the way, and Eddi called Carla.

"They've got him, all right," Eddi said. "Looks like they grabbed him from the rehearsal space."

There was a long pause. "Shit," Carla said.

"Stay put tonight," Eddi told her. "Meet at the practice room at three tomorrow. Either we'll know something then, or we won't be able to stand it anymore."

"Jesus. Isn't there *anything* we can do in the meantime?"

"Is Dan there?"

"Yeah."

"Then what are you asking me for?"

Carla laughed, if reluctantly. "I'll tell him you said so."

When she'd hung up, she stood for a minute looking out through the wet glass of the booth. She'd found a spot under an awning to park the motorcycle, and the phouka sat on it, his arms crossed over his chest, his head down. In the window beside him a neon beer sign flashed on and off. It lit the rain in his hair with red reflections and tinted his profile. She wondered if it was the light that made him look sad and tired.

She ran across the street through the drizzle. When he looked up, she kissed him.

"I love you," she said.

"Whatever gave you the idea that I needed to hear that now?"

"I don't know."

"Well, whatever it was, I'd like to thank it." The bleak look was gone from his face.

They rode home through the gathering storm, as the thunder caught up with the lightning. When they pulled up behind the apartment building, the weather struck in earnest. The rain pounded them, and they ran for the back door and left puddles on the stair landings. Once inside the apartment, neither of them moved to turn on a light. Rain slapped the windows like hail; the lightning strobed through the room.

Eddi went to the windows. "Have you ever noticed how lightning takes the color out of things?" she said. "Every time there's a flash, it looks like a bad print of a movie."

"Eddi . . ." The phouka clutched the back of the armchair, looking down. "Nothing is as I would have wanted it, but I . . ." He flung his head back, shaking water out of his hair. Between one roll of thunder and the next, she heard a frustrated sigh.

She knew suddenly how it would feel to touch him: sliding her hands across the wet, chilly fabric of his shirt and finding his skin warm underneath. She shivered.

He stepped forward and laid his hand on her upper arm. "You're cold."

She put her fingers over his, to keep him from pulling them away. They stood like that for a moment before Eddi lifted his hand. She touched it to her lips, one fingertip at a time. His other hand curled around the back of her neck and drew her to him. She relinquished his fingers and kissed his mouth.

"Come with me," she said at last, when her head felt light and her heartbeat rattled her like the thunder did the windowpanes. She led him through the lightning into the bedroom.

He stood very still beside the bed. He might have been reluctant—but she heard him breathe, saw his face and his closed eyes in the intermittent light. She slid the damp brocade coat off his shoulders and let it drop to the floor, then unbuttoned the waistcoat beneath. That followed the coat, and she began to work on the tiny pearl buttons buried in the ruffles of his shirt. She heard him laugh breathlessly.

"I could make it all vanish if you prefer."

"Don't you dare. I enjoy this."

"I can tell." He drew her damp hair back from her face and kissed her temples. "So do I. You'll forgive me, won't you, if my knees become too weak to hold me up?"

"I think so." She finished with the buttons, and began to slip the shirt off his shoulders.

"Cuffs," he murmured, and attended to them himself. Eddi watched, fascinated with him. There was a remarkable, pleasurable tension in it—she knew he was conscious of her gaze on him, and yet he didn't raise his eyes until he'd dropped the shirt on the floor. Then he shook his hair back and faced her, unsmiling, his chin up in the haughty pose that meant he was scared. The streetlight in the alley filtered through the blinds, painted highlights on the muscles of his chest and abdomen and shone on the tight-curled hair growing there.

He took her chin in his hand and kissed her. "I haven't the faintest idea how to get you out of this, you know," he said, tapping the velvet on her shoulder.

Eddi realized why he'd seemed so absorbed in his cuffs—she was seized with shyness as she undid the zipper under her arm and pulled the blouse over her head.

"Ah," he said softly. "That's where it is. I can manage the rest, I think." He did, his hands careful at her waist. Hers shook over the buttons of his pants. The most vulnerable moments in lovemaking were in undressing, Eddi decided. She would have examined the notion, but her thoughts wouldn't settle down long enough for study.

She was half-afraid to hold him naked against her, but only half. He was all smooth, soft skin over hard muscle, all hungry mouth and inquiring hands. She turned away long enough to pull the bedcovers back. He sat on the edge of the bed and pulled her to him, but she kissed him swiftly and shook her head. "Lie down on your stomach," she said.

He raised his eyebrows, but obeyed.

She wanted to make it last. She would only have one chance to make love to him for the first time; though arousal was itself a powerful glamour and clouded the mind, she chose to linger over his body. She kissed his neck, beneath the crisp black hair. She stroked his shoulders with her lips, and sketched his spine with kisses. His fingers stretched out tense and then curled, like a stroked cat's paws. She heard a hiss of indrawn breath when she reached the small of his back, and again at the insides of his thighs. She nudged lightly at his waist with one hand, and he rolled over.

She knelt over him, and kissed his mouth and eyelids, his ears, down his throat. He fastened both hands on her hips, then let his palms slide upward, over her stomach and ribs and breasts, across her shoulders to her arms. Then he pulled her down against him. His excitement fueled hers—his breathing fast and harsh, his heart pounding under her spread fingers.

The world shrank slowly, steadily, until it was a tight-fitting envelope that barely held the two of them, the continuous, two-colored surface of their skin and all the sensations that coursed along it. Her thoughts were blurred and broken; she moved by instinct, through pleasure like a brewing storm. Then he cried out beneath her, and all her senses failed in light and darkness. When she had skin again, and a body, she found that he did, too, and they were sweat-damp and drained, twined around each other. They dozed like that, and the warm, grassy smell of his hair invaded her dreams and made them sweet.

The first time she woke, the sky was lighter outside the bedroom blinds. The phouka lay on his side next to her, asleep. With his restless energy set aside, his eyes closed, and the lines of his mouth softened in sleep, he looked about seventeen. She drew the sheet up over his shoulder and shut her eyes again.

When she woke again the sun was up, and he was awake, propped on one elbow and watching her.

"Mm." She smiled at him. "What're you doing up?"

"I need very little rest. Do you know that when I tickle your nose, you frown at me in your sleep just as you do when you're awake?"

"When were you tickling my nose?"

"Just now, to make you wake up. You see? I told you that you frown."

She tried to throw her pillow at him. That led them, through devious routes, to another kiss, which in its turn led them to lovemaking.

Afterward, she said sleepily, "What time is it?"

"A little before noon, I think," the phouka replied, playing with her hair.

"D'you figure Her Ladyship has made up her mind yet?"

"We can hope. Would you like me to find out?" He swung his legs over the edge of the bed. She watched him go out into the living room, brown and graceful. For a moment she felt a wordless, longing ache, as if he were a line of music she couldn't reproduce.

He stood at the kitchen table, doing something to a piece of paper from the telephone notepad. She slid out from under the sheet and went to lean in the bedroom door.

"What's that?"

"You'll see." He was folding the paper, his fingers quick and certain. Just as she recognized it, he held up the finished paper airplane. He went to the living room window, blew softly on the plane, and launched it out over the alley. "You thought I was joking, didn't you?" he grinned.

"When you said you got messages by paper airplane? Of course I did." The plane was a scrap of white, spiralling over the next roof in an updraft—and then it was gone. Not carried out of sight, but vanished between one moment and the next.

The phouka came and leaned on the other post of the doorframe, so that their hips barely brushed. "Of course, the very idea is a joke of sorts. We're fond of children's toys and games. The best of them have the power of symbol and ritual, polished and perfected through years of repetition."

Eddi smiled. "I think it's just your essential juvenile nature coming out." She went into the bathroom to start the shower.

"Oh, a good bit of that, too," the phouka said over the sound of the water. "But you'd be amazed. Centuries of mortals seeking to master magic, pursuing blood sacrifice and self-denial and all manner of unpleasant studies. And if only they'd known the trick of it, they could have slain their enemies with a game of jackstraws."

Eddi stepped under the flow of water and looked out at him. "Can I slay *my* enemies that way?"

His mouth took a sudden wry twist. "Unfortunately, no. You have the wrong sort of enemies."

"Good."

"Good?"

"If it was that easy, I'd feel sort of obliged to do it. And I'm not hot to start killing people."

He stepped into the tub and pulled the shower curtain closed behind him before he answered. "It may come to that, you know," he said quietly.

"But it might not. Pass the shampoo?"

They took pleasure that was only slightly erotic in scrubbing each other's back, and they stood embracing under the shower head, so that the water would rinse them both at once.

Eddi went into the bedroom to dress. The phouka's costume from the night before was gone. *I'll never have to pick up his dirty socks,* she thought. Then she noticed that her clothes were gone, as well. She opened the closet and found them there, the skirt clean and pressed, the black velvet blouse unmarked by last night's rain. Meg, of course. She fingered the velvet and nodded.

She pulled on a jade green boat-necked T shirt and baggy trousers of white cotton, and went to see what the phouka was doing.

He was just coming out of the kitchen with a plate and two forks. He'd conjured up a pair of tight paisley jeans but no shirt. Eddi paused to admire the shape of him, compact and slender, wide-shouldered and narrow-hipped and muscular without bulk.

The plate was full of omelette. "Eat hearty," the phouka said and handed her a fork. "You won't regret you did."

She paused over the food, stabbed by a little blade of guilt. What did Willy have for breakfast today? The phouka looked up at her swiftly, as if he'd seen her hesitation and understood.

"Eat," he said. "It's all you can do, just now."

She nodded and took a bite. "Did Meg leave this?"

"Mm-hm."

"But it's still hot."

"I know," he said, with wicked amusement. "It's magic."

"Phooey." Then she realized that the centerpiece on the table was a little paper airplane, light green. "What's it say?"

"It says that our presence is requested in Loring Park, at the fountain, in half an hour. So eat up."

"Hmph," she said, but she did.

The day was clear and hot, and owed nothing to the past night's thunderstorm. They walked the few blocks to Loring Park. It was a shallow, grassy scoop of land with a meandering ornamental pond in the bottom, an arched wooden bridge, two pretty stuccoed park buildings, a couple of tennis courts, an unroofed bandstand—and the fountain. It bloomed at the edge of the park like a white dandelion head made of water. There were no old men on the benches there, no kids playing on the wall—an unnatural state. Then she saw three figures on the other side. The details were blurred by the curtain of spray, but she knew them by their bearing, and by the uncanny air that was always a part of them. She stepped forward to greet the Queen of the Seelie Court and her honor guard.

The queen wore her customary pale green in a short tank dress, with a wide white leather belt studded with silver. A silver maple leaf, the size of the real thing, hung from one of her earlobes. Her blood-red hair was loosely clubbed at the nape of her neck. Oberycum was dressed in a beige linen suit and a dark green silk T shirt, and looked as if even so elegant a compromise chafed him. Nothing about him was quite appropriate to modern dress. The other member of the queen's company, a man of the Sidhe with striking deep-gold hair, wore a black muscle shirt, camo-print parachute pants, and mirrored sunglasses. Eddi wanted to ask him where he'd left his Uzi.

The queen gave them a stiff nod as they came up. The phouka showed no inclination to kneel; perhaps the meeting was informal.

"Good afternoon," Eddi said, not knowing what else to do. "How did you manage to get the place all to yourselves?"

"A work of no great moment," the queen said, and gestured to Oberycum. He raised one hand, as if signaling a waiter. The wind changed direction, grew stronger, and water from the fountain spattered the benches on the opposite side.

"Uh-huh," said Eddi. "I'll remember that next time I'm on a

crowded bus.'' She wondered at her own rudeness, and tried to subdue it.

"You urged us to decide quickly on the matter of Willy Silver,'' the queen said, her face and voice composed. ''We have done so. You need concern yourself no longer.''

Eddi blinked. ''Does that mean you're going to give up Como Park after all?'' She was dismayed, but it was the sort of grand gesture she'd come to associate with Faerie.

"No," said the queen. An expression, or the shadow of one, crossed her face and was gone, before Eddi could tell what it was. Beside her, the phouka shifted his weight nervously.

"What *are* you going to do?''

"You have not the right to question us,'' the queen replied, too quickly. Eddi felt a flutter in her nerves, and knew she was hearing bad news. ''Your choices are not ours, you have responsibility for no one but yourself.''

All the pieces fell together in Eddi's head. They must have done the same for the phouka; there was dread and denial in his face. ''You're going to give him to her, aren't you?''

"Do you censure us for that? Is it not the judgment of mortal rulers, that for the good of the greater number, the few must sometimes suffer? I have but taken my example from your kind. Do you say that it is a bad one, an unjust one?''

She had seen the queen in the grip of anger. This, too, was anger, but with something else in the mix—a core of pain. Eddi felt no fear of her, no awe. If anything, she pitied her. So bound by the past, by her heritage, that she was half-blind. . . . ''Someday,'' Eddi said, fighting the distraction of her own thoughts, ''I should talk to you about mortal rulers. Have you sent word to the Unseelie Court yet?''

"It is not,'' said the queen in a glacial voice, ''your place to ask.''

Eddi made a fist and took a deep breath. ''What if I told you I could do something about it? Would it be my place then?''

The phouka looked quickly at her, then looked down. The queen studied her narrowly. ''And *can* you do aught to mend this? Be warned, we'll not countenance idle talk now.''

"In other words, put up or shut up? If you've already told the Unseelie Court that you won't deal with them, I can't do anything at all.''

"We have sent no message,'' the Lady said grudgingly.

"How many of your people know you've decided this?''

"All who know stand within this circle now."

"Good. Make sure it stays that way." In the back of her head was a horrified voice telling her to behave in the presence of the Lady, but she hadn't time to listen. "If anyone asks, say that you haven't decided yet. Will you promise me that?"

"To what purpose?" asked the queen.

"If you tell her you won't give her the park, she'll kill Willy. Boom. She's got no reason to keep him around."

"She will kill him all the same, in the end. What can you accomplish by the delay, but the extension of his suffering?"

Eddi looked into that cold, proud face and saw a strange thing: not hope, not quite yet, but a plea for some reason to hope.

"I'll tell you as soon as it's safe," Eddi said. "Do you promise not to send any word to her?"

The queen lifted her chin. "You have my promise."

Eddi turned to Oberycum and the Sidhe in the sunglasses. "How about you two?"

Oberycum raised one eyebrow, but finally nodded, and the other man followed his lead.

"Right." She was grinning and wasn't sure why. This was akin to the mania that often grabbed her on stage, that sometimes led her astray. "I'll be off, then."

"Send us word immediately you are able. You will risk our displeasure else. You are dismissed."

Eddi and the phouka bowed and backed away, a performance that the queen did not stay to watch. She and her retinue strode off toward the trees.

"Come on," Eddi said, and started across the park at a fast walk.

"Mmm." The phouka kept pace with her easily. Not until they'd retraced their route back to the edge of the park did he say, "Very well, my primrose. Will you tell me now what you're up to?"

"Sure. You're going to get word to Hedge that we're meeting at three, and we're getting the bike and going to the rehearsal space."

"Eddi . . . *Do* you have a plan?"

"Hell, no."

"Then what, by seven leaves from seven holy oaks, was all of that?"

He was as exasperated now as she had ever been with him, in their early days together. But she didn't have time to enjoy that properly. "No, I don't have a plan. Yet. But I'm damn well going to have a plan, if I can keep the Lady from cutting her own throat first. If I told her I didn't have any good ideas, but would she please do this as a favor to me, do you think she would have listened?"

"No," the phouka admitted.

"Tell me what's happening with Willy right now." the phouka frowned, and she added quickly, "I don't mean gory details. Where's he being held? How do they manage to hold him at all, given that he's got all the powers of the Sidhe?"

For a moment he was silent, thinking. "The difficulty, beloved, is in the 'where.' Faerie is outside the boundaries of this world. And even if you could cross into it without the heavy price such a crossing entails, you would have to find him still."

"Could you find him?"

"No, worse luck. In Faerie there are layers of being and place. There are lands encysted in other lands, undiscoverable. Somewhere in all of that she holds Willy prisoner, and not the Lady herself could find him without the Dark Queen's cooperation."

"Then he won't be in reach again until Como Park, when she pops back in at the Conservatory. Damn. What else? How does she hold him?"

He glanced at her, and she saw some of her excitement in him. "The Dark Queen's power is greater than any in Faerie save that of the Lady. Her magic can control Willy's, and her strength can keep him weak."

"What if you don't want to go head-to-head with her? Is there anything you can use against her?"

"Several things, depending on the circumstances. Rowan, salt, various herbs. But none of them will hold her long. All that can truly bind her is superior power, or her own sworn word."

"We may not need very long. We'll see."

"Tell me, love—you're determined to make no mention of any of this to the Lady?"

Eddi stopped in the middle of the sidewalk and shook her head at him. "You're the one who said there's a security problem in the Seelie Court."

"Yes, but—the Lady and her consort?" He raised his eyebrows.

Eddi shrugged. "What she doesn't know, she can't veto. Now, how do we get hold of Hedge?"

He looked smug. "I attended to that this morning."

"You're good, did you know that?"
"Oh yes."

Eddi cleaned up the signs of what had happened in the practice room. The phouka had offered to do it, but she'd turned him down; he watched, concerned, while she went about it. The brisk progression from task to task helped her restlessness. She bundled up the sheet, took it downstairs to the parking lot, and stuffed it in the dumpster. She set the mike stand up and tested the mike in it. She opened all the windows to blow the burnt smell away. And she changed the broken string on Willy's guitar.

The replacement came from Willy's guitar case, though opening it seemed like an invasion of his privacy. Were she to look in Hedge's case, she knew, she would find the plush unmarked and barely crushed, the hinge on the inside compartment still stiff, and nothing in it but, perhaps, an unopened set of spare bass strings. Willy's guitar case had more character.

The lining was torn down one side and threadbare in most places. It held a litter of dog-eared papers written over in a compact, ornamented hand that Eddi knew must be Willy's. She couldn't resist looking at them quickly. For the most part they were song lyrics and the accompanying chord progressions, with notes on the lead parts. Some of the songs were Eddi's. On one of them, in the margin next to a verse, there were a pair of exclamation marks. Symbolizing what? Amusement? Surprise? Pleasure? On another there was a quickly drawn staff with three measures' worth of notes on it. She played them in her head and found they were the lead riff she'd suggested for that spot. Next to it he'd written, "Yes."

There were guitar picks scattered throughout, some of them broken. In the accessory compartment she found a jumble of strings in their paper packets; two empty packets, crumpled but never thrown out; a yellow newspaper clipping about a bluegrass festival in West Virginia; an address in Detroit written on a napkin in blue ballpoint; a chrome bottleneck; three dimes; a rhinestone earring; and a battered bluejay feather.

"What have you found?" asked the phouka over her shoulder.

"Mostly that I don't know anything about him." She sighed, chose a string that seemed like the right gauge, and closed the case. She pulled Willy's guitar into her lap and stripped off the broken string.

The phouka dropped onto the couch. For a while he seemed

absorbed in studying the ceiling; when he spoke, he sounded pensive. "Sometimes I think he's the best of a bad lot. He's the youngest of the Sidhe, you know, and one of the very few native to this country."

"He told me things about himself, when we first . . . Were they true?"

"I don't know what he said, but I imagine so. He has spent a long time out of Faerie, traveling, living alone or among human-kind. For the Sidhe, he is a puzzle—not a disgrace, but full of things that seem alien to them. They think his concerns are too much those of mortal folk."

"Shows you how much they know about mortals," Eddi muttered.

The phouka smiled. "It's true that Willy has learned the surface of mortal life, and missed much of the substance. But not all of it. He is hunting something, and he doesn't hunt it in Faerie. However much that may distress his kin, I've taken it as a hopeful sign."

Eddi tuned the new string to her guitar, and tried a few chords. Willy's axe was an excellent one, with good electronics and action. Other than that, it was a perfectly ordinary guitar. "You mean, that the next generation will rule better than this one? Just because one of 'em is restless and hangs out with mortals?"

"If the failing of this generation is complacency, yes."

"I wouldn't say your queen is complacent right now."

"Now," he said softly, "neither would I."

They heard people on the stairs. It was Carla, Dan, and Hedge, all at once. Eddi saw Carla look around the room for things out of place.

"Have a seat, guys," Eddi told them. "The news is pretty strange."

She told them about her meeting with the Lady. Dan looked grim. Hedge looked pale and sick. "They're gonna let him *die?*" Carla wailed, as if the Seelie Court had failed to consider the consequences of the decision, and by sheer volume, she could remind them.

Eddi paced once to the windows and back. "If we do anything about this, guys, it could be us, too."

" 'S enough."

It was Hedge who'd said it; they all stared at him. He un-folded from the floor and faced Eddi.

"Can't listen. Wouldn' want me to, if y' knew. May's well leave." He shot a glance at all of them, out from under his hair, and turned sharply to go.

"Hedge!" Eddi's voice stopped him, though it wasn't harsh. "If we knew what?"

"Nuthin'," he muttered, his back to her. " 'F I go 'way, won' matter."

"Tell me."

The phouka sat at the edge of the couch. His eyes were on Hedge.

Hedge took a step toward the door, and Eddi said, "Please?"

It was too much for him. He spun around, his face snarled with pain, and said, "Awright! 'L tell ya! Been talkin' to th' Dark Court, that's what!"

It was a moment before any of them realized what that meant. Then, "All along?" the phouka asked, almost gently.

Hedge nodded. "Didn' think it'd hurt much. Didn' care, at first. Just some human, make e'rybody die—who cares wha' happens to 'er?" He looked up at Eddi, his brown eyes big with anguish. "I didn' know! Didn' know *you!*"

The phouka rose, and it was a dreadful coiling movement. *Don't, don't, don't,* Eddi thought at him.

"Does this have to do with Willy?" she asked Hedge, though she thought she knew the answer.

Hedge squeezed his eyes shut, as if they hurt. "Wanted me t' help get Willy. Wouldn'. Too late, though. Already told 'er enough t' do it. 'S my fault."

"You told them who and where she was," the phouka said at last, slowly. "You would have tossed her life to them and thought nothing of it." Eddi realized that he was talking about her. She put her hand on his arm, squeezed it, and he stayed quiet, but only barely.

"Just at first! Wouldn' after a while, just told 'em little stuff, nothin' 'bout Eddi, 'r th' band even. Last week, decided t' shut up 'bout all of it, f'rget th' whole thing. Knew you guys 'd say it was wrong t' talk. An' then she asked me t' get Willy."

"Why didn't you *tell* somebody?" Carla snapped.

Hedge scowled at her; then the corners of his mouth crumpled, and he turned his face away. "Scared to," he muttered.

The room filled up with silence and tension in the seconds that followed. The phouka stood poised for some action, if he could only decide which one. Carla stared at Hedge as if she wasn't sure he was a good idea. Dan looked puzzled and hurt and shaken, and Eddi realized for the first time how much he loved this band, how much like family they had all become.

She took the few steps necessary to reach Hedge, and put a hand on his shoulder. "Do you want a chance to help fix things?" she asked him.

He looked up swiftly, his face intent.

"Did you break with the Unseelie Court yet? Did you tell them you wouldn't spy for them anymore?"

Hedge winced at the word "spy," but shook his head. "Scared to," he repeated.

Eddi breathed in deep. "Are you too scared to make up for it?"

She watched him as he covered his face with both hands. She felt far away, and calm. There was a bright spot in the back of her head, growing steadily, and the more she looked at it, the more it seemed to be the beginning of a plan. She decided to speak some of it aloud and see what happened to it. "I need somebody to feed bullshit to the bad guys, and get a little information out of them, besides. If they think you're still on their side . . ."

Hope made Hedge look young and frail, as if light would shine through him.

"It's dangerous—you know better than I do what would happen to you if they found out. But I'm going to bust Willy loose. Somehow. And I need all the help I can get."

"All *right*," said Dan, his voice low and fierce. Carla whooped and flung her arms around him. Hedge just smiled. But it was one of those smiles, the kind that radiated like heat from a stove. He stuck out his hand, and Eddi shook it. At the corner of her vision, she saw the phouka; his face was full of love and something like awe.

CHAPTER NINETEEN

When the Generals Talk

The weather turned suddenly to damp heat, the kind that settled on the shoulders and made people walk as if they were twenty pounds too heavy. It pointed tempers and blunted energy, and gave despair a great seductive power. But they had only three days; they couldn't wait for the heat wave to break.

Eddi primed Hedge with rumors of disarray in the Seelie Court, disaffection in the band, and unwillingness in either group to deal with the other. He offered his cautious opinion that these were falling on fertile ground. Eddi hoped so; if the Dark Queen believed them capable of organizing a counterstrike, she might do something about it. But Hedge had no luck finding out where Willy was held. Eddi abandoned the faint hope that he might be a prisoner somewhere other than Faerie, that they might attempt a rescue before their deadline. At the Conservatory, the Queen of Air and Darkness would be most on her guard.

Dan and Carla hunted for equipment to rent. Eddi and the phouka went to scout out the terrain. It was only as they were negotiating the gracious sweep of parkway toward the Conservatory that Eddi realized her mistake.

"Ohmigod," she said, and stopped the bike. "There's bound to be a critter or two from the Unseelie Court around here. If they spot us, they'll know we're up to something."

The phouka cocked his head. "Is that all? There's an easy remedy for that, my sweet."

"Hightail it out of here?"

"Not a bit. Turn your shirt wrong way out, and put it back on."

"*What?*"

He was already stripping off his jacket (raw silk, in tangerine) and pulling the sleeves inside out. When she sat and stared at him, he grinned. "Once you would have thought this an elaborate practical joke."

"What makes you think I don't anymore?" she asked weakly.

"Because you trust me." He looked wickedly pleased, and as if he might leave it at that. But he relented. "I have told you that magic has much to do with symbolism. This is more of it. When you turn your coat, you are wearing your recognizable self face inward. To those who see the magical surface of things, you are invisible."

"Good grief. Will you still be able to see me?"

He met her eyes in a way that made her shiver pleasantly. "I see you in a great many ways. It would be hard to blind me in all of them."

She was wearing a shirt over a tank top; she shrugged and took the shirt off. "Won't people stare when they see a couple of weirdos with their seams showing?"

The phouka only raised an eyebrow at her.

"You're right. So what." Eddi buttoned the shirt over her breast as if it were armor, and drove the rest of the way to the Conservatory.

She'd been there once many years before, with college friends on a picnic. She remembered only a splendid glass building without details. The decaying grandeur of the thing that rose before her now left her staring, wondering how she could have forgotten it.

The center was an immense double-curved dome of glass, the Moorish fantasy of some early twentieth century Minnesotan, topped with a glass cupola and a stubby spire like a playing piece from a game of Clue. Glass wings stretched out from it on either side, one with an arched roof, one with an angular one. The entryway was itself a little greenhouse, with a pointed roof and glass between the white-painted pillars. The wide, shallow steps up to it were studded with tubs of petunias, purple and red and white. The scent of them was thick in the hot air.

Inside, the Conservatory was as hot and damp as the outdoors, and the air could not be called perfumed. The smell was of moist earth and peat, fertilizers, wet bark, and plants that weren't grown for their fragrance. But it was a rich, intoxicating smell. Eddi was disoriented by an impression of living things, so many of them, full of small motions. She realized after a moment that the phouka had taken her elbow and was looking at her closely.

"I think it's the heat," she mumbled.

"No. It's not. This is a place of power, my heart, leashed and tended and concentrated to a fearful degree. Magic breathes under every leaf here, and mutters to itself." He stared at the base of an enormous palm tree beside them, as if it were much farther away. "I should be able to tell you the character of this magic, whether it serves the Dark Court or the Light. And I cannot. This is a wild power. She is rash to do her business here."

Eddi was glad of his distraction. It gave her time to catch her breath, to feel her heart slow down. Whatever had overwhelmed her had retreated to background noise. "Let's go. We've got work to do."

There were only a few people in the Conservatory; a gardener passed them once, and two women with babies in strollers wandered the paths, absorbed in conversation. After studying them suspiciously for a moment, Eddi decided that they were what they seemed.

The central domed room of the Conservatory was given over entirely to palms. In the middle, on a raised, paved area, was a wishing fountain with a bronze sculpture of a woman dancing on the crest of a wave. Dolphins poked startled-looking faces out of the curl beneath her foot. The woman's beauty, her unselfconscious grace, reminded Eddi of the creatures of the Seelie Court.

Would the Dark Queen hold her meeting here? For such a large room, it had little open space, only widened spots on the flagstone path for benches. It seemed like the wrong sort of room for her.

They peered at the walls and ceiling, looking for anything they could put to use in rescuing Willy. There was infuriatingly little. "I don't suppose the Unseelie Court melt if you squirt them with a garden hose," Eddi said sourly.

"No, more's the pity. Garden hose does seem in plentiful supply."

"Maybe we can trip them with it. Let's see the next room."

The next was the north wing, with its angular roof. It was Oriental and exquisite. There were citrus trees and bamboo, holly and oleander and magnolias, pine trees and one extraordinary California redwood. At the heart of the room, like a close-kept secret, there was a pool where water dripped musically from a source somewhere in the roof. The end of the wing was a Japanese rock garden fronted with stone benches.

"Maybe here?" she said.

The phouka looked thoughtful. "Perhaps. There are things here that are hers—vervain and pomegranate and myrtle. But . . ."

"Right. *But*. It's too . . . secretive, or something."

He eyed her for a long moment. "She can be secretive."

"I bet she can. But she wouldn't stage this like a KGB spy exchange. She'd want to make a production of it. Wouldn't she?"

"Hmm," he said, and they went on to the next wing.

It was the fern room, and even more unsuitable than the rest. It was a long, narrow corridor. The ferns grew thick and high, and curtained the view from anywhere in the room. If, indeed, Willy's release was to be a production, there was no place to put the audience.

"I feel like I'm trying to find a site for a concert," Eddi grumbled as they came back to the palm house, the hub of the wheel.

"For what it's worth," said the phouka, "I favor the north wing."

Then they turned right through a set of double glass doors and stopped.

"May I change my vote?" the phouka asked.

They stood on a terrace at a wrought-iron railing, looking out over a formal sunken garden. A keyhole-shaped pond ran most of its length, the water almost hidden by water lilies. Boxwood and laurel, pruned in stately shapes, marched along the glass walls. At the far end six Italian cypress rose tall and thin, like great dark sentinels. They stood guard over an arched alcove. It was too far away for Eddi to see what was in it.

Steps led down from their terrace on both sides. Beside each flight a bay tree grew, the shiny dark leaves massed in a spreading mushroom-cap shape. The flagstone path traced the shape of the pond, from one flight of steps to the alcove and back to the steps on the other side. Lamps hung from the ceiling down the center of the room, made of leaded panes of glass in the shape of many-pointed stars.

The plantings blurred before Eddi's eyes, turning into streaks and pools of color. Then they came into abnormally sharp focus: gloxinias and begonias, mounded geraniums and chrysanthemums, coleus and baby's breath, tall nodding roses in red, white, yellow, pink, and clear orange. The lily pads in the pond stirred at the edge of her vision; then she saw the red-fire streaks of the goldfish sheltering under them. For a moment, the whole glass room seemed to be dancing. But she blinked, and everything around her was formal and still again.

The phouka frowned at her, but stayed silent.

"This is it," Eddi said. "If it isn't, my last name's Van Halen. Come on, let's get serious."

They walked slowly down the stairs and along the path. They found things, though they weren't sure how to make use of them. There was a watering system, a network of tubes like capillaries that fed each potted plant. There was a reflecting ball on a pedestal at the end of the pool. There was another paved terrace before the alcove, and a fountain in it.

The phouka dropped down on one of the benches on that terrace. "Little to work with, I'm afraid."

"Oh, I don't know. I've got some ideas. What *are* those things under her feet?"

The phouka looked at the fountain, where another bronze girl was dancing. "Frogs, I think."

"Yuck."

"What are your ideas?"

Eddi shook her head. "The snapdragons have ears. Tell you later."

She woke early the next morning. She unwrapped herself from the warm cocoon of the phouka's arms, and he was awake at once, though she'd been gentle. He came out of sleep quickly and alert. She wondered if he always did, and felt a moment's terror that she might never know.

He raised his eyebrows at her.

"Gonna see if Meg's here," Eddi whispered. "Go back to sleep."

"I doubt if I can. But if you prefer it, I can lie here and be still."

"Probably a good idea." Eddi grinned at him and kissed his nose. "She thinks you're full of nonsense."

"She's lamentably ignorant of my better qualities."

"You mean she hasn't seen you with your clothes off?" Eddi thought he blushed.

She wrapped her kimono around her and went quietly into the living room. At first, she thought Meg had already gone, or hadn't come yet. Then she saw a herd of dustballs roll out from under the couch in what, had they been alive, would have been panic. She waited until they'd clambered up the side of the wastebasket and thrown themselves in. Then she said cautiously, "Meg?"

The nose came out first around the back of the couch, followed by the scowling brown face. "Tha hair wants combin'."

"I'll get to it, I promise. Meg—"

She disappeared behind the couch again. "I'm worrrkin'," she said gruffly.

Eddi sat down in the armchair and propped her chin on her hand. She'd think this was just Faerie perversity—but Carla was like this sometimes, when something needed discussing, and Carla was afraid to do it. "Okay," Eddi said. "You work. I'll talk. You've heard about Willy, I suppose?"

The rustling behind the couch went on, but Eddie didn't think she was being ignored.

"Well, the Lady has decided that she can't give up Como Park for him. I can understand that. Willy would probably even understand it. You can't throw away the good of the whole Court for one guy."

Behind the couch, there was a thump.

"After studying the situation, I've decided that this is a job for a third-party contractor. So I'm going to rescue Willy."

The reaction to that was silence. Finally Meg came out from behind the couch, wearing an expression eloquent of not-very-patient suffering. "Wha's that tae do wi' me?"

Eddi sighed. "I'd like you to help."

"Nay," Meg declared, lifting her chin. "I'll nae help."

Eddi had to bite her lip for a moment to keep her mouth closed. Then she said, "Why?"

"The young laird's nae charge o' mine. He's walked his road. If he canna thole what's at its end, worse luck tae him."

Eddi studied the little brown woman before her, standing so stiff and proud. The phouka had told her that the brownies were solitary, disinclined to bow to the wishes of the Sidhe. But she thought there was something uneasy about Meg's independence.

So she looked long at her, and said at last, "I wonder where you'd be now, if I'd thought like that at Minnehaha Falls?"

Meg's face screwed up with fury and anguish. "It's na' fair! Tha's got nae call tae fling what I owe in my face!"

"What do you owe, Meg?" she asked, knowing quite well.

"My life," Meg spat. "Tha may ask what tha will o' me, and I canna refuse aught."

Eddi laced her fingers together across her knees and stared at Meg until the brownie stared back. "I saved your life. The way I see it, your life is beyond price, right?"

Meg nodded shortly.

"Good. There are two ways to look at that. In one of them, you owe me a debt that you can't ever repay, and I pretty much own you." Eddi paused for dramatic effect, though she felt like a wretch for doing it. "But I told the phouka once that I *didn't* own you, and I still believe that. Lives *are* beyond price, and to treat them as if they have some kind of barter value is obscene." Meg looked puzzled, and Eddi continued, "I saved your life because it was the right thing to do."

She unfolded her hands and stood up.

"Lass!"

Eddi felt something sweep over her skin, a rush of hot or cold. It must have come from the sudden jump of her heart. She turned back to Meg.

"Lass . . . The Dark Lady, she's the de'il himself. She'll hurt tha dreadful if she can."

"Are you afraid?"

"A' course I am! Tha should be, too."

"Well," Eddi said, leaning on the back of the chair, "I am. But I have to do this anyway. And I hope you'll help me—but not because you think you owe it to me. Do it because you want to do me a favor, or Willy a favor, or because it's right. Or don't do it. I can't blame you if you don't. All our necks will be on the line, and there won't be anybody to save 'em if it goes wrong."

"The Lady and her folk?" Meg asked.

"They don't know anything about it. And they won't, till it's over. We're going to play by mortal rules, and I don't think the Sidhe would like it if they knew."

Meg screwed her mouth up, and rubbed her nose vigorously. "If I said aye—what would I do?"

Eddi sat back down in the armchair and leaned forward. "How are you at gardening?"

The sensible thing to do, on the afternoon of the battle for Como Park, would have been to take a nap. She couldn't, of course. Instead she and the phouka made love. They gave each other comfort and strength and pleasure, and took the same things back. And each pretended to be certain that it would happen again.

When Eddi left the bedroom to start a pot of coffee, she found her armor lying on the kitchen table. Black motorcycle leathers: zippered jacket, pants, knee-high boots. On top of the pile was a black Bell full-coverage helmet. On the side of it, she saw the design of the pin the phouka had given her, the five-petaled flower in the square, inlaid in gold and silver.

"Phouka?" she called, a little unsteady.

He was at the bedroom door almost instantly. "Ah," he said when he saw what she was looking at.

"Where did all this come from?"

"I think from whence your breakfast comes, love."

"This is Meg's work?" Her eyes burned, and she squeezed them shut firmly. "Maybe she doesn't want to have to mend my jacket again."

The phouka came and put his arms around her. "If you want to cry, you may, you know."

She turned and put her head on his shoulder. "No. If I do, I won't stop. I'm wound up too tight." She looked up at him and smiled a little. "This is worse than Minnehaha Falls. This time I *know* how much trouble I'm in."

"That, sometimes, is a kind of protection." He stroked her face, and she kissed his palms.

"What's with the little flower?" she asked, in a blatant change of subject.

The phouka nodded at the helmet with its insignia. "Every noble house has its colors and its device."

"Since when have I become a noble house?"

"Since first you came among us." His voice was barely more than a whisper, but it was full of that langorous power she'd heard there only rarely. "That we were all slow to recognize it makes it no less true."

He kissed her, as if in ritual, on the lips, and walked into the bedroom. She stared after him for a moment. Then she gathered up her armor and went to put it on.

The weather had broken, finally; there was a wind blowing. It was full of the chill of impending rain, and Eddi was glad of the leathers. The moon rode high, barely more than a quarter, and clouds boiled across it. She could see better than could be accounted for by that dim light, or the streetlamps, or the Triumph's headlight. But she was getting used to that. When all this was over would she keep the Faerie magic she'd acquired? If she lived long enough to see it end?

They met on Como Avenue, at the edge of the park. Carla's wagon was pulled up to the curb, and Hedge was leaning against the fender, in a tight T shirt and torn jeans, his hair in his eyes. Eddi drew up next to him and took the helmet off. His eyes widened when he realized who it was, and she grinned. "You're the very picture of juvenile delinquency," she told him.

"And *you* look like an ad for a movie," Carla said, leaning out the driver's side window.

"A good movie," the phouka said.

"Got a call just before we left my place," Carla told Eddi. "I didn't know whether to laugh or cry, under the circumstances."

"What?"

"We're gonna play First Avenue for the Fourth of July."

Eddi gaped. "We are?"

"Yep. Three-band bill, the third band cancelled out. We're replacing 'em."

"Ye gods. In the mainroom?"

"With all the flashing lights. Now we *really* have to get our guitar player back."

Eddi raked a hand through her hair. She understood what Carla meant about laughing or crying. "You've got all the stuff?"

"Down to the last patch cord. Now relax. We're gonna knock 'em dead."

"Carla, are you *enjoying* this?"

" 'Course she is," Dan sighed from the other side of the car. "Girl thinks she's in the middle of 'Mission: Impossible.' "

"Well, you're not, damn it," Eddi said fiercely. "This is real, and if anything screws up, you'll be dead."

Carla glanced down for a moment; when she looked up at Eddi again her expression was very different. "I know. But I may as well play this for all it's worth—just in case."

Neither of them wanted to talk about in-case-of-what, so Eddi put her helmet back on. "You know the drill. Follow in fifteen minutes, set up, and wait 'til you see us." She wished she could think of something cleverer to say than "Break a leg," but she couldn't. Instead she revved the bike and headed into the park.

The Conservatory was dark. Eddi parked in the curving drive in front, pulled off her helmet, and tucked it under her arm. She and the phouka walked warily up the steps. The outer doors stood open.

They stood in the palm house feeling naked beneath the pale

glass arch of the roof. The shadows were deep under the leaves, and full of rustlings. Eddi hoped it was just a ventilator blowing.

There was a glow to her left, very soft. She turned and saw the frame of the double doors into the sunken garden faintly luminous, and felt a rush of relief. If they had been wrong, if the Dark Queen had chosen the north wing after all . . . She tugged the phouka's shirt sleeve. He nodded and followed her.

The sunken garden was dim, the colors extinguished by the faint moonlight. What light there was bounced off the water of the pond between the lily pads, like puddles on a wet road. Eddi stepped to the edge of the terrace and clutched the iron railing.

Light leaped up—both electric and eldritch. The star-shaped hanging lamps glittered. The flagstones of the path shone softly at all their edges. The struts in the arched roof were streaks of pale light. It was more than enough to show the Queen of Air and Darkness, in a gray jumpsuit and a long gray coat, on the far terrace before the alcove. Her guards were ranked among the trimmed boxwood. Then a wet, dark-green creature shambled out from under the bay tree toward them. The phouka stepped quickly between it and Eddi.

The queen's lovely, throaty voice carried the length of the room. "I'm afraid you'll have to submit to a search." She sounded amused.

The thing, which seemed to be animate pond scum, had quick, cold fingers. She stood very still and tried not to shudder. There was nothing to find on either of them, and the creature seemed irritable about it.

"Very well," said the queen. "Come in and make yourselves at home."

They walked down the glowing path side by side, though there was barely room for it. A little snarling mud-colored creature thrust a spidery hand from beneath a coleus and grabbed Eddi's ankle, and she stopped.

"Control yourself," the queen said coldly, and the creature drew back.

They stood at last at the foot of the steps that led to the queen's terrace. "So," she said cheerfully, "what can I do for you?"

Eddi felt terribly cold; it even made her lips stiff. She swallowed and said, "We've come to ransom your hostage."

"Ah, of course." Her long dark eyes narrowed with catlike pleasure. "It is a very good joke, you know, that the pale bitch sent you as her envoy. She must hate you dreadfully."

Eddi felt hope like a spike of flame in her. Hedge's rumors had reached their destination, and the Dark Queen was not suspicious.

The queen looked over her shoulder and snapped her fingers. Two of the gray, milky-eyed monsters that Eddi so feared stepped from behind a cypress. They supported a figure between them, a figure in black jeans and a torn, bloodstained white T shirt. His arms were bound tightly behind him. There was a hood over his head, but it was unmistakably Willy.

They forced him to his knees beside the queen and pulled off the hood. At first he refused to look up. Then the queen twined her fingers in his hair and pulled his head back. He saw Eddi and the phouka, and his eyes went round with surprise. He closed them quickly.

Eddi was torn between anger and relief. There was dried blood at the corner of his mouth, and blood still stained the white streak in his hair. But he could walk, and think. They wouldn't have to carry him out.

"Do you know, I shall miss you," the queen said to Willy's upturned face.

"I'm afraid," Willy said, baring his teeth, "that I can't say the same about you." There was a dreadful cold fire in his green eyes. With a yank, he pulled his hair out of her grip.

"Now!" Eddi snapped. And out of the infinite closet from which he conjured all his clothes, the phouka summoned his coat.

Eddi plunged her hand into the pocket of it as it appeared around him. She pulled out a handful of what they had put there, and threw it at the Dark Lady. Rowan berries.

The queen stumbled back, her fact twisted with fury and disgust. Her magic unravelled for just a moment—but she was the only one in the room with the power to hold Willy, and in that moment, her hold broke. With a great wrench, he snapped the cord that held his arms. His right hand blazed with white fire. He flung that light and heat at the ceiling, at the bracket that held one of the star-shaped lamps, and it plunged, still lit, into the pond. Sparks plumed in all directions. Then he leaped off the terrace, as the phouka swatted down one of the gray things that had lunged to stop him.

The room was a scene out of hell. The tubes of the watering system had all reared out of their pots and begun to spray an extract of St. John's Wort at random. *Nice work, Meg,* Eddi thought. In the pool, where the lamp was shorting out, some-thing green thrashed, showing dreadful glimpses of limbs or tail or snake-jawed head. Creatures of all sizes and aspects dashed from the now-toxic flowerbeds toward the walls and began to climb the roof trusses.

They plunged through the chaos toward the double doors. One of the gray long-snouted horrors dropped down at them from the ceiling. Willy raised his burning hand and blasted it as it fell; it rained on them in foul-smelling cinders.

"No more of that for a while," Willy panted. "Hope you've got reinforcements."

"Not until we get outside," said the phouka, and kicked a redcap into the pond. It shrieked as the green thing pulled it under.

They were on the terrace. Eddi turned, looked back—she didn't know why. She felt the bay trees shaking on either side of her, reaching out and down. . . . But not for her. She felt the boxwood grow thorns as if they sprouted from her own skin. The cypress breathed fragrant poisons with her every exhalation. The roses twined and tangled and tripped the fey feet that blundered among them, and she felt the pull against her own fingers. For an instant, she heard the wild and terrible music that the garden danced to. Then the phouka grabbed her and yanked her out the door.

The fight had reached the palm house. She heard a dull smacking sound, and looked round to find Hedge holding a tire iron and trotting past an enormous heap of fur that must have been an attacker before he hit it.

"I told you to stay the hell outside!" Eddi yelled. He muttered and swung at one of the little mud-colored things. She lost sight of him behind the trunk of a palm.

Carla stood at the inside door, holding a pair of black drum-sticks as if they were daggers. "Graphite and epoxy," she said. "Damn near unbreakable."

"I told *you* to stay outside, too," Eddi grumbled.

Hedge loped out of the trees, ferocious triumph on his thin face. The phouka and Willy hit the doors a moment after he did. They set their backs against them, and the phouka pulled two pairs of very dark glasses out of an inside coat pocket. He flipped one to Willy. Hedge took his out of his jeans pocket. Carla had hers on already. Eddi pulled her helmet on; the faceplate was tinted.

"Ready?" she said.

"Hell, I hope so," Carla gasped. "Here they come!"

Before she turned toward the door, Eddi caught a glimpse of the creatures of the Unseelie Court boiling out of the undergrowth. She had no desire to look again.

They shot through the entryway and out into the night. Which became day. The first of their pursuers came through the door into the white glare of the carbon arc lamps mounted on the roof of the station wagon. Eddi watched for an instant, appalled, as one of the gray things reeled back with skin scorched black and falling away in strips.

"Move your ass!" Dan yelled from the car. "Batteries won't last much longer!"

Eddi leaped onto the Triumph and kicked it alive. The phouka pushed Willy onto the back of it.

"But . . . !"

"I'm faster than he is," the phouka said through his teeth. "Go!"

"Shit!" She twisted savagely on the throttle and sent the bike tearing down the hill, across the grass, to meet the Seelie Court's assembled might.

They were ranged across a vast open lawn, their white horses stamping and tossing their manes, their banners snapping in the high wind. Eddi braked hard and slammed the bike around, skidding wildly and scraping up turf. Willy leaped off and swatted her across the shoulders.

"Go get him!" he screamed against the wind and the roar of the cycle. "Hurry!"

Eddi popped the clutch and took off back toward the Conservatory.

The phouka was backed against the trunk of a tree by a long pale woman who smiled with a mouthful of white needles. Her expression turned to terror just before Eddi ran her down.

She stopped the bike and sat shaking until the phouka jumped on the back. He held her tightly as they rocketed back across the grass. Eddi knew it wasn't just to keep himself on the bike.

"Where are the others?" she yelled.

"They got away in the car."

"Hedge, too?"

"He was on the tailgate. He seemed to be enjoying himself."

Everybody does but us, she thought vaguely. "Are they heading home?"

"No. Did you really expect them to?"

"And Meg?"

"Out the back, through the growing houses. I doubt they had time to realize she was there."

And of course, she had been there all along, a homey, unobtrusive little spirit in a back room, unnoticed until she became a tornado to sweep them all up. Was it she who had set the plants themselves in motion?

She wheeled the bike when she got to the assembled Court, and drove along their line as if she were reviewing it. She could see the enemy on the opposite slope, a glittering darkness. At the end of the line she let the bike idle while she hauled off her helmet.

"Hot in this thing."

"Mm." He kneaded her shoulder muscles through her jacket. "What do you suppose the Lady had to say, when she saw you deliver Willy?"

Eddi snorted faintly. "Don't I wish I knew. No time to ask her now, though."

"No, I suppose not."

Then Willy himself came toward them through the fey army. He still wore his torn T shirt; his only concession to his place among the Seelie Court was the weapon he carried, the long white lance of the Sidhe horsemen. He saw the phouka on the back of the bike. "Good," he said, with a quick nod.

"Good," the phouka sighed. "I am saved from certain death, and all he says is 'Good.'"

Willy tried not to smile and failed. "That and 'Thank you.'"

Eddi looked up, startled. He'd said it as if it were in a foreign language—or as if the words had power. And, of course, they did.

"The bitch-queen said that Hedge had spied for her," Willy continued.

"She wanted him to help capture you," Eddi said quickly. "He refused."

Willy nodded. "Something about the way she told me made me think that he hadn't been all she'd hoped." He chuckled softly. "And he's a good man with a tire iron. But where did the St. John's Wort come from?"

"Hairy Meg."

Willy's grin faded, and wonder took its place. "Meg the brownie?"

"Yeah."

He looked down, then swiftly back at her. "You shame me—no, you shame us all. I hope we have the sense to recognize it."

The phouka's hands went stiff on her shoulders. "Showtime, my children," he said quietly. "You'd best put your helmet on again." When she turned to him he pointed with his chin. The black line on the other side of the field had begun to move.

Nothing that happened after that made sense. Or rather, it made perfect sense, but only within itself. They were all in a bubble of time and place where killing and dying happened and disappeared, like events passed on the roadside. She saw terrible things, had a constant nagging feeling that she was doing some of them. But caught up in the press, she was flung from one occurrence to another too quickly to be sure. She saw Stuart in the fighting, his features rearranged by fear and fury. Perhaps hers were, too. Then something hairy jumped in front of the bike, and she lost sight of him. She had to stop once to wipe drops of blood off her faceplate. She didn't know where it had come from; that disturbed her more than the blood itself.

They gathered together gradually, finding her by the sound of the bike: Dan, wielding a baseball bat as if he'd done it before; Carla with her drumsticks; and Hedge with his tire iron. Eddi and the phouka acted as cavalry on the Triumph. They worked their way through the chaos as a very loose unit, splitting up and reforming as the fighting demanded. Then the rain began.

It fell in sheets, in blinding curtains, and the grass under them was a field of mud in minutes. Eddi dumped the bike twice before she got it to higher ground and the trees.

Trees. She looked around dully. The fighting had swept across a street somehow—she should remember driving over the curbs, shouldn't she?—and it had all broken up into smaller engagements when they reached the wooded land. She slid off the bike and let it down on its side. It would be useless in the trees; she'd run into one and kill herself.

The phouka trotted up the slope beside her and propped himself against a tree. He looked drained.

"How're we doing?" Eddi asked, tugging off her helmet. Her hair was soaked with sweat and sticking to her forehead.

"I defy anyone to tell from here," he replied sourly. "But we seem to be at the eye of the storm, just at the moment."

"It *is* awfully quiet."

"I won't dignify that with the stock reply."

A shout and the sound of blows gave the lie to Eddi's words. "Well, there you go," she said, about nothing in particular, and they ran up the slope through the trees.

Hedge was in a little clearing, facing three of the enemy. He clubbed at one, a thick-limbed, thick-furred bearlike man, and missed. It showed its teeth and drew one great clawed hand back to strike him. Then a shaft of white cut through the gloom and into the bear-man's gut. Willy was on the other end of it. The remaining Unseelie folk fled into the undergrowth. Hedge looked startled, but Willy grinned and winked at him, and after an instant, Hedge smiled back.

Across the clearing, Eddi saw a man's silhouette through a break in the trees. She reached out and touched the phouka's arm. The man's shape was familiar, his size and stance. The brown brush of his hair—it was Stuart. She saw light glance off the steel barrel—

She probably screamed, but she couldn't tell. The sound of the gun filled up all her hearing. Why were guns never so loud in movies? She would never hear again, she knew it; she would never hear anything but that gunshot, going off forever.

A red watercolor blossom opened on Willy's soaked white T shirt. He stepped backward, wide-eyed, as if to catch his balance. The gun roared again, like a digital echo of the last shot. Willy sank to his knees. Eddi could see in his face the sudden knowledge of what was happening. There was horror there, but still no pain. The gun fired twice more, and Willy's shirt was red. He folded up onto the wet grass.

The phouka was fast, always so fast—why was he only halfway across the clearing, barely ahead of her? It had happened slowly, she had seen it.

Stuart turned and fired at the phouka. So slow. Why didn't he dodge? The bullet hit somewhere in the left half of him. Eddi heard the phouka's sharp cry, saw him turn with the impact and slip and fall hard.

Stuart was so *slow*. Eddi stepped toward him, toward the little mouth of the gun. She saw it waver, saw terror cover Stuart's face like ice over a pond. It made him pitifully ugly. What the hell was he afraid of? Hadn't he killed everything in the clearing that could scare him? She wrenched the gun out of his frozen hands and flung it away, heard it go off when it hit. It finally sounded like a gun in a movie: muffled, someone else's problem.

Stuart staggered backward until he bumped into a tree and slid down it. Eddi paid him no more attention. She started toward the phouka, but he had already risen to his knees. His right hand clutched his left shoulder.

"Never mind me! See to Willy!"

She crossed the clearing. Hedge was crouched over Willy, sobbing, one fist jammed in his mouth. She knelt beside the still figure on the grass, brushed the wet black-and-white hair out of his face.

He opened his eyes. The emerald brilliance was draining out of them, as the lit-from-within quality was leaching out of his pale skin and leaving it like white ashes. She was watching the victory of entropy, of mortality over magic. It made her sick.

His lips parted, and there was blood behind them. "Love and death," he whispered, and smiled. "I guess it's death, after all." His eyes squinted shut suddenly, in pain. They never opened again.

She couldn't breathe, her chest wouldn't move, her throat wouldn't let anything through. The rain had unaccountably turned salty. When she looked up, Hedge had rolled himself in a shaking ball on the other side of Willy's body. The phouka stood behind him, head down, hair dripping water slowly.

"He's dead," Eddi whispered, because someone had to admit it.

The phouka covered his face with both hands.

Carla and Dan stood at the edge of the trees. They didn't seem to believe it yet, not really. Stuart, on the other side of the clearing, sat propped against his tree, his knees pulled up, his hands over his eyes.

People had fought in this open space, and they had all lost. Death had won. Death had won all night, and would do it again, on and on at every battlefield. . . .

She ran from the clearing, past the phouka, past Carla and Dan, as fast as she could through the trees to where she'd dropped the Triumph. She pulled it up, started it, plunged down the slope on it. It wouldn't be hard to find what she was looking for. She could follow her own rage and hate, her own pain, the despair that threatened to empty her of herself. What she would do when she found what she wanted . . . something would occur to her.

The rain had stopped, and the smell of blood and smoke had risen in its wake. She knew now where the burning came from.

She remembered Willy lashing out with fire in the sunken garden, and she cried out with the bitterness of the memory. They had rescued him, they had saved his life. . . .

She had nothing white to use as a flag, was not even sure that Faerie recognized the convention of a flag of truce. All she could offer the Dark Queen's guard as proof of her intentions was an upraised empty hand. They parted before her—more out of surprise, she thought, than anything else.

The Queen of Air and Darkness waited for her, all her playacting stripped away. She was still in the jumpsuit and long coat, but they were a mockery now, human clothes on an inhuman creature. She seemed to be outlined in burning black. Eddi knew that if she had come to attack the queen, nothing would have penetrated that blackness.

She killed the engine and let the bike fall almost at the Dark Queen's feet.

"In spite of everything, you fascinate me," the queen said. Her voice, her commonplace tone, seemed horrible in context. "What are you here for?"

"To put a stop to it."

The queen's eyes narrowed. "Interesting. How did you plan to do that, by killing me?"

Eddi shook her head. "No. That's more of the same. I . . ." The words sounded stupid in her head, but she said them anyway. "I'm challenging you to a duel. A fair fight."

For a moment the queen only stared; then she laughed. "But you don't want me dead?"

"No. Just—out of her. You and your people. We're all dying for pieces of ground, and the pieces of ground don't mean anything. They're just poker chips for you to count at the end and see who's won. I want you gone, *now*, and I don't want anyone else dead getting rid of you. What do I have to do?"

The Dark Queen looked at Eddi, her face full of growing amazement and delight. "Splendid! The challenger has set the terms. Now it's the challenged party's right to name place and weapons."

Eddi had a dreadful certainty that matters had been wrenched from her hands. Then she heard the phouka's voice from behind her.

"Indeed it is. They must, of course, be in agreement with the challenger's terms, but I'm sure you'd no intention of ignoring the words, 'fair fight.' Had you?"

Eddi turned to look at him, and he gave her a pale, drawn smile. He was still holding his left shoulder. A little blood leaked between his fingers.

The Dark Lady frowned at him, shrugged, and said, "Me? Certainly not. I shall, in fact, be more than generous. Does your band play again soon?" she asked Eddi.

Eddi was suddenly cold and sick. Willy was dead. There was no band.

"First Avenue, July Fourth," she said with a toss of her head.

"Excellent. And would you say that you're better at music than at anything else?"

Eddi could only nod.

"Then surely no one will object to the conditions of my proposed contest." She regarded the phouka coldly. He stared back. She returned her attention to Eddi and smiled. "You will use your music to sway the crowd in your favor. I will use my magic to try to sway them away from you. All right?"

"My God. No. A whole club full of innocent bystanders—"

"I don't propose to maul them. They will be our unwitting, unbiased judges, no more than that."

Eddi's mouth was dry. "If I win, you pack up and leave without a fight?"

"I do," she smiled.

"What happens if I lose?"

The Dark Queen looked past Eddi and raised her eyebrows. "I doubt your allies would consider your loss theirs, would they?"

They were the center of a tight ring of fey folk, Eddi realized. It was Oberycum the queen had glanced at as she spoke; he stood behind Eddi in his battered green-and-gold armor. He shook his head slowly, as if it was a hard thing to do.

"Then I cannot ask the Seelie Court to give up its claim if you lose," the Dark Lady continued. "We'll simply take up where we left off, fighting for our 'poker chips.' I'll be angry, of course, over the waste of time and energy. And if my anger prompts me to some immediate, vengeful act . . . well. No need to worry over that now."

Eddi rubbed her eyes and thought frantically. It was madness to do this. The Queen of Air and Darkness wielded more of the magic of Faerie than anyone but the Lady herself. How could she expect to go up against that power and win?

But she was not going up against it, not really. She had only to match it with power of her own, of a different kind. The

phouka had said that nothing would bind the Dark Lady but
superior strength, or her own word. She had been offered that
word, if she could win it.

"It's a deal," Eddi said. She heard the murmur of reactions go
around the circle, and wondered what they were. "I'll see you
on the Fourth." She turned her back, knowing it was an insult.
The phouka held out his hand, and they walked out of the circle.

Carla stood just outside it.

"How much did you hear?" Eddi asked.

"Too much. Are you crazy? We can't play First Avenue.
Goddammit, Willy is *dead!*"

"We've got bass, drums, keyboard, and guitar," Eddi said
savagely. "We've got four good voices. More than a lot of
bands have. We're still Eddi and the Fey. And we're going to do
this. If you want out of it, get out now."

It was only then that she realized Carla was crying, had been
for some time from the looks of it. "If you want me out, you
better throw me out," she said, hurt and proud and stubborn.

Eddi shook her head. She started to say several different
things at once, and none of them came out. Instead she put her
arms around Carla, and Carla put hers around Eddi. They stood
in the mud and wept, while the phouka watched over them, and
the hosts of Faerie counted their wounded and their dead.

CHAPTER TWENTY

I Have the Touch

The phouka found someone to tend his shoulder. The outward sign of his injury was a prosaic white sling, but Eddi saw more than that. There was a tension around his eyes and his generous mouth that was not so much pain as the recent memory of it, the fear of it.

"How do you feel?" she asked.

He smiled, a pale version of his usual one. "Disinclined to shrug, but otherwise well enough, considering. We *do* heal quickly."

Eddi heard what he didn't say: "When we heal at all." She looked involuntarily toward the trees, then pulled her gaze away. "Do you feel strong enough to ride for a while?"

He raised his eyebrows. "That depends, my wild heart, on what you want to ride into."

"I just . . . if we go home, I'm going to look around and remember Willy sitting in the living room. And I don't want to do that."

The phouka looked up at the sky. It was still overcast, tarnished silver from the city lights bouncing off the clouds. "I've a fancy to stay out-of-doors, if you've no objection."

She didn't. They drove aimlessly for a while, making slow progress toward the river. She felt as if she needed to see and touch everything in town, to prove to herself that it was still there, unchanged. Surely something had changed. Unthinkable that she could leave Como Park and find no mark of what happened there on the rest of the world.

They cruised from St. Paul into Minneapolis, through downtown, until they found themselves on the parkway around Lake of the Isles. The grand houses that fronted it were quiet and dark, but their gardens made the air sweet. Eddi was aware of the mud on her, the prickly feeling of dried sweat on her skin. She turned off the parkway on Franklin Avenue and made her way through Kenwood, over the railroad tracks, and onto a half-wooded dead-end street.

The phouka looked around. "Are we lost yet?"

She felt guilty suddenly for dragging him around town. "Would you rather go home?"

He shook his head. "If you're worried about me, love, then be at ease. The open air is better for me than anything else."

"All right. But if you want to leave, tell me."

Eddi led him down a dirt track into the woods. Maybe the world had changed, after all. There was nothing threatening about the darkness under the trees, no menace in the night. It was full of the quiet comfort of silence between friends. It was full of sorrow, too. But that was a bearable ache here, not the sharp anguish that left no room for thought.

Or maybe, Eddi decided, *it's just me.*

At the end of the track they came out from under the trees, and onto a sand beach. Cedar Lake lay before them.

"Ah," said the phouka softly. Whether it was recognition, pleasure, or something else, Eddi couldn't tell.

They sat on the sand, watching the dull light catch on the wind-ripples until the lake looked like gray corduroy. In the weeds along the shore, frogs and crickets made music. More rarely, a fish would rise and add a watery pop to the mix.

"I want to go swimming," Eddi said.

"Then you should."

She was about to tell him that there was a law against swimming nude. He must have known what she was thinking, because he threw back his head and laughed.

"Ah, my heart, my heart. If you wish to remain unseen, you have only to will it so. You are a creature of Faerie, after all."

She was too tired to question him, and the lure of the water was too strong. She took off her clothes, dropped them on the sand, and walked into the water.

She floated on her back, staring up at the winter-colored sky. The water soaked the dirt from her, tugged at her hair until she could feel it fan out around her head. She wished it could wash her thoughts away as quietly. Memories of Willy kept rising in them. There he was on the edge of her bed, playing her guitar; swaying at the edge of the stage at the Uptown Bar in an ecstatic trance, fiddle under his chin; falling with a studied lack of grace into the couch in the practice room. *We're all immortal until we die.*

Finally she paddled back to shore. The phouka lay on the beach, propped on one elbow, watching her.

"You *are* a creature of Faerie," he said as she stood up in the water. "You're very beautiful."

"What's that word that Meg says at times like this?"

"Havers. But it's not." His voice was soft. "You look more fey than I do—all pale and shining with water, your hair streaming with it, rising from the lake. Yes. You're very beautiful."

She lay down next to him, and the sand stuck to her wet back Any other time it would have been annoying, but tonight it felt pleasantly abrasive, like a back brush. The phouka rested his head on her stomach, and she stroked his hair.

"Phouka?"

"Mmm?"

"When Stuart . . . when Stuart shot the two of you. I took the gun away from him. What was he so scared of? Why didn't he shoot me, too?"

She felt a shiver go through him. "I'm not certain of the answer to the second question. The answer to the first is 'You.' "

"He was scared of me?"

"For those few moments, beloved, *I* was afraid of you. But he was not only afraid. Perhaps," he continued, more thoughtfully, "that is the answer to your second question. You shamed him, and he couldn't shoot you."

"Shamed? What do you mean?"

"He saw in you what he might have become, had he been stronger."

She thought about Stuart as she'd last seen him. "What'll happen to him?"

"If you mean, at the hands of the Dark Court, nothing. But I think he's crumbled away inside. What happens to mortals with broken minds?"

Eddi looked down at the phouka. His eyes were open, staring at the sky, and he seemed sad and restless. She asked, "Could he have been stronger? Could it have been him, instead of me?"

"I am not an oracle," he said heavily, "and I'm glad of it. I cannot tell you."

That left silence hanging around them, and a collection of thoughts that neither of them wanted to be alone with. The phouka changed the subject. "Why here?" he asked.

"What do you mean?"

"The city is full of lakes. Why this one, this place?"

"I'm not sure. I guess . . . all the other lakes are so public and civilized. Even this one is, in places. But sometimes you can forget you're in a city at all, here."

"Tell me about it," he said. "Or about anything, I suppose. Chase away the silence for me, love."

She knew what he meant. So she told him, as best she could, about Cedar Lake. She described the quiet, almost rural lawns that bordered one bank. She told him about drifting in a canoe under the summer sun, past white, pink-throated water lilies the size of coffee mugs and wild iris hiding in the weeds like beautiful feral children. She remembered for him the red-winged blackbirds that dived at her when she got too close to the cattail thickets that sheltered their nests. She told him about the turtle she'd watched, soaking up sun on a floating log. It had let her get within reach before it dropped into the water.

As she talked, she felt him relax, saw his eyelids droop. "Asleep?" she said softly.

"No." His voice was low and drowsy. "I was pretending I was a turtle in the sun."

"Good. What kind of bodyguard falls asleep on a beach at night?"

"An out-of-work one."

Eddi raised her head and frowned at him.

"You are entirely safe until you have played First Avenue. Who in the Unseelie Court is fool enough to harm you before then? It would rob the Dark Queen of her sport."

Eddi felt the dropping sick feeling of fear in her stomach. "Phouka," she said, her voice unsteady, "am I going to lose?"

He sat up, winced, and scowled at her. "If you thought you would lose, why did you propose the contest at all?"

That was no comfort. He shouldn't have to ask that, surely. "Because I had to."

"Because we might all die?"

"No. Because we might either kill or die, and neither one was any better than the other. And I had to do something to stop it. All I could think of was to fight her by myself, in some way that I wouldn't have to kill her to win."

He looked out over the lake for a long time. "The Dark Lady is as much a paradox as any of us. She would not have suggested the form of the contest if she did not think she could win at it.

Yet if she thought she could not lose, there would be no sport, and she would not bother to venture a contest at all. How your enemy judges you may tell you more than the judgments of your friends. Your enemy's opinion of you seems to be a good one.''

Eddi stood up and began to brush sand off her skin. "I suppose you couldn't just say, 'Of course you'll win'?"

"That would be too close kin to lying," the phouka said apologetically.

They had a week, and Eddi and the Fey spent it practicing. They were mourning; they were building a memorial; they were honing their revenge.

The hole that Willy's death had made in them could not be mended. They missed the sound of him, and the sizzling energy of his presence that they'd looked to more than they'd known. It was a different band without him—but they didn't dare believe it was a weaker one.

Dan and Hedge elaborated on their arrangements, filling up the space that Willy had occupied. Hedge sang more. Eddi played guitar more often, and flung herself into every song as if she didn't expect to come out again. Even so, some of the band's best material was not as strong as it had been. To construct the set list for the Fourth of July, they had to rebuild each song as if they were starting over.

The fierce heat that sometimes took possession of Minneapolis in midsummer had settled in. For long, nightmarish hours they worked in the oven that the rehearsal room became, trying to keep the equipment from overheating and their own sweat off the instruments. Sometimes in the middle of a song, Eddi would remember vaguely that there was magic in the world, that she had some of it, and that she needed it for this. But magic had to come second to the music, and the music took everything out of her.

When they were done, they were again the best band they could be. None of them wondered aloud if that was good enough.

They packed the station wagon as if this were any gig, and split up to rest and eat and dress. Eddi found she couldn't manage the first two.

Carla and Dan, she knew, would dress to kill. Only heaven and the Queen of Faerie knew what Hedge would wear. Eddi wore her armor. It would be hot under the stage lights, and black leather was at odds with the sound and style of the band. But she was going into battle, after all.

By the time Boiled in Lead, the second of the three bands, went on stage at First Avenue, the crowd was large and noisy. Eddi stood backstage and listened, trying to judge the mood and character of the audience from the commotion.

"As soon as all the fireworks let out, there won't be room to inhale out there," Carla said.

"Mm. You've been out front already?"

"Just for a sec." Carla smiled and thumped her on the shoulder. "Lighten up, girl. They look like our kind of people, and they're all here to have a good time."

"Hah. Wait 'til the Queen of Air and Darkness starts in on them."

She looked around the little room at her band. Carla smoked a cigarette and leaned over one of Dan's keyboards. Dan was playing it unplugged, scales to keep his fingers limber. Scales without sound, only the precise rhythm that his fingers made hitting the keys. Carla's hair hung like a black satin curtain around her face, brushing the electric blue of her sleeveless blouse. Dan wore a pale pink baggy linen suit, a light gray shirt and a white tie. On his lapel was a button that read, "When MIDI talks, money walks." He was completely absorbed. Hedge was wonderfully well-dressed, at least for Hedge: an enormous shirt in a red-and-black Japanese print, and tapered white pants with cuffs. He was reading a comic book, a copy of *Swamp Thing* that someone had left in the room. He giggled now and then.

They seemed impossibly calm; that and Eddi's nerves made her want to hit them. She felt her own tension on the air, so thick it didn't seem breathable. "Be right back," she muttered, and stalked into the hall to find the phouka.

He was leaning against the wall, pretending interest in the toes of his patent-leather boots. He'd found something to wear that at first glance looked like a tuxedo. But the jacket was shorter than that, and the pants narrower, and the white tie that nestled under the wing collar was a little too softly knotted. His shirt studs were cabochon emeralds.

"I have to circulate a little," she told him. "Want to come with?"

He smiled. "Is it becoming too much for you?"

"Hell, yes."

"Me, too."

Eddi leaned against him and sighed. "The guys—they're nervous, and they're worried, but . . . Carla reminded me yesterday that the worst that can happen is more of the same, more Faerie war. And she's right. So why do I feel so scared?"

He put his arm around her, and they walked down the hall like that. "Because you know more of Faerie than Carla does. Particularly more of the Dark Lady. If you lose. . . . Once the terms of the challenge no longer apply, she needn't fight fairly."

Eddi looked up at him quickly. "I'm right to be worried, then?"

"I don't know. But I am perfectly terrified, and I would hate to think there was no reason for it."

They came out from backstage into the wall of music that Boiled in Lead was building. The dance floor was full, and Eddi remembered Carla's pronouncement about the fireworks. "Lucky bastards," she yelled, watching the band tear gleefully through "The Rights of Man." "I wish we'd already played."

"No, you don't," the phouka shouted in her ear. The first set crowd would have needed warming up. By third set, the audience would be addled with music and dancing and drink, generous and ready for wonders. It would be harder for the Queen of Air and Darkness to dim their vision.

They wandered through the crowd, seeing nothing more unusual than on any night at First Avenue. There were a few of the polo-shirts-and-chinos crowd, what Carla called "the tourists." There were women in vintage finery and new-wave splendor, men in antique tailcoats with their braided queues hanging down their backs, and people in the latest from the trendy departments of Dayton's. Eddi suddenly loved them all, desperately.

At last she made a stop at the ladies' room, leaving the phouka to wait on the balcony. The restrooms were the only places in First Avenue where the lights were bright. The sound of the band was muted there, too, and people came to talk, or repair makeup. Only in the restrooms did the club reveal its earlier life as a bus station; though the stalls had been painted, they were the original ones, as were the old black-and-white tiles and the row of sinks. Eddi bent over one of those to wash her hands, between a woman in pale makeup and red lipstick, and two college women who were doing each other's hair with setting gel.

"So, all ready for the big show?" the low voice said behind her, obscenely pleased. Eddi looked up, looked into the mirror, and found the Dark Lady standing behind her. She was dressed in dark gray brocade threaded with silver. She wore her black hair unbound, and it made a cloud down her back. Tiny tendrils of it were spit-curled around her face. There were huge silver disks in her ears, and her lips were the color of strong wine.

No one else in the room seemed to take special notice of the Dark Queen. To Eddi, however, she wore her uncanny nature like heavy scent, a dark fragrance that made the head spin. She met the queen's black eyes in the mirror.

"I'm ready," she said. "Are you?"

"I quite look forward to it." The wine-colored lips curved upward. Eddi swallowed and wished she'd go away.

Then Eddi saw a bright figure behind the dark one, and spun round in surprise. The Lady was there.

Other women in the room *did* notice her. She was hiding her true nature, Eddi realized, but not the fey beauty that was part of it. She was a powerful presence in the room; she commanded it as if by a sword or sceptre.

Her streaming red hair had been cut, and it curled and frothed over her forehead, sparkling with a dusting of gold. Her white features were too beautiful to be imagined, too perfect to be real. She wore a slender tunic that flashed when she moved, as the light bounced off the pale green spangles and sequins that covered it, the rhinestones (or diamonds, perhaps) around the high collar. She wore stockings of the same color in some shimmering stuff, and short silver boots.

The Queen of Air and Darkness looked over her shoulder. Her lips pressed together at the sight of the Lady. "You do not, I take it, come to watch quietly from the shadows."

The Lady's white lips twitched at that. "This would be ill garb for that, certainly. No, cousin, we come to watch our champion fight."

Eddi looked swiftly from one to the other. The Dark Queen's eyes widened as if she'd been struck, until anger replaced surprise. The Lady held out a long hand to Eddi, palm up. It was the same gesture, the same hand, with which she had offered the morsel of Faerie bread, so many weeks ago.

In her palm lay a pendant, a woven knot of silver and red enamel. No, not red enamel. It was a strand of the Lady's hair.

"It is our token," she said to Eddi, in a voice that made her shiver, "and our pledge. The Seelie Court shall abide by what transpires here; we shall stand or fall with our champion."

The Dark Queen's face was feral and eager. "If I win, then, you agree that these lands are mine."

"And if Eddi McCandry wins, you shall forfeit them, yourself and all who bow to you. It shall be so for seventy times seven years, and any who would defy that banishment shall be cast out of Faerie."

The Dark Lady showed white teeth. "Which applies equally on both sides, of course. Yes, this gives the evening a great deal of spice."

Eddi reached out and took the pendant from the Lady's hand. It shone a little more brightly than she thought it should, but she felt no great power in it. It was not a weapon—only a symbol, as the Lady had said. She slid the chain over her head and let the token fall against her chest.

No one in the restroom seemed to find anything odd in their words or actions, Eddi found when she looked up. Though the Lady was stared at, no one stayed to do it; there was no crowd gathering.

"With the stakes so much higher," said the Queen of Air and Darkness, "I would like some guarantee against false dealing."

"You have my sworn word," the Lady said coldly. "You need no better."

"Oh, that will bind you, and all your Court. But—forgive me my prejudices—I cannot trust it to bind a mortal." She directed a dazzling smile at Eddi.

"You can have my promise, too," Eddi snapped.

The Dark Queen looked her up and down, and drawled, "How much is a mortal promise worth?"

Eddi felt an angry heat shoot through her. The Lady's pale eyes blazed, and she seemed about to speak. But before she could, the Dark Queen continued. "I'm sure we can find some more tangible symbol of our agreement." She nodded to Eddi and the Lady, and walked out of the room.

Eddi closed her hand around the Lady's token. "Why?" she said finally, hearing despair in her words. "Before, if I won you got what you wanted, and if I lost, you were no worse off than if none of this had happened. Why did you *do* this?"

The expression on the Lady's face sat so oddly there that Eddi barely recognized it. It was sorrow.

"To be our champion is an honor, Eddi McCandry, and one you have earned. You have shown yourself loyal and beyond reason courageous. You have served the Seelie Court more wisely, perhaps, than I have ruled it. For you to stand against the Queen of Air and Darkness and not bear our blessing—it would be black insult to you, and dishonor to my house.''

''I can't say anything about the dishonor,'' Eddi said with a ferocious quiet, ''but do you think I give a good goddamn about the insult?''

''No,'' said the Lady fiercely, ''I do not. You are free to ignore it, or forgive it. I cannot. We are inflexible, aye, and you have scorned that. Yet that is why we speak naught but the truth, and why our sworn word will bind us though the earth swallow us up. Does that seem such an ill thing to you?''

Eddi met her burning eyes and finally shook her head.

When the Lady spoke again, her voice was gentler. ''I would deny you this if I could. Were Willy alive, he would try to turn me from my purpose—and even for love of him, or his memory, I could not spare you this. We are a hard people, and we think perhaps overmuch of the weighing of rights and wrongs, of favors and slights. I could not rule Faerie if I did not live by its precepts.'' She went to the mirror and starred blindly into it. ''So I must mete out your due, for good or ill. Then I shall stand and see the consequences of what I have done, and take them as they come.''

Eddi rubbed the pendant between her fingers, and studied the Lady's bleak white face in the mirror. ''I'll do my best,'' she said at last. ''For both of us.''

A spasm of pain crossed the alabaster features. ''For all of us. Have you not guessed the surety the Dark Lady will demand?''

Eddi frowned. The pity with which the Lady regarded her finally sank in. ''The phouka,'' she whispered. ''No. She can't.''

''She is within her rights to ask a hostage of us. She will ask for him. She holds him, and you, in bitter hatred for freeing Willy. If you lose to her, she will take his life before your eyes, and be revenged on you both.''

Anger and fear were scrambled in Eddi's head. When she spoke, she didn't know which emotion it was from. ''When Faerie and my world intersect, does anything good ever come of it?''

The Lady gave her a cool glance, one of bitter amusement. ''Think on your lover, Daughter of Eve, and answer for yourself.''

She, too, swept from the room. Eddi was left leaning on the counter, feeling cold and ill.

When she reached the balcony, only the phouka was there. He

knew what had happened; she could tell from his expression. They held each other in silence, and he buried his face in her hair. "Do what you can, my primrose," he whispered at last. "I love my life better than I ever have, now that it's at risk. But even so, I love you better still."

She strangled on a sob, and kissed him. Then he straightened his shoulders and lifted his chin in that familiar way, and walked until the crowd swallowed him.

She would have run backstage, but the press of people kept her slow. When she reached it, Carla saw her face and stood up with a snap.

"What's wrong?"

Eddi leaned against the wall and breathed deep and slow. Carla hurried over, took her hand, and Eddi wanted so much to cry, to collapse and let Carla take care of her.

"They just changed the stakes," she said finally. Her voice sounded flat in her head.

"What do you mean?" Carla asked. Dan stood at her shoulder, alarmed, and Hedge looked horrified, as if he'd already guessed what the stakes must be now.

"If I lose . . . then the Unseelie Court gets the city, and the phouka dies."

After a moment, Carla squeezed her shoulder hard. "What do you mean, if *you* lose? You mean *we*, girl." Eddi stared at her, and finally nodded grimly.

They said things to her after that—even Hedge said something. But she didn't hear them. She sat down in a corner and put her axe in tune. Boiled in Lead finished their set with a manic, thrash-band rendition of "The Gypsy Rover," their equipment was whisked off the stage, and Eddi and the Fey's replaced it. When they went down the corridor to the stage, Eddi was still shaking off her mental fog.

They stood ready at their mikes, while an amplified voice from the sound booth announced their name into the dark room. The crowd cheered—Eddi hadn't expected that. Were there people out there who'd come to hear *them?* Carla tapped three beats on the rim of her snare. The fourth fired the stage lights and Hedge's bass. No turning back now.

They had ten songs. In ten songs, they had to catch and hold an audience, overthrow a queen, free the phouka, and save the city. Put like that, it was the stupidest thing Eddi had ever heard. So she didn't think of it that way again.

They opened with Peter Gabriel's "In Your Eyes." Perhaps they should have chosen something louder and faster, something that would grab the dancers right away. She couldn't see the dance floor past the stage lights, couldn't tell what was happening. Where was the Queen of Air and Darkness? Where would she position herself, in such a time and place?

Once Eddi thought to ask the question, the answer was obvious. She raised her head and scanned the VIP balcony.

The Dark Queen sat watching from a little table, ignoring the drink in front of her. She met Eddi's eyes and nodded. Behind her the phouka stood, one hand on the railing, his face set and tense. She saw a glimmer of light at his wrist, and squinted. It came from a thin cord of some magical weaving, and it bound his wrist to the top rail. Eddi stumbled over the next chord change and saw the Queen of Air and Darkness smile.

There were shadows in the sound booth, silhouetted against the second-floor bar. There were shadows on the dance floor. She would be a shadow of a different sort if the Dark Lady won, and Carla and Dan and Hedge with her. Here in this room was what she fought for, this wild human energy, this fast-burning mortality that made so much light. There was a dark cloth laid over it now, dimming, smothering. She could feel it. She could almost see it. Pull it back, shred it, smolder it away with sound and light. . . .

She lost track of what she was singing. Were they her words? She was driving them up out of the middle of her like flame from a dragon's mouth—they must be hers. Hedge stood on one side of her, braced as if against a gale, head thrown back, eyes closed. He clawed the Steinberger wtih eagle talons, climbing a spiral of bass notes into the hot blue air. Dan danced behind the keyboards, with feet and hands and mouth, mad and swift as a striking snake. Carla summoned up the beat of pounding water and falling stone, rhythms that had not faltered since the universe took shape.

And still the darkness lay over them all, the Dark Queen's barrier to light and noise.

Eddi shot out a hand and plucked the lights from the ceiling, fired all the neon at once. She made it rain flash pots like falling stars. The video screens roiled with color, throbbed with beat, trembled with images that seemed to want to break their surface tension and spill out onto the dance floor.

The darkness shouldered up to meet them.

Sparks leaped and spat all over the stage, under Eddi's fingers, singeing them, bridging the beads of sweat on her face. Current crackled and arced over the dance floor, around the metal balcony railings. The room glowed blue for an instant, as if struck by lightning.

At the back of the room, near the balcony stairs, the Lady stood pale and shining. Oberycum was beside her, tall and knightly, gleaming in green and gold and his hair like bleached wheat. In that flash of blue he nodded to Eddi, the solemn salute of equals, but she had no time to nod back.

She hammered down on three chords, repeated them, heard Carla roll sticks across the snare like a forest fire. Hedge screamed down his low *E* string, the sound of a descent into hell, and they began "For It All." The neon lashed the ceiling again, and Eddi saw the light-dyed faces of the dancers turned up to her, flowers following the sun. She demanded their minds, then insisted that they think for themselves; stole their ears and made them fight to get them back. Their dancing bodies she did not take by force—those she sought humbly, and each one given to her was a treasure. She felt their sweat running down her skin, felt their arms cutting shapes in the air around her, her muscles aching with the motion of their dance. Darkness and light ran together around them like confluent rivers, like braided streaming hair, black and red, like tangled patterns of cloud and sky.

Her guitar was gone; she didn't know where. She thought her mike was in front of her, but she couldn't see it, hadn't the attention to spare to sing into it. She took a breath, then let her voice spill out:

> *Fire coming down the sky*
> *On a horse of wind*
> *Beckons to the naked eye*
> *And who can see?*

Carla backed the words with the thunder of deep drums, Hedge with the rolling voice of his bass, Dan with wild flying piano like flocks of birds.

> *Those who look up,*
> *Hearts that hurt for height and heaven,*
> *Those who look up see*
> *What never falls to earth.*

The music grumbled under her voice like something large coming closer to them all, approaching swiftly through the earth toward the surface. Carla and Dan and Hedge sang up a net of light behind her, a veil of sun and shadow that trembled with the deep instruments.

On the balcony, the Dark Lady was a pillar of black fire, hands clenched on the balcony rail, face turned upward. A devouring silence roiled where she stood, pressed outward. But a powerful wave of music was rising against her.

> *Armies hurled against the hall*
> *Cannot breach the outer wall*
> *The castle built of thundercloud*
> *Will only yield*
> *To those who look up*
> *Hands held out aloft and empty. . . .*

She pointed and the dancers all turned to see it, laughing with delight when it *did* look like a castle.

Thunder boiled up, from Carla's drums and the air above them. Ozone smelled bright and mind-clearing and sounded like Dan's synthesizer. Eddi pointed again to the tarnished silver sky, where the thunderheads raced toward them like flying mountains.

> *Tall ship on the hungry sea*
> *An ark, a saviour sent to free*
> *Those who see the ladder tossed*
> *And jump, and catch, and climb aloft. . . .*

The thunderhead was low, low in the sky, and the rain would come soon. They had better take the cloud itself and ride above the storm. She leaped into the air, legs tucked up. Was that a tugging at her ankles? Gravity, or pulling hands? A laughable bond, weakening with each second. She kicked it off. When her feet came down they hit the cool mounded white top of the cloud, and it crunched like snow. The dancers laughed and yelled, sprang aboard without missing a beat. In the dark blue altitudes it was easier to dance, easier to whip through the thin air. They would never be tired now. Even gravity, with its dark shrouding hands, had slipped off them. Eddi pulled the wind into her lungs and laughed, felt tears pouring down her face. They were the dancers' tears, too, who cried with joy because there was too much of everything. She wept fiercely and her voice never wavered with it.

Whatever was coming up from underneath, whatever made the growing thunder, was almost upon them. Dan and Hedge and Carla opened up the golden net they'd made and let it through.

> *Ears tuned to the sounding stars,*
> *Wings stretched to catch the wind,*
> *Here comes the jet to cut the clouds,*
> *To take us home.*

Silver flashing up from beneath, through the whiteness—so fast, but not too fast to reach out and touch. They all did, brushing their fingers against the cold, wet metal in wonder. Eddi's face burned with the salt on her cheeks.

The song was free, rising above them as they rose. It filled everything with its roaring, it pushed the walls down around them and walls for as far as thoughts could range. The silver shape above them changed, widened, climbed through blackness and the unshuttered stars on a pillar of fire. The cloud was gone, but they didn't need it now.

The dancers sang without words, Carla, Hedge, and Dan sang with them, and Eddi weaved like wildfire in and out of the voices. And though they'd left the room behind, she could still see the Lady and her Consort at the foot of the stairs, bright as the stars around her, singing. She could still see the balcony where the Dark Lady, a tattered shadow, hid her face in her hands, where the phouka tore his wrist free from the railing, flung his head back, and added his voice to Eddi's.

She was on her knees at the edge of the stage, still crying, and people were pressed forward to touch her, laughing and crying just as she was. Carla pulled her to her feet and flung her arms around her. Eddi reached out to Hedge and hauled him into the embrace, and Dan, too. Then the phouka was there. She fell against him, too weak to stand without her friends' arms around her. They had to carry her off the stage.

There was no magical change in the city; what they'd fought for, after all, was the city the way it was, the way they loved it. But the air *seemed* cleaner, the light stronger, the colors more certain. If it was only that they'd taken them a little for granted until then—well, that at least was different.

It was not a concert to be walked calmly away from. They could not pack the car, go to their separate homes, and fall asleep. So they went to the Ediner, and when that closed, they went to Denny's, and when they couldn't stand that any longer, they went to sit on the shore of Lake of the Isles. A park police car cruised past, but Eddi pretended that they weren't there, and it never slowed down.

Carla shook a cigarette out of her pack, lit it, and paused, staring at the glowing end. Then she stubbed it out in the grass. "That some kinda symbol?" Dan teased her.

"Nah. But just for tonight. . . ." She rolled over on her back and grinned at him. He leaned across and kissed her nose.

Hedge sprawled on his stomach, playing kazoo on a grass blade between his thumbs. He looked pleased and sleepy. Though he didn't speak, he looked up and smiled at Eddi now and then, and she smiled back.

"And so it's done," said the phouka softly. No one seemed to hear but Eddi.

"Is it really? What about all the things you wanted to see changed, all the things in the Seelie Court?"

He smiled down at the grass. "I'd intended to plant a seed or two, and wait to see what grew there. Things grow slowly in Faerie, my beloved."

"So you're just going to see what happens?"

"I don't know. I'd thought in terms of seeds, you see, and never dreamed that what I had loosed on the Court was a madwoman with a crowbar."

"What, me? I'm flattered."

They watched the moon dance on the lake and listened to Hedge play his blade of grass. "Well," Eddi said at last. She thought irritably, *Why is it that at times like this, every sentence starts with 'Well'?* She bit the inside of her lip. She wanted to ask him if he would stay, if he *could* stay. Where he would go if he didn't, she wasn't sure, but she knew it was someplace she couldn't follow. She remembered his words at Midsummer— "What will you do, when our war is done, and we withdraw from your life?" She still had no answer.

He stood up, crossed the grass to her side, and sat down again next to her. "I've been instructed to give you this," he said, and pulled a packet out of the inside pocket of his jacket.

She unfolded the white silk and found a silver maple leaf—the earring the Lady had worn in Loring Park. Her eyes burned. She knew a parting gift when she saw one.

"I think you did her a world of good," she heard the phouka say smugly above her. "Though Earth and Air know I would never say it aloud in her hearing."

"When are you going?" she said softly.

"Going where?"

She looked quickly up. He was smiling, and that soft, adoring look was on his face.

"I was just about to ask you," he said, "if you thought we ought to tour."

If you enjoyed *War for the Oaks*, you'll enjoy *Falcon*!

"*Falcon* soars! Exciting, evocative and entertaining. I couldn't put it down and was sorry to reach the end." — Chris Claremont, author of *FirstFlight*

"Stark and strong: strict science fiction, purely myth, a perfect novel." — R. A. MacAvoy, author of *Tea With the Black Dragon*

"Emma Bull combines an elegant style with high adventure and thoughtful speculation. *Falcon* is one of my favorite novels. Read it. If you don't like it, write to me and complain." — Steven Brust, author of *Jhereg*

"A world it is actually a pleasure to visit, and a wrench to leave." — Lois McMaster Bujold, author of *Falling Free*